INSIDIOUS

Dark desires...
Deadly secrets...
Devious deceptions...

Disclaimer

A Smart, Sexy Thriller

Mature Adult 18+ Only

This novel is a work of fiction and contains sexual situations and violence that may be disturbing to some readers.

Read at your own risk.

INSIDIOUS: *proceeding in a gradual, subtle way, but with harmful effects*

PROLOGUE

Past

APPREHENSIVELY, the patient settled against the paper-covered examination table and lifted her flimsy gown. Her eyes fluttered between the technician and her husband as she waited for the gel to be applied to her growing midsection. Goose bumps rose on her exposed flesh as the cold, condensing liquid oozed onto her skin. Saying a silent prayer, she closed her eyes.

"With high-risk cases, we like to keep everything monitored," said the young woman in scrubs. "This is just routine. There's no reason to be concerned. Have you had any problems since your last appointment?"

"Not since the last scare. I haven't had any more bleeding or cramping since I was discharged more than a week ago," the patient replied, trying to hide the obvious trepidation from her voice.

Squeezing her hand, the man at her side smiled reassuringly. "It will be all right. Everything has been going well. We've done everything the doctor said."

Applying the large wand to the patient's midsection, the technician smiled.

Waiting for the monitor, the man said, "Listen to that…" The room filled with the reverberating sound of *thump, thump, thump.*

"Yes, that's a very strong heartbeat." The technician responded reassuringly.

"Heartbeat?" the man asked, obviously perplexed.

The fuzzy image began to clear as the wand found its perfect spot. "Yes, sir. See right here…" She pointed toward the screen. "…your baby's heart is strong."

"Baby?" the patient again questioned, her eyes filling with tears. "What do you mean *baby*? I'm having twins! There are two babies! We've seen them."

The young technician's smile faded as her brows knitted together. "Um, the other one is probably hiding. They do that." Her words faded as she frantically moved the wand from side to side.

"Where is it? Where's our other baby?" The man's voice became louder with each question.

"Sir, the doctor will be in soon. He can explain…"

"I know you know what you're seeing. Tell us. Tell us what you see!"

The patient's arm covered her eyes as tears continued to stream, pooling on the white paper. The image on the screen, though somewhat distorted, was clear. One baby dominated the screen. As the wand moved, a ghostly image, smaller than the other, seemed to float unmoving on its own. Between breaths, the patient asked, "Did this happen after I left the hospital? How? What's happening with our other baby?"

"The doctor…"

The man interrupted the technician, "Tell me our son survived. Tell me that you see a boy."

"Sir, the doctor…"

"Tell me!" he demanded.

Just then, the door opened and the doctor entered. "Excuse me, what's happening in here?"

Unable to respond, the patient looked toward her husband. Straightening his shoulders, he glared toward the screen. "She said our *baby* is healthy. We're having *two* babies. My wife is pregnant with twins, fraternal twins, a boy and a girl. Last week at the hospital you said there was a size differentiation, but you said it wasn't significant. Now she…" He pointed toward the technician. "…is saying there's only one baby. What happened?"

Taking the wand from the technician, the doctor looked

comfortingly toward the patient. "How have you been feeling?"

Holding back her sobs, she replied, "Tired, but the cramps stopped…"

Staring toward the screen, the doctor smiled. "This can be difficult. But let's concentrate on the positive. You have a strong, healthy girl. Sometimes things like this happen. The body understands if both fetuses can't be supported. In those cases, the stronger one survives. Your daughter…"

The man didn't hear the rest of the doctor's statement. Glaring momentarily toward his wife, he opened the door and walked away. The entire room fell silent as the helpless door bounced against the wall, filling the room with only the sound of the echoing slam and the steady *swoosh, swoosh, swoosh* of the fetal heartbeat.

CHAPTER ONE

Present

THE BACKDROP of blue did little to temper the stagnant Florida heat. Peering through the windshield, I watched the hot, muggy air ripple through undetectable waves, as the impressive Miami skyline appeared to bow and arch in the heat-induced optical illusion. Stepping from the cool car, I longed for a breeze anything to shatter the oppressive weight of the unseasonal autumn humidity. Moist air saturated every void as my heels walked upon the concrete streets and between the glass castles. I was where others longed to be. This was the best of the best: the homes, offices, and shopping mecca to the elite of Miami society. To the unknowing tourist, or even the unaware Miamian, these buildings and monuments were an enticing testament to the power of wealth and influence. However, in reality, they were but a beautiful façade waiting patiently to entrap the unwilling participant. I should know. At one time I was that unwilling participant, dragged into the depths of malevolence. That was years ago. I've learned my lessons well and played my role. No longer willing to be a victim, today I'm insidious.

"Thank you, Mrs. Harrington." The saleswoman's voice reverberated throughout the pricey boutique.

Nodding in response, I took my purchase and strode toward the door. The five-hundred-dollar shoes weren't a necessity. Hell, they weren't even for a purpose: a dinner, a benefit, or any other excuse to show me off and parade me around Stewart's business associates. They were just because: because they were tall and sleek, with a slender heel, and a thick platform. And because they were red. Red, as in the color of emotion: emotion that remained pent-up until its only acceptable outlet was a mundane visible reminder, a way to flaunt the loathing within to the world outside. Oh, I had covertly exercised other modes of release, yet at the moment, a pair of red shoes would suffice.

The gentleman in uniform spoke as he opened the door. "Thank you, Mrs. Harrington. Please come back to see us again."

"Yes," I said, my expression inscrutable.

"Ma'am, we're all praying for your husband."

"Thank you." I looked down and bit my lip before I returned his gaze, bravely smiling, and added, "I'm afraid that's our only hope."

His eyes dulled as he sadly nodded, allowing me to exit through the open door. Rarely did a day go by that someone didn't offer me his or her support or encouragement for Stewart, as he fought his unwinnable battle. I'd practiced my responses well. After all, very little went unseen. While we'd made headlines when we married, mostly surrounding our age difference, we were making them again as the tabloids and magazines discussed my impending widowhood at the young age of twenty-eight.

Moving onto the sun-drenched sidewalk, I covered my eyes with the dark glasses and braced myself for the wave of heat. Up from the depths of hell, like fire fanned by the devil himself, my legs tingled with the contrast in temperature. I bit my lip again, stopping the genuine smile that threatened to shatter my mask of grief. Assuming hell was real, soon it would have another resident. Before the bun of long brown hair secured low on my neck could mold to my skin, I settled into the backseat of the waiting taxi.

Though my car was parked only a few blocks away, I knew the wonders of technology. The GPS would show that I'd spent my afternoon in the Harbor Shoppes—at least until I was ready for it to indicate otherwise.

"To ONE Bal Harbour Resort," I instructed, as the driver pulled the car into midday traffic.

After spending most of my life in southern Florida, I found little beauty in the city of Miami. What appeal it had was completely lost on me as I scanned the screen of my phone, reading my text messages. A sense of suffocation loomed omnipresent as I read one from my husband:

"WE HAVE A GUEST COMING TO THE WAREHOUSE THIS AFTERNOON. BE THERE AT 4:30. DON'T BE LATE."

I closed my eyes, hid my expression behind my designer sunglasses, and sighed. Thankfully, due to Stewart Harrington's recent rapid decline in health, we'd not visited the warehouse in some time: his text was sent months ago. Nevertheless, I refused to delete it. It served as my fuel and my daily reminder: a reminder of a time I refused to forget.

I would not. I could not.

I scanned back to the message I'd more recently received, one I'd first seen late last night:

"I NEED TO SEE YOU."

I gave it one more glance, grinning at the shared sense of desperation, before I hit delete. I waited until this morning to respond:

"TODAY?"

After I'd hit send, his response came back almost immediately:

"NOW."

We both knew that NOW hadn't been an option, but a minor tweaking of my schedule and a slight juggle of my responsibilities would allow LATER to be a possibility. Smoothing the silk of my sundress over my lap while trying desperately to ignore the sweat-ladened stench of the taxi, I relished the reality: *later* was almost upon me. If only the car could fly instead of fight the midday traffic.

As Stewart's time on earth drew nigh its end, I worried about the legalities of our prenuptial agreement. With Stewart's network of good ol' boys, finding an ally, someone to look out for my interests, had been difficult, but thankfully not impossible. Since I'd made my alliance with Brody Phillips, junior partner at Craven and Knowles, there was nothing I wouldn't do to continue the flow of information. Besides, sex was nothing more than a tool, a weapon. It had been used against me, but I'd learned to use it in my favor. If sex helped me obtain my goal, there was no fucking reason not to use it.

Minutes upon minutes later, the cab pulled under the covered drive of the resort, allowing me to exit in the much-appreciated shade. With an assuming smile, I handed the driver cash for the fare and a generous tip. I confidently placed my high-heeled sandals on the steaming pavement and walked toward the resort. With the efficiency of a drill sergeant, I moved dauntlessly toward my objective. Merely a pretentious nod of my head and the door was opened. A crisp one-hundred-dollar bill at the bellman's desk and I was armed with the key to a suite on the eighteenth floor. Walking toward the elevator, I shifted my gaze, daring anyone to question my presence. No one did. I'm Mrs. Stewart Harrington.

Within less than a minute, I was ascending the tower toward the eighteenth floor. Although I was confident that Brody had chosen the hotel suite with other goals in mind, that wouldn't happen today. I'd opened myself up—a little—to him for one reason: it wasn't sex.

It wasn't as if I always denied him sex. As a matter of fact, we had an array of locations littered throughout the city where I hadn't denied him, but honestly, there was something about Brody that made me uncomfortable. Sex was a mechanical act for me, a time to leave my body and zone out. Each time Brody and I were together, that was increasingly difficult. I didn't want to face that reality or even the internal questions that it raised.

As I disembarked the elevator and peered down the long hallway, the fleeting sense of anticipation took me by surprise. Rarely did I find myself aroused. However, as I realized that it had been almost a month since I'd been alone with Brody, my insides involuntarily tightened.

Brody Phillips, esquire, was, among other things, my informant.

As a junior partner at Craven and Knowles, the prestigious law firm that handled all of Stewart's personal legal needs, he was privy to information that affected me. The common good ol' boy attitude shared by most in the firm was that as Stewart's wife I didn't need to know, or couldn't possibly understand, the legalities that affected me. Thankfully, I'd found an ally who disagreed. After all, it was my name, Victoria Conway Harrington, on the documents. Despite my husband's obstinacy, I had a right to know.

Our alliance had started slowly. Every man was suspect, especially anyone within Stewart's circles. I hadn't planned on allowing Brody to get to know me—few people did. However, with time and patience, he pulled me into a sense of camaraderie. Unlike the men who saw me as nothing other than an available fuck, Brody spoke to me with sincerity. It was years into our clandestine friendship before we took it to the next level. However, once we did, turning back wasn't an option.

A quick swipe of the key and the lock mechanism clicked. Before I could fully open the door, Brody's strawberry blonde hair and smiling eyes stopped me momentarily in my tracks. He was the perfect man next door: innocent and sweet. Yet I knew from experience, he was equally cunning and shrewd. There was no way he'd have survived in the world of Craven and Knowles if he weren't. However, there was something about his eyes. From the first time we'd met, I was fascinated. His eyes were unlike any I've ever seen. They weren't the color blue nor were they green: they were more of an aquamarine hue. It wasn't only the color that pulled me in: it was the way he looked at me, really looked. With a glance, even in a crowded room, he made me feel vulnerable and exposed. That did strange things to me, things I didn't like. It was as if he could see a side of me that no one else could: he could see through my façade. Taking him in, the small lines at the corners of his eyes and the slight gleam, implored my gaze to travel lower to his raised cheeks and welcoming smile. Involuntarily, the tips of my lips moved upward.

With his suit jacket and tie missing, my eyes traveled down his starched, fitted button-down shirt to his trim waist. His dark gray Brooks Brothers' slacks accentuated his long legs and firm physique. Hearing the sound of his voice returned my attention to his remarkable eyes.

"Vik-ki," he said, elongating my nickname. "I was worried you wouldn't make it." The temperature of the room increased as he reached for my shoulder and leaned near. His lips brushed my cheek with the teasing promise of more. The lingering scent of his aftershave filled me with memories of freshly laundered sheets, so unlike the heavy masculine cologne my husband wore. I fought the urge to reach up and stroke Brody's cheek, to feel the slight stubble beneath my fingers.

Taking my hand, he led me inside the spacious suite. The wall farthest from the door was nothing but windows filled with the familiar blue. Though there were many things about Miami that I detested, the view of the water going on forever was not one of them. Now it momentarily took my breath as well as my response away.

"This is stunning."

"Not as stunning as you," he said, removing my sunglasses and staring deeply into my steel-gray eyes.

"Brody, I can't—"

His lips captured my words as his firm chest pressed me toward the wall. The tingle of anticipation I'd felt moments earlier grew like a fire—wind to a spark on dry grass. I gave into desire and moved my petite hands to the sides of his face, feeling the stubble I'd longed to touch. My fingers lingered as our tongues united. I didn't want to admit that I was afraid to let go, afraid of not remembering the feeling smoldering inside of me. The sound of our breathing filled the suite, as my beating heart echoed in my ears, momentarily drowning out reasoning, filling me instead with hunger for what he could provide.

"God, Vikki," Brody finally said, breaking our seal and pushing me slightly away. His gaze deepened as he asked, "God, you taste so fucking good. I've missed seeing you like this."

I reached for his chest and buried my cheek in his shirt. With the sound of his steady heartbeat, my body melted. Pent-up tension oozed from every pore until all that was left of me was liquid, held in place by his embrace. Fighting the desire to take our vertical connection horizontal, I stiffened my neck. "Brody, I-I can't. Not today."

"Are you all right, baby? You seem so... I don't know... like you're ready to explode. Or implode?"

I stepped back and walked toward the sofa, adjusting my dress and ignoring the part of me that longed to be lost in his arms.

"Why would you think I wasn't coming?" I asked. "Our agreement was for 1:00 PM, and it's barely one."

"You didn't reply to my last text. I was afraid someone else might have seen it."

"No," I said definitively. "Believe it or not, my phone stays with me. I did delete the text. There's no sense taking unnecessary chances. Now, tell me what's happening?"

His brow furrowed. "How's Stewart?"

I shook my head and looked down. It was the same speech, with the same all-important non-verbal cues that I'd given to anyone who asked. "Not well. The doctors seem to think that it could be any time. When he's awake he's lucid, but when he's out, he's out! I think it's the medications. Though he hasn't complained, the doctors say that this form of rapidly progressing leukemia is extremely painful. They have him pretty drugged up on painkillers. They're doing all they can do to help him go peacefully."

Brody reached for my hand. "Bravo. That's a beautiful speech, Mrs. Harrington. Now tell me how the motherfucker is really doing."

My downturned lips twitched as my eyes darted toward his. "He's dying. He's suffering. Karma's a bitch and though he deserves every damn second, I wish Karma would get her ass in gear and finish him off. Watching him die is sucking the life right out of me."

"Oh…" The aquamarine of his eyes shimmered. "I'd be glad to suck some life into you."

The tension of the last few months seeped from my taut shoulders. "Don't tempt me, Mr. Phillips. I'm not a stable woman."

"Don't say that. You're a fucking rock. I'd wish more years of suffering on him, if it wouldn't be so hard on you."

"I met with his oncologist yesterday. They've exhausted all the treatment options. It really is just a matter of time. But now he is arguing about the pain medicine. I like that it makes him sleep. I'm hoping one day he will go to sleep and not wake up."

Brody's forehead furrowed. "Did you know Parker was at your apartment yesterday?"

"No." I bristled. I didn't like the idea of Stewart meeting with his private attorney and one of the founding partners of Craven and Knowles without me. Honestly, I didn't trust either one of them.

"He was," Brody confirmed. "It was yesterday morning."

"I was out," I said reflectively, thinking back over the last twenty-four hours. "The first and third Wednesday of each month I meet with the Harrington Society. My sister's spearheading another medical mission trip."

Brody nodded. "The good Doctor Conway. There isn't a selfish bone in her body."

"No." I genuinely smiled. When it came to saints, Valerie was next in line for canonization.

"I got the feeling that timing was everything," Brody continued. "Parker made a comment about you not letting Stewart out of your sight or vice versa."

The small hairs at the back of my neck stood to attention. "Do you know what they discussed?"

"Not for sure. Last evening, I overheard him asking his assistant to pull some old files. When I heard your name, I texted you. From all of my snooping, the only thing I could determine was that it involved Stewart's will, but I know for sure she also pulled the contract."

I stood and paced the length of the room. "Why? Why would they be looking at that contract?" I lowered my head to my hands to think. "Brody, everything, all of our investments, all of his stock, holdings, *everything* is in both of our names. Tell me, what could he possibly do in a will to combat that?"

"As long as they stay that way, I predict *nothing*. Maybe he just wanted to be sure everything was in place. You know? If he's feeling the finality of his situation, he probably doesn't want anything to be out of place." Brody shrugged. "Being the standup guy that he is and all."

My mind raced. "My name was added after our marriage, over ten years ago. I've followed that damn contract to the letter."

"Vik, you don't want that contract going public. Let's watch. I wanted to see you today to let you know I have my eyes and ears open. I'm watching your back. You don't need to worry."

"So help me God, if he screws me… after everything."

Brody's brow arched. "I'd say you've been royally screwed already, but what are you going to do, Vik? Kill him? The man's dying."

He wouldn't be the first person I had killed. Slowing my breathing, I said, "I know Craven and Knowles represents Stewart, but, damn it, they're supposed to be representing *my* best interests, too."

Brody's whisper brushed across my hair as his arms encircled my waist from behind. "Vik, I'm here. I'm watching out for your best interests. You never need to doubt that."

Leaning into his embrace, I craned my neck until our lips met. The emotion bubbling within me rushed forth as his tender yet firm lips willingly accepted my kiss and encouragingly demanded more. Spinning me around, our tongues once again fought for supremacy, wrestling and submitting, tasting and savoring. Again, the fire within me sparked to life.

"How long has it been since someone has really held you and loved you?"

Brody's question brought a deep ache deep to my chest. "How long has it been since we've been together?" I replied. From the way we were standing, I could see shimmers of light from the ocean below reflected in his unique irises.

"Jesus, Vik. I want to pick you up and throw you on that bed." He lifted my chin and peered deep into my eyes. "Look at me, damn it. I'm not like the others. I don't want to fuck you." A deep rumble came from his chest. "That's not true. I want that too. But..." He brushed my cheek with the back of his hand. "What I want more than anything is to make love to you, to hold you, to watch you sleep, and be there when you wake. I want to love you so hard that when those beautiful eyes are closed, I have no doubt that you're dreaming about me. And when you wake, I want to be the one to make every one of your dreams come true."

"Brody, please, please, don't make promises you don't intend to keep."

"But I do. I'd do it right now, if you'd let me." He tugged my fingers though I stayed fastened to the carpet, refusing to budge. His forehead wrinkled as his cheeks rose. "I make good money. Tell

Stewart to go fuck himself. Tell all the ass-wipes on his board of directors and Parker Craven to shove it. I know you said it could be any day, but it could also be a week, a month, or more. Don't subject yourself to him and his fucked-up idea of loyalty any longer."

I shook my head from side to side. "Stop. I told you that I'm a mess right now. And you're not making sense." Without admitting the truth, that no one had ever proclaimed undying love to me, I rallied, "I haven't devoted ten years of my life only to walk away when the prize is within sight. It isn't just about the money. It's the satisfaction I'll get when I whisper in his ear that I made it. He underestimated me, and my ability to handle everything he threw my way. I want his last thought to be of me in control of everything he holds dear."

"You deserve that," Brody said dejectedly.

"I do. I'm not feeling guilty for wanting what I deserve."

Again he wrapped me in his arms. "Victoria Harrington, I know without a doubt that I don't deserve you, but I'll be damned if I feel guilty for wanting you."

The ringing of my phone stilled us both. Stewart's distinctive ring cut through the chilled hotel air. Hurrying to my purse, I put my finger to my lips and said, "Hello?"

"Tori." My husband's voice was stronger through the phone than it had been earlier in the morning. Obviously he'd succeeded in decreasing the pain medicine.

"Stewart, is everything all right?"

Brody's eyes widened.

"Hardly," Stewart replied sarcastically. "Travis said that you're at the Harbour Shoppes?"

"Yes, do you need me home?"

"No," his tone gained strength. "I want you at the warehouse in an hour."

Shit! My stomach sank. "Stewart…" I could argue, but he knew I wouldn't. Despite his weakened state, he'd already proven he could still orchestrate. My only option was to pray it would be the last time.

Once Stewart was gone, the warehouse would be the first thing I sold, or maybe I'd torch it? The thought brought a feeling of resolve. Swallowing my retort, I replied, "I'll be there," and hit disconnect.

Brody's hands brushed my arms. "What is it?"

I looked away. "I need to go. Please keep me posted."

His eyes opened wide as panicked concern infiltrated his voice. "Why, Vik? Where do you need to go?"

I didn't answer, but picked up my purse and headed for the door. Before I walked away, I heard Brody, his voice a low growl. "I hate that damn motherfucker. I swear, if he weren't dying…" The closing of the door drowned out the rest of his sentence. But I knew what he was about to say.

CHAPTER TWO

Present

MY HANDS SHOOK as my body trembled. Why was I even surprised he'd gone back on his word? The fucker had promised! He'd promised to always be with me!

Holding my midsection, I doubled over as revolt took hold and my lunch was purged onto the concrete of the private garage. The sound of my distress wouldn't bring anyone's attention. There was no one there. I knew that. I knew once the *friend*, as Stewart liked to call them, was done, he was gone. It was one of the ways they tried to secure their anonymity. Besides, Stewart's voice had told me that he was gone, told me to stay where I was, not to move until he said the word. I'd disobeyed in the past. I no longer considered that on option. Stark naked on the freaking four-poster bed, I waited as the damn music came through the headphones.

Sometimes I hated the music as much as his voice. For almost nine years it had been the same eerie playlist. When I asked, Stewart refused to tell me the names of the songs, only that they reminded him of a time long ago. As the years passed, I think I found reassurance in the predictability of the order. Without my sense of sight, it gave me something to hold, something expected. Each time he restarted the music, it was always from the beginning. I'd heard the first melody so many times it haunted my dreams. One day I searched and searched the Internet until I found it: *Fatal Lullaby*. Knowing the title made it even more depressing—if that were even possible. *Death Dance* came next. All of the songs he chose were composed by Adrian von Ziegler and were only instrumental music. None contained words, only dark, tortured strains that resounded through my ears as I struggled to make sense of the world around me.

Closing my eyes, I reached for my car. Fleeing the stench of the garage, the warehouse, and my life was my only thought. Without a doubt, I needed to get away from this place.

After so many visits, somehow not having Stewart present had made it worse. But then again, he was. He was there through a new system of cameras. With this new system, he could watch from our home. Our home. In one afternoon, he'd taken away the separation of warehouse and home: one of my last refuges.

My hands trembled as I pulled my car door closed. I fought with the new reality: Stewart's voyeurism wasn't over, not as long as breath still entered his lungs. With this newly installed technology, his favorite sick form of entertainment would continue. The last two months of reprieve as he fought against the cancer was only that, a momentary break. The sadistic motherfucker would keep this going until the bitter end.

I turned my eyes—devoid of makeup—toward the rearview mirror. Thank God there was a shower at the warehouse. I hated the smell of the men. Again, the loss of sight heightened my other senses, including that of smell. I wasn't supposed to know who his *friends* were. It used to give Stewart a rush as we'd enter a party or a function and he'd taunt me with the idea of whom I knew and who knew me. Closing my eyes, I still heard his sadistic tone as he paraded me on his arm.

Of course, the men never let on. They never came forward, but smell was a powerful sense: whether cologne or aftershave, a breath mint or body wash. When I'd least expect it, an aroma would remind me of the warehouse, the music, and Stewart's incessant directions. Then I would know. I would know that the man smiling sweetly at his wife, or taunting me with his stare was one of Stewart's *friends*.

This afternoon, his friend wore cologne similar to Stewart's. When we first married, I loved the erotic combination of rose and sandalwood, and oud. I'd noticed the unique scent the first day we met. I remember finding the bottle in his room and reading the name: Tom Ford Oud Wood. There was even a time when I would lay my head on his pillow just to inhale the scent.

That was before, before the warehouse, and before death grabbed him by the balls. No longer did he walk in a cloud of expensive cologne. Now the scent of death and denial hung in layers around him and his makeshift hospital room.

The great Stewart Harrington wanted to die at home. He wanted to be surrounded by the luxury and opulence of his hard work. *Bullshit!* Stewart Harrington wanted to live. Going to the hospital and being attached to their equipment would admit defeat. I couldn't imagine him admitting that until words were beyond his control.

That knowledge refueled my strength. The motherfucker was going to die: of that I was confident.

Turning up the radio, I tried to drown out the wordless dark tunes in my head. Slowly, I put the car into reverse. Exiting the garage, the sunlight steamed through my windshield, blinding me as I reached for my sunglasses. *Damn, it was still daytime. This fucking day wouldn't end.* I looked toward the clock when the screen on the dash changed. STEWART flashed on the screen indicating an incoming call.

I choked back the bile and hit the CALL button that allowed my husband's voice to replace the music and fill the car.

"What?" was the best greeting I could manage.

"Are you coming home?"

I turned the car right, not sure where I was headed, only that it was away from our penthouse. "No."

"No?"

"You fucking lied!" I'd played the role so long that my unexpected outburst no doubt took Stewart by surprise. "You said you'd always be there. You weren't *there!*" The road before me blurred from my tears as I fought to regain my semblance of control.

"Tori," his voice was soft, though his pet name made the bile return to my throat. "Come home. Let's talk about this."

"No. We're not supposed to talk about *this* at home. It's supposed to stay separate from home. You ruined everything."

"Come home." Unlike his tone through the damn headphones, these words were spoken more as a plea. "The doctors want to give me more medicine. I want to see you first. I want to tell you how good you were. How proud I am of you."

He fucking wanted to do more than that, and I knew it. I gripped the steering wheel and weaved through traffic, not even the slightest bit concerned with my destination. "I'll be home, just not until later."

"You know, you don't have the right to be mad. I checked the contract. There was nothing in there saying I would *always* be present."

"Well, Stewart, I haven't read the fucking contract since before we were married. But I have heard you tell me that you're there, with me. I hate it! I've always hated it. But at least… Shit!" I slammed on my brakes and threw my weight onto the horn. Stupid fucking tourists, walking in the damn street.

"What happened?"

"Nothing. Take your damn medicine. I'll be home when I'm home."

"I want you to come home now. You're my wife."

"I am your wife. I'm Mrs. Stewart Harrington and I'm going out. I'm calling my sister or something. I've followed your rules. I played your whore. Now I'm doing something for me. I may not have read the contract recently, but I do remember there's nothing in it restricting my activities." Before he could refute my comment, I went on, gaining strength with each word. "I'll tell you what I'm *not* going to do this afternoon. I'm not going to sit in a chair and watch you die." *Because if I did, I'd grab a pillow and accelerate the process.* The words were right there. Thankfully, I had enough self-control to bite them back. "Goodbye, Stewart. Get some rest. *You've* had a busy afternoon."

I hit the disconnect icon.

As my car filled with the music from the radio, my surroundings came into view. I was near the offices of Craven and Knowles. My mind started turning, playing Stewart's words over in my head. He said he'd recently reviewed the contract. That was the opening I needed. If he'd reviewed it, I could review it.

Jumping two lanes of traffic and ignoring the horns, I pulled into the parking garage and found a space. It was nearing 5:00 PM. No doubt the secretary wouldn't be pleased to see me so close to closing time. Too damn bad. I'm Mrs. Stewart Harrington.

I took off my sunglasses and looked in the rearview mirror. I never went out without makeup. My eyes looked red, as did my lips; yet, my cheeks were pale. Reaching for my purse, I found some mascara, eyeliner, and lipstick. My damp hair was tied in a knot at the back of my neck. Pulling a few loose strands from the sides, I let them dangle beside my cheeks. Sliding my sunglasses back into place, I decided it would have to do. I'd driven to the law firm for a reason, even without thinking about it. For the first time in over ten years, I wanted to see the damn contract.

"Mrs. Harrington? I-I'm sorry. Did you have an appointment?"

"No, Trish. I did not."

She shifted uncomfortably. I knew she didn't want to spend her precious nail-polishing time on me. Honestly, I didn't know how this woman had kept her job as long as she had. She was probably giving blow jobs under desks. It was the only possible answer. Her skills as a receptionist certainly lacked: maybe she excelled at fellatio?

"D-Did you want to see someone?"

"Trish, I want to see *something*. I need to speak to Mr. Craven's assistant. I believe she'll be able to help me."

She looked toward her computer. "I'll be happy to schedule—"

I put my hand on her desk. "I'm here now. Now would be a marvelous time to schedule. Don't you agree?"

"Y-Yes. Let me call her. I know Mr. Craven has been out. If she's available—"

My skin crawled. "Trish, I suspect that even if Mr. Craven's assistant is busy, she can find time for me. I'm not leaving until I see what I came to see."

Trish stood. "If you'll follow me, I'll get Maggie."

"Thank you." I nodded as I followed her to the center conference room: the fishbowl with the blinds. It was the same one I'd been in many times. Within seconds she'd hit the switch, changing the windows to opaque.

"Mrs. Harrington, may I get you something? A coffee perhaps? One with cream and two sugars."

"Thank you."

I wasn't a coffee drinker, but her request made me smile. It was one of my first lessons in being Mrs. Harrington. At that time, I'd seen so much potential. Funny, I shouldn't have. Perhaps there was a time I'd been as positive as my sister. Leaning back against the plush leather chair I huffed. No, that had never been the case.

My purse buzzed and I pulled out my phone. There were three text messages. The first was from Brody:

"I'M WORRIED ABOUT YOU. WHERE ARE YOU? ARE YOU OK?"

I grinned as I replied:

"IN YOUR OFFICE. IN THE FISHBOWL."

The second was from Stewart.

"NOT ANSWERING YOUR PHONE? VERY MATURE. COME HOME NOW!"

My grin quickly disappeared. He may have the power to make me participate in his sick-assed fantasies, but never during our marriage had he had the ability to control my comings and goings.

"I DIDN'T TURN OFF MY RINGER. I MUST NOT HAVE HEARD IT. I WILL BE HOME... LATER."

The final message was from my sister Valerie.

"I JUST GOT A CALL FROM STEWART. WERE YOU PLANNING ON COMING TO SEE ME? I'D LOVE TO HANG OUT, BUT I'M ON CALL TONIGHT. TOMORROW?"

I sighed. I'd find something else to do. All I knew was that I didn't plan to be home until Stewart was amply medicated and sound asleep.

"LET ME CHECK. TOMORROW MIGHT WORK."

As I finished my last text the door opened. The young paralegal, probably about my age, in her late twenties, entered. I didn't recognize her, but then again, young women working for Parker Craven came and went with some regularity.

"Mrs. Harrington," she said with a tight smile. "What can I do for you?"

Trish came in the open door and set my cup of coffee on the table. After she left us alone, I replied, "Maggie, I presume?"

"Yes, ma'am."

"I would like to see a contract that Mr. Craven prepared for my husband and me before our marriage. I know it's available: my husband told me he'd recently reviewed it—yesterday, I believe. He recommended that I also review it." The mention of Stewart seemed to dispel some tension. I remembered my recently washed face and removed my sunglasses. Obviously feigning a smile I went on, "I'm sorry I didn't call first. As you can see, I'm not truly prepared to be out. It's just that with his health... well, Stewart wanted me to do this right away. So here I am."

Her shoulders relaxed. "Yes, I'm so sorry about your husband. I was worried because Mr. Craven is currently with a client, but if Mr. Harrington sent you here..."

"He did. I'd recommend that you call, but with the medication, he's probably asleep right now. That was why I wanted to do as he asked before he woke again."

Her light brown eyes glowed. "Of course. Let me get it for you. I haven't sent the contract back to the filing room yet. It's on my desk."

I dramatically massaged my forehead. "Thank you again. I hope this doesn't put you out."

She shook her head. "Not at all. You stay and review as long as you need. Anything to help Mr. Harrington in his hour of need."

I managed a smile, with my jaws clenched tightly together. It was the best I could do.

A few minutes later, I was alone with my coffee and the document. *Why was he truly reviewing this? Was there something I missed ten years ago?* Hell, undoubtedly I missed something. At eighteen I had no idea what all the clauses and addendums meant. It wasn't until he later explained that I realized I'd signed a legal document with the devil himself.

I began to read:

This agreement is hereby entered into willingly and without coercion between Stewart Allen Harrington, hereinafter referred to as Mr. Harrington, and Victoria Ann Conway, hereinafter referred to as Ms. Conway. Mr. Harrington and Ms. Conway hereby agree on May…

The terms of this binding agreement between Mr. Harrington and Ms. Conway are as follows:

1. Mr. Harrington and Ms. Conway agree that all that occurs under the terms of this contract are confidential and consensual.

The door opened. Expecting Maggie or even Trish, I turned impatiently. Parker Craven's dark glare bore into mine as he entered, a cloud of heavy cologne hanging around him. The realization of his afternoon whereabouts paralyzed my movement until I straightened my neck and returned his stare.

"Victoria, what are you doing?"

The tips of my lips moved slowly upward. There was no way it reached my eyes. Loathing was all I could feel. The rush of blood that filled my ears and eyes narrowed the scene to a tunnel. No one else existed. I felt his sweaty hands on my skin. I couldn't allow him to see my hatred. It was my fuel, my energy to carry on.

Refusing to show him my reaction, I opened my eyes wide, and said, "Parker, nice of you to tend to me personally. Your assistant said that you were with a client."

He looked down at the document. "I asked you a question."

"Yes, you did. I'm reviewing the contract that Stewart and I signed."

"Why?"

I lifted my brows innocently. "Because he told me to. After all, he said he'd reviewed it with you and I should do the same. Didn't he tell you?"

"He told you that? When?"

My teeth ached from clenching. "Why, it was this afternoon."

He inhaled deeply. "This afternoon. He told you that this afternoon?"

"Am I stuttering?"

He glared in my direction. Before he could respond, I softened my tone. "Oh, Parker, sometimes he doesn't know exactly what he's saying. I'm very concerned about the decisions he's making. Why, just this afternoon, I was with him at home and he told me that you'd been to the apartment. I'm sorry I missed you."

Parker Craven reached for the document. "I don't know what you think you're—"

I slapped my palm on the pages. The clap echoed throughout the small room as my eyes bore into him. "Mr. Craven, I believe that you and your firm have been hired by my husband and me. If you want that arrangement to continue in the foreseeable future, you will not attempt to stop me from seeing documents that pertain to me: this or any other."

"I can't allow this without Stewart's permission."

My grin widened. "Do you not believe that he sent me?"

"That he sent you this afternoon? No."

I leaned back, still holding the document. "Why? Why would you doubt me?"

"Mrs. Harrington? Oh, Parker." Brody said, opening the door and interrupting the palpable confrontation. Looking from Parker, to me, and back, Brody continued, "Maggie mentioned that Mrs. Harrington came by and needed assistance. I thought you were with another client." Brody motioned toward the door. "If you need to get back to your other client, I'd be happy to help Mrs. Harrington."

Parker narrowed his gaze. "Brody, this is a delicate matter between Mr. and Mrs. Harrington. I believe it would be better if—"

"Thank you, Mr. Phillips. I believe my husband has put his trust in you and I will too. Now, run along, Parker. I'm sure you have catching up to do. I hear you've been out of the office."

I'm not sure if the senior partner had ever been told to *run along*. But by the crimson seeping from his cheeks to his ears, he wasn't happy about it at this moment. Without a word, he left the room and Brody gently closed the door.

In a hushed tone, he asked, "What are you doing? What did I walk in on?"

"Brody, can you make a copy of this for me?"

"I suppose."

"Do that. Then you and I can go through it with a fine-tooth comb."

CHAPTER THREE

Present

I DIDN'T KNOW if I could trust Brody enough to share my revelation about Parker. Truthfully, I wasn't sure I could stomach saying it aloud. Memories of my first meeting with Parker Craven, thoughts of discussions and dinners, as well as time spent with his wife, playing tennis, attending charity functions, all combined to bring back my nausea from before. I knew in the pit of my stomach that today hadn't been our first encounter. The ghostly scent of his cologne seeped through years of sexual encounters until all I wanted to do was bury them in a deep, bottomless tomb.

Brody touched my knee, bringing my thoughts out of the pits of hell and back to the ONE Bal Harbour Resort suite. "Hey, we have a copy of the contract. We don't need to go through the whole thing tonight. Besides, this is sick-assed shit and you've had a rough day." His eyes widened as his hands went up in surrender. "I'm sorry, Vik. I don't need to know what you went through, or what he made you do, but just being here, sitting next to you… you're different than you were this afternoon. I feel you pulling away. Don't give him that power."

My neck straightened. "I'm not. That's why I went to the law firm. I'm not giving him the power. If I had, I'd be home right now."

"Home with him? Why?"

"He called me, after…" I blinked unnecessarily. "…I yelled at him.

I can almost tell you the number of times I've yelled during our entire marriage. Honestly, there haven't been many. It's just that he made me a promise. From the very beginning of this *sick-assed* thing..." I motioned toward the contract and emphasized Brody's words. "...he made me a promise and today he broke it."

"And you're surprised? A man who made you sign a contract like this... you're surprised he broke a promise?"

My chin fell to my chest. "Stupid, isn't it?"

Warmth enveloped me as strong arms pulled me closer. "No, Vik. It's not stupid and you're not stupid. You were tricked into marrying the devil. It's only natural that you'd try to justify his actions and hold on to any shred of moral high ground."

Inhaling Brody's fresh clean scent, I allowed myself to melt against his chest. His words, tone, and actions were exactly what any normal woman would want to hear. But then again, I wasn't normal. How could I be? I'd been told since before I could remember that I was venom. If there were even a small part of me that had feelings for Brody, the best thing I could do for him was to keep my distance. Then again, I needed his help, at least until the nightmare named Stewart Harrington was buried deeper than my memories.

"Stop it," Brody commanded.

My eyes widened. "Stop what?"

"You're still doing it. You're retreating to wherever you go in that beautiful head of yours."

He was right. It was safer there. I could control the world in there.

"Vik? Look at me."

Clearing away the fog of broken promises, I peered into the tranquil aquamarine of his gaze.

"That's it. Now, stop thinking about anyone or anything else: live in the here and now, with me."

I shook my head. "I can't. I need to go home. I'm sure Stewart's asleep by now, but if I'm not there when he wakes, he'll ask questions."

"When you spoke, what did you tell him you were going to do?"

"I said I wasn't going home right away. I told him I was going to go out with Val."

Brody's brows peaked expectantly. "Do you ever spend the night at your sister's?"

I couldn't stop the smile. "I have, but not often. Stewart doesn't approve."

"But… you yelled at him, right?"

I nodded.

"He knows you're mad?"

"Yes, I made that pretty clear."

"Why aren't you with Val?" he asked.

"She has rounds at the hospital tonight. I remember her saying that she's covering for some other doctors, ones who'll be covering for her while she's in Uganda."

"Uganda?" Brody repeated.

"Yes, that's her latest project. With the help of the Harrington Society, she's been and will continue to bring cancer treatment to remote villages. It's pretty remarkable. She's organized a big network. There are volunteers there all the time, but as the administrator of the grant, she has to be the one to monitor and help with transporting the necessary drugs."

"Isn't it dangerous?"

"She assured me that there are more dangerous areas of the world," I replied, remembering how I'd asked Val the same question. "That doesn't mean I don't worry about her. I asked her why she couldn't offer the same services here in the United States. There are still millions of people here who can't afford the necessary treatment. Especially with Stewart's diagnosis, it made sense. Why not start Harrington Cancer Clinics in the US?"

"Great idea. What did she say?"

"She laughed and told me she'd get a grant proposal to me as soon as she could."

"I love the way your beautiful eyes glow when you talk about your sister."

"She's the only good thing to come out of this."

"No, she's not," Brody said matter-of-factly.

Pressing my lips together, I didn't respond.

"How many people has she helped through the Harrington Society?"

"Hundreds, maybe thousands. But who's to say she wouldn't have done that—"

"You're doing it again, Vik. Don't sell yourself short. You made a deal with the devil and managed to promote good. Damn, beautiful, you're the one who deserves sainthood."

He couldn't have been more wrong. Sainthood was not in my future. Well, unless the devil had an apprenticeship program. I mean, he did start out an angel. I chuckled. Perhaps the devil did have a program. Unfortunately for him, I'd been a very good student.

"You're doing it again." His tone was demanding, as he proclaimed, "Stay with me."

"I can't."

"Not the night, though I want that. Stay here in this suite, with the ocean view." He gestured toward the windows. "Stay here. Don't go back into the darkness."

If he only understood: that was where I was born and where I'd lived. It was who I was. Nothing he could do or say would change that.

"If Stewart's already asleep," Brody began, "give me two hours. I'll search the contract tomorrow and text you. We'll work out another time and place to discuss it. Just, please, give me two hours tonight."

My lips quirked to a one-sided grin. "Why, Mr. Phillips? What could we possibly do in two hours?"

Lifting my hand, Brody stood. "Come with me, Victoria, let me show you."

My gaze fluttered toward the floor. "I-I don't..."

"Please," he implored. "No sex. Let me hold you. Just the two of us, in the light."

The anxious twisting in my stomach told me what I already knew: I should leave. I shouldn't allow my darkness to pollute his light. However, before I could argue, Brody had arranged the bed pillows and pulled me toward his broad chest. The beating of his heart echoed in my emptiness. It resonated with an ache more painful than the shame I used to feel from the warehouse or Stewart's comments.

That humiliation was no longer present. It had been, but I'd learned to shut myself off. It was like this afternoon. My body engaged in the activities instructed by the voice through the headphones, but my mind and my heart were shielded. As Brody continued to whisper loving things, the pain within me grew. Shouldn't I like this? Maybe my heart wasn't shielded; maybe it was dead? *Then again, can an organ ache if it no longer existed?*

I lifted my face to his and ran my fingers through his soft, short hair. In the natural light from the open windows, the hint of strawberry that graced his blonde was difficult to distinguish. Lifting my chin, I kissed his lips. The innocent connection deepened as our tongues united.

"Whoa," he protested, pulling away. "I'm being a gentleman here. What are you doing?"

Sitting back on my heels, I reached for the hem of my sundress and pulled it over my head. In one dramatic gesture, I threw it to the floor in a pile of silk. Wearing nothing but my panties, I palmed my heavy breasts, exposing and twisting my taut nipples. "Mr. Phillips," I began breathily, "you now have less than two hours to make me forget everything. I want you to fuck me so good that everything else in the world goes away. I want my only thoughts to be of you deep inside me." I lifted my brow, as I reached for his hand and placed it over my breast. When our eyes met, I asked, "Do you accept the challenge?"

From the look of his slacks, the tenting growing higher by the moment, and the sultry expression emerging from where moments ago I'd seen compassion and concern, I knew he did.

"Vik, I want you to know that I think of you as more than a fuck —"

I put one finger on his lips. "Brody, right now, I want to be fucked. I want to be fucked by someone who I can see and hear. I want to be the person in control of my movements and responses. I want *you* to fuck *me*. Fuck me like no one else has ever fucked me." My thumbs found the waistband of my panties. "Will you please do that for me?"

Unfastening his belt, he smiled my direction and said, "All but one thing. Just for the record, I'm in control of your responses." Before I could refute, he continued, "I'm not going to tell you what they are, but you'll know it was me who brought them on. I'm not stopping until I get what I want. Fuck the damn two-hour time limit." With my panties gone, Brody pushed me back against the large mattress and climbed my body, raining kisses from my breasts to my lips. "That is the challenge I accept."

I could do this. I could spread my legs and disappear. It was my specialty, my survival technique.

"One more thing," he said, grasping my chin and moving my eyes to his. "You're going to stay with me. I want to watch you come."

I needed to leave to escape. This connection wasn't what I wanted. "I-I don't..."

"Vik, right here." He calmly demanded as he pointed to his eyes. "Look right here."

When I did, his hand slid down my stomach. The path he'd traveled tingled from the warmth of his touch and ignited my skin. I reached for his shoulders as one then two fingers slid inside of me. In and out. With my gaze set on him and my hands holding him tight, my hips moved to his rhythm.

"That's it. Stay with me. Oh, baby, you're getting so wet for me..."

Lifting my hands toward the headboard, I refused to listen as Brody continued to talk. I hadn't gotten wet for anyone, not even Stewart, in years. That was what lubricant was for. Most of the *friends* were too stupid or too self-centered to know. Most probably gave themselves kudos for how easily their puny, condom-wrapped dicks slid inside. Little did they realize that the mere thought of their presence turned my body to dust. Sometimes I imagined that dust blowing away...

The way his aquamarine gaze penetrated, I knew this was different. I'd cleaned myself well at the warehouse. I was truly aroused.

"Vik, I'm going to use a condom."

Refocusing on his words, I nodded. It didn't matter. I wouldn't get pregnant. Stewart required monthly birth control injections as one of the clauses of the contract. I'd recently learned they weren't necessary, at least not where he was concerned. At one of his doctor's appointments, I'd accidentally found out that, years before our marriage, he'd undergone a vasectomy. Apparently, it wasn't something he felt the need to share. I presumed that the shots were added protection against accidents that could occur during his little shows.

"Oh!" I stared into the depth of his gaze as the head of Brody's hard cock pressed against my entrance. Despite the wetness, with each inch, his cock pushed the limits of my core. The delicious fullness demanded my attention as I readjusted my hips, encouraging him to fill me to the brink. Again, I reached for his shoulders, longing for that connection. My small hands caressed his rippled muscles, as he fulfilled my request. The scent of musk permeated the suite replacing his fresh aftershave, drawing me toward him. He didn't speak, but sounds of lust and approval filled my ears, capturing all of my senses.

His hips bucked harder and faster as I fell into his rhythm. Reaching for my ass and supporting us on his elbows, he pulled me closer, until finding where one of us began and the other one ended was beyond comprehension. We were one. Sounds escaped my lips as his heavy balls slapped against my ass.

"You feel so good. I-I…" Brody murmured as his eyes glazed, and he let go of my ass and found my clit.

As he fondled the swollen bundle of nerves, the suite around us disappeared. It had been so long since I'd had a real orgasm, the overwhelming sensation took me by surprise as fireworks ignited and flashes of light electrified my body from within. I couldn't let go of him, fearful that if I did, I'd be washed away in the waves of pleasure flowing from my fingers to my toes.

Pounding into me, Brody found his release as he let out a roar that echoed through the suite. When the final ripple of unbridled pleasure subsided, Brody kissed my forehead and rubbed his cheek against mine. "You're incredible."

Smiling, I moved my hips, sending messages to where we were still connected. "I don't think that was me."

His expression lightened as the small lines came to the corners of his eyes. In a smooth flip, I found myself on top, straddling him, his cock still buried deep inside of me. "I'm pretty sure there's no one else here. It was all you." He lifted my hips slightly and lowered me. The friction brought life back to where it had begun to descend. I moved to adjust as he stretched my already pleased core.

"That's it Vik. Keep moving. I don't believe my time is up."

I leaned back, allowing him to fondle my breasts. Skillfully, Brody twisted and taunted the already hard nubs, his ample fingers bringing both sparks of pain and waves of pleasure. Each sensation moved from my breasts to my core, magnifying each thrust of his hips. With the building tension, I questioned my ability to remain upright. As if reading my mind, his fingers entwined with mine, supporting and holding me as I enjoyed the mounting friction. The wildfire that had exploded earlier re-ignited, burning a path that threatened the destruction of my finely constructed walls.

The suite filled with clamor as primal sounds escaped my open lips and Brody, too, growled above the din. We continued to move as one until our words and noises reached their peak.

"Fuck! Vik, you're so fucking hot!"

His back arched and fingers dug into my flesh as his cock throbbed within me. Unable to hold back, the walls of my core milked and contracted while satisfied sighs stilled our movements and quieted the suite. Like a cloud of peace, the room—hell, the world—fell into a climax-induced calm.

Unable to face the aquamarine that saw inside of me, I fell, shattered beyond repair, onto his chest. As I reeled with my reality, strong arms enveloped my shoulders. It had been unlike any orgasm I could remember. Surely, I wasn't whole. I couldn't be. In the depths of my haze, I knew that I was no more than a million disassociated pieces vulnerable to the winds of life.

Yet, before I could be blown away, Brody again kissed my forehead and brushed my cheek with his. He pulled me into his warm embrace and held me as I melted into his side. Without hesitation, I laid my head on his shoulder and drifted to sleep.

"Vik," Brody's startled voice pulled me from the depths of slumber.

Oh shit! Despite the open drapes, blackness filled the suite. "Fuck! What time is it?"

"It's after midnight."

My head spun as I threw back the covers, rushed from the bed, and searched for my clothes. "I need to go."

"Where's your car?"

My car? "Fuck! It's at the hospital."

Brody reached for my hand, his words slow in comparison to the mayhem in my sleep-dizzy mind. "It's all right. If he questions you, tell him you were at the hospital with Val." Brody reached for his slacks and continued, "You two were discussing the new cancer clinics when she was called to help with an emergency. You fell asleep waiting for her to return."

My eyes widened as I secured my dress. "That's good. I just need to get Val on board."

"Will she be?"

I shrugged. "She's my sister. We look out for one another."

"Let me drive you to the hospital."

Nodding, I reached for my purse and pulled out my phone: two missed calls from Travis. It figured. If it weren't Stewart, it was his informant: his eyes and ears. Oh, well. I would deal with it in the morning. There was nothing I could do now.

As we walked toward Brody's car, I asked, "How did you come up with that alibi so fast?"

"Why, Mrs. Harrington, I'm your attorney. It's my job."

CHAPTER FOUR

Ten years ago

"Miss Conway?"

Travis, the man who'd come to get me, had moved without my realizing it, walking toward an elevator. Hurriedly, I stepped to catch up to him, reaching him just as the doors opened. The control panel held only one button: PH, which I assumed meant penthouse. A million questions swirled through my mind, but from my limited experience, I didn't believe that this driver would be the one with the answers.

Since I'd agreed to attend this meeting that my parents had arranged, I'd been given no more information. All I'd received was the outfit to wear with a note telling me that my presence was imperative for all of our futures.

Attempting to hide my uneasiness, I did my best to appear calm and stay quiet in the small, uncomfortable space as the elevator ascended toward our destination. When the doors opened, the most stunning view and exquisitely decorated living room was before me. The tall windows illuminated the room, overpowering the light-colored furnishings with the intense blue of the sky and sea.

"Thank you, Travis, I'll take Miss Conway from here."

I turned toward the woman's voice. About my mother's age with short blonde hair and soft blue eyes, she didn't give me the same uncomfortable feeling I felt from Travis. Before I could speak, she reached for my hand. "Welcome, Miss Conway. It's nice to meet you. My name is Lisa. If I can be of any assistance, please don't hesitate to ask."

"I'm sorry, Lisa, where am I? Whom am I supposed to meet?"

Her eyes opened wide. "Miss Conway, you're here to see Mr. Harrington. We're in his Miami penthouse. Surely you recognize the city through the windows."

My heartbeat approached a normal cadence with her honesty, and I glanced again toward the windows. "Yes, I recognize the city. I just didn't know where *in* the city I'd been brought."

Her expression softened as she asked, "Would you like to freshen up before seeing Mr. Harrington? If not, he is ready to see you."

Lowering my voice, I asked, "Lisa, who is Mr. Harrington, and why does he want to see me?"

Concern danced across her expression. "Miss Conway, I'm not sure why you haven't been informed. Perhaps it would be better for Mr. Harrington to explain." She squeezed my hand. "After you speak with him, I'll gladly help clarify anything I can for you."

Uncertainty and apprehension twisted in my empty stomach. I was suddenly happy that I hadn't eaten. Swallowing the growing lump in my throat, I squared my shoulders, and replied, "I believe I'm ready to see Mr. Harrington."

"You look lovely, dear. Let me show you to his office."

I followed as Lisa led me through the large white living room. Lush green plants and accents in the hue of blue complemented the tile floor and white leather furniture. With the color of the ocean outside of the windows, it all flowed together beautifully. The tile changed in shape as we approached a long hallway. I couldn't help but wonder how big the penthouse was; however, before I could give it much thought, Lisa paused. Looking me in the eye, she whispered, "Harrington Spas and Suites, International. Perhaps you weren't to know that yet, but I believe it would be beneficial for you to know whom you're dealing with."

Before I could respond, she turned away and knocked on the door. My mind was a blur. Of course I'd heard of Harrington Spas and Suites: it was one of the most exclusive hotel chains in the country, probably the world, since Lisa had said *international*. The main reason

I knew about it was that my stepfather Randall's medical practice had an exclusive contract with the Miami Harrington location. According to my mother, it was a very sought-after account. The fact that Randall had been involved in securing the partnership was an accomplishment that my mother felt the need to flaunt at one of our rare dinners.

I also remembered hearing something about Harrington Suites in one of my classes. The academy that I attended prided itself on its college-preparatory classes. An introduction to business was essential for the children of the elite. In one of those classes I recalled a discussion about transitions in business and the repercussions when a family-owned business was passed from one member to the next. As I recalled, Mr. Harrington's father started the Harrington Suites a long time ago, but when he passed away, his son—the man behind the door—inherited the controlling shares of the company. He created an uproar by wanting to modernize the already successful chain. There was more than a little trepidation on the part of the board of directors. Nevertheless, the younger Mr. Harrington stuck to his guns and included spas in all of the facilities. From what I'd read, they were remarkable top-of-the-line spas.

As I heard the greeting of *come in* from behind the door, I tried to remember the news reports I'd seen and the biography I'd been required to read. Funny, at the time it didn't seem important. Now, I'd give anything to have retained more. I did recall reading that the younger Mr. Harrington grew up with the world at his fingertips and had quite the reputation for living life to its fullest. I also thought I remembered that his wife passed away at a relatively young age. Nevertheless, by today's standards, they'd been married for a while.

When the door opened, I stood dumbfounded. *That was Mr. Harrington?* I'd expected him to be older. It wasn't that he was young, like me, but I was expecting ancient. He looked like he was perhaps forty, give or take a few years. He definitely looked younger than my parents, and my mother spent a lot of money and time with her plastic surgeon to look as young as she could. Immediately, his gaze went to me and a grin came to his lips. "Miss Conway, Victoria…" He extended his hand as he came around his desk. "…I'm so glad we were able to make this work."

I took in his casual attire—jeans and white t-shirt—and suddenly felt overdressed. Though the heels gave me height, with each step he took toward me, I felt smaller and smaller. Next to him, my five-foot-six-inch frame was dwarfed. He had all the tell-tale signs of a man who lived in Miami, the sun-kissed skin and blonde hair.

Yet, all I could wonder was why on earth would this well-known business owner want to see me?

Slowly I accepted his hand and looked down. Instead of shaking mine as I'd expected, his grasp lingered. The warmth of his touch was in stark contrast to the cooled air within the penthouse suite. When I lifted my gaze, his deep-set blue eyes devoured me, as his grin broadened. My insides twisted again as the fine hairs on the back of my neck stood to attention. Unabashed by my obvious trepidation, he leaned back and scanned me up and down.

My discomfort grew with each passing second. With my hand still in his, I turned for help, looking for Lisa. Perhaps she'd show me some sign of support or reassurance. However, as I turned, all that I saw was the door as it closed, leaving me completely alone with this man I didn't know. Summoning any strength I could find, I worked to articulate without fainting. "Mr. Harrington, I'm afraid I don't know why I'm here."

His mouth twitched as he cocked one brow. "Miss Conway, is it usual for you to frequent unknown places for unknown reasons?"

Was he amused by my discomfort?

Freeing my hand, I gripped my purse and squared my shoulders. "No, Mr. Harrington, it is not. As a matter of fact, I'm a bit uncomfortable. Please tell me what this is about or I will leave."

"I believe you should hear me out." He gestured toward me. "I mean, look at how beautiful you look. You're all dressed up."

Blood rushed to my cheeks.

He stepped back and casually leaned against his desk. "Let's start with you calling me Stewart. Formalities seem unnecessary."

Unconsciously, I closed my eyes and sucked in my lower lip. My body trembled with uneasiness as I tried to understand what was happening. Before I could speak, Stewart cupped my chin and lifted my eyes towards his.

His ease with touching me made me even more uncomfortable. I stepped back and replied, "Stewart, I don't know—"

His tenor dropped. "Victoria, your parents and I have discussed an agreement to resolve a situation they seem to have gotten themselves into. I find it interesting that they apparently didn't feel it was necessary to fill you in on your role."

I did my best to remain stoic, mistakenly believing that I could no longer be surprised by my parents' actions.

He continued, "They have arranged for you to settle their debt for them."

Settle their debt? "I don't know what you mean... I don't have money..."

My words trailed away as he once again secured my hand and led me to a sofa: one that I'd not even noticed until that moment. Once we were seated, he said, "Victoria, we are to wed."

"What?!" I pulled my hand away. "I'm not marrying anyone. I haven't even graduated from high school." Stewart was almost as old as my parents. There was no way in hell I was marrying him or doing anything else with him.

Smirking, he went on, "I realize that wasn't exactly a romantic proposal. I'll be honest: I'm not looking for romance. You may or may not know that your family is a bit dysfunctional."

Dysfunctional? He had no fucking idea.

Though my nerves were stretched to the point of fraying, I tried to quiet the hysteria in my mind, as I comprehended the idea that I could never have possibly foreseen this, or that once again, I underestimated my parents' ability to ruin my life. Fighting my flight response, I gave Stewart Harrington my full attention and calmest voice. It was a trick I'd taught myself as a child, a way to appear calm to others when in reality all hell was breaking loose on the inside.

"Stewart, I'm eighteen. I don't have to do anything my parents say. I make my own decisions."

"Yes, you do. You won't be forced to accept this arrangement, but before you decide, I recommend you hear the entire story."

Fine, I'd hear him out. Years of private education and finishing school taught me manners. I'd hear him out, and then politely tell him to fuck off.

"Your stepfather has an affinity for gambling. He has made a few bad choices."

Yes, like thinking that I'd ever be willing to sell myself to save his ass. The scenario was too obscene to comprehend. "I don't really care what Randall has—"

"Victoria, don't interrupt until the facts are out there."

Taking a deep breath, I nodded.

"As I was saying, Randall likes to play the horses and dogs and well, anywhere he can place a bet, he does. Your mother has a secret, too. She may have kicked the alcohol, but her new drug of choice can be as equally destructive. It's shopping. She's been known to spend a hundred thousand in an afternoon. The two fuel each other. She needs his winnings to support her addiction. That all works well, as long as Randall wins. When his streak first ended, he thought he could gamble his way out. That's what happens with the addiction. Every next bet has the potential to save both him and his reputation. However, as you can imagine, since we're sitting here, it hasn't worked. Each bet dug him deeper and deeper into debt—"

"Randall is a doctor. He makes good money."

Stewart's gaze darkened at my interruption.

I didn't care if he approved of my speaking or not. This was my life and my future we were discussing casually, like a movie or book. I needed clarification. "I still don't understand…"

"Perhaps you should try listening?" he said, somewhat condescendingly.

Pressing my lips together I stared, lifting my brows for him to continue.

"As I was saying, Randall's debt grew. He tried to work a deal with the gentleman who loaned him the money. These types of gentlemen are not interested in deals and they don't take kindly to unpaid debts.

"Randall came to me for help. I have money that I can lend. The thing is…" He paused. "…I don't need it. Therefore, I decided that in exchange for the money, I wanted something else…" He reached for my knee. "…something less conventional in return. You see, since my wife passed, I have found myself in need of companionship. I have a reputation, and there's nothing like a pretty, sexy young thing like you to send the world of stuck-up assholes into a frenzy. I want them to talk and notice; however, I don't want to feed the paparazzi. A young wife is better than the string of dates or dealing with hired women to fill the roles I desire."

Did he equate the two? A wife or a prostitute? My voice raised an octave or two. "I'm not a whore. I cannot be bought."

"You are *not* a whore, and I don't mean to insinuate that you are. However, anyone can be bought. You come from a socially acceptable family, and though young, you can be taught to deal with those stuck-up assholes. And, because you're young, you can be trained to fulfill my requirements."

No longer able to sit, I stood and paced about the large room. "This is ridiculous. I'm not for sale, and I'm not a dog. I won't be trained."

"Victoria, I assure you, you're not a dog. Bestiality is not my thing. As I said, you're not a whore, but once you agree to this marriage, you will be *my* whore."

"I don't understand. I'm not selling myself to save Randall or Marilyn. They wouldn't lift a finger for me. Why would I do this for them?"

"Didn't you wonder why they weren't willing to pay for your continued education?"

"No," I answered unequivocally. "I know why."

Stewart lifted his eyebrow in question.

"They hate me and everything about me. That's fine, I don't need them. I have a job arranged."

"At a small insurance company, as a receptionist, making a little over minimum wage."

My mouth opened. I hadn't shared my job with anyone—anyone except Val. "How do you know about that? How do you know so much about my family?"

"Vic-tor-ia," he said, standing and drawing out the three syllables. "I wouldn't be offering you this opportunity if I hadn't had you thoroughly investigated. I know everything there is to know about you. I can't have a wife with skeletons in her closet."

"I'm not marrying you."

Coming closer, his words slowed. "Because a studio apartment and minimum wage is better than living between this penthouse and my estate just outside the city limits? Or because you don't want to help your sister?"

What did he know about my sister? Val meant everything to me. I would do anything for my younger sister. After all, it wasn't like our parents cared. We were all each other had. Keeping my eyes away from Stewart's smug expression, I asked, "What do you know about my sister?" Before he could respond, I walked toward the windows; the ocean was rough with white-capped waves glistening out toward the horizon.

Stewart's voice came from behind me, his tone steadfast in his knowledge. "I know everything about both of you. I know everything about your no-good stepfather, your mother, and their spoiled boys. I even know about your biological father."

Tears unexpectedly filled my eyes. Despite my better judgment I turned back toward this man who had many more answers than I imagined. "I haven't heard from him, ever. My mother said he hasn't contacted her since Val was little. What do you know about him?"

Grasping my shoulders, his large hands ignited my skin as his knowledge and power flowed through his touch. For just a split second, concern showed in the depths of his blue eyes. "I know he doesn't need to be your concern." Maintaining his grip, he continued, "Now, to your other questions. I know that Valerie won't be able to stay at the academy for her senior year of high school nor will her post-high-school education be paid. I know that you have every reason to hate your parents, and perhaps you do, but you don't hate their boys, your half-brothers. I know you don't want them to lose their home and very likely their parents."

"What do you mean?"

"Those men to whom Randall owes the money—they won't accept less than payment in full. If they don't get it soon, Randall's life will pacify them for a short time. It'll appear like an accident, but it will happen. How do you think your mother will handle that? Do you really want to be responsible for his life?"

Did I? It wouldn't be the first life I'd been blamed for taking, yet would it end at Randall? Did I care? Did I care if my mother drank herself into oblivion? I didn't know. Then again, what about Marcus and Lyle? What about Val? What would happen to them?

"Stewart, I don't even know you…" my words trailed away as I turned back to the window. Randall and my mother could dive into the ocean as far as I was concerned, but the boys? They're still so young… and Val? One more year before her future can begin. It was too much—too much to comprehend.

Fighting the emotional overload, I closed my eyes and tried to grasp what had just happened. As I did, Stewart's warmth alerted me that he was directly behind me. With my overwrought nerves, I startled when his hands brushed my arms.

"Victoria…" Stewart's voice resonated deeper, more breathy. "…you're beautiful. I've had time to consider this agreement. I have to admit, as I've watched you for the last few weeks, my anticipation at getting to know you has increased. You're truly astounding: so strong despite the lack of support you've been offered." His hands continued to brush my arms in a ghostly caress.

"But I don't know you. I don't love you."

His voice echoed near my ear, each word closer than the last. "You will get to know me."

I began to turn toward him, to stop the uneasy feelings his proximity spurred, when he stopped me, his tenor leaving no room for compromise. "Don't turn around."

Involuntarily I shuddered at his command.

"Put your hands on the window. Let me see those pretty little fingers."

I'd never heard a man speak with such unquestioning authority. Obediently, I splayed my fingers on the cool glass, thankful that I'd left my purse on the sofa. Caging me within his arms, his hands came to rest beside mine. The contrast in size was as startling as his deep voice as it exhaled breathily onto my neck.

"I'm sure you're concerned about our age difference. Let me reassure you, I've taken good care of myself. That's the thing: most women my age haven't. As I said before, I have preferences, things I like and things I don't."

One hand disappeared from sight, and soon brushed the side of my right breast. Sucking in a gasp, I closed my eyes. *Why was I allowing this?* I should scream or run.

His head dipped to my shoulder as a shudder went through me

and a new sensation stirred within me. "Victoria, I like that strength I mentioned. I like that even though you don't know me, you've been honest with me about your family. I like that you haven't left these negotiations and are considering this agreement. I like that from this view I can see your hard nipples beading under that black dress. I like that you didn't turn around when I told you not to, and I like that you're aroused."

"I'm not," I lied, as the unusual feelings made my core clench. It made no sense. I didn't know this man, didn't want this man, yet his mere words were doing something to me.

The hand that had brushed my breast came back up and slipped down the front of my dress. As I gasped and began to move, his deep voice stopped my movement. "I said to keep your hands on the window. I didn't give you permission to move. Did I?"

When I failed to respond, his fingers found my nipple and rolled the hard nub, in a painful twist. "Victoria, I asked you a question. Answer me, or I'll need to get your attention another way."

It took all of my concentration to form the words and not think about what his hands were doing. I didn't know if I liked it or hated it. My mind and my body were at war, and I was caught in the middle. As his fingers sought the other nipple, I remembered how to speak. "No. You didn't give me permission."

"Good girl. Now, don't move your hands and tell me the truth. This is turning you on, isn't it?"

"I-I don't know… I'm scared."

His lips brushed my neck. Instead of fighting, I tilted my head back against his chest to give him better access.

Sighing, he moaned. "Damn, girl, you're sexier up close than I ever imagined. Do you know how hot that answer was?" His fingers that had just painfully twisted my hard nub caressed my same breast. Suddenly, his touch was warm and electric. "You may be frightened, but it's not of me: it's of what you're feeling. Your nipples are telling me you're feeling the same thing I am. They're saying that you like this." With both hands on my breasts, he lowered the top of my dress, fully exposing me to the window. Thankfully, we were stories above the city. "Do you know how else I know you're aroused?"

Forming words had become increasingly difficult. Therefore, I shook my head.

"I smell it, and darling, you smell fantastic. I bet you taste fantastic." Nuzzling my exposed neck and shoulder, he continued, "Have you ever let a boy go down on you?"

"N-No, I've never…"

"There're so many things that I can show you, so many highs. Darling, if you and I can make this agreement happen, I promise you highs like you've never imagined."

"This-this isn't right."

"Does it feel wrong?"

I wanted to say yes, it felt wrong, but it didn't. "My parents can't do this to me. It isn't fair."

Continuing his torment of my breasts, Stewart continued, "They aren't the first. Think of this like an old-world arranged marriage. Do you think those lords and ladies didn't think of their daughters as a commodity, as a means to an end? Their daughters were nothing more than a way to infiltrate into a better family, a better way of life. Just like a young virgin married off to a king, consider yourself a payment to save your family's standing. If you agree to this, they can go on fooling the upper-crust snobs."

"B-But I don't care about them—"

"No? What about your sister? Do you want Val to have the education she deserves? Would you like to have so much money and influence that you could tell your mother to fuck off?"

I'd never dreamt of that, never even considered it. *Was that the opportunity staring me in the face? Did I want that? Wait! No, I wasn't selling myself for them—but Val?*

My internal debate came to an immediate end with another painful twist of my nipple. "Ouch."

"I asked you if you wanted to help your sister and outclass your mother at the same time."

"I want to help Val." Once I spoke, the pinch morphed to a pleasant caress. "I-I don't know about my… Oh!" Stewart's hips tilted forward, stalling the thoughts of my family. He pulled me against his chest and introduced my lower back to what I was sure was a huge erection.

"Victoria, I can only imagine how tight and wet you are right now.

I know my cock will stretch that tight pussy in the most incredible way."

I'd never heard anyone speak this way. As much as I wanted it to disgust me, it didn't. Powerfully, he pulled my ass against him.

"You're worried about my age. I like your age. I like that you aren't a virgin, but that you have so much more to learn. I guarantee I'm not like that kid from Kinsley Preparatory: I'm a real man who knows what he's doing. I'll do things to you that you've never imagined."

"H-How do you know what I've imagined? And how do you know about Wesley?" He was from Kinsley and the only boy I'd ever been with. Our first time was a blundering of sorts. Neither one of us knew what to do or how to go about it. The next time didn't hurt as much, but being with him had never been nearly as erotic as standing here against a window with my hands being the only thing I could see, besides the gorgeous blue ocean view.

"I've told you: I've been watching you and doing my research." With one arm above my exposed breasts and the other around my waist, he pulled my ass tighter against his erection and swayed his hips. "And like I said, I'm glad you're not a virgin. I don't want that responsibility. That said, other than the fact that you had one guy's dick inside of you, I promise, when it comes to what I have planned, you've never experienced anything like it."

His words and hips created a delicious rhythm rocking me against his solid chest, as well as other parts of him. Without thinking, my body moved in sync.

"Please..." I needed this to stop. The painful tension building within me caused my insides to ache. "...please, Stewart."

His arm tightened around my waist. "Yes, Victoria, *please* what? What do you want me to do? Do you want me to fondle that deliciously lickable breast again and pinch that hard nipple or do you want more than that?"

"I-I want..."

"If I lift this dress, I could expose your slick thighs. You're wet for me, aren't you?"

"S-Stewart, you're right, I'm not a virgin, but I've never felt this way. I don't know what to do."

His hand lowered to the hem of my dress and began to lift. "Let me see how wet you are."

Was it a question? Was he asking me or telling me what he was going to do? I couldn't think straight. Brushing my inner thigh, I knew he'd find what he wanted. I was wetter than I'd ever been.

His voice was low as his fingers slid over my thighs, so near, yet not touching where my body wanted him. *Did I want that?*

"Victoria, you're a naughty girl. If I put my fingers inside of you, would you fuck them? If I told you to?"

"W-What are you doing to me? I-I don't want this." Throwing caution to the wind, I gathered what little strength I had, pushed off from the window, and spun into his chest. "Stop. You're a pervert, and I told you I'm not a whore."

His blue eyes were the color of the water, deep and dark. With a smirk, he lifted his finger to his lips and sucked. After making a show of it, he grinned. "Once you're my wife I can do that whenever I want. Allowing your husband to finger fuck you isn't being a whore. Like I said, you will be *my* whore."

Righting my dress, I moved around him. The sound of his chuckle filled the otherwise quiet office as I made my way to a chair and sat. "I'm sorry Randall has made poor decisions, but that isn't my concern. I have a job lined up. I'll support Val. We'll make it."

Stewart walked to his desk, his erection visibly tenting his jeans as he sat. Lifting two manila folders, he slid both of them toward me. "Victoria Conway, this offer has not been made lightly. I've given it a lot of thought and consideration. I've even had my legal team work out the necessary legalities. In this folder..." He touched the one on my left. "...is an agreement to do as we've discussed. It includes a do-not-disclose statement regarding what happened today as well as an agreement for us to wed, next Thursday. Along with that is a contract that I'll sign. One that will guarantee the payment of necessary funds to repay your stepfather's current debt as well as give you access to any monies necessary to fund your sister's education at the academy and any undergraduate and post-graduate study she chooses. I believe she's interested in medicine." His eyebrows rose. "Medical school can be expensive."

I swallowed. *How did he know so much?* That was a lot to offer.

Could I truly make her dreams come true?

Stewart continued, "And in this folder..." He touched the one on my right. "...is a nondisclosure agreement for what happened today and a check made out to you for fifty thousand dollars. I want you. I want you to be my wife; however, if you choose to walk away today, I don't want you to be beholden to the likes of Randall and Marilyn. You deserve better than that. This money will help you, post-graduation, and you can use as much as you'd like to help your sister, your mother, whomever. The choice is yours."

"Fifty thousand? All I have to do is sign and I have fifty thousand dollars? The only stipulation is that I can't tell anyone what happened here today?"

He leaned back and nodded. "Darling, your mother's little secret shopping issue would be nothing for you if you sign the other contract. Within reason, your access to my fortune won't be restricted. You'll not only live in the best of the best, vacation at the most exclusive Spas and Suites, but you'll have whatever you desire. Fifty thousand wouldn't even be a limit on one of your charge cards."

"But, why me? And what will I have to do for all of that?" My voice was gaining confidence with each question.

"Why you? Randall. But that was only the beginning. I've watched you; I saw how incredible you are. I waited for you to become legal. Then today, I saw that you're everything I imagined and more: so sexual, so responsive. I could have so much fun with you. That would be what you'd need to do: let me do what I want with that sexy body."

Goose bumps materialized. "What does that mean? Will you hurt me?"

He leaned forward. "When I twisted your nipples, did it hurt?"

I looked down and back up to his eyes. I refused to let him intimidate me with the subject of my own body. "Yes, it did."

"Did you enjoy it?"

Blood rushed toward my cheeks. "It hurt, but then you made it feel better."

"And?"

"I guess I liked it."

"As Mrs. Harrington, your pleasure, as well as your pain, will work together toward my pleasure. You'll be my wife and my whore. Ms. Madison will be responsible for getting you ready for the role of my wife. She'll teach you how to act, respond, and how to deal with some of the issues that'll arise. I'll assume the responsibility of teaching you about your sexual role."

My sexual role? What the hell? One thing at a time. "Ms. Madison?" I asked.

"You met her when you arrived."

"Lisa?" I asked.

"Well, yes, Lisa. Interesting that she gave you her first name."

"What if I try this and I can't do it?"

"Look through the documents. Everything is spelled out: what will happen if *I* chose to terminate the contract, what will happen if *you* chose to terminate it, as well as other options. You should read it all carefully before you decide."

I couldn't believe I was actually considering this. "When do you need an answer?"

"Tomorrow morning, by seven-thirty. If you choose to sign the nondisclosure statement then you have school to attend. If you choose to fulfill the contract, we have a wedding in less than a week."

"B-But what about my graduation?"

"You will graduate. I'm one of the biggest donors at the academy. They will not refuse my wife's graduation.

I stood. "I guess I need your number so that I can call you in the morning."

"No." He smirked.

"No?"

"You'll be staying here tonight. During that time you can speak to Ms. Madison and ask her questions. If in the morning, you opt for leaving, Travis will drive you to class."

"I'm not sleeping with you. I'm not agreeing to that as part of the deliberation process."

Playfully, Stewart put his hands in the air. "My cock will not enter that tight little pussy until you ask for it. Until you beg for it."

Jerk! "Well, then that will make our arranged marriage rather easy on my part. I have no intentions of begging for anything."

"Really? I barely touched you today and you creamed those pretty little panties of yours. I'm confident that you'll be begging to have my dick inside of you before we tie the knot."

I suddenly thought of Val and her ice cream, waiting for my return. "I-I need to call Val."

"Of course. She'll be concerned; however, at this time, the nondisclosure is effectively in place, since both options include that clause."

I gripped the back of the chair. *How was this happening?* "I have to speak to her. What can I tell her?"

Stewart grinned. "Victoria, you are truly my dream. If there is any more I can do to entice you to sign that contract, don't be shy about a counteroffer."

He didn't know the truth. All his research didn't tell him that I wasn't a dream: I was a nightmare. I'd been told that my whole life. Pushing those thoughts away, I replied, "That doesn't answer my question. I don't lie to my sister."

"Did you tell her about Wesley? Did you tell her about the job with the insurance company or the deposit you put on that small apartment?"

His intimate knowledge of my personal life was starting to piss me off. "I eventually told her about Wesley. I will tell her about the apartment and job. I didn't want to worry her right now. She still thinks I'm going to the University of Miami."

"So, darling, my point is that you have indeed lied to your sister." His blonde brows lowered, and his eyes squinted. "You won't lie to me. As you can see, I have ways of learning things."

"I can tell her that it was a meeting about a possible opportunity and since it was elaborate, I'm staying in the city, at a fancy hotel. She'll be excited for me." That wasn't a lie. She would be. My sister could take any scenario and make it optimistic. I on the other hand was unsure if it were possible to spin this whole thing to the positive. "Now, where am I to stay?"

"Ms. Madison will show you to a room, but know that once we're married, you'll share a room with me."

"*If* we are married," I corrected.

Another chuckle. Stewart looked down at his watch. "You have almost twelve hours to make up your mind. In less than one hour you've gone from *it's not happening* to *if*. Perhaps I'll have my begging before the night is done?"

Smug bastard. That was one challenge I didn't mind accepting. "Not happening." I turned toward the door. "Where do I find Lisa?"

CHAPTER FIVE

Ten Years ago

LISA TOOK me on a tour of the penthouse. It comprised the top two floors of the building—the entire floors. It was humongous. How could one man live in all that space? There were sitting rooms, as well as the large living room that I'd seen upon my arrival. There were multiple offices; apparently the smaller ones were for his employees. There was a beautiful kitchen, dining room, outside patio, and pool, as well as an exercise room. I lost count at the number of bedrooms, or more accurately, suites. The only one that mattered to me was the one I was to call my own. Although Stewart made it clear that after we wed I'd be sleeping in his room, for the night, I found refuge in my own space. It was all too much to process. Lisa asked me repeatedly if I wanted food. Eating was not on my short list. The more my mind churned over the proposal before me, the more my stomach twisted with confusion and doubt.

I knew that I needed to talk with Val. Truthfully, I should've called my parents and asked them what the hell they were thinking. I should've demanded that they tell me the truth about the situation and why on earth they thought I'd come to their rescue. However, talking to either of them while managing the aftershocks of their bomb blast was not something I wanted to do. Talking to my sister was. We were so close that I worried she'd catch on to my deception. If I'd really been in a fancy hotel, I would've called and chatted leisurely. So, I did. I put on my façade of a sister interviewing for a job and talked with her on the phone for over an hour. My concerns were unfounded: she spent most of the conversation talking about my graduation and the TV show we were simultaneously watching. It was one we watched every Sunday evening. Together we'd laugh about the ridiculous way the women treated one another. The situations the contestants found themselves in had seemed ludicrous. That was until I watched the reality show, lying on a big-assed bed, in a huge opulent bedroom, with a TV the size of our dorm room. Suddenly, life competed with reality television for the absurd. For a few minutes I even considered the fact that maybe I was a contestant. Maybe this whole thing was nothing more than a new reality show.

To that point, I searched for cameras as Val and I spoke. Granted, my knowledge of hidden cameras was nonexistent; however, I was thankful that I didn't find any.

As soon as our call ended, I turned off the TV and attacked the manila folders. Since I had a pretty good idea what the nondisclosure agreement would say, I only opened the option B folder to confirm the existence of the fifty-thousand-dollar check. I'd only planned on glancing at it, being sure it was there, but then I saw it. *Victoria Conway* typed out on the payee line, $50,000 in the small box and spelled out underneath my name, Stewart Harrington's name and information above, and his signature sprawled in the lower right corner.

For longer than I cared to admit, I held the check and contemplated the possibilities. I may not be able to tell my mother to fuck off with only fifty thousand dollars, but I could walk away from my graduation with confidence in my future. Marilyn might need expensive shopping, but I didn't. I could make that amount of money last a good long time.

But at what expense?

Was Stewart telling me the truth? Was Randall truly in that much debt? What would happen if I said no? Would I need to live with another death on my hands?

Each moment that I held the check, my guilt lessened. After all, what had Randall or Marilyn Sound ever done for me? And fifty thousand could help Val too... but what about our half-brothers?

What about Marcus and Lyle?

With trembling fingers, I put the *walk-away* check back into the folder and reached for the other folder: the one with a contract for my life. The one with a contract to buy me, to make me—as Stewart had so eloquently called it—his whore. I wouldn't let myself think of the possibilities. Hell, I couldn't think of the possibilities. My sex life was too nonexistent. I didn't even read the books that some of the other girls at the academy read. They'd blush and giggle as they sent screen shots of highlighted passages to one another, all the while shifting in their seats. I'd always found it hard to believe that mere words could have that much effect on someone's libido, but then again, that was all Stewart had used. With words and proximity he'd made me wet, wetter than I'd ever been.

Slowly, I opened the second folder. *Shit!* Why was I even considering this? Why didn't I just laugh in his face earlier in the afternoon and tell him to shove it?

My neck straightened as I fought with my answer. I didn't really want to tell my mother and her fancy-ass husband to fuck off; I wanted her to know that I had that ability. I wanted, just once, for her to look at me like I wasn't a horrible monster. I wanted her to look at me like she looked at Marcus and Lyle. I wanted what I'd never had. The question was how far would I be willing to go to get that?

I stared down at the multipage document in my hand. What I knew about legalese could be summarized on a subject line of an email and still have room for more. Reading the name of the law firm at the top of the page, I knew I was in over my head. Craven and Knowles sounded not only impressive, but threatening. I began reading:

This agreement is hereby entered into willingly and without coercion between Stewart Allen Harrington, hereinafter referred to as Mr. Harrington, and Victoria Ann Conway, hereinafter referred to as Ms. Conway. Mr. Harrington and Ms. Conway hereby agree on May —

I shook my head in disbelief. It was dated for tomorrow. Stewart was either confident or extremely cocky. As I continued reading I began to decipher which.

The terms of this binding agreement between Mr. Harrington and Ms. Conway are as follows:

1. Mr. Harrington and Ms. Conway agree that all that occurs under the terms of this contract are confidential and consensual.

The hairs on the back of my neck stood to attention. I may not know much about contracts, but could he really contract my consent? Wasn't that something that I'd need to give as each instance occurred?

---

2. Specific information regarding the personal and sexual activity of Mr. Harrington and Ms. Conway may not be disclosed by either party to anyone outside of the experience. Failure to comply with this term will result in immediate breach of contract and void of all financial compensation.

What the hell does *outside of the experience* mean?

I went to the desk in the corner of the room and searched through the drawers. Finding paper and a pen, I went back to the contract and started making notes. If I were actually considering this ridiculous proposal, I wanted my questions answered.

Two hours later, with two pages of questions, including clause numbers and addendum citations, my head spun. The knock on the bedroom door pulled me from my concentration. Bristling, I sat straight and glanced toward the sound. Somehow I'd become safe within the cocoon of the four walls. It was true: I was engrossed in the contract, clauses, and addendums that could very well define my life, but upon the plush silk sofa with a view that marveled the one in the living room, I'd found security.

Stewart had promised that we wouldn't have sex before I made my decision. No, he'd said not until I asked—or begged. That seemed impossible, but then again, what part of this scenario was possible? What if he were the one knocking? Did I want it to be him? Would seeing him again help me make a decision?

I hadn't seen anyone except Lisa since I'd left his office, over—I looked at my watch: 10:30 PM—five hours ago. The knock came again.

"Just a moment," I called as I made my way toward the door. Opening it only a crack, I peered around the edge.

"Miss Conway?"

I exhaled the breath I didn't realize I'd been holding. "Lisa, it's you." I opened the door wider.

Smiling, the kind woman said, "Yes, miss. I'm about ready to go to my room for the night. However, I first wanted to be sure you were comfortable. Is there anything I can get for you?"

"Lisa, could you please come in for a minute?"

"Certainly." She stepped across the threshold. Her grin widened, making her light blue eyes shine. "I see you found the clothes. I'm glad they fit."

I looked down at my bare feet peeking out from the end of the yoga pants and the unbelievably soft t-shirt that hung from one shoulder. It was just the kind of thing I liked to wear around the dorm room in the evening, much more comfortable than the heels and dress that my parents had instructed me to wear for my mystery meeting.

"Yes, I found these as well as a few other things. Thank you."

"You're very welcome. However, it wasn't me. It was Mr. Harrington. He wants you to be as comfortable as possible."

I edged toward the window and gestured toward the sofa and chair. "Would you mind having a seat for a few minutes? I've been reading this contract for hours, and I have so many questions." Suddenly I thought about the nondisclosure clause. Would talking to her be a violation of that clause? Would all of this have been for nothing, even if I opted for the *walk-away* agreement?

The concern must have been evident. Lisa reached for my hand and using a reassuring tone said, "It's okay. You can talk to me about it. Mr. Harrington showed me the documents. He assumed you might be more comfortable talking to me than to him."

"S-so… if we speak about it, it doesn't constitute my breaking the do-not-disclose clause or agreement?"

"No." Lisa sat and looked at the table where I had left the contract and my notes. "I'm glad you're taking this seriously. I was concerned that with your…"

"My age?" I asked, finishing her sentence.

"Yes. I don't mean any disrespect, my dear. It's just that Mr. Harrington is an intense man. He didn't make his offers lightly. This arrangement has been thoroughly researched and dissected. I was concerned, before I met you..." She added with a nod in my direction. "...that you would think it to be a flippant offer."

I closed my eyes. My head ached from all the deliberating. "I assure you, Lisa, I'm not a silly child. I may be only eighteen, but I've been making life-altering decisions for much longer than I should. I've not had the most stellar parental support."

"Given the circumstances, I presumed. How may I help you?"

After trying to understand all the verbiage in a purely technical manner, having Lisa's kind words and expressions brought emotion where I'd worked to keep it away. I didn't want emotion. Even at my young age, I'd found that my head made better decisions than my heart.

I abruptly stood from the chair near Lisa and walked to the window. With the night sky, the ocean below was dark: the only exceptions were the scatterings of lights here and there from ships, yachts, or boats. From the height of the penthouse, the expanse was enormous. I searched for the horizon: the place where the black water met the darkened sky. The moonless, starless night made the differentiation difficult.

Keeping my eyes fixed toward the ocean, I asked, "You have used the word *offer* twice. Do you really see this as an offer?"

"What else would it be?"

I shrugged, turning back toward her and fighting the impending tears. "I guess, technically, it is an offer. But I feel like I'm agreeing to a sale, not a proposal. I mean, if I understand all that I've read, and I agree." I rephrased. "*If* I agree, I'm in essence accepting money, housing, the repayment of my parents' debt, and Stewart's name in exchange for my life. M-my body... m-my future." I lost the fight with the emotions as a few renegade tears cascaded from my still-painted eyes.

"In essence, isn't that the way it is with every marriage proposal?" Lisa asked. "In marriage, doesn't the woman give herself over to her husband in exchange for his protection? When she does that, doesn't she usually choose to take her husband's name and financial support?"

I nodded. "Yes, but..." The next words sat heavily on my chest. "...most women marry for love. I never imagined marrying anyone, but if I ever entertained those fantasies, I imagined candlelight dinners and walks on the beach. I assumed I'd know—really know— my husband, and he'd know me. I never, in a million years, imagined a fifteen-page contract and a twelve-hour deadline."

Lisa looked down. There truly was no answer. No one imagined his or her life would be orchestrated the way I found mine to be. Well, no one in the twenty-first century. Maybe as Stewart said, kings, queens, and nobility did it in the sixteenth century, but not today.

I continued, "This isn't even like an online dating service. With that I'd at least be able to look at his profile."

A spark of excitement came to Lisa's light blue eyes. "Did you Google him?"

My nose wrinkled. "No. I guess I've been a little busy with these contracts."

"Do that, dear. Google him. Learn all you can."

"What can you tell me?"

She shifted in her seat. "I've worked for him for over ten years." She didn't offer any more.

"And?" I asked when the silence began to loom.

"The death of Mr. Harrington's father was difficult for him on many levels. By the time I was employed his father had passed, and he'd taken over Harrington Spas and Suites, International; however, I heard things. I knew that assuming responsibility for his father's business presented him with many challenges. During that time, Mrs. Harrington was the light of his life, and he was a devoted husband." A shadow cast over Lisa's features as she looked toward her lap. "Her death changed him in more ways than I can say. In the time since, he's different."

I didn't like the foreboding feeling I felt from her words. "What do you mean *more ways than you can say*? Are there restrictions on what you can tell me?"

Her bright eyes looked up. "No, not at all. Mr. Harrington implored me to be honest with you, and I am being honest. He's a private man. Even after all of these years, I know that there are sides to him that I know nothing about."

"Like at his work?"

She shook her head. "That, but something else. I know that he has another apartment, one he sometimes frequents. I don't know why he has it or what he does there. I just know that he doesn't talk about it. I inquired a few times, but was told that it didn't concern me."

I sat with a huff. "I'm nuts! I'm absolutely crazy for even considering this."

"Miss Conway, I'll always be honest with you. I don't know what I'd do in your situation. I know that there could be worse offers from far worse people. I believe that Mr. Harrington is seeing his youth pass by. I believe that in you, he hopes to recapture some of that. I also believe that the person with whom you should be discussing this is him."

She went on, "You're right, there isn't love, but there can be respect. The best way to facilitate that is honesty. I know Mr. Harrington expects and respects honesty. In return, he'll be honest with you."

You won't be a whore, but you will be my *whore.* If those words were spoken in honesty, what did they mean?

As I contemplated, Lisa stood. "It's getting late. Is there anything I can get you?"

"No, thank you. Thank you for talking with me."

She squeezed my hand. "Anytime. I'll admit, for selfish reasons, I hope you agree."

I didn't answer, but raised my brow.

"Ever since Mrs. Harrington died, the house has been quiet and often boring. I'm excited to have someone else to care for and talk with."

Her smile warmed me. *When had someone wanted to take care of me?* It was another emotional question I wouldn't allow myself to contemplate.

"Thank you, Lisa. I'll start my Google search right away."

"If you want anything to eat, there's plenty in the refrigerator. Help yourself." With that, she was gone, and I collapsed on the bed with my phone. Opening the browser, I entered *Stewart Harrington* into the search engine. Most of the recent findings were business related. It wasn't until I searched further back that I found anything personal. It seemed that before he married Lindsey Harrington and after her passing, he went through a rather wild time. There were pictures and articles about his escapades. As time passed, I kicked off the yoga pants, washed my face, brushed my teeth, and climbed under the incredibly soft covers.

With the clock nearing midnight, my cavernous bedroom filled with the sound of my rumbling stomach. *Perhaps I was hungry?*

Still barefooted, I quietly made my way down the long corridor, down the stairs, and to the kitchen. I'm sure there was a more direct route, but with the dimmed lighting, I was unsure of my surroundings. Once my feet hit the textured flooring of the kitchen, I searched for the refrigerator. There were many, all filling a corner of the restaurant-grade kitchen. They were stainless steel and large.

I'd lived most of my life in boarding schools. I didn't know much about cooking, but this kitchen was nothing like the one at my mother and Randall's house. Without turning on the lights, I saw wall ovens and multiple stovetops with large hoods. Near a row of cabinets there was a stand-alone refrigerator. I decided to check in there first.

When I opened the door, the bright light flooded the kitchen. As soon as my eyes adjusted, my cheeks rose, revealing my smile. On the first shelf were multiple containers with notes that all read *Victoria*. Pulling the first from its place, I opened it and discovered a salad, complete with a container of dressing. The second was filled with fresh fruit. Each one was a gift, made especially for me, by someone who truly wanted to help me.

As I reached for the last container, the energy of the room shifted. It wasn't that I heard anyone or physically felt anyone, but I knew. I knew I was no longer alone. Before I could speak, a large hand came from behind and held open the refrigerator door. I didn't need to turn around to know Stewart was there.

CHAPTER SIX

Ten years ago

STEWART'S warm breath skirted across my hair, a stark contrast to the coolness coming from the refrigerator. Goose bumps materialized on my arms and legs as I became hypersensitive to his proximity, as well as keenly aware of my clothing. I was standing in Stewart's kitchen in nothing more than a long t-shirt and panties.

"May I help you?" he whispered near my ear.

Shuffling my feet, I reached for the final container. With a quick turn and a confident smile, I replied, "No, thank you. I think Lisa has taken care of everything."

Now, nearly nose to nose, Stewart took a step backward and scanned me from head to toe. "Pity."

I arched my brow.

"I hoped there was something you needed, something Ms. Madison wasn't able to give you."

"I-I didn't eat earlier. She said I could get something..."

He stepped closer, his firm chest grazing my erect nipples. Taking the container, he reached for my hand. "Come, Miss Conway, let me show you the view."

Like an animal to its slaughter, I followed, bare feet silently padding the hard tile surface until our destination came into view. Seeing the small table with the flickering candle, I gasped. Once he led me through the glass doors, the salt-scented humidity assaulted my senses while the warmth brought back feeling to my air-conditioner-cooled fingers and toes. Glancing at the table, I watched as the small flame protected within a glass chimney illuminated the beautiful balcony, creating a contrast to the dark ocean beyond.

"Stewart, this is beautiful. Did you talk to Lisa?"

His expression blanked. "I have, but not recently. Why?"

Was he an honest man? Could I take his reaction to mean that he'd planned this himself, perhaps, without my comment to her about candlelit dinners?

I shook my head, my dark hair cascading around my shoulders. "It doesn't matter. It was just something I said to her."

"You don't like the ocean breeze?"

"No, I do. I like it very much. I always wanted to spend time at the beach, but even growing up near Miami, I rarely did."

Stewart reached for my hand. "Tonight I don't want to talk about your decision or the contracts. If you have questions, ask me tomorrow. We'll talk, early. Tonight, I want to learn more about you, and if you want, I can tell you more about me."

My lips pursed. "Do you swear you didn't talk with Lisa?"

"I swear." He crossed his heart with his finger. "Our last conversation was about breakfast tomorrow morning. It'll be at six." He glanced at his watch. "Which is getting closer by the minute." With a raised brow he asked, "Do you want me to double-dog swear? I will."

"No." I giggled. "No need to go to all that trouble." I looked out at the water, the same water I could see from my room a floor above. "This is beautiful."

"It is," he agreed, though his eyes weren't on the water, but on me. "More beautiful than I dared imagine."

Blood rushed to my cheeks as I looked down to my lap. Before I could respond, his fingers reached for my chin. "Tori, don't look away. Never look away. You're much too beautiful for that."

"Tori?" I questioned. No one had ever called me Tori.

"I like it. I like that it's my name for you and mine alone. When I call you Tori, you'll know it's our connection."

I didn't know what to say. *Our connection? Did we have a connection?* "Stewart, please tell me more about you. I know you lost your wife—you mentioned that. Did the two of you have any children? Do you have any children?"

He shook his head. "No. We tried. Lindsey even tried in-vitro. Some things even money can't buy." The cloud of sadness took away his self-assured façade.

"I know you said not to talk about the contracts, but there's a lengthy clause about children, about not having them. Can you tell me why?"

Stewart opened the container that held grapes and popped one into his mouth. "I can, and I will, but not tonight. My turn to ask questions. Why didn't you run? Why did you stay here tonight?"

"I don't know. I'm scared and intrigued. I'm trying to not make a rash decision. After all, this will be the biggest decision of my life." I sat straighter. "Can I believe you?"

"Implicitly."

"So everything you told me about Randall and about his debt is true? His life is truly in danger?"

"That's the reason for the deadline. If he doesn't come up with the money by tomorrow afternoon... well, I suppose technically it's *this* afternoon. He needs the money by *this* afternoon."

I reached for the grapes, feeling the rumbling of hunger. When I did, Stewart pulled the container from my reach. "Let me," he offered.

"I'm capable—"

"Shush, let me..." Taking one grape from the container, he held it near my lips.

Obediently, I opened my mouth. The grape was sweet and juicy as I closed my lips and bit through the skin. By the time I swallowed, he had another one waiting.

As I opened my mouth, he spoke, "Tori, I didn't know how this would work. I still don't. I didn't plan on truly wanting you, but since you walked out of my office this afternoon, you're all I can think about."

When I closed my mouth on the next grape, his finger and thumb lingered between my lips. Instead of moving away, I sucked them, pulling them into my mouth and licking them clean. The groan that came from deep in Stewart's throat told me what I'd suspected: I had power. Over this wealthy, older man, I had power. The realization gave me strength.

"You didn't expect to want me?" I questioned. "Then why would you offer to marry me?"

He ran his finger over my lips. "I expected to want to fuck you. Who wouldn't? But that was all, as I said, to have you available, to not have to mess with the uncertainty of buying companionship, or the annoyance of dating."

Shaking my head, I tried to comprehend. "You would choose marriage over dating?"

"I told you that I didn't want to talk about specifics of the contract, but you did read both of them, didn't you?"

I nodded.

"Dating requires time and commitment. I don't want to do that. If you sign the contract, our future is secure for at least the next ten years. You can get mad at me, I can piss you off, or..." His words slowed. "You may be happy and content. The point is, for ten years, it won't matter."

"There was a clause to void—"

"Yes, there is a clause that gives either one of us the right to void the contract and our marriage. However, as I'm sure you read, it comes with serious repercussions. While we're married, you'll have access to my wealth, more access to more wealth than you can imagine. If you decide to void our contract before the ten-year benchmark, you forfeit everything: everything you've accumulated during our marriage, anything you stand to gain in a divorce, and anyone else who benefits personally from your generosity as a result of our marriage will be subject to terms of repayment."

I'd read that part. "Like Randall?" I asked.

"Yes, and your sister if you choose to pay for her continued education."

My eyes widened. "I can do that?"

Stewart brought another grape to my lips. "As Mrs. Stewart Harrington you can do almost anything you desire."

The *almost* floated in the air as I swallowed the sweet juice and accepted another.

Stewart continued, "After ten years, you'll have claim to a quarter of my fortune with no clause for repayment by any of the benefactors of your generosity."

"You keep saying *my* generosity. It's your money."

"As long as we're married, it will be our money. I have no deep-seated desire to help your family. If helping them makes you happy it benefits me. The decision to help them will be solely on you." Another grape brushed my lips. "After twenty years of marriage, you'll be entitled to half of our accumulated fortune. If I void the contract before ten years, you'll automatically receive fifty percent." Stewart leaned forward. "My darling, that is more money than you can even comprehend. I assure you that I will not be voiding the contract."

"Tell me more about Val, Marcus, and Lyle—mostly about Val. As long as we're married, I can pay her undergrad and graduate school?"

"Tori, we have already spent more time than I wanted discussing the contract. However, if it eases your mind, I'll repeat: once we're married, you'll have access to enough wealth to allow your siblings *carte blanche* at any university they desire. Now..." The flickering candle reflected in the shimmer of his heavy gaze as his finger lingered on my lips. "...tonight I want to learn more about my possible future wife."

His touch was cool and tasted sweet from the grapes. While the gentle ocean breeze blew wisps of my hair around my face, I watched Stewart's lids grow heavy, as if he were seeing me, yet imagining more than was before him. How did he expect to learn more if he didn't want me to speak?

With only the hum of the waves stories below, the silence on the balcony grew louder until the only sound I heard was the swish of my pulse resonating in my head. Without my realizing it, Stewart had moved from his chair and was mere inches away: his cologne lingered in a cloud surrounding both of us with the masculine scent. Moving his finger from my lips, he traced my cheek and a line along my chin. Without thinking, I inclined my face toward his soft touch.

"Stand for me," he said, offering me his hand. Though his command was soft, it was a command.

I obeyed.

"Tori, all I can think about is pushing you against that wall, ripping off those panties, and showing you what it's like to be with a real man."

With each word, I became suddenly aware that my t-shirt did little to conceal my sensitive, disloyal nipples. Trying to not give myself away, I fought to keep my eyes on his. It didn't work.

Looking down, a smug smile came to his lips. "You want that too, don't you?"

"You said that you wouldn't... that we wouldn't..."

"And I meant it. That doesn't mean I don't want it."

Taking my hand, he rubbed it over his not-so-hidden erection. What he offered behind his jeans was big and hard. I wondered what his cock would look like if it were released from its denim confines. The image of him inside of me scared as well as fascinated me, all the while making me wet with desire. His blue gaze drank me in as I continued to allow my hand to rub up and down the bulge.

Humming, he continued, "You have no idea how badly I want to free myself from these jeans. Just having your hand there..." He nuzzled my neck. "...knowing you're this close. You have me ready to come right now." His warm breath on my collarbone, he purred, "Tell me you don't want the same thing. Tell me you don't want to be fucked right here, against this wall. Tell me you don't want me to fill that void you're feeling and satisfy the tension building within you."

God! He was so right. My insides ached with need.

"You're wet for me already, without my even touching you, aren't you?"

"Y-Yes, I'm wet." Part of my brain told me that this was wrong, and that even having this conversation was wrong. The problem was that I could barely hear that part of my brain: the blood thundering through my veins as well as the sound of his heavy breathing overpowered everything else. As the stubble of his cheek brushed against mine, he pulled me closer, pressing me against the wall.

Before I registered the sense of entrapment, I stood on my tiptoes and kissed his neck.

"Fuck," he growled, pushing his knee between my legs, spreading them apart.

Despite my position, my sense of empowerment returned. I reached again for his erection, not freeing it, but rubbing, on my own, without his guidance. His jeans strained as his cock twitched below the material.

"Do you remember the question I asked you this afternoon?" he whispered, hot, needy breaths bathing my skin.

Hell, I couldn't remember my own name. There'd been too much. "Which question?" I asked through panted breath.

"If you would fuck my fingers… I promised you no sex until you're ready, but damn, girl, you're so fucking ready. You just don't know it. Let me give you the best orgasm of your life. If I can do that with only my fingers, then you can just imagine what I can do with my cock."

"S-Stewart, I-I don't—"

He reached under my shirt, stopping my words with the caressing of my breast, teasing the taut, hard nub of my nipple. "You don't *want me to stop*? You don't *think you should say yes, but you want to*? You don't *know what it's like to have an orgasm*?"

I buried my face against his wide chest, hiding my embarrassment in his cotton shirt. Everything he'd just said was true. It wasn't how I'd planned on finishing the sentence, but nonetheless, it was true. Again, the amazing scent of cologne overpowered my already overloaded senses.

Continuing to fondle my breast, he reached for my chin and brought my eyes to his. "Don't hide from me. I want to see every emotion behind your incredible eyes. That's what I want out of this agreement. I want to watch those eyes as I take you places you've never been."

I nodded.

"Words, Victoria, I need to hear it."

"I want what you just said."

His nose nearly touched mine, as he probed, "What did I just say?"

Damn him! He was going to make me say it. "I want to feel your fingers. I want to have an orgasm."

Letting go of my face, he reached for the waistband of my panties and teased the elastic band. "Have you ever had an orgasm?"

I shrugged. "I think. I'm not sure."

A low chuckle rumbled in the back of his throat. "Darling, if you're not sure, you haven't. Now, I still haven't heard exactly what you want."

The tension continued to build as his hand found my thighs.

"Shit, girl, you're so wet, you've soaked these panties."

Again, my cheeks blushed. "I-I should have worn the yoga pants. It's just that…" I shyly admitted, "…I was about ready to go—"

He reached down and shifted his growing erection. "Fuck!" he interrupted. "Tell me what you want before I rip these panties right off of you."

Gathering strength from his need, I reached for my own waistband and pushed the satin and lace down over my hips. "Stewart, I want you to fuck me with your fingers. I want an orgasm."

His smile grew, while his eyes shimmered with seduction. "Tori, my darling, that's one request that I'll never deny you."

The rough texture of the wall bit my back as his body once again pressed me against the outside of the building. When he lifted one of my legs with his knee, I reached for his shoulders. Before my exposure registered, his fingers opened my swollen lips and spread my wetness. I tensed at the intrusion until one of his fingers slid between my warm folds and inside of me. Simultaneously a long hiss filled my ears. It took me a moment to realize that the sound was coming from me. Everything he was doing felt incredible. It wasn't awkward or uncomfortable like it had been with Wesley.

"Oh, fuck! You're so tight."

Bouncing on the balls of my feet, I fell into the rhythm of his thrusts when without warning he added another finger. "Oh, God!" I breathed against his chest. Never had anything felt so good. Never had I been wound so tight. Each time his fingers probed deeper and deeper, I had the sensation of climbing a mountain: higher and higher. My breathing labored as I neared the precipice. As the peak showed itself in the distance, he expertly brushed my clit and ignited a fire storm within me. An uncontrollable whimper escaped my lips as he rubbed the sensitive bundle of nerves.

"Relax, baby, let me give this to you. Don't fight it."

Was I fighting? It sure didn't feel like fighting.

I nodded, closed my eyes, and floated against his chest. His knee bounced, lifting me up and bringing me down. In and out his fingers slid. It was all in perfect rhythm, a harmony of sensation as my mind and body reached the crescendo that he'd orchestrated. Then in perfect timing, in unison, he pinched my clit and my nipple. My world exploded. Flashes of light like I'd never known sparkled behind my closed eyes. Every muscle in my body tightened and imploded. Though it came upon me fast, it didn't end the same way. No. I held tightly to his shoulders as waves of pleasure rippled through my body. It wasn't until I fell slack against his chest that I realized I'd been yelling out.

My legs gave way as embarrassment washed over me. Stewart picked me up and sat me in the chair. Awkwardly, I realized I was still bare-assed. He knelt before me, lifted my chin and placed his fingers to his lips. Inhaling deeply, he said, "Tori, you're incredible."

Slowly, he sucked my essence from his fingers and licked his lips. As he reveled in his display, mortification overtook me. I tried again to look away, but his words stopped me.

"No, I want you to watch. Can't you see how good you taste? I could go down on you all day. Tori, you have no idea how fucking hot you are, how sexual. There are so many things I can teach you, but I can't teach that. You're fucking perfect."

Slowly, my mind processed my still-exposed sex, as my cheeks once again blushed. "I think I need to get dressed," I muttered as I reached for my panties.

They were too far away, and my muscles were Jell-o. Chivalrously, Stewart reached for my underwear. With a grin, he placed it near his nose, closed his eyes, and inhaled.

"Please..." I said, self-conscious of the wetness of my panties.

"Please?"

"I'm..." I truly didn't know what to say.

"You're *perfect*. That's what I said, and I don't say what I don't mean." He lifted my feet one by one, placing them into the leg holes of my panties. His blue eyes bore through me, as if he could see something others couldn't. I remained silent as he slid the soft material up my legs. When they were almost in place, he said, "Tori, don't ever be embarrassed about your reaction. It was beautiful and honest. That's what I want from you: honesty. Now, tell me what you're thinking."

My mind was mush. "I have no idea," I replied honestly with a giggle. "I *am* embarrassed, but I don't know why." I lowered my eyes.

"It was unbelievable. I've never…"

Helping me stand, he secured my underwear over my hips and whispered near my ear. "Remember what I said. My cock is much better. You haven't experienced anything yet."

The dark sky beyond our bubble reminded me of the late hour. "I think I'd better get some sleep."

"Yes." He grinned. "Tomorrow is a big day. Can you find your way back to your room?"

Nodding, I replied, "Yes. I'll see you in the morning."

"Good night."

CHAPTER SEVEN

Present

"WHERE THE HELL WERE YOU?"

The words echoed through my bedroom suite, bouncing off the walls and windows as I blinked my eyes. The flood of sunlight assaulted my sight, burning my vision, where moments earlier I'd seen only peaceful dreams. I'd been sound asleep, alone in my bed. With my drapes suddenly opened, I struggled with reality. *What was happening?*

Before I could acclimate, the soft blankets cocooning my world moved, and cool air struck my warm, suddenly exposed skin. Thankfully, I still had the protection of my nightgown and panties, as I squinted against the light and focused on the faces before me.

"What the hell?"

As the haze faded, both my husband and his right-hand man came into view. Stewart was beside my bed, in the wheelchair, and Travis was standing near the open drapes. I had no doubt that Travis had been the one to wheel Stewart from his downstairs room to my suite.

Stewart continued his glare. "Where the hell were you last night?"

Reaching for the blankets, I covered myself and scowled toward Travis. "Get the hell out of my room."

It took every ounce of my energy not to jump from my bed and slap the smug expression off his arrogant face. Instead, I scowled toward Stewart with my lips pursed in silent disobedience. Finally, he turned toward Travis. "Leave us. I'll call for you when I'm ready to be taken back to my room, or..." He looked at me. "...Mrs. Harrington can tend to her husband. After all, isn't that what good wives do?" Stewart shrugged. "But then again, good wives aren't out until all hours of the night." He nodded. "Go now."

"Yes, sir," Travis replied, all the while his eyes fixed on me.

Fighting the sickening feeling I always had in Travis' presence, I taunted, "Yes, Travis, run along. I'm sure there's someone else who you can make miserable for a few minutes."

"Always a pleasure, Mrs. Harrington."

I stared his direction as he walked the length of my suite taking his time before he finally closed the door and left us alone. Turning toward Stewart, I asked, "What the fuck? You let him come in here while I'm sleeping?"

Despite his disease-ridden body, his eyes were quick, dark, and responsive. "I asked you, my wife, a fucking question—twice. Where were you last night?"

Throwing back the covers, I eased myself from the bed, and walked toward the bathroom. "With Val; I told you I was going to go out with her."

"At the damn hospital?" His voice came muffled from the suite, echoing as it traveled into the tile-covered bathroom. "You went *out* with your sister at Memorial Hospital all night?"

After doing my business, I washed my hands, and splashed water on my face. While making Stewart wait, I tied my long hair back into a low ponytail, grabbed my robe, and casually re-entered the bedroom. "Yes," I said, as I tied the cord around my waist. "We didn't go *out*. She had rounds. As you may have inferred from our conversation, I was pissed, and I didn't want to be here."

"Victoria, you were gone until one in the damn morning. You're Mrs. Stewart—"

"I goddamned know my fucking name! I was at the hospital with my sister. We were discussing a new project for the Harrington Society, a string of cancer clinics here in the US. Tell me, Mr. Harrington, what part of that was inappropriate for your wife?"

"The one-in-the-morning part."

"Check the damn hospital records: about ten o'clock there was some big emergency, a pile-up on I 95 or something. They needed Val in the ER. I waited for her in the doctors' lounge. Honestly, I fell asleep." My gray eyes narrowed. "I'd had a rather emotional day."

Without a smidge of remorse, his clouded blue gaze remained fixed.

Thankfully, there had been a big car accident. I'd heard about it on the radio on my way home. A quick call to Val's cell phone and my story was solidified.

I continued, "She woke me when she returned to the lounge and I came home. It's a pretty fucking torrid story. I mean, seriously, I'd hate for your wife to be doing anything without you present, oh, like getting fucked."

His unwavering gaze matched his steady tone. "What did you just say to Travis?"

My mind spun. "I don't remember. I told him to get the fuck out of my room."

"No. You told him to *run along*. Like some goddamned child."

My breath quickened as I looked around my room. *Shit!* This wasn't all about the late hour. This was about my visit to Craven and Knowles. "Travis has no right; you have no right, to allow him in *my* room."

"This isn't your room. Your room is in my room—our room. It always has been. I don't like you sleeping in here and it's going to stop."

I blinked slowly and took a deep breath. "Well, I may have promised to sleep in your bedroom, but you made me promises too."

Stewart's blue eyes paled, and his ashen face fell toward his chest. "Take me back to *our* room. I'm not feeling well and we'll talk about it there."

A sense of duty nudged at my conscience as I looked at the remnants of the man I'd married. No longer was he the larger-than-life mogul. The cancer had taken his strength and his pride.

"When was the last time you had your pain medicine?" I asked with less than a tinge of concern and more of a desire to have him medicated.

"Last night, after I'd finally given up on you coming home."

"It's time for more, don't you think?"

He grimaced as he lifted his eyes. "No. I want to talk about this."

I turned his chair toward me and sat on the edge of the bed. "Then talk. I'm not having this conversation in front of Travis or any of your harem of nurses. You want to talk, let's talk."

"I was there. Tori, I've never lied to you."

"Virtual presence isn't the same as being there." I fought the absurdity of our conversation.

"I-I can't physically be there anymore. You know that. There are so few enjoyable things left in my life. There's such a short time... can you blame me for wanting pleasure where I can get it? I'm still a man with needs. I want that." He lifted his hand toward me. "This."

If we'd been talking about almost anything besides the topic at hand, I could have felt a pang of sympathy. But we weren't and I didn't. "Yes, I can blame you. You're the only one I can blame."

"That's not true. I heard you went to Parker's office." *Of course he did.* "You looked at the contract. Tell me whose signature was on it?"

"Yours and—"

"And yours," he stated matter-of-factly. "You agreed to this before we were married. Like I said, nowhere in that document does it say I must be *physically* present. It states that you'll comply. You could still hear my voice. I could still see you."

I stood abruptly, securing the robe around my waist and fought the *Dark Lullaby* threatening to replay in the recesses of my mind. "I fucking complied!"

His cold, clammy hand reached out to mine. "Tori, you were perfect, as usual. Give me a private show right now. Let me see my sexy wife in real life. I wanted that last night too. You know how much I enjoy having some of you after I watch. By not coming home, you denied me that pleasure."

My heart sunk. "Stewart, I have to meet Maura today..." I looked toward the clock on the bedside stand. It was almost eleven o'clock. *Shit! I'd slept late.* "...in about an hour."

His clouded eyes narrowed. "I've received many requests from our friends. As you know, we haven't been able to accommodate them, but now we can. Is that what you'd prefer? Say the word, Mrs. Harrington: a private show for your husband or another visit to the warehouse?"

I closed my eyes and inhaled. The ghostly scent of Parker's cologne whiffed unmistakably through my suite. I opened my eyes abruptly. He wasn't with us. We were still alone; it was only my imagination. I fought the growing nausea as I assured myself I wasn't losing it. "Please…"

A sadistic smirk emerged from his graying complexion. "All of this is of your own free will, my Tori, completely consensual. Now, tell me, which do you prefer, here or the warehouse? Perhaps both? The day is young."

"Stewart, what about Maura?"

He nodded toward my bedside stand. "Your phone is flashing. Maybe she's left you a message. Maybe she's unable to attend. If not, you can call and cancel or postpone."

Debating my options, I walked toward my phone. Each step on the plush carpet seemed as though I were stepping through quicksand: the next step more difficult than the one before. Picking up my phone, I read the screen. There were three text messages. It didn't take long to see that none of them were from Maura. I closed the app. I knew who at least one was from, and I couldn't stomach Brody's kind words with Stewart's darkening blue gaze watching my every move. I kept my back toward my husband as I said, "The messages are from Val. She was worried about my driving home so late."

I turned to his raised brows.

"What's your decision, Mrs. Harrington?"

Exhaling, I turned back away and searched my contacts. Finding Maura Craven's name, I hit CALL.

Catching her voicemail, I made my tone as light as possible. "Maura, I'm sorry to do this to you on such short notice. Stewart's having a difficult morning. I don't think I should leave him today. Please, dear, give me a call and we'll reschedule."

I disconnected the call and turned back toward my husband. My chest became heavy as I saw his flaccid penis. He'd obviously lowered the edge of his sweat pants and exposed himself while I spoke.

Not hiding my cruel tone, I asked. "Did you beat off while you watched yesterday?" I knew the answer. He couldn't get off with a Hoover vacuum. The disease and medicine had taken away more than his ability to stand.

71

"Come here."

Resigned, I moved forward. My new concern was getting to the bathroom in search of lubricant. Without it, there was no way that cock would get inside of me. Momentarily I remembered my arousal from the night before. If only I could relish the idea of Brody's come being there with Stewart's dick. Maybe, just maybe, I could find a way to enjoy the irony. Seductively, I leaned down and kissed his lips. Summoning my most appeasing voice, I said, "Let me go get ready for you. I'll be right back."

He reached for my hand and placed it on his dick. "No. You can get ready right here." His hand tugged at the cord around my waist, opening my robe and exposing my nightgown. "Mrs. Harrington, you are overdressed for this show. I believe you know my rules."

Allowing the robe to fall from my shoulders, I pulled the nightgown from my head.

"Panties. Tsk tsk. Those were never needed when you slept where you're supposed to be sleeping."

"I can't sleep with the nurses checking on you all night long. You know that."

"Panties. Off."

The lace fell to my ankles.

"Now, I want to feel those marvelous lips. The ones I watched suck our friend's come yesterday afternoon. Let me feel that beautiful mouth on my cock."

I fell to my knees as the overwhelming scent of sickness infiltrated my senses. Fighting back the bile that threatened my throat, I reached for his limp cock. It flapped in my grasp. As I tried to direct it toward my lips, revolt spurred in my empty stomach.

"That's my girl. So good at following directions." The hairs on the back of my neck stood to attention. It was a phrase he used in the warehouse: his idea of praise. In reality, each time he said it, I felt more like a well-trained dog.

Up and down my head bobbed, my lips chapping as time passed with no result.

Unabashed, Stewart reached for my hair and pulled my eyes upward. "You're losing your touch, darling. I think you might need more practice."

I reached for his sagging balls in desperation.

"Oh, yes, I feel it."

I was glad he did. I didn't. Maybe I could convince him of an ejaculation he didn't really have. I quickened my pace, willing saliva where only dust remained. Dramatically, I changed my pace, gagging with the sound of forced swallowing.

"That's it!" he exclaimed as his head wobbled backward and he exhaled an ethereal breath. Pushing me away, he demanded, "Now show me that sexy pussy. It used to be so tight, so wet."

I leaned back on my ass, spreading my legs and fingering my lips.

"You used to be tight." His eyes gleamed. "I know what's still tight. We can have some fun with that."

My heart raced as I leaned farther back, exposing myself completely.

"Move my chair to the edge of the bed, and lean over that mattress. I want to fill that tight hole."

My feet moved, but just like at the warehouse, my mind went away. When his fingers went inside of me, a hiss left his lips. "What's wrong with you? Where's my dripping-wet little whore?"

I wonder? Maybe you don't turn me on at all?!

When I didn't respond, he continued, "Go get some lubricant. Damn, you're dryer than the fucking Sahara."

No shit, asshole. I would've done that earlier if you weren't such a dick! Of course, I didn't say that. However, the idea of saying it brought a private smile to my thoughts.

Once he situated me on the bed, he spread the lube, first fingering my slit and then thrusting into the destination he'd sought. "Oh, yes, darling... that's what I like. No wonder so many of our friends enjoy pushing their dicks inside your ass. You've still got it there."

He thrust his finger in and out. As I was getting used to that, he told me to find him the glass plug. Though it was much thicker and longer than his fingers, the smooth surface combined with the lubricant gave little resistance.

I obeyed, moving appropriately and making the sounds he required. However, the entire time with my eyes closed, I longed for the blindfold of the warehouse, and without the headphones, I had to imagine the *Dark Lullaby* melody in my head.

Thankfully, his energy was quickly spent. Slapping my ass, he declared, "We're done with this. Wheel me into the bathroom. You can continue the show in there: a little shower dancing. I can watch as you suds up that pussy."

Like the good wife, I complied, loathing bubbling beneath the surface and a serene smile on my face. After all that he'd done, having him watch as I showered was truly nothing. As the bathroom filled with humid air, I took my time and embraced the warm, cleansing spray. At least I didn't have the scent of his come to wash away, only the stench of his impending death.

When I opened the glass door, I found Stewart with his eyes closed, chin on his chest, and slumped in his wheelchair. Though his brow glistened with perspiration, I held out hope as I touched his wrist and prayed.

Fuck! He still had a pulse.

CHAPTER EIGHT

Present

DESPITE WHAT HAD HAPPENED UPSTAIRS, the lower level of our apartment appeared as it always did: perfect. Being only a little after one, the afternoon haze had not yet settled, allowing the Florida sun to glisten as sparkling waves and crystal-clear sky filled our living room with light.

"Mrs. Harrington?" Travis questioned from behind me as I stood momentarily watching the view.

Without turning, I replied, "Mr. Harrington is asleep. He's in his suite. The nurses are attending to him."

"And… you are going?" he asked. As I turned I saw him eying me from head to toe, no doubt trying to assess my plans by my attire.

"Travis, stay here and do what you do. Watch over Stewart. We wouldn't want him to wake to both of us gone."

Travis stood taller, appearing the intimidating bodyguard he truly was. "Ma'am, after we were unable to reach you last night, Mr. Harrington asked that from now on I drive you. He would prefer you not to be out alone."

My lips pressed together as my neck straightened in rebellion. "I can assure you that I'm capable of driving myself. Your services are neither needed nor welcomed." When Travis started to reply, I leaned closer and lowered my voice. "Back the fuck off and remember who'll be in charge when Stewart's no longer here."

Lisa's voice severed the mounting tension. "Mrs. Harrington?"

Travis and I both turned.

"Yes, Lisa? I'm on my way out."

"Yes, I wanted to catch you before you left. Your mother called, again. She said that she can't seem to reach you on your cell, and she desperately needs to speak with you."

I closed my eyes. I had enough shit to deal with, without adding the great Mrs. Sound to my platter. "Lisa, please inform Mrs. Sound that I'm terribly busy and preoccupied with my husband. I don't know when I'll have the opportunity to return her call."

Travis' obvious huff at my *preoccupation* with Stewart received another narrowing gray-eyed glare from me.

"I'll let her know." Lisa tilted her head to the side and pursed her lips knowingly. "She doesn't take rejection well."

"That's too bad; she dishes it out like a pro." Securing my purse, I hit the button on the elevator. "I plan to be back before Mr. Harrington wakes. If I'm not, well, Travis, I know you have my number."

"And where am I to tell Mr. Harrington that you went?" Travis asked.

"Check my car's GPS," I said as the doors closed.

I knew it drove Travis crazy that he couldn't access my whereabouts with my phone. He'd tried multiple times. Thankfully, money worked both directions. Stewart could afford the means to track me, and I could afford the means to stop it. Continual scans of my number and account by the privacy firm I'd hired stopped any and all GPS apps that mysteriously found their way onto my personal device.

Stewart had told me before we married that he wouldn't monitor my movements. Whenever he questioned my phone's GPS, I innocently reminded him of that promise. One time when he pursued the topic, I gave him two options: A—leave my phone alone and I'll answer it, or B—monitor it and I'll leave it at home. Grudgingly, he chose A.

Starting my car, I thought about its GPS. The privacy firm offered to disable it, and I'd considered it for a while. Then I decided that I liked the false sense of empowerment it gave to both Travis and

Stewart. While leaving my car and taking taxis wasn't my favorite activity, thus far it had worked well.

I glanced at the text message I refused to allow myself to read earlier in my suite. It was from Brody, received at 6:54 AM. I grimaced. *Like I'd ever be awake that early?*

"DID EVERYTHING GO ALL RIGHT?"

There was a second one, sent later.

"I'M WORRIED YOU HAVEN'T RESPONDED. BTW – I THINK I FOUND SOMETHING THAT IS IMPORTANT. LET ME DO SOME MORE RESEARCH AND I'LL GET BACK TO YOU."

The third was from Val. I'd already accessed it and replied.

"SORRY ABOUT THE EMERGENCY? HOPE YOU MADE IT HOME ALL RIGHT. WE NEED TO CATCH UP."

My response:

"I'LL BE OVER THIS AFTERNOON. TEXT ME IF YOU'RE BUSY."

Since I hadn't heard from her, she was my first stop.

~

My knuckles rapped on the door of the small apartment not far from Memorial's medical center. Within mere seconds, the door opened and I was greeted by the same gray eyes I saw every day in the mirror.

"Hi, sis, come on in," Val said with a welcoming grin.

Our gray eyes were our familiar personal trait. Other than that, we looked much different than one another. Many people didn't realize we were sisters. Val's light brown, short, spiky hair was about as different from my long, dark hair as possible. Hers was thick and took on a life of its own: the absolutely perfect style for the busy life of a doctor, while mine was sleek and shiny. I often wore mine pulled back, but if I left it down, it easily reached the middle of my back. We also varied in size. Val was shorter and more petite than I. Her body shape was more like our mother's. Though we were both fit, my five-feet-six-inches held more curves than her five-foot-two. When I wore my usual three- to four-inch heels, I towered above her.

"Hi," I greeted, eying her suspiciously. "Have you even slept? What time did you get home from the hospital?"

"Yeah," she waved me off. "I'm fine. I didn't want to pass up a chance to see you. Besides, I felt bad for turning you down yesterday, and I wanted to hear more about that cryptic text." Her brows rose in question. "Umm, so, we hung out last night?"

"We did," I confirmed. "Has anyone called to question it?"

"Like your husband, or that creep, Travis? No, but if they do, I'm good. I think I've got the story straight. We were talking about the U.S. cancer clinics and due to the pile-up on 95, which, by the way, really slammed us hard last night, I was called away."

"Yes." I nodded. "And I fell asleep in the doctor's lounge waiting for you. You found me, woke me, and I finally left after midnight."

Val's head shook from side to side. "I know Stewart's been an ass, but, damn, his days are limited. Keep your ducks in a row for a little while longer. You don't want to screw everything up now."

I fell into her overstuffed sofa. "It's complicated. I didn't mean to be out so late. I was mad, met up with a friend, and believe it or not, fell asleep."

Her eyes widened. "Jeez, I know I'm exciting company, and falling asleep in the doctor's lounge is totally feasible, but your friend must be a riot if you really did fall asleep. Unless..." Her eyes widened. "...it's a friend who you happened to be seeing in a horizontal position. Which makes sleeping much easier," she added with a grin.

I shrugged and reached for the tall glass of iced tea Val offered. "Thanks. When are you leaving for Uganda?"

"Two weeks. So, see, I would've been awake anyway. I have a ton to get done. Right now..." She pointed to the table near the side of the room covered in papers, folders, and her laptop. "...I'm getting all the forms completed. I'll be meeting with the representative from Doctors Without Borders next week."

"Why? Your project is fully funded through the Harrington Society. You don't need to answer to anyone else."

"I'm not *answering* to anyone. They're helping me. Vik, you don't get it. It's not like I'm transporting antibiotics around the world. The drugs I'm transporting could start an epidemic or perhaps even a pandemic if they fell into the wrong hands."

"I thought your clinics were all about treating cancer."

She smiled. "They are, but the drugs used in chemotherapy and radiation therapy could conceivably be used in more devious ways. You know the Harrington Cancer Treatment Centers receive donations from all over the country. It isn't all funded through you. If it were, I doubt Stewart would be as open and giving." She put her hands in the air. "I don't know for sure. Call it intuition, but these drugs are expensive. Anyway, hospitals, doctors' offices, and clinics welcome a legitimate way to rid themselves of expired or nearly expired drugs as well as equipment and other resources. They want a way to write off the expense for tax purposes and not eat the loss. There's an entire facility here in Miami devoted to nothing but receiving and cataloging those donations. I need to match those donations with the needs at our clinic in Uganda. Some items are easier to get. I mean, as a whole, medications such as Cytoxan, a common chemotherapy agent, are frequently donated. However, the cesium radioactive pellets, like what went missing a couple of years ago, were not. The facility that donated those pellets expected and deserved the tax break they should've received from their donation."

I nodded. I'd heard the story from other members of the foundation. Hell, I'd spent hours on the phone with the representative from the clinic that made the donation. I obviously knew more about it than she thought. After taking a sip of tea, I said, "That's why we now have the checks and balances. To be honest, there's no way of knowing for certain if that clinic ever really donated the pellets or if they only claimed that they did. For your information, I'm the one who spearheaded the new facility. Now, donations are accepted, cataloged, and receipts are immediately issued. Everyone knows exactly what's happening." I tilted my head. "Unfortunately, there's a lot of potential for abuse with so many volunteers. Believe it or not, I'm rather fond of what you've accomplished with the Harrington

Society. I love that you got this all started while still in med school. And I do know what's going on, both from you and the board. They report to me. They always have. Stewart's never cared about the money the Harrington Society has cost; he truly never gave a damn about the foundation. However, he did like the publicity. And…" I leaned forward. "…he wasn't happy when that was tarnished. Since that incident with the pellets, I've made sure nothing like that can happen again."

"Vikki, I wasn't implying…"

"Yes, you were, and I understand. I know I'm not a doctor, but I know my way around the world of money, taxes, and philanthropic organizations. I was thrown neck-deep into that muck over ten years ago. I think overall I've done damn well."

Val reached for my hand. "Stop. Of course you've done well. You're kick-ass. I'm in no way insinuating lack of knowledge or your ability to oversee. I just mean with everything happening with Stewart, well, I know you have other things to worry about than if a shipment of Adriamycin or a vial or two of powdered Cytoxan has gone missing."

"Are those things missing?"

"No. They're not. They're just drugs that could be used, as an example."

Pondering her choice of drugs, I watched my glass as the ice melted and floated near the top. "Theoretically," I asked, "why would anyone take one of those drugs?"

Val leaned back and sighed. "Well, if we're talking epidemic or pandemic proportions, it would take more than a vial or a shipment of twelve bottles. You see, Cytoxan is commonly used to treat breast cancer. Since it has a relatively short half-life, it's transported in powder form. Before administering it to a patient, it's made into a solution—a liquid."

I rolled my eyes. "I may not have gone to college, but I know a solution is a liquid; thank you very much."

"Well, it's not the liquid that's the issue. It's the powder. It only takes a small amount of the powder to create the therapeutic dose. Yet, when in that form, this chemical is actually toxic. If that same small amount, or even less, of the powdered Cytoxan is absorbed through the skin, it can be toxic. In a very short amount of time the exposure would result in a dramatic decrease in white blood cells." She nodded. "Which you know opens the floodgates for infection. Not just infection, like the flu or a cold: with exposure to this chemical a person's immune system would shut down. It would be like HIV amplified. In only a matter of days, perhaps hours, sepsis could occur. Just imagine if enough was stockpiled? It could be released on an unsuspecting population, and they'd all be dead before anyone ever knew what happened.

"Adriamycin is known as the red devil. It's a chemotherapy agent used to treat many kinds of cancer, including breast, lung, ovarian, and bladder. It's commonly used as part of a three-part regimen. It's administered over a period of time intravenously. It has serious side effects: low white and red blood cell count, low platelets, hair loss, and mouth sores. That's when it's given as directed. If it were to be absorbed through the skin or ingested at higher doses, those side effects would be amplified. The effects would be similar to the Cytoxan, but the symptoms would come on slower."

"Wouldn't people know that they were having symptoms?"

Val moved her head thoughtfully from side to side. "Probably. They'd know something was different, but they wouldn't know the cause. I mean, a symptom like hair loss can be brought on by something as benign as a change in hormones. Honestly, most doctors wouldn't take it seriously, taken by itself. Besides, it wouldn't matter. By the time the drug's in someone's system, nothing could stop it." She shrugged. "Adriamycin also has been shown to have a toxic effect on the heart muscle."

"So it could cause a heart attack?" I asked.

"Essentially."

"Damn, you're like a doomsday postcard."

Val laughed. "Hey! I'm not trying to predict doomsday. It's just that one of my professors at Johns Hopkins was big on hematology and the lack of real knowledge on blood cancers. He sparked my interest."

"Blood cancers, like the leukemia Stewart has."

"Yes, like that, as well as non-Hodgkin's lymphoma, many other lymphomas, and even multiple myelomas. My professor would talk about the incidences of each etiology and how the CDC was watching for hot pockets."

"Did they find any? Hot pockets?"

Despite missing my final, that year of advanced biology was kicking into gear. I'd always loved this kind of thing. I'd even been accepted into the University of Miami before my life took an abrupt turn. With either this kind of conversation or Stewart's private shows as a potential use of my time, I much preferred sitting with Val and listening to her dire discussions.

"Yes," she answered thoughtfully. "They found clusters of concentrated diagnoses in areas like Chernobyl as well as Hiroshima. The fall-out in both cases was extensive. However, even with Chernobyl being as recent as 1986, the lack of technology, compared to current day, limited the data."

Val's expression lit up, as it did whenever she was excited. "Actually, my professor is among a group of researchers studying the population around Fukushima, Japan. They have so many more resources today. Since the reactors only melted down in 2011, the results won't be found for a long time, but with this incident, they have a better idea what kind of base data to retrieve." She looked wishfully into her tea. "I'd love to know what they've learned. It's all so exciting."

"But those cases aren't some form of bioterrorism like you were insinuating earlier."

"No. Those were all incidences of radiation exposure. We all know that radiation is a known carcinogen. So based on the exposure, they can learn a lot. However, of course, the CDC is also on the lookout for hot pockets of unknown etiology."

"Ha! Like a few missing drugs from our clinics could cause that."

Val's expression darkened. "Well, Vikki, that's how it starts: a few drugs from one clinic, a few from another. It all adds up. Suddenly, things are happening without cause. People are losing their hair and becoming ill. Think about it: some Cytoxan in powder form, distributed through an HVAC system in a building that houses or employs thousands of people could make a real mark for a terrorist organization."

"Would it really be that easy?"

"No. Something like that would cause residue. The perpetrators would be caught or end up killing themselves. Where it would work better and be less likely to cause red flags is on a smaller scale. For the average murder, it could work well. That makes an assassination attempt a concern."

"God, Val, this is heavy shit. Maybe you should decide to write a crime novel?"

"It is heavy. That's why there are so many forms to fill out and hoops to jump through."

I shook my head. "I'm sorry to bother you with my alibi. I know you have bigger concerns."

A candid smile came to her lips. "Honestly, Vik, I'm there for you anytime. I know Stewart isn't the love of your life. I also know you've done all you can do to make the best of it. I don't mean to concern you with the everyday shit of the clinics."

"But," I asked, "if you were to start U.S. clinics, would there still be so much scrutiny?"

She shook her head. "No… and yes. No matter where the clinic is located, everything needs to be accounted for. However, there's a normal, acceptable amount of natural attrition. I mean, shit happens. Solutions are mixed incorrectly and vials are discarded. Of course, it should all be documented, but sometimes the nurses get overwhelmed and things happen. That's all taken into consideration during audits." She reached out and grabbed my knee. "Besides, it doesn't matter. I haven't had time to put together the proposal for the U.S. clinics yet."

"Honey, I like that idea much better than having you traipse all over the world. I mean, if terrorists groups are looking for these drugs, I don't like the idea of your traveling with them." Changing the subject, I stood and walked to Val's shelf of pictures. I lifted the picture in the middle; it was a photograph of the two of us, taken during my senior year of high school at the academy. We both looked so young, so innocent. There were also pictures of Marcus and Lyle and one of mom and Randall. That reminded me of something. "Guess who's been trying to contact me?"

Val looked down. "I know. She's called me too."

I spun. "Why? Why the hell would she be bothering you?"

"Because she can't reach you. She asked me to ask you to call her."

I pinched the bridge of my nose. "Do you know what she wants?"

"No," Val answered curtly. "I can guess."

"Tell me that she hasn't asked you for money."

"She hasn't. Well, not since the time you laid her out and explained the difference between my work as a doctor and Randall's."

"Good," I said matter-of-factly.

"I believe it has to do with money for Marcus' education." Val volunteered. "She's very excited that he's attending the University of Miami. It's very difficult to get into."

"I know," I said dryly.

"Yes, I know. You were accepted there too. Well, I'm guessing her constant calling has to do with the tuition. The second semester will be coming due soon. Mom blew through Randall's life insurance money pretty fast."

I shook my head. "What kind of a mother blows through millions of dollars when she has two sons who need an education?"

Val shrugged. "I'm going out on a limb here, but I'd say one who has a daughter who could buy the damn university if she wanted."

"Fuck," I mumbled under my breath. As much as I didn't want to save her skinny ass, I also didn't want Marcus or Lyle to suffer. I mean, damn, he'd been accepted on his own merit.

My mother blamed me for her second husband's early demise. *Another body to my count,* as she so eloquently put it the afternoon of the funeral. I'd been the one to turn down Randall's request for cash. It wasn't enough that I'd sold my body and soul for them once. He had the audacity to fall into the same trap: over a million in debt to a bookie.

Stewart left the choice to me. All I needed to do was say yes and Randall's debt would've been paid. But, damn! I'd done that once, as well as secured Val's education. And what thanks did I receive? Marilyn and Randall played the perfect parents pretending to be the one helping their daughter through undergrad and medical school.

So when faced with the decision again, I decided to be the one to place the bet. After all, perhaps it was time I was the one to enjoy the exhilaration of gambling. Besides, there'd always been a part of me that doubted that the inability to pay a debt would truly result in a death. This wasn't the Wild West, was it?

Two days after I placed that bet, I lost. Randall's car drove off an embankment into high tide. The investigation showed an accelerator malfunction, which allowed my mother to receive the life insurance money. A significant portion went to paying off Randall's debt; however, that still left her with more than enough to save and invest.

Marilyn Sound and I have only spoken occasionally since Randall's funeral; however, according to Lisa and now Val, she still felt the right to approach me for money. I'm sure that if you asked her, she'd say she was entitled.

Stopping the tirade of thoughts, I looked at my watch. "I need to get home before Stewart wakes. He wasn't pleasant this morning."

Her expression mellowed. "Vikki, I've watched many patients go down the same road as Stewart. His diagnosis was especially difficult on him. It's understandable. Statistically, he's too young for the aggressive type of cancer he has. I'm sure that's made it even more difficult for him. He's a man who's used to getting his way; nonetheless, neither his money nor standing could save him.

"What I've learned in my practice is that with a diagnosis like Stewart's, he hasn't just had to come to terms with dying. He's also had to face loss of control. It doesn't matter if someone is a seventy-year-old grandmother or the fifty-year-old CEO of Harrington Spas and Suites—it's difficult.

"It isn't uncommon for patients in his position to try to exert control in any way that they can. I'm sure that things like him wanting to know your whereabouts is annoying. But right now, it's all he has."

I remained stoic. There was no way I could let her know the ways he liked to exercise his control.

"In many ways," she went on, "what happened to Randall was more humane than what's happening to Stewart."

Karma.

When I didn't answer, she reached for my hand and continued, "I've also watched the spouses of those patients. I know this is hard on you. I wish you'd consider counseling. Grief and bereavement counseling doesn't need to wait until he's dead. You deserve support."

I leaned over, gave her a hug, and said, "I know you're busy, but I've loved getting together. Hopefully we can do it again, just the two of us, before you leave. Let me know your schedule, and we'll work something out."

"Sure thing, sis. Don't worry about any of the foundation stuff. I've got the drugs all handled."

I smiled, nodding my head, as I recalled a similar conversation a few years ago, one that proved very helpful.

"Val," I asked, "what are those pellets used for? I mean, why would you have radioactive pellets in the first place?"

"They're implanted into cancerous tumors, usually not permanently. However, when implanted, their radiation kills the cancerous cells."

"Can they cause damage to the healthy cells?"

She shrugged. "When there are quickly multiplying deadly cells, that's our number-one priority."

"What if there weren't?"

Her brow furrowed. "Then you wouldn't implant them. Seriously, exposure to that level of radiation could result in the mutation of healthy cells. It would be just like Chernobyl on an individual scale."

Val touched my shoulder. "Vik, think about it."

My eyes opened wide. "Think about what?"

"The counseling. It's all right to get it. You're too young to be going through this. Facing the death of your spouse is hard. That's why they have counselors. Sometimes it helps to talk to someone who isn't as close to you."

I shook my head. *What I needed was for him to be dead.* "Call me. Next time let's talk about something a little less morbid."

"Hey, I don't use these drugs for morbid purposes. I use them for good. Remember that."

I gave her one last hug. "Oh, I do."

CHAPTER NINE

Present

BEGRUDGINGLY, I SWEPT the screen of my phone. Though I refused to acknowledge the vibrations while with Val, I couldn't help but notice the on-and-off-again motion coming from my purse. The icon for text messages practically jumped off the screen with the number eight flashing wildly. Eight fucking messages. I'd been gone from home for less than two hours. I continued reading: two were from my mother, two were from Brody, one was from the Harrington Society Clinic, and three were from Travis.

Touching Travis' number was like ripping off a Band-Aid. If I did it fast, I could get it over with and move on to better things. A closed-lip grin came to my face. *Wouldn't my mother be pleased to know that I considered her a better evil?*

Message 1: *"MR. HARRINGTON WANTED ME TO REMIND YOU THAT HE EXPECTS YOU HOME UPON COMPLETION OF YOUR VISIT WITH YOUR SISTER."*

Really? My jaw clenched. From the first time I met Travis, he rubbed me the wrong way.

Message 2: *"MR. HARRINGTON WOKE AND WANTS YOU HOME NOW."*

There was no way that Stewart was awake. I watched the nurse pump pain medicine into his IV after I'd assured them it was what he wanted. Because it was more of what I wanted seemed irrelevant.

I wasn't sure what kind of power play Travis thought he was making, but I didn't plan on participating. I'd already been sucked into one set of fucked-up games. My quota had been filled. Each thought of Stewart's right-hand man made my blood boil as well as my stomach churn. It was no secret that I detest everything about Travis: quite honestly, the feeling continued to be mutual. It was during Stewart's warehouse training period that we finally laid our cards on the table. The looks, glances, and smirks that he'd given me during the first year of my marriage finally made sense the first and only time I was faced with him as a *friend*. Well, not faced. I was blindfolded. I wasn't sure how either of them thought I wouldn't recognize the man who'd, for over the last year of my life, spent every waking hour mere inches away from my husband.

Though I handled the situation completely wrong, I learned from it. I also learned that in some ways I could still influence my husband.

Settling into the leather seat of my car, I mused: if that asshole was stupid enough to think I'd keep him employed after Stewart died, he was dumber than he looked. It had been nearly nine years since Stewart's right-hand man put his cock near me, yet whenever I saw his slimy sneer from the corner of my eye, my stomach lurched. I remembered that day like it was yesterday. I remembered it with the clarity that comes from the first time.

"This is the big test, Tori. We don't want you disappointing our friends. They're all anxious to get to know you."

My hands trembled in his grasp. The tone with which Stewart spoke was as if we were asking me to organize a dinner party, not put myself on display for strangers—or worse, for men I knew. Ever since he'd first brought me to the warehouse, I knew this day was coming. He'd laid it on the line with no room for discussion. This was his desire, his fantasy, and the reason he'd chosen to make me his wife. This was what I'd agreed to do when I signed his contract.

I could choose to walk away. He'd told me that too. I could accept the clause of the contract that voided our agreement: voided our marriage and freed me from this hell. But at what cost?

Stewart had done everything he'd said. He'd fulfilled his promises: Randall's debt was paid. My ungrateful stepfather's life was spared. My mother was able to maintain her façade of perfection while now being able to boast about her daughter and new son-in-

law. He'd provided me with every luxury a woman could imagine. Never did he question my expenditures or anywhere I chose to spend money.

I steeled myself against my emotions as he slowly removed my clothes, placed the blindfold over my eyes, and headphones over my ears. With each impending second, I knew I would willingly give up everything. I didn't give a damn about the money. Randall could make his own fucking way in the world and as for my mother's social status, I didn't give a rat's ass. What kept my hands on the headboard, holding tightly to the wrought-iron spindles, was the realization that Val would not be able to attend Johns Hopkins University.

She'd worked hard to make her grades at the academy. Johns Hopkins was one of the top pre-med programs in the country. It was exclusive and prestigious with only a seventeen-percent acceptance rate. She'd made that cut. Tuition alone was nearly fifty thousand dollars a year. Despite all of Randall and Marilyn's posturing and proclamations of devotion, they'd never ante up for her tuition, not to mention her room and board.

It wasn't that Val wasn't a hard worker: she was. However, was it fair to offer her this opportunity and take it away? That was what would happen if I decided to exercise my right to leave. As long as I played Stewart's game, I could support my sister and anything else my heart desired.

His voice came through the headphones. "As we've discussed, I could tie your hands, but if I do that, I take away your freedom of choice. Nod if you understand."

I refused to let him know how much this disgusted me. So I summoned all my strength, straightened my neck, and nodded.

"Good girl. Stay focused on me. I'll be right here with you. Can you hear me all right?"

I nodded.

Of course I could fucking hear him. We'd been playing this game alone, just the two of us, for months.

"Remember, don't speak. You can make sounds—I love to hear your sounds—but no words. Nod if you understand."

I nodded.

"Today you're going to meet our first friend."

My legs twitched, aching to close and cover myself. The way Stewart had placed them they were slightly bent with my knees to the sides. I was completely exposed.

"No, Tori. I want our friend to see you, to appreciate that sexy, fuckable pussy. I want him to see those luscious tits of yours. I'm sure he'll enjoy coming all over them as much as I do."

I closed my eyes and unsuccessfully tried to drown out his voice.

He continued, "I promised you condoms during penetration and that will always be followed. I'm here for you, darling. However, don't be surprised if some of our friends take them off to bathe your gorgeous tits or your perfect ass; others may let you suck them. Remember to be a good girl and swallow." His words taunted and demeaned, while his tone was sultry and encouraging. It was a cruel game.

My arms ached before our friend ever made his presence known. And despite the cooled temperature of the warehouse, my sweaty palms made keeping my grasp difficult.

"Don't let go of those bars. You're not allowed to touch our friends unless I tell you what to do. There's no sense in your trying to figure out who they are. It makes this game so much more fun that way, don't you agree."

I didn't nod. I didn't agree. There was nothing fun about any of this.

I don't know if the friend spoke. I couldn't have heard him if he did. He made his presence known by touch. I gasped when I felt it, immediately knowing it wasn't Stewart. There was nothing remotely compassionate in the way this rough hand seized my breast, pinched my nipple, and pulled it tight. Despite all of Stewart's training, I flinched away.

"It's all right, baby," Stewart's voice attempted to calm me.

My legs slapped closed as my skin tingled in disgust. For a while I heard nothing, only music. All I could imagine was that the two of them were discussing what this friend was going to do.

Finally, Stewart's voice came back through the headphones. "Come on, Tori, I know you can do this for me. Don't make our friend mad. You don't want to be punished."

The hairs on the back of my neck sprang to life. There was no fucking way... and then I knew. I don't know how I knew, but I did. His warm breath was near my neck, and the same sickening feeling I'd had since the first time I met Travis overwhelmed me.

Though I was working blindly, I reacted by instinct. My knee went up. At the same moment I let go of the headboard, leaned forward, and sunk my teeth into whatever was in front of me. My knee hit pay dirt as I felt the bed shift. Ripping the blindfold and headphones from my head, the room of light and sound momentarily blinded me as the world spun.

It wasn't just the assault to my senses that set it spinning. It was the back of Travis' hand as he struck my right cheek.

"Stupid bitch!" He screamed, surveying his bleeding shoulder and his wounded balls. "You fucking kicked and bit me!"

I was a damn cat with claws extended. Without thinking, I sprang from the bed. I didn't give a damn about the rage-filled glare I saw in Travis' eyes. Ignoring my throbbing cheek, I scratched at his exposed skin.

"Get the fuck away from me. There's no goddamned—"

Stewart reached for my shoulders, pulled me away from Travis, and yelled, "Stop!"

His voice was harsher and more demanding than I'd ever heard. Before that moment, I perhaps had thought I'd seen my husband angry. I'd been wrong. Nothing compared to what I now saw and heard. His hands trembled as his face reddened with fury. Knowing I was outnumbered, I prepared myself for his promise of punishment, closed my eyes, and waited. My punishment never came.

My husband spun toward Travis. His voice was strong, not at all trepidatious about remonstrating this monster of a man. Spit rained forth with each word. "What the fuck do you think you're doing?"

"The bitch bit me! She kicked me in the goddamned balls." Blood oozed from his wounds as his body too shook with anger. "What the fuck do you think I'm doing?"

Stewart stepped toward him. As their proximity decreased, Travis' body shrunk. "Don't you ever fucking lay a hand on my wife again. How dare you think you could strike her? You're a fucking idiot. You know how this goes down. If you plan on being with me one more day, you'll recognize that you just had your one chance and you blew it." His finger prodded Travis' bare chest. "You fucking blew it!"

When Travis failed to respond, I peered from behind the perceived safety of Stewart's back and said, "Mr. Harrington just told you that you blew it. Nod if you fucking understand."

Stewart's arm came out to stop Travis from lunging forward. "Get the fuck out of here. We have our own car. Go. You and I'll discuss this later."

"There's no way you're going to have her ready for the sena—"

"Shut the fuck up, or I'm going to be the next person to hit someone and you're going to be that someone." Stewart's voice lowered an octave. "Leave now. Don't make me say *it again."*

With one last glare my direction, Travis turned and walked away. Stewart stood statuesque and waited until Travis was in the bathroom before he exhaled and turned toward me. His expression softened as he ran his finger over my already raised cheek. "We need to get you some ice. Baby, I'm sorry. That'll never happen again."

Tension seeped from my muscles as I fell against his chest.

"Tori, I should never have allowed Travis... I thought it was a safe test, but I'm not an idiot. I've seen how he's looked at you since the first day he brought you to the penthouse. I promise I'll never allow anyone to treat you like that, ever again."

I looked up at his face and tried to read his thoughts. "But you'll let others fuck me, still, after this?"

He stroked my hair. "Don't you see? It's as much for me as it is for them. I'll get off watching them with you. I want you to come." He once again touched my cheek. "I don't want this, ever." He looked back into my eyes. "This is about pleasure: our friends', yours, and mine."

"I don't want pleasure with anyone except you."

"I'll be here. I'll always be here. You can know that when someone else is fucking you and you're about ready to come, so am I. Once they're done with you, you can tend to me, because that's what good wives do. That, my darling, is what you agreed to do. I never intended for anyone to hurt you."

I stood as tall as I could, barefooted and naked. "You don't think that this whole thing hurts me?"

"No," he answered. "I want to see your pleasure. The only pain you'll endure is the stimulation to something more pleasurable." He bent down and kissed me. "Mrs. Harrington, you have my word."

"Fire him," I said, when our lips disengaged.

Stewart's expression blanked.

"I said, fire him. Fire Travis tonight so I never need to see him again."

Stewart pulled me against his chest. "Darling, Travis has been with me for years. I need him as much as he needs me. He knows too much about too much." He motioned toward the bed. "Like this. You don't want him in a position to tell the world about this."

"I don't want anyone to be in a position —"

Stewart's finger covered my lips. "Stop. I'm not firing Travis, but you have my word that he'll never be a threat, and as for others, know that there will be others. This..." He gestured toward the bed. "...will happen. Therefore, unless you plan to invoke your ability to walk away from this marriage, this conversation is done."

When I didn't respond, Stewart asked, "What happened? I thought you were ready."

I wanted to say that I'd never be ready; instead, I shrugged. "I knew it was him. The way he's looked at me over the last year has given me the creeps. I just knew it was him, and I couldn't stand the idea of him touching me. And he was being rough. You're never..."

Stewart captured my lips with his—kissing, caressing, and calming. "I don't want to be. I don't like that. That's why I need to know that you're doing this willingly, to make me happy."

It was such a fucking lie. My emotions couldn't keep up. I loathed his existence, yet he was my savior. What would have happened if he hadn't stepped in? What would Travis have done? Eying the blood beneath my nails, I knew that whatever it was, I wouldn't have taken it lightly.

The ringing of my phone brought me back to present. I was still in my car, sitting in the parking garage, zoned out on putrid memories, and willing my jaws to unclench. Taking a deep breath, I read the number: *HARRINGTON CLINIC RECEIVING FACILITY.*

I started the car and inhaled the cool air from the vents. After the third ring, I answered, "Hello."

"Mrs. Harrington?"

"Yes," I answered, more curtly than necessary.

"Ma'am, I'm sorry to bother you, but Dr. Conway has submitted a manifest and without your signature or that of Mrs. Keene's, we can't release the drugs."

"I'm the second name on that list for a reason. I have a few other —"

"Ma'am, I'm sorry. I know you're busy with Mr. Harrington. It's just that Mrs. Keene is out of town with the senator. I'm afraid if we wait for her return…"

"I'll be there in twenty-five minutes."

"Thank you, ma'am."

I disconnected the call, without acknowledging her gratitude, and worked my car into traffic. Focusing on the cars about me, I sighed at the unexpected duty. Truthfully, I welcomed the distraction from my life and memories. I didn't know what brought that particular memory back with such vigor, yet by the look of my reflection, you'd think I'd just experienced it all again. Refreshing my lipstick and covering my eyes with my sunglasses, I straightened my neck and shoulders. I was Mrs. Harrington, Mrs. Stewart Harrington. *I could fucking do this.*

As my internal monologue worked to convince myself, my phone rang again.

The name on the small dashboard screen read: BRODY PHILLIPS. Taking a deep breath, I hit the receive button. "Hello."

I listened as his voice came through my car speakers. "What's the matter? Are you all right?"

I looked down at the hands grasping the steering wheel too tightly. "I'm fine. I've been with Val. Did you find out anything?"

"I did, but not about the contract."

I waited. Finally, I prodded, "Brody, I have a lot going on. Don't give me clues. What the hell did you find?"

"Vik, I want to sit down with you and talk about this."

My phone buzzed with another text message. This time STEWART flashed on the screen on the dashboard. "I can't. Not today. I need to run by the Harrington Clinic's receiving facility and sign off on a few things before Val can get the things she needs for Uganda, and then I have to go home."

Brody's tone lowered. "This is serious. I'm concerned that it'll upset you. I want to be with you when you hear the details."

I steered my car toward the distribution facility. "Brody, if it's something I need to know, tell me."

"Can we plan for tomorrow?"

I shook my head. Fine, I'd make it work, somehow. "Sure. Can I meet you around lunch time? You work for my husband: he's ill. Let me meet you for lunch?"

"No, Vik. Not in public. Not with what I need to tell you. I'll get a room at the Viceroy. Tell Stewart you're meeting someone at 15th and Vine for lunch. I'll text you the room number. You won't need a key. I'll be waiting."

"Jeez, Brody. You're stressing me out. If it isn't about the contract, what's it about?"

"Stewart's will, Vik. He's drafted a change to his will. He's added an inheritance clause."

"What the fuck? Isn't the entire will about inheritance?"

"This isn't about money or even property. You get all of that. This is something new under specific bequests and devises."

I struggled to focus on the late-afternoon traffic as I processed Brody's words. "I don't understand," I admitted. "If he isn't willing money or property, what is he willing?"

"Proprietorship of your contract."

The air left the car as I gasped for breath.

CHAPTER TEN

Ten years ago

WALKING BACK TOWARD THE BEDROOM, my mind flashed to the patio scene with Stewart. *Oh my God!* Did I really allow him to fuck me with his fingers? Had I really asked him to do it? What the hell was wrong with me? I hadn't even known this man for twenty-four hours and I invited him to put his fingers inside of me! Was I honestly considering marrying him?

I thought back to the afternoon. Stewart had said that his cock wouldn't enter me until I asked—until I begged. When he'd said that, I'd thought he was a narcissistic asshole. But after what just happened, I wasn't sure.

Those thoughts and more danced through my head as I struggled to find sleep. Looking at my phone, I wanted to call Val and ask her advice. Perhaps I needed her calm, positive demeanor. Would she truly be able to look at this situation and see the positive, or would she tell me I was crazy and to run away as fast as I could?

The knock on the door brought me back to consciousness. Opening my eyes, I realized that despite all my tossing and turning, I'd finally fallen asleep and morning had arrived. Panic struck as I jumped and fumbled for my phone. *Oh my God, what time was it?* After being up so late with Stewart, did I oversleep? Before I could read the time, the knock came again.

"Miss Conway," Lisa called from behind the door.

The numbers came into view: 5:30 AM. With a sigh of relief, I answered, "Come in."

"I'm sorry to bother you so early. I know Mr. Harrington said that you have until half past seven, but he was hoping you'd have breakfast with him in his office and discuss any questions or concerns you may have. The final answer must be made by seven-thirty so that you can be taken to school if your answer is no."

I exhaled, securing the covers around my lap. "Thank you. I'll be there as soon as I get dressed."

Motioning toward the closet, Lisa said, "There are some jeans and shirts as well as underwear and bras in the closet. I believe they should all fit. There're even some more comfortable shoes. I didn't think you'd want to wear the black dress and heels back to school."

"Lisa?"

Her eyes opened wide.

"I can't believe I'm considering this."

Her pursed lips tipped upward and the gleam came back to her eyes as she stepped toward the bed. "You are? After I spoke with you last night I got the feeling…"

I cocked my head. "Did you tell Mr. Harrington about our conversation? Did you tell him I had questions?"

"Not last night. It was late. I went to bed. However, I did tell him this morning that we'd spoke." When I didn't respond, she went on. "He asked me what time it was that we talked. Then he asked me to be sure you were awake and to ask you to join him in his office." She sat on the edge of the bed and patted my blanket-covered leg. "My loyalty is to this household. Right now that means Mr. Harrington, but if the future contains a Mrs. Harrington, rest assured that I'll be loyal to her as well." With a wink she added, "Perhaps I already am. Now I'll let you get ready, unless you need my assistance."

Smiling, I replied, "No, thank you. I'll be to his office as soon as I can."

Tipping my head back, I heard the door shut and tried to concentrate on my questions about his contract. While clauses and addendums should have been front and center, memories of his hands, words, and warm breath filled my thoughts. Before I realized what I was doing, my hand snaked below the blankets and massaged my overly sensitive clit.

I'd never been one to spend much time masturbating. It was difficult when you shared a room; nevertheless, when I had, it was more of a way to relieve stress than a way to find pleasure. I'd been honest when I told Stewart I didn't know if I'd had an orgasm. The relief I felt when my fingers rubbed my clit was nothing like the overpowering wave that hit me last night. I couldn't help but wonder: if his fingers felt that good, would his cock be even better? How big was he? My hand moved faster as I imagined the possibilities. With the tension building, I remembered why I was in the luxurious penthouse and this enormous opulent bedroom. I remembered why my life was about to be sold and who was responsible. My hand stopped. There wasn't enough self-pleasure in the world to make me come while thinking about my parents. Ultimately, this was all Randall's fault. He was the one in financial trouble. He was the one who mentioned me to Stewart. If he hadn't done that, Stewart Harrington wouldn't even know my name, and I'd be sleeping in my dorm or studying for my advanced biology exam. No matter how great I felt coming apart on that balcony last night, nothing made up for what Randall had done to me. Nothing.

I continually reminded myself of that as I showered, dried my long brown hair, and secured it in a messy bun at the back of my head. Though the bathroom cabinets contained all kinds of cosmetics, I opted for a little mascara and lip-gloss. Rarely did I wear more than that. Well, I had worn more yesterday, but that was different. Today I looked more like me: an eighteen-year-old about to graduate high school.

The clothes Lisa mentioned fit perfectly. The jeans hugged my hips with tight, stretchy material and the top was a snug red t-shirt that showed just the right amount of cleavage: not too much to be slutty, but not too little to be prudish.

From the expression on Stewart's face, when I entered his office and he looked up from the *Wall Street Journal*, I knew I'd done well. He looked different than he had yesterday too. Today he wasn't as casual, dressed in a tailored gray suit with a teal tie. The color accentuated the ocean blue eyes that met mine and then slowly, unashamedly scanned my frame, up and down. Standing, he greeted,

"Good morning, Miss Conway," as he pulled back a chair.

Miss Conway? What happened to Tori?

Summoning my most sincere smile, I laid the tablet with my questions beside my place setting, accepted the chair he offered, and replied, "Good morning, Mr. Harrington."

Just then, Lisa entered the office with a covered dish and set it before me. Raising the lid, she smiled and said, "I hope you like eggs and bacon." Before I could answer, she asked, "What can I get you to drink?"

"Um, I'm fine with water."

"Come, dear, we have many other options: coffee, tea, juice?"

Her endearment made me smile. "Thank you, orange juice would be wonderful."

After she left, Stewart asked, "So you're not a coffee or tea drinker?"

"Not really. I drink coffee sometimes when I'm studying late." I glanced toward the cup near his plate. "But you are a coffee drinker, I see."

"I am." He smirked.

"What?"

"It seems as though we're learning more and more about one another."

I lowered my eyes to my plate. "I also don't eat meat. I don't mind that other people do. I just don't."

He reached across the table and scooped up the bacon and deposited it on his plate. "We didn't know. What about eggs?"

Lifting my fork, I grinned. "I eat eggs, and scrambled is my favorite."

Stewart leaned back and watched as I ate. Truthfully, the few grapes I'd eaten last night did little to suppress my hunger. With pink filling my cheeks, I remembered what had taken my mind away from food.

Looking toward my tablet, Stewart said, "I'm going to interpret your wanting clarification as a good sign. At least that means you weren't prepared to come down here and just tell me no."

Swallowing, I shook my head. "I believe it's best to explore my options."

Lifting his brow, he replied, "Hmmm, I like to explore as well."

Shifting slightly in my seat, I asked, "What if I said yes right now? What would happen?"

"We'd wed on Thursday."

"No, not that. What would happen with Randall and Marilyn, Marcus, Lyle, and Val?"

Stewart cleared his throat. "*If* you said yes, you and I would immediately leave here and go to my attorney's office to sign the contract. We need witnesses, and Parker wants to go over some finer points with both of us present."

"Parker?" I asked, feeling very intimidated. What attorney in his right mind would write up such an elaborate agreement, much less want to sit and discuss it?

"Parker Craven, of Craven and Knowles. He's been my lead attorney for years."

"I-I don't know. Some of the things in the contract are pretty personal. I mean it spells out specifics about things like…"

"Sex." Stewart volunteered. "Yes, Miss Conway." *Again with the Miss Conway?* "If we are to wed and you're to share my name and money, I expect sex. I expect birth control. I have many expectations centering on the way I want things. From our limited experience, I don't foresee any of that being a problem; however, if you were to decide to withhold my desires from me, it would be grounds for termination of our contract. The only way to make that legal is to spell it out."

"But I don't know him. I don't want to discuss my sex life with him."

Stewart smirked. "You will know him. Though your parents believe that they live among the elite in Miami, they aren't even close. This is a whole new world. Sometimes there'll be instances that make you uncomfortable. When that happens, tell me. I'll do what I can to help you. In this instance, I'll be there with you. However, to make this all legal, the conversation with Parker is unavoidable."

"Speaking of my parents, after we sign the contract, *if* we do, what happens to Randall?"

"I'll give the go-ahead for the withdrawal of funds. Travis will take the funds to where they need to be, and Randall's life will be spared."

"Are you going to call him, let him know my decision?"

Stewart studied my face before answering. "Perhaps you'd prefer to make that call?"

My cheeks rose. "I haven't made a decision. However, if I do, I think I'd like to wait until he calls me. After all, he and my mother put me in this situation, and other than a package with clothes and a note, I've yet to hear from them."

He nodded approvingly. "Damn, sexy and bitchy. You, Miss Conway, get better by the minute. That is the perfect combination for success in my world."

"And if I decide *no*, I also believe he can call me."

"Yes, you, my darling, could make this work. So *if...*" he emphasized the word, "...you say yes, I'm assuming I won't be burdened with my mother- and father-in-law's presence?"

I shook my head. "It would probably be the first time in my life that they wanted to be around me. So, no fucking way. They want to sell me off to save their asses—that's their business. But if they think I'm going to welcome them with open arms into this new crazy-assed life, they're dumber than I imagined."

Reaching across the table, Stewart secured my hand as his expression morphed. No longer did I see the business tycoon in a designer suit. His countenance softened, eyes widened, and he leaned toward me. "Tori, I've decided to make a change to the *no* file."

My heart raced and body tensed as I awaited his explanation.

"I've changed my mind. If you chose to walk away today, I'll double the amount of the check. You're right: your parents have put you in an incredibly unfair position. One hundred thousand dollars should help you and your sister. As a matter of fact, if you keep your word, maintain your silence about what occurred here yesterday and today, and you ever need more money, don't hesitate to contact me. I'll give you my private cell number."

The immediate excitement over the increase in money quickly faded. "I-Is that what you want me to do? Do you want me to leave? Is that why you keep calling me Miss Conway?"

He exhaled, leaned back, and resumed his businesslike tone. "I'm calling you by your name. Until the time that you choose to marry,

Miss Conway is your name. This is a business deal. Formalities work best in business. Emotion clouds the real issues."

I pulled my hand away. "So what was that last night? Was *that* clouding the issue? Because, to be honest, I was pretty *clouded* when I made my way back to my room."

"No, Miss Conway, you were not clouded. For the first time in your life you were satiated. And if you make the right decision, it won't be the last."

"You just said to walk away."

"I said it's an option, one that just doubled in appeal."

I squared my shoulders and straightened my neck. "Are both offers still on the table, or have you removed the second offer?"

His jaw clenched as he eyed me suspiciously. "Is it your intention to make me beg? Do you intend to hear me specify that I want you to take the offer of marriage so that you can turn it down?" His arms crossed his chest. "Miss Conway, let me make myself clear: I don't beg."

My façade of a smile remained unwavering yet inside, I wanted to scream. *What the hell was this guy's problem?* If there were an award for sending mixed signals, he'd definitely be in the running. Hell, I'd nominate him myself. Finally, prying my pursed lips apart, I said, "Well, Mr. Harrington, neither do I."

Stewart looked at his watch. "Your time is ticking. You have almost twenty minutes before it's time for your decision. Do you want to ask any of those questions?" He tilted his head toward my paper.

Did I? Or was I ready to tell him to fuck it? I looked down at my writing, scanned the questions—those that last night seemed of monumental importance—and replied, "No."

"No?"

"No," I repeated with confidence.

Stewart uncrossed his arms and leaned forward. "Interesting. That's all it took?"

"What do you mean?"

"It only took an extra fifty thousand dollars for you to walk away and stand up to your stepfather?"

My mind spun. "I haven't said I'm walking away, although you seem to be pushing me in that direction."

"You just said no."

"I said no, I don't want to ask any of those questions. Instead, I want clarification."

Stewart exhaled.

It may not have been begging, but it was the closest sign of his desire I'd seen during our morning discussion.

"Clarification on what?" he asked.

I fought the urge to pace, instead busying myself by smoothing nonexistent wrinkles from my jeans. Summoning courage from some unknown source, I began. "I'm eighteen years old. I don't want to be held prisoner in your home. You have a lot of shit in that contract about my obligation to sex. What are my other obligations? If I marry you, will I have a life? What about my contact with my sister and brothers? What about school? What about work? I want to know what I'm signing up for today. Tell me there will be more to my life than sex."

He grinned. "Oh... if only my time permitted me to say no, but alas, I too have work and obligations. Therefore, you'll have plenty of time for other activities. As long as you present yourself in all situations in the decorum I know you've been taught to maintain, there'll be no restrictions on your activities. I have no intention of monitoring you or your communications. School is done; your graduation is this Saturday. Work is unnecessary, and Lisa will help you integrate into the world of the elite. She'll help you find proper activities. Who knows, you may become friends with some of the uptight bitches who grace the arms and beds of my associates."

"Are we arranging playdates now?"

His hands slapped the table. "Miss Conway. That bitchiness is not welcome when it's directed toward me."

Ignoring his rapidly disintegrating demeanor, I concentrated on his earlier answers. "*If* I marry you, I won't be at my graduation?"

"No. We'll be on our honeymoon. That doesn't make the graduation any less valid."

"Honeymoon? Do you have this all planned?"

"Yes and no," he said. "We'll have a clandestine destination wedding."

"I feel there's more to it than that."

"Of course, it'll be leaked to the press. It'll appear as though we've had this secretly planned for a while. You'll have everything a bride dreams of for her wedding."

"Unless, of course, I dreamt of a long engagement and maybe love."

Stewart's eyes narrowed: his agitation was showing. It didn't take a genius to recognize that he didn't appreciate my comebacks. Too damn bad. I wasn't the one who made him the marriage offer.

"Miss Conway..." he elongated my name, his tenor lower.

Hearing his tone of admonishment, I sat straighter and said, "Listen, Mr. Harrington, I've done pretty damn well without parental support for eighteen years. I don't need it now."

"Obviously, your parental provision has been stellar." He leaned forward, his blue eyes simmered with a combination of annoyance and lust. "Let me assure you, there's nothing remotely close to parenting in my plans for you, or in our contract."

The way he looked at me made my mind stop arguing while my insides twisted. He was right: everything in the contract was a much more direct discussion of a sexual relationship, made legal and binding through the act of marriage. Nevertheless, the sultry sheen to his icy blue eyes returned my sense of power.

I looked at my phone, 7:26 AM. "If you'll give me a minute to brush my teeth, I believe we have an appointment with your friend Parker."

"And at this meeting... which contract will we be signing?"

"My stepfather will live to see another day."

Stewart's cheeks rose revealing a pearly white smile. "I'll phone Parker to alert him to our arrival."

"But not Randall."

"No, not Randall."

~

THOUGH I WAS uncomfortable about visiting his attorney, Stewart remained true to his word. He stayed with me every step of the way. When we arrived, I did my best to appear to be a woman about to marry one of the wealthiest men in Miami—hell, maybe the country.

Yet the entire time I feared that my pounding heart or sweaty palms would give away my secret. I wasn't worthy of this offer.

I'd been reminded of that all of my life. My presence contaminated and infected those closest to me. It would take some time, but one day Stewart would realize that this was a deal he shouldn't have made.

As soon as we entered the prestigious leaded-glass doors to the cavernous foyer of Craven and Knowles, a tall, slender woman with a black pencil skirt greeted Stewart warmly. "Mr. Harrington, it's our pleasure to have you visit today. Mr. Craven will be right with you." The entire time she spoke, she purposely avoided looking in my direction as her peasant-style blouse teased with the promise of her barely hidden breasts.

"Trish," Stewart began, focusing her attention my way. "Let me introduce my companion, Miss Conway. In the future, I expect you'll be as happy to see her as you are me."

A crimson hue settled on her cheeks as she shamefully lowered her chin, and for the first time, looked in my direction. "Hello, Miss Conway, I apologize if I was rude. It's nice to meet you. Let me show you to the conference room. Mr. Craven will be with you in a moment."

Stewart placed his hand in the small of my back as we followed Trish to a glass room. Located near a multitude of desks and doorways, the room had glass on all four sides. When Trish flipped a switch the walls of windows instantly turned opaque and previously invisible blinds created a secluded, private room for our meeting. "Please have a seat." She gestured toward the table and plush chairs. "While you wait for Mr. Craven, may I get either of you anything to drink? Anything to make the two of you more comfortable."

Stewart looked my direction with a raised brow. Truthfully, I found her fawning amusing. I did my best not to laugh. "Would you like a cup of coffee, my dear?"

Trish failed to hide her flinch at Stewart's term of endearment. Nodding, I stifled my amusement. "Yes," I turned toward Trish. "Thank you, Trish, coffee would be wonderful."

"And coffee for me, also," Stewart volunteered. "I'll take mine black. Miss Conway prefers hers with cream and two sugars."

Trish immediately repeated the instructions and retreated from the room.

When Stewart reached for my hand, I grinned and asked, "What the hell?"

"As Mrs. Harrington, you're going to see a lot of that. I thought you might enjoy having a little fun. Besides, ordering something you have no intention of drinking will only help your reputation. I guarantee she's in the coffee room right now gossiping with anyone who'll listen. When she finds your full, untouched cup, it will make the company email."

"Ha, ha, I thought maybe you forgot that I didn't drink coffee."

"No, I don't forget. The world you're entering is full of piranhas. One day you'll be able to swim without me, but in the meantime, I'll be glad to help you grow your teeth."

I never thought of myself as someone who needed help. The whole concept seemed foreign; however, before I could give it much thought, the door opened and Parker Craven entered. Unlike Trish, who avoided looking in my direction, Parker seemed incapable of looking away; his large, brown eyes almost came out of his head as he took me in. I saw something sinister in his gaze, predatory and frightening. As much as I wanted to turn toward Stewart for the help he'd offered, something told me this would be a recurring theme with the good ol' boys in Stewart's circle. The sooner I learned to deal with it, the better. I maintained my composure and thinned my smile.

It was a look I'd seen my mother do throughout my life. It was her I'm-a-bitch-and-pretending-to-play-nice face. As the silence grew, it seemed appropriate. From my peripheral vision, I watched Stewart slowly stand. Parker Craven was a tall, handsome man, with dark hair and olive-colored skin. However, Stewart's stance, in some unspoken show of alpha-male superiority, dwarfed Parker's presence. Finally, Parker turned to Stewart, and exclaimed, "Holy hell, are you shitting me?"

Stewart unbuttoned his jacket and retook his seat. With his arm casually around the back of my chair he said, "Parker, this is Victoria Conway, whom I've mentioned."

Parker extended his hand in my direction. "Victoria, my pleasure."

When his clammy touch enveloped my hand, I immediately regretted not offering a nod instead of contact. As quickly as possible,

I retrieved my hand and repressed the desire to wipe it on my jeans. I couldn't believe I needed to sit with this man and discuss the contents of the contract. No longer did I wonder about the attorney who had the fortitude to compose such a ludicrous agreement. I knew in the pit of my stomach that he was as slimy as some of the clauses.

"I'm not sure how Stewart convinced you to get this far," Parker began, with a licentious grin, "but I must say, I'm glad that he did."

Clearing his throat, Stewart brought everyone's attention to him. "Park, today is about the contract. To avoid the obvious repercussions to Victoria's stepfather, we need to finalize this sooner, rather than later."

"Yes, yes of course." He opened the folder before him. "By that statement, I'm looking for confirmation that the two of you are willing to endeavor upon the marriage contract?" He looked from one of us to the other. "I need verbal confirmation from both of you."

"Yes, that is correct," Stewart replied.

Both sets of eyes turned toward me. *Fuck!* It was truly the precipice of my life. On one side I had life as I'd known it, except without my stepfather and with the aftermath of his untimely death, while on the other hand I had…

A promise?

A contract?

A life sentence?

"Victoria?" Stewart asked, bringing me back to the table of decision.

I squared my shoulders and fought the trembling. "Yes, Mr. Craven, that is correct." With that, I signed my life away.

CHAPTER ELEVEN

Ten years ago

MY HEAD ACHED as we stood to leave Parker's office. The contract discussions hadn't eased the uncomfortable feeling I got from Stewart's attorney. When we stood to leave, Stewart shook his hand, but remembering the clamminess of his contact, I only nodded. "Goodbye, Mr. Craven."

"Miss Conway, I look forward to getting to know you better."

I used my play-nice-bitch-face; honestly, I'd been getting a lot of use out of it since we entered Parker's office. Ignoring the rest of the conversation, my thoughts went to my phone. As Stewart once again placed his hand in the small of my back and spoke with Parker, my purse vibrated again. It had been happening periodically throughout our meeting as we dissected and discussed clauses and addendums. Willingly, I allowed Stewart to lead me out to the car. When we neared, I saw Travis opening the door and giving me a feeling similar to Parker.

Once the door was closed, Stewart squeezed my hand. "Are any of those messages from Randall?"

"I-I haven't checked," I trepidatiously replied. Pulling my phone from my purse, I scrolled the text messages, all nine of them. I had six from Valerie. I hadn't spoken to her since last night, and I'd missed my last advanced biology study session. Surely, she was concerned. My last, final examination was tomorrow, and it wasn't like me to blow off obligations. I had two text messages from friends in my advanced biology class, probably also concerned with my uncharacteristic absence, and one text from my mother. "No, but I do have one from my mother."

I accessed the message:

"VICTORIA, AS YOU CAN IMAGINE WE ARE ANXIOUSLY AWAITING A MESSAGE FROM YOU. THIS IS YOUR CHANCE TO REPAY ALL OF RANDALL'S GOODWILL. I CERTAINLY HOPE YOU DON'T PLAN ON DISAPPOINTING US."

I bristled in my seat as the magnitude of my decision weighed heavily on my chest.

"Do you care to share?" Stewart asked.

I couldn't look his direction. Everything had me on edge. I wasn't one to cry, yet with my eyes stinging from the impending tears, I handed him my phone. There was no need to pretend I had a great family. In three days, Stewart would be my husband. That wouldn't even be possible if it weren't for Randall. Stewart was obviously aware of how totally fucked-up Randall and Marilyn Sound were.

His body tensed next to mine as he read. Finally, he handed me back my phone with a simple observation. "She's really a bitch."

I couldn't help but laugh. It was better than crying. "I know we signed the contract, but do you really want to be part of this messed-up family?"

He reached for my thigh and gave it a reassuring pat. "No, I have no desire to be part of Dr. and Mrs. Sound's fucked-up family."

My eyes opened wide. *What the hell?*

Stewart continued, "But I believe you feel the same... am I right?"

I nodded.

"Three days, my dear. In three days you'll be Mrs. Stewart Harrington. You can tell them to never contact you again." He leaned closer, and kissed my cheek. "In all actuality, you can tell them that now. We may not be legally wed, but the ink on the contract is dry. There's no backing out now."

"In three days I'll be Mrs. *Victoria* Harrington," I corrected.

"In this town, darling, you'll be Mrs. Stewart Harrington. Get used to it."

I inhaled, feeling the muscles in my neck strain as I peered at the traffic outside the tinted windows and tried to change the subject. "Has Travis delivered the money?"

"Not yet. He's taking me to my office and you back to the penthouse. After that, he will."

"I want to take my advanced biology final tomorrow. I know it sounds juvenile with all that's happening, but I've worked hard for it. If I score the top in my class, I have an automatic scholarship to the University of Miami."

Stewart had pulled out his phone and was reading. Without turning he murmured, "Mrs. Stewart Harrington needs neither an advanced biology grade to graduate nor a scholarship to attend college. Your next two days are fully booked. Currently, there are tailors and seamstresses waiting at the apartment to take your measurements." He briefly turned my direction. "In three days, you'll not be seen wearing these kinds of clothes, and the work on your wedding dress will commence immediately. There's also a personal shopper coming later this afternoon to determine your preferences. She'll get your closet fully stocked. Besides the wedding gown, you'll need a nicer version of off-the-rack until the custom-made items can be produced."

My preferences? "What if my preference is what I'm wearing?"

Stewart didn't respond; instead, still looking at his phone he continued, "You also have various appointments scheduled on Tuesday and Wednesday with hair stylists, manicurists, and cosmetologists. With facials, highlights, waxing, *et cetera,* your schedule is full. On Thursday we leave for Belize."

"Belize? I don't have a passport."

He looked at me and shook his head. "You will. I'll call Parker and have one expedited. You may need to squeeze in a visit to the Department of State Passport Agency into your schedule, but it can be done."

I wanted to say that I thought it took more than three days to get a passport; however, I knew if I did, I'd hear what I'd been hearing all day. *It will happen.* Before I could reply, my phone rang. Looking at the screen, I saw MARILYN. "My mother," I whispered.

"I'd give you privacy, but there isn't anywhere for me to go," Stewart offered, trying to lighten my mood.

It rang again.

"Are you going to answer it?" he asked.

Was I? Was I ready to have this conversation?

"Hello, Mother," I said as I hit the speaker button. I didn't want to repeat the conversation, and besides, I wanted Stewart to hear what I dealt with, firsthand.

"Victoria," her voice was uncharacteristically relieved. "Why wouldn't you return my message? What's wrong with you? You had to have known that we've been worried sick."

My eyes met Stewart's. I was beginning to read his agitation by his clenched jaw and narrowed gaze. "It's so nice to hear from you too."

"Don't be cute, young lady."

The absurdity of her tone made me laugh. I had to cover my mouth to keep my amusement silent. "I don't think you've ever accused me of being cute. What exactly have you been so worried about, Mother? My life? My future? Truly anything about me?"

"Victoria, don't be selfish. Randall is right here. We want to know that you didn't disappoint our family."

"Seeing as how I've been a disappointment all of my life, I don't know how you'd think this would be any different."

The voice changed; it was now Randall. "Victoria, I've tried several times to reach Mr. Harrington. I can't seem to get past his secretary."

I smiled at Stewart, who nodded.

Thank you, I mouthed. "Why, Randall, why are you telling me this?"

My mother gasped in the background. Her shrill voice cut through the speaker of my phone. "Don't tell us that you didn't go to the meeting we arranged for you yesterday." *Was it really only yesterday?* "Don't tell us that you didn't discuss an arrangement with Mr. Harrington."

"Oh, I went."

"Vikki, I know this seems like a big favor we're asking of you—"

I cut off Randall's unfelt words. "A big favor? No, sorry. *Please pick something up at the store* is a favor. Sell yourself to save my ass is not a favor."

"Don't speak to your father—"

This time it was Stewart who spoke, interrupting my mother. "Mrs. Sound, from now on, you will not ever speak to your daughter with that tone. Is that understood?"

In our brief time together, I had never heard such command and authority in Stewart's voice.

It was Randall who next spoke. "Er, Mr. Harrington, can we assume that this means our arrangement is complete?"

"Dr. Sound, I'm waiting to hear your wife's answer to my question."

Oh my God. Listening as Randall's voice wavered and my mother was being called out for the bitch she truly was made my body tense with excitement.

"Mr. Harrington," my mother began, "I understand. Thank you."

An apology to me. How hard would that be?

Stewart watched my expression as I listened. As if he read my mind, he said, "Mrs. Sound, Victoria is waiting to hear an apology, not only for your outburst, but for the situation in which you and Dr. Sound have placed her."

"Umm, yes, of course. Vikki dear, we're both sorry."

I shook my head and squared my shoulders as the car came to rest.

"We're at my office," Stewart whispered.

"Mom and Randall, I need to go. I obviously went to meet Stewart. He and I have an agreement. Where that leaves the two of you has yet to be determined. Don't bother me: I won't bother you. In the meantime, Randall, look both ways before you cross the street. Goodbye."

My mother's gasp was the last sound we heard as I hit the red END CALL button.

Though Travis had the door open and the hot, humid Miami air filled the interior of the car, Stewart sat unmoving. "I'm not sure I should leave you right now."

"I'm fine. As you said, I have many appointments."

"What about Randall and the money? I promised you I'd pay it. Do you still want that?"

I touched his cheek. "Please, I do. Send Travis to pay it, but as for

Randall and Marilyn, I think they can sweat about it for a little while."

His blue eyes crinkled with small lines as his cheeks rose. "Tonight, Tori. Tonight, I'll make you forget about all of this, I promise."

Tori. I smiled. "We'll see, Mr. Harrington."

"Yes, we will."

～

WHEN SUSAN, my new personal shopper, finally left the apartment, I collapsed against the sofa and stared out at the ocean. Though the sun was still high, shadows from the tall buildings hid the beach below. It was there, so close, yet out of sight. Out toward the horizon, the late afternoon sunlight shimmered on the waves, creating prisms of color in the distance. The stunning view was hypnotizing. Without realizing it, I found myself lost in the wonder of the glistening hues. *How had my life changed so drastically in a mere twenty-four hours?*

I recalled my conversation earlier this afternoon with Val. Not surprisingly, she was shocked.

"What the hell, Vik?" Her voice came through my phone, loud and clear.

"I'm getting married Thursday. I know it sounds sudden." Due to the nondisclosure, I was limited on what I could share.

"Sudden? Oh my God! You went from *I have a job offer and I'm staying at some fine-assed hotel* to *I'm engaged and marrying some old, rich guy.*"

"He's not that old," I replied defensively.

"I don't get it."

"Listen, I can't say anything to make it make sense. But it's true, and I want you to be part of it. Will you?"

Val's voice lost some of its edge. "What do you mean?"

We went on to talk for almost an hour. I had people waiting. I knew I did, but Val was my sister, my connection throughout my life. I needed her to understand. I let her know that this was to be a very small, private wedding; therefore, neither Mom nor Randall was invited to attend. Funny, with all the craziness, the thing that seemed to bother her most was that I wouldn't be taking my advanced biology final. She more than anyone knew how hard I had studied, how much time and energy I'd devoted to it.

It was one of my top concerns too. Convincing her that it didn't matter anymore was one of the most difficult lies I'd ever told. Mostly because it did matter: it mattered to me. Closing my eyes, I sighed. I truly was to be Mrs. *Stewart* Harrington, not Mrs. Victoria Harrington. Victoria would take her exam. The realization increased the tension in my neck, twisting the muscles until I rolled my shoulders for relief.

I was in over my head, and though I wasn't the one who put me there, ultimately I was the one who signed the contract. Yet while I sat on the white leather sofa, I knew the blame went beyond me. For that reason, I held no regret for not informing Randall or my mother of my decision. I knew Randall's life was no longer in danger. *Could I say the same about mine? What did I truly know about Stewart Harrington?*

As I wrestled with my thoughts, Lisa broke my trance. "I'm sorry to disturb you, Miss Conway. I wanted to inquire as to what you'd like for dinner."

"Will Stewart be home?" Damn, I sounded like some lonely housewife.

"Yes, miss, he will. I just thought if you had a preference..."

Preference? Susan used that word; so had Stewart. *Was anything truly my preference?*

"Lisa, I honestly can't even think about food. I'm exhausted, which is funny, because I don't think I've done anything all day."

"That's not true."

I tilted my head with a grin. "You've done more for me today than anyone ever has, and then there was Susan, Fritz, and all the other people. I can't even imagine what tomorrow will entail."

"Miss, I think you're overwhelmed. There's been a lot of change in a short amount of time."

"I was just thinking," I said wistfully, "I came here about twenty-four hours ago. I didn't even know Stewart's name. Now, we're getting married. I keep thinking this isn't real."

"It's real, but you need to unwind. I suggest you go to your room and take a nice bath. Mr. Harrington won't be here for another hour. I'll discuss dinner with him after he's home."

I remembered the large tub in the bathroom off my room. "I think

I'd like that."

She patted my knee. "Then it's settled. Don't worry about a thing. I'll let Mr. Harrington know where you are."

Wearily I stood. "You know what?" I asked rhetorically. "This morning when Stewart said I would be busy all day, I didn't believe him."

"Oh, miss, if there's any advice I can share with you..." Lisa looked down.

"What? Please share."

"I shouldn't offer. If you ask, I'll answer, but it isn't my place to offer."

I reached for Lisa's hand. "You've been wonderful to me. I'm asking. Please offer me advice, anytime you feel the need."

With a smile, she said, "Don't doubt Mr. Harrington. He's too busy of a man to not be straightforward. If he told you that you would be busy, you will be busy."

"Thank you, Lisa. I believe I'll take that bath now."

"Do you need me to draw it for you?"

"No, thank you," I said with a smirk. I'd always imagined someone sketching a picture when I'd heard that phrase. "I think I can manage."

Wearily, I made my way to my room. *My room? When had I started to think of it that way?* It wasn't really my room. Once we were married I'd be staying in Stewart's room. He'd said that the first afternoon, and if I were to believe Lisa, I shouldn't doubt that he meant it. Hell, I hadn't even seen his room, but then again, yesterday morning I hadn't seen him.

As the scent of jasmine bath salts filled the bathroom's sultry air, I stood nude before the large mirror. With my long hair piled on my head, I wondered how I would continue to change. Tomorrow I had appointments with cosmetologists, estheticians, and manicurists. I already knew my wardrobe was changing. Truly, Susan had taken my preferences and molded them into the most incredible fashions. Would these beauticians do the same? Would my desires be taken into consideration? My hand slipped down toward my trimmed sex. I'd never thought about waxing. I'd heard about it, but the idea seemed too intrusive: I never wanted to be that exposed to anyone.

Yet, when Stewart mentioned it—in the grand scheme of my situation —it seemed insignificant. Now, the idea added tension to my already taut nerves.

Easing myself into the hot, silky bath, I closed my eyes with an appreciative sigh. The warm water soothed my sore muscles and the remnants of bath salts coated my skin. Unconsciously, I caressed my arms, enjoying the smooth texture. My thighs and calves ached from hours spent standing in heels higher than I was accustomed. Between the measurements for my wedding gown and future wardrobe, I'd been tugged and pulled in every direction. Massaging my calves, my hands unconsciously moved upward.

My thoughts turned to Stewart: last night on the patio, with the sea breeze on my skin and his fingers inside of me. I remembered his voice as he spoke to Marilyn and Randall. *Why didn't it bother me that he'd interrupted my conversation? Perhaps, because, by using the speaker phone, I'd essentially invited him to participate.* Nevertheless, it wasn't that he'd intruded: it was how. His voice held more than enough power and authority to stop Marilyn Sound in her proverbial tracks. With merely a few words, he'd given me more support than I'd ever known.

The silky jasmine salts coated my legs as my fingers continued to move to my inner thighs and found the swollen lips of my sex. The sensation wasn't even close to what I felt with Stewart's fingers, but it was something: something to relieve the tension of the day, of the last thirty hours.

I let out a sigh as my fingers plunged inside my core.

With my eyes gently closed, I imagined Stewart's handsome face. For a man so much older than I, he was incredibly handsome. His blue eyes could be so intense and yet so understanding. On the patio they'd been filled with lust, yet in the car, empathy and protection. Could I possibly be seeing so much? Or was it my youthful imagination?

My lips pressed together as the tension from the day found its way to my core. My hand moved faster, my fingers concentrating on the swollen bundle of nerves. My sole desire was to find release, one that I knew was near.

"Damn…"

I jumped as Stewart's deep, raspy voice shattered my bubble of seclusion. My eyes sprang open and water sloshed about the massive tub.

"...you're fucking beautiful."

Instinctively, I stopped—stopped everything—moving, breathing, and thinking. Standing in the doorway, with the deep blue eyes from the patio staring down at me was the man I'd agreed to marry, the one in my current fantasy. Bashfully, I looked away from his gaze, only to see the tenting of his custom-made slacks grow before my eyes. Though his jacket and tie were gone he screamed importance. The bulge that continued to grow screamed something totally different.

"Don't let me stop you, Tori. Watching you come is quickly becoming my new obsession."

"S-Stewart, you startled me," I said as I reached for a towel.

A shake of his head stilled my movements.

Biting my lip, I watched as he removed his shirt and marveled at the hard, massive chest I'd clung to the night before. His voice was velvet soft and yet rough. "When Ms. Madison told me that I'd find you in here, I had no idea what I'd find." His lips quirked into an approving grin as he scanned my body, totally exposed through the water. "I'm sorry I didn't find you sooner."

Stewart knelt beside the tub. His warm, uncovered skin radiated a heat exceeding the hot water around me. Bashfully, I reached again for the towel, but this time, he touched my hand. "No, Tori, I want to see more of that sexy show." He gently kissed my fingers and led them back toward my clit. "Give yourself pleasure. I want to watch."

Blood flooded my cheeks. "I-I'm not sure I can." It took all my effort to manage words through my embarrassment.

"You can."

His strong, powerful hand engaged mine, surrounding and dominating it. Soon we were moving together, our rhythm not unlike the one from before. Since removing my hand seemed out of the question, I closed my eyes, leaned my head back and moved as he instructed. My mind concentrated on the man beside me, the rich, woodsy aroma of his cologne, and his controlling touch. When his hand left mine, my eyes opened.

"Keep going, Tori. Don't stop. I want to watch you come."

There was no anger in his tone. It wasn't like the one I'd heard in the car, yet it also left no room for debate. I felt compelled to comply, moving my fingers in a tight circle. My breaths came faster as I applied a little more pressure to my ever-quickening caress. The water and Stewart's eyes no longer mattered as I brought myself higher up the mountain. When the tension settled in my groin, I knew this was going to be more of an orgasm than I'd ever given before myself. It wasn't the peak that Stewart had reached last night, but without a doubt, in a matter of seconds, I'd be falling to unknown depths.

As Stewart's large hands found my breasts and pinched my nipples, sounds unlike I was accustomed to making, escaped my lips. My mouth formed a tight O, and the rigidity in my legs gave way to release.

Slowly, my reality came back, and I opened my eyes. Before I could look away, Stewart reached for my face and caressed my cheek. "My beautiful Tori, that was incredible." Reaching for my hand he encouraged me to sit up. "Look at the water. Do you see it?"

To my horror, I did. There was a faint cloud, floating suspended in the silky water.

"Do you?" he asked again.

"Yes."

"Do you know what it is?"

I felt the blood again rush to my cheeks. "Yes."

"Tell me," he demanded. "Tell me what you see."

"It's me. It's my come." I hated saying the crude words, yet I knew instinctively he'd settle for nothing less.

"Yes, it is, and the next time you come, it won't be in a bath. Although, let me tell you, it was fucking amazing. I know it's been a long day, but if we're going to get the world talking, we need to be seen together. I want you to get dressed. On your bed is a dress that just arrived. Will you let me take you out for dinner?"

Though I wondered about Lisa's plans, I didn't have the strength to question. Instead, I nodded. *Was no even an option?* My insides twisted. There was something about being seen in public that made this situation even more real than the stupid contract. With his hand again gently caressing the side of my face, he leaned closer.

"Let me tell you about tonight." He didn't wait for me to approve. "I want you to wear the clothes on your bed, *only* the clothes on your bed. There's a dress and a pair of matching shoes." He reached into the water and possessively stroked my slit from back to front, leaving my swollen clit suddenly wanting. "I want to know that this warm pussy is waiting for me, uncovered by any obstacles. I want you to know that when you look in my eyes, I'm thinking about what I watched you do, and I'm thinking about your come floating in this water. Do you know why I'm thinking about it?"

Speaking seemed out of reach. Thankfully, he allowed me to shake my head.

"Because after I share my beautiful fiancée with the world, I'm going to bring you back here and bury my face in that perfect pussy. The next time you come, it won't float in a tub. No, darling, it will cover my tongue, my lips, and my chin. I'll be dripping with your sweet juices."

Oh my God!

"And you will *not* be sighing contently, as you just did. No, you'll be calling out—screaming out—my name. Because as of today, that's your job—to come, to show me how amazingly sexy you are. Because this little orgasm was nothing like what will overtake you when we get home."

I was shocked and appalled at his candor, and, at the same time, I was freaking turned on and hot as hell.

"Tori," his voice washed over me with more of his velvety tone. "Will you do that for me? Will you wear only the dress and shoes? Will you let me go down on you and make you scream my name? Will you wash my face in your juices?"

What does someone say to that? I'd never been asked something so intimate so casually.

His warm breath bathed my neck. "Tori, will you indulge me this evening, fulfill my desires, knowing that you too will receive yours?"

"Yes." It was the only word I could possibly articulate.

CHAPTER TWELVE

Ten years ago

I TOOK one last look in the mirror and smiled approvingly. My long hair was curled at the ends, allowing it to flow freely down my back, and I'd done my best to replicate the makeup from the day before adding a bit of blue to highlight my gray eyes and complement the dress. It was the dress Stewart had mentioned and was the color of cobalt, with a flowing skirt and a halter bodice that accentuated my breasts. With the open back, I couldn't have worn a bra if I'd wanted, and thankfully, the skirt was lined and showed no hint of my lack of panties.

When I stepped into the foyer, Stewart's appreciative gaze gave me the strength to continue.

"My darling, you're stunning." He leaned near my ear and whispered, "And I hope you've followed my instructions."

Maintaining my need for a semblance of control, I stared into the depth of his eyes and replied, "Yes, Mr. Harrington, to the T."

He nuzzled my neck. "Then, for good girls, I have a surprise."

Unknowingly, my eyes drifted to his slacks. His deep laughter filled the entryway. "Yes, I have *that* surprise, but I believe I'm waiting for someone to ask."

I fought the reddening in my cheeks. I hadn't meant to look, but once I did, I recognized how truly close I was to asking.

"Tonight," he continued, "I have another surprise, before we make our dinner reservations."

Stewart helped me to the car, where Travis was waiting. As we approached, his driver scanned me up and down, almost as if he knew I was nude beneath my dress. My mind told me it was absurd, nothing more than a combination of paranoia and my overactive imagination.

A little time later, the car came to a stop in front of a well-known, exclusive jewelry store in downtown Miami. The sign near the entrance indicated that the store was closed. Undaunted, Travis opened the car door, and Stewart helped me out. Before I could question his motives, the door to the store opened and a slight gentleman in a very nice suit came our way.

"Mr. Harrington, welcome! And Miss Conway." He bowed respectively. "I was exceptionally pleased to receive your call. Please, if the two of you will follow me."

I looked around the interior. Though it was closed for business, the cases were lit and members of the staff stood at the ready awaiting their directions.

"Would you like to peruse our cases, or would you prefer to see the private collection?"

Stewart didn't hesitate. "Alfred, the private collection. I don't want my wife wearing a ring that just anyone could purchase."

A ring? I tried to keep the look of shock from my face. *Of course, I'd have a ring. I was getting married.*

We followed Alfred into a regal private office, complete with a large desk. Stewart and I sat on one side, as the jeweler settled on the other. Before he could begin, a woman entered, carrying a tray bearing crystal fluted glasses and a bottle of chilled champagne. "Excuse me. May I pour you each a drink, something to celebrate this monumental occasion?"

I looked toward Stewart. I wasn't old enough to drink, not legally.

"Thank you," Stewart said with a nod.

I waited, wondering what would happen when they asked me for identification. However, they never asked. Instead, Alfred began, "Mr. Harrington, from our brief conversation, I believe I've selected the finest gems our company has to offer. I must tell you, one of these rings was already promised to another client, but for you, I've postponed our meeting."

Stewart's lips formed a straight line. "I assure you, Alfred, you don't need to apply high-pressure sales tactics or I'll willingly take my business elsewhere. If my fiancée likes what she sees, we'll buy it. It's that simple."

"Of course," he muttered, as he pulled a black velvet case from a drawer. Fixing his eyes on me, he said, "We can have any one of these rings sized for you by tomorrow. Please concentrate only on the unique settings, quality, and flawless stones."

My heart fluttered as he opened the case. There were only four rings, each with a stunning center diamond. The one that caught my eye had a beautiful emerald-cut yellow diamond.

Stewart looked at me. "What do you think?"

"I-I think they're astounding." I looked from the case to my fiancé. "Do you truly not want more information before I choose?" *Like maybe the price?*

"Alfred, are any of these rings doubles? I emphasize the need for an original."

The jeweler's eyes opened wide. "No, sir. Each creation in this collection has been made by one of our world-renowned designers. Each one is as unique as the love the two of you share."

So they're all fakes? I couldn't help but think; however, before I could turn toward Stewart, he squeezed my hand. A not-so-subtle reminder that this was another step in convincing the world we were real.

"Alfred," I said, "I think the yellow diamond is beautiful."

The jeweler's grin grew. "Miss Conway, you have wonderful taste. The center stone is a flawless 4.7-carat yellow diamond, surrounded by another 15 carats of white diamonds. This is the ring that I mentioned. I say that," he clarified, "because it has already been sized, but it too can be readjusted."

He removed the ring and handed it to Stewart. After a brief inspection, Stewart asked, "Would you like to see if it fits?"

It was the closest thing to a proposal I'd hear.

"Yes, thank you," I said, extending my left hand. Slipping snuggly over my knuckle, it was as if it had been made for me. "It fits. I love it."

Stewart turned back to the owner. "Do you have the matching band?"

"Oh, yes, Mr. Harrington."

When he handed the diamond-embedded band to Stewart, he also handed him a note that I assumed contained the pricing information. Stewart barely looked at the paper, placed it on the counter and extended the band in my direction. "Do you like this, too?"

"Miss Conway," Alfred informed me, "the band has another 16 carats of white diamonds."

I didn't respond to Alfred as I positioned the two rings together and secured them both on my fourth finger. The sparkling band fit perfectly, accentuating the large yellow diamond. Looking up to Stewart's watchful gaze, I smiled. "I do."

Stewart extended his hand to the jeweler. "Thank you, Alfred. We appear to have made our decision."

I handed both rings back to Alfred who placed them into a velvet-lined box and handed the box to Stewart. "Thank you, Mr. Harrington..." He nodded and reached for my hand, lowered his lips to the top and said, "...and Miss Conway, we're honored that you came by our humble establishment."

Once in the car, Stewart removed the velvet box from his jacket and extracted the large yellow diamond engagement ring. "Miss Conway." His blue eyes softened. "Tori, in two more days this agreement will be irrevocably sealed. Thus far, I'm not disappointed. Allow me to place this ring on your finger as an outward sign of our mutual arrangement."

Was I expecting a declaration of love and devotion? What we were doing was an agreement—a contract—and the sooner I accepted that the better. I squared my shoulders, steeled my gray eyes, and extended my left hand. "I signed the contract, and I accept your ring."

His brows lifted. "You may want to work on your enthusiasm, my darling. In a few minutes we'll be on the rooftop of the Beach Club, which I'm sure you recognize as one of the most exclusive private clubs in Miami. I anticipate seeing many associates, perhaps even some of your esteemed stepfather's colleagues. While some of this is for show..." He leaned closer. "...because I am so looking forward to showing you off—as I'm sure you're keenly aware—there's more than an element of attraction. As I'm introducing you this evening, I want you to remember what I plan to do with you tonight." His lips parted slightly and brushed my suddenly blushed cheek. "As I take a drink of my wine, I want you to know, I'm imagining drinking you." He nuzzled my neck. "As I'm inhaling the aroma of our perfectly prepared meal, I'll be anticipating your sweet scent. When the food hits my tongue, I'll be thinking about my tongue inside of you, with your sexy legs wrapped around my face."

Oh my God! I knew I was getting wet just listening to him.

"Tonight," he went on, "when I have you back at my penthouse, I'll be doing what every man whom you meet will want to do, what they will envision doing, what they will be doing with their wives but imagining my fiancée. You, my Tori, are stunning." His hand found the hem of my dress and moved under the soft material toward my thighs. "Tonight and every night I'll be the envy of every other man. You'll be starring in their wet dreams while you star in my every fantasy." His fingers inched upward. In a mere inch or two he'd learn for certain that I followed his instructions. "Spread your legs for me, Tori."

The car we were riding in wasn't a limousine. There was no partition between the two of us and Travis, no sound barrier. My eyes darted to the rearview mirror. With the setting sun, Stewart's driver wore sunglasses. The dark lenses covered his eyes and his expression, keeping the focus of his attention hidden.

"Tori," Stewart's tone was more demanding. "Don't make me ask you twice. Spread those beautiful thighs. Give me an appetizer, a promise of what's waiting for me."

His words shouldn't have been turning me on, but they did. I knew with a shift of my legs he'd find the wetness he sought. Once again, he'd gotten me totally aroused with only his words. "Oh, Stewart…"

"Shush, Tori, moan into me."

I shifted my legs farther apart, as his lips covered mine. It was our first kiss, the first time his tongue danced with mine. Yet that was not what had my attention; my entire body ignited as his fingers plunged between my swollen folds. I widened my thighs more to give him better access. Within seconds, the world disappeared and all that mattered was his touch and his kiss. When he found my clit, I did as he'd said: I moaned.

Our sounds intermingled as he removed his hand with an approving hiss, and cooed near my ear, "Yes, so wet, always so wet."

Oh my God! I wanted more. I wanted my mountain. As he brought his fingers to his mouth my cheeks blushed.

He spread my arousal on his lips and licked. "Just a taste of sweetness." His eyes shimmered. "Later, I'll dine."

What was happening to me? He was making me want things I'd never even considered.

My knees wobbled as Stewart led me from the car into the Beach Club. Then, as if nothing had just happened, he greeted the *maître d'* and led me toward the private elevator. Once alone inside the elevator, he brushed his nose against my neck and whispered. "Nothing here will taste as good as you. My darling, I hope you don't mind if we skip dessert."

～

I'D NEVER BEEN SO busy and yet done so little. What Lisa didn't do for me, she had someone else who could. The next two days flew by in a flurry of rush and wait. The days were monopolized by fittings, primping, and beautification. My long, dark tresses were highlighted, not in shades of blonde as I'd imagined, but tints of chestnut and lowlights of mahogany. When sunlight hit my hair, the various shades came alive in a truly surprising array of color. My skin was moisturized, waxed, hydrated, and massaged. Cosmetologists spent hours applying and teaching me to apply just the right amount of makeup. With the guidance of Zhen, a cosmetologist, I became an expert at creating the most dramatic eyes.

The wedding dress that Lisa had chosen—yes, she said that she argued with Stewart and won, not allowing him to see it until the wedding—was stunning. Before my first fitting, it was close to my size. By Wednesday afternoon, it fit like a glove. The flowing chiffon and fitted bodice worked together to create the perfect look for a destination beach wedding.

I'd also learned a little more about my fiancé. Though his homes were in Miami, his hotels were all over the world, and thus he spent quite a bit of time traveling. He said there would be times he would travel alone but probably more times he'd want me to accompany him. Though he never truly demanded, the way he asked, the way he inquired, left me little room for debate.

Beginning Monday night at the Beach Club, I was introduced to his friends and associates. Never once did he hint that our union was anything other than what it appeared. We were the topic of conversation, not only in Miami, but also around the country. Even the television gossip programs talked at length about the unlikely pairing. Of course, pictures with my engagement ring went viral. News of the wedding had yet to hit the press, but Stewart had no doubt it would be front-page news by Friday morning. That was why he'd decided upon a Thursday evening wedding. Our nuptials would hit the wire before the weekend, making an impact before being lost in the end of the week drivel.

Though I'd kept my word and hadn't begged for his cock, it was becoming increasingly difficult. Since Sunday night, I'd reached higher heights with Stewart than I knew existed. He'd gone down on me multiple times. It was everything he offered with his fingers and more. I didn't fight to journey to the top of the mountain, because falling off was my reward for the hard-felt expedition. When his tongue and fingers worked together, no matter how hard my hips bucked or my thighs squeezed, I was helpless against the precipice that exploded and sent me falling, not in one piece, but in a million shards to a cushion of sedation. Though he liked to watch as I began the journey on my own, not once had I seen what lay beneath his slacks. Each time I reached for his hidden erection my curiosity grew, and I knew it was only a matter of time before I did as he'd predicted and begged. My goal was to make it to our wedding.

The night before our departure for Belize, Stewart came home from his office earlier than usual. Lisa was out and I was sitting by the pool with Susan, completing the final arrangements on another order of clothing. This one was a special selection of designer casual dresses, ones that Lisa proclaimed were a necessity for my everyday activities.

Stewart's booming voice echoed across the rooftop pool as we both looked up to see him approach. Though he wore his custom suit and his blonde hair fell perfectly styled over his brow, the expression he wore was unlike one I'd ever seen. "Where the fuck is your phone?"

Susan's eyes widened as I looked around the table, moving magazines and sketches, I replied, "I-I don't know. In my room?"

Eyeing Susan, Stewart's demeanor shifted. "Ms. Jennings, I believe your services are no longer required today. Please contact my wife after we arrive home from our honeymoon."

"Yes, Mr. Harrington," she replied, standing and collecting her material from the table.

"Victoria, come to my office, now." With that, he was gone from the pool deck in a cloud of regal perfection and fury.

"Miss?" Susan inquired once we were alone, her eyes peeking questionably toward mine.

I wanted to assure her that everything was fine, yet I didn't know. Nevertheless, I smiled and nodded encouragingly: perhaps in an attempt to reassure myself. "Thank you, Susan. I'll see you in a week. Do you need me to see you out?"

She forced a smile. "No. If you have any last-minute concerns over this order, you have my number."

"I'm pretty sure the order is just fine," I replied.

I'd faced my parents' wrath on more occasions than I could count; I could face Stewart's. In some ways he'd been kinder to me than they ever had. Whatever was upsetting him, I believed I could handle. That, however, didn't lessen the anxiety that grew with each step as I made my way toward his office. When I entered, I asked, "Stewart, what—"

He reeled at the sound of my voice. "Did you find your goddamn phone?"

"No." My neck straightened. Though his clenched jaw and darkened expression filled me with dread, I was about to be his wife, and I didn't appreciate his tone. "I came to your *goddamn* office. That's what you said."

He paced behind his desk. "I've been trying to reach you. What's the fucking purpose of having a damn phone if you're not going to have it near?"

"Stewart," I slowed my rebuttal. "What happened? Why have you been trying to reach me?"

"I tried the apartment phone. I couldn't even fucking reach anyone here. I finally got through to Ms. Madison, but as you know she is out and couldn't reach you either."

"You're here now. What is it?"

His expression of anger morphed into one of uncertainty. "I paid the fucking money. I did it. Travis delivered it on Monday."

What money? My mind spun: so much had happened in such a short time.

"Victoria, your stepfather's in the hospital."

My knees gave way to a wave of nausea. *That money.* I hadn't called Randall or my mother. I'd been too caught up and busy, and to be honest, I liked the idea of making them sweat. "Hospital? What happened?"

"I don't know. Get your purse. We're heading over to Memorial."

Blankly, I nodded, trying with all my might to hide the fear rippling through me. *Oh my God. If he died, it would be another death on me.*

On the way to Memorial, I checked my messages. There were multiple text messages and voicemails from Stewart, some from Val, and one voicemail from my mother. I listened, not putting it on speakerphone.

"Why? Why Victoria? Do you hate us this much? Randall's at Memorial Hospital."

I looked to Stewart. "My mother's message doesn't tell us anymore than you already know. She only said he's at the hospital."

He reached for my hand and held it as we walked through the corridors on our way to ICU. I spotted Val first. We hadn't seen one another since Sunday afternoon. Until our eyes met, I hadn't realized how much I had missed her: three days were suddenly a lifetime. Her puffy eyes met mine.

As soon as they did, our mother's gaze followed Val's, and Marilyn stood. Years of being a judgmental bitch came into practice. It took her only a second to scan me: my new clothes, hair, and engagement ring. Almost instantly, her neck straightened. I held tightly to Stewart's hand, knowing without a doubt that he was the only thing keeping her from telling me exactly what she thought.

With more decorum than I knew she possessed, she took a step toward us. "Mr. Harrington, please allow me to speak to my daughter in private."

He looked possessively in my direction. I didn't want to let go of his hand, but I knew I should. Before I spoke, Stewart did. "Mrs. Sound, how is your husband?"

"He's in critical condition. There isn't anything they can do, but wait."

"Mother?" I asked, "What happened?"

"It was a heart attack. The doctors believe it was brought on by stress." Her last sentence dripped with accusation. Nevertheless, my lungs took in a much-needed breath as the tension left Stewart's grip. It hadn't been an accident. Nodding to Stewart, I let go of his hand and walked toward my mother. Abruptly, she turned and led me to a small family-consultation room. Once we were alone, she turned, striking like a viper.

"Are you happy? Is this what you wanted? Look at you, dressed like damn arm candy, with that giant rock on your finger. Do you think Randall told Mr. Harrington about you so you could reap the benefits and leave us out to dry? Where's your sense of loyalty after all that Randall has done for you? You and your selfish ways did this! You can't stand to see me happy, can you? You have to ruin every relationship I've ever had."

Though her icy tone dripped with hatred and accusation, I tried for more information on Randall. "What's his prognosis?"

"Do you even care?"

The fire in my veins melted the ice she sent my way. "Do I even care?"

"Maybe I should warn Mr. Harrington," Mother said, her volume low and threatening. "I should warn him what a deadly bitch he's dressing up for his arm. Everyone you touch dies: everyone who's naïve enough to get close. Even his money won't protect him from you."

"Are you listening to yourself? You fucking *sold* me without so much as a warning or regret."

"I should have known it would take something of more value to help us."

I clenched my jaw and willed my tears to stay at bay. Beyond the glass panel of the closed door I spotted Stewart. He was standing in the perfect place, leaning against a wall, and looking directly at me. His presence gave me strength. I lowered my tone. "Randall's debt is paid. It has been since Monday afternoon. His current crisis is the result of his fucking addiction and yours. You've made your decision. Don't contact me again—ever." My eyes left hers and found Stewart's. He stood straight and walked in my direction.

Dumbfounded at my outburst, Marilyn Sound glared at me. As she collected her thoughts, Stewart opened the door causing her to spin, suddenly muted by his presence. Rallying my strength, I said, "Marilyn, this is Stewart Harrington. I believe you have something to say to him."

Her eyes opened wide.

Turning toward Stewart, I continued, "Stewart, my mother would like to thank you for saving their asses."

I had the choice to concentrate on her icy glare or his smirk. I chose his smirk.

Marilyn extended her hand. "Thank you, Mr. Harrington. From the rock on my daughter's finger, I presume congratulations are in order."

"Mrs. Sound, I expect you to heed my earlier warning, and as for congratulations, yes. We're saddened that you and Dr. Sound will be unable to attend the festivities; however, it appears that your attention will be needed and welcomed elsewhere." He reached out to me. "Victoria, I believe we need to leave."

Reaching for Stewart's hand, I looked toward my mother. "Give Randall my regards. Oh, and let him know I said *you're welcome*."

My emotions stayed in check until we made it to the car. At that point, everything bubbled out: years of humiliation, of being a disappointment, and of being unwanted. As I collapsed into Stewart's embrace, I whispered, "Please, I'm begging."

Pushing me slightly away, Stewart looked down into my tear-filled eyes. "Victoria?"

"Please take me home. I need you to make me forget. I need you inside of me."

Raising his voice, he commanded, "Travis, take Miss Conway and me back to the apartment."

I held tightly to his hand as he walked me to the master bedroom, on the first floor of the penthouse. It had the same floor-to-ceiling windows as the living room, filling the massive space with natural light. Pulling me close, Stewart demanded, "Say it. I need to hear it."

"Please, please…" Unabashed, I fell to my knees. "I'm begging you to make me forget. I'm begging you for your cock. I need you inside of me."

"Victoria?"

I looked up at the massive, powerful man before me. Offering me his hand, he said, "Stand up."

I did, though on trembling knees.

"That, my darling, will be the first and the last time you'll ever beg. Do you understand?"

I didn't, though I nodded.

"Thursday, you'll be Mrs. Stewart Harrington. No one—not your mother, your father, nor your stepfather—no one but me will ever again have the power over you." He raised my chin. "Do you truly understand?"

"I do."

"Are you confident of what you want?"

Reaching for Stewart's belt, I said, "I am."

He grasped my hand. "While I appreciate your enthusiasm, darling, this is my area of expertise. Let me."

Nodding, I released his belt, but rubbed his hidden erection.

Spinning me around, Stewart lowered the zipper of my dress and removed the straps from my shoulders. The soft fabric fluttered to the floor as his low hiss filled me with a much-needed semblance of power. With my back to him, he secured the waistband of my panties and reverently pulled them toward the floor.

"You are so fucking beautiful." He turned my nude body to face him and gingerly kissed my lips, holding me close. The beat of his heart reverberated in his massive chest as his arms warmed and shielded me from the air-conditioned air. Taking my hand, he said, "Climb on our bed and show me your wet pussy. Spread those legs. I want more than your words—let me see your body beg."

While I did as he said, Stewart removed his jacket, shirt, and belt.

With each action, his eyes stayed fixed on me. Kicking off his shoes, he undid the button on his slacks and let them drop to the floor. His boxer shorts were incapable of hiding what I'd yet to see. Lying back upon my elbows, I brought my knees together and gasped. Never in all of my life had I seen anything so large. His penis stood erect, nearly touching his navel.

"Oh... I-I don't know... if..."

Removing his boxer briefs, Stewart climbed onto the bed. His blue eyes shimmered with lust as his words reassured me. "I've wanted this since before you walked into my office. Tori, I'm going to make you forget everything. All you'll be thinking about is the incredible stretching in your tight pussy." His anticipation was evident as he asked, "Do you trust me?"

Naïvely, I did. "Yes."

Spreading my legs, he kissed the inside of my thighs, each kiss moving closer and closer to my sex.

"I'll never get tired of your scent, so sweet." His tongue lapped my slit. "So good." Another lick.

I wanted more. "Please," I said as I gripped the sheets in anticipation.

More carefully positioned licks and kisses, so close yet not penetrating and not touching my clit. "What do you want?" he taunted.

"I want your cock," I proclaimed with confidence.

When I opened my eyes, I saw Stewart kneeling between my legs, his cock right in front of me. "Touch it, Tori. Feel what's going to be inside of you."

Uncertainly, I reached out and stroked the smooth, stretched skin. He moaned as it twitched with veins protruding and balls hanging heavily below. A drip of pre-come shimmered at the head.

"That's it. Stroke it."

My hand surrounded it: my thumb and fingers unable to touch. I looked up to his approving gaze. "Are you sure it will fit?" I asked.

"I'm sure."

Reaching for a condom that I didn't realize he had, he slid the sheathing over the length and eased his body over mine. "Relax, Tori. Open for me."

I lifted my knees. Slowly he moved over me. When the head of his cock pushed against my entrance, I gasped.

"It's all right. Let me in."

I closed my eyes and concentrated on his words as slowly his cock moved in and out, in and out, each time penetrating deeper than the time before. The only thing I could think about was the stretching of my core as pain gave way to pleasure. Sounds came from my lips as I once again grasped the soft sheets and fought the urge to pull away, but with each thrust that buried his hard cock deeper inside of me, I knew there was nowhere for me to go. Pain and pleasure intermixed as he filled me to my core.

"Fuck! You feel so good, so fucking tight."

Nothing else in the world mattered. With his balls against my ass, he stilled. When I opened my eyes, I saw only him. His voice filled the bedroom suite.

"God, you're amazing. Are you all right?"

I was. I was stretched, sore, and filled. Nodding, I smiled while a tear trickled from the corner of my eye.

Stewart lapped the tear with his tongue and rained kisses on my neck and breasts. Teasing my nipples, he sucked each one, creating taut, hard nubs. All the while, his cock moved in and out of me. In no time, the ache in my thighs gave way to a building tension that was forming inside of me. Subconsciously, I began to move in sync with him. My hips danced with each of his thrusts as his pace increased. The internal pressure was like nothing I'd ever known. It was nothing like what his fingers or mouth had been able to produce. Grabbing my ass, he pulled me closer, willing my already spread thighs farther apart and pounded his cock against my core.

We were almost there, almost to the peak of the mountain, and then with one final thrust he brought me to the top. The orgasm hit all at once. There was nothing else in the world: no aching muscles, no extended family. It was only the two of us. With his warm skin burning against mine, I fell. No, he threw me to the depths below. Screaming his name, I plummeted until there was nothing left. My only movement was the spasms flowing inside of me from head to toe.

"Fuck! I love the way your pussy milks my cock," he said as he continued to pump. "You're not done. Not yet."

How did he know I wasn't done? I was lying in pieces, unable to move. He reached between us and rolled my already swollen clit between his fingers. I called out at the delicious pain. I didn't know how much more I could take. The friction of his cock, in and out, the movement of his fingers. I couldn't breathe as the mountain formed in the distance. Again his lips and teeth found my breasts. Kisses gave way to nips. The mountain had the highest peak I'd ever seen and the journey was long. Undaunted, Stewart pushed me upward, thrust, by thrust, until my entire body hung precariously on the ledge.

"Now!" he demanded, pinching my clit and drilling into my depth. My second orgasm hit harder than the first. My newly painted nails dug into his broad shoulders. It was the only way to keep from washing away as each new wave roared through me. Stewart screamed, "Oh, fuck!" as he slammed into me one last time. His engorged cock pulsed inside my now tender core as he collapsed on top of me.

Paralyzed and mute, I lay below my fiancé, surrounded by his warmth. When he finally moved, I was left feeling empty, until he pulled me close to his side and kissed my hair. "Go to sleep, my Tori. Tomorrow we leave for our wedding."

CHAPTER THIRTEEN

Nine years ago

IN CINDERELLA, the handsome prince saved the poor girl from her wicked stepmother. In Snow White, the handsome prince saved the young, unwanted princess. Children's fairytales of happily-ever-after began the process of planting the seed in young girls' minds that princes truly existed. Many of the stories didn't begin that way: instead, they originated from tales of brutality and violence devised by the brothers Grimm. With that in mind, perhaps the fairytales shouldn't center on the prevailing of good, but the presence of evil. For without evil was there truly good?

The fairytale I'd been sold, the one that made the reality of my sale bearable, gave way to the true nature of my situation a little over a year after I became Mrs. Stewart Harrington. The façade of my prince shattered with my introduction to Stewart's *other* apartment. With all that had happened, I'd forgotten about its existence, until that was no longer possible.

"Remember the contract, my darling," Stewart said as he led me from the elevator in what appeared on the outside to be a warehouse in a more secluded part of town.

Though this was the first time he'd mentioned the contract since before our wedding, I wasn't sure how he thought I could forget.

Up until the evening when I first saw the warehouse, my days were spent integrating my way into the world of the socially elite. I'd been welcomed with open arms and knives at the ready. As Stewart's wife, no one dared publicly forbid me entrance into the clubs and organizations frequented by the upper one percent. Yet, I wasn't naïve enough to assume that the welcome I received was the one shared behind closed doors. After all, I was younger than some of my new friends' children, perhaps even grandchildren. There was more than what I saw on the surface. I would soon learn the depth.

I saw the looks as I was introduced. The women who invited me to play tennis and plan events were no more my friends than the girls at the academy had been. Thankfully, like most women, I'd been initiated early and I could hold my own. Being female enabled one the keen ability to smile politely and loathe internally. My mother's influence continued to seep into my dark core. Stepping into her shoes had never been my plan, but plans change. To fulfill my new obligations, I wore the proverbial bitch boots proudly.

It didn't take long for me to forget how Stewart and I began. I hadn't expected love, but what I found was as close to it as I'd known. My heart leapt when Stewart praised the things that I did. I loved the gleam in his blue eyes as I walked beside him or held to his arm at the elite social events. No longer did it feel as though we were for show. I genuinely enjoyed his company and it seemed that he did mine. Whether at the apartment or at our sprawling mansion outside of the city, he was attentive and engaged.

Often, I'd accompany him on business trips, proud to be Mrs. Stewart Harrington. He'd been right when he told me not to worry about his age. I marveled at his prowess in bed and took each new introduction—each new position or toy—as an adventure. Never had I imagined the life I lived, and never did I regret my signature.

Not until that night.

Unlocking the door to his warehouse apartment, Stewart led me inside. I soon realized that we'd entered on the second level. As Stewart hit switches, the cavernous room below came into view. Standing at the banister, I saw the stark contrast to our downtown apartment near the beach. As opposed to floor to ceiling windows, this place had none; instead, the perimeter was nothing but tall brick walls void of decoration. Two stories above was the only possible source of natural light: a large skylight. Given the late hour, it appeared as dark and dense as the bricks.

In a corner of the room below was a kitchen with a granite-covered bar and three stools. In another corner were sofas, chairs, and a TV. The starkness of the furnishings reminded me of a struggling bachelor or college student. Though Stewart had only been married to me for a year, *struggling* hadn't been a word that could be used to describe him, perhaps ever.

As I looked around, I couldn't help but wonder why, with our downtown apartment and large estate outside of Miami, was this extra residence necessary? Silently, he led me down the stairs. When the staircase turned, my gaze settled on the area of the room that was not visible from the entry. My curiosity turned to horror as my heartbeat intensified and my footsteps stalled. Taking in the raised platform containing a large four-poster bed, bile rose in my throat. Near the platform was one large, overstuffed chair.

Though the contract had outlined specifics regarding consent for sexual activities, up until that moment, Stewart had never proposed anything that I deemed out of the ordinary. With everything he initiated, I'd willingly followed. There was no doubt that he'd taken me to places I'd never been. However, I innately knew that there was something vile about the scene before me.

Tugging my hand, he encouraged my steps. "Don't stop now, Mrs. Harrington."

"Stewart? What is this?"

"This is where my fantasies come true."

My neck straightened as I tried to comprehend. "I-I don't understand? We have sex. We have a lot of sex. Why do you need an apartment for it? What's wrong with our home?"

Though my mind spun, my feet continued to move. Nearing the bed, he said, "I'm not complaining about our sex life, Victoria. I like what we do at home. This is different. This is why I married you. This is what our contract was about."

The contract came back to me: clauses and addendums. One particular sentence came back: *outside the experience. What the hell?*

"Stewart, what happens here? What do you expect of me?"

"Nothing has happened here since our agreement. I'm not sleeping with other women, if that's what you're asking. I did before we met. I have needs." He directed me to sit upon the bed and touched my cheek. With a difference in his tone, he continued, "As of late, Mrs. Harrington, most of those needs have been very well met."

"Most?" My stomach continued to churn. "Just say it. What do you think I'll do here?"

His grin twisted. "I *know* what you'll do here. You'll do as I say. We have a contract, a legally binding agreement."

"I-I still don't—"

He touched my lips. "I've maintained my side of our deal. You have my name, access to my money. Your sister has been accepted at Johns Hopkins." He tilted his head. "Have I denied you anything?"

"N-No," I answered with obvious trepidation.

"And you will *not* deny me. I told you before that if something made you uncomfortable, I would be there for you. You'll never be here alone. I'll always be here."

I shook my head. "I don't understand! Why wouldn't you be here? If I'm supposed to do something, something to do with sex…" my words trailed away as the upheaval in my stomach became impossible to ignore. A quick look to the side showed me a door. I prayed it contained what I needed as I bolted from the bed, flung the door wide, and vomited my dinner in the toilet.

With my head pounding and my body shaking, I moved to the sink and, cupping water, rinsed my mouth. With my head on the sink, I turned toward my husband and demanded, "Just say it!" My volume rose. "Don't make my imagination take me places I don't want to be."

Reaching for my hand, he helped me stand upright. "Where exactly is that beautiful imagination going?"

I already knew that Stewart enjoyed watching me pleasure myself. Often, he'd encourage me to masturbate, even introducing me to use toys so that he could watch as I came apart. "It's something about watching, isn't it? That's why there's a chair. Please tell me that there'll be no one else here besides us."

"I can't."

My brows rose as I repeated, "You can't?"

"You're a beautiful woman. I've told you how many men want you. I wasn't lying. They do. And I love watching those beautiful lips cry out. I want to be the one orchestrating; I want to watch as other men use you. I want to be the one to give you that pleasure."

"No!"

"No?" he quirked. "Mrs. Harrington, that word was removed from your vocabulary the day you signed my contract."

"I-I can't. I don't want to be with other men. I want to be with you." *At that moment, even that wasn't true.*

"And you will. You'll be with me. I still want to be with you. The idea of watching is making me hard right now. I bet if I lifted the skirt of that pretty little dress, I'd find that you're wet thinking about it."

"I'm not!" I answered honestly. "Who? Who are you willing to share me with?"

"You see, that was the part that had me stumped. When it was prostitutes, it didn't matter. But as my wife, you're expected to be on my arm." He placed my petite hand in the crook of his arm and led me back to the bed. "And I like having you there. I've decided it would be better for you not to know."

What the hell?

"That doesn't make any sense. How could I possibly be doing... whatever it is you want to *orchestrate*..." I emphasized his word, "... and not know who I'm with?"

Stewart stopped again at the bed. "I believe I've worked that out." He reached under the bed and pulled out a box.

I stood speechless as he opened the lid.

Inside I saw an array of sex toys, but that wasn't what he sought. Stewart removed headphones and a blindfold. "These headphones will cancel out the sound of the other person's voice, and the blindfold will do what blindfolds do. You'll neither be able to hear nor see the person with you." He removed a Bluetooth and placed the headphones over my ears. His voice came through the headphones. "Speaking through the Bluetooth, you'll only be able to hear me. When I'm not speaking, I'll have music playing, all in an effort to conceal your partner's identity."

It creeped me out to have him talking casually about *my partners*. I removed the headphones. The sound of his voice was beside me. I didn't need to hear it through electronics. "But, but the other person will know it's me. Even if I don't know who it is, he will."

"*They* my dear; not *he*. Plural not singular." Stewart placed the blindfold over my eyes and the headphones once again on my ears. With my world dark, he continued, "You're so hot, and you're so right: *they* will know. However, you won't. Each time we attend a function or accept an invitation to dinner, you won't be burdened with the knowledge of the man across the table having had his dick inside of you. As you're playing tennis at the club, you won't be comparing the husbands of the women you see. All you'll know is what I choose to share with you."

As I reached for the blindfold, Stewart's words brought my hands to a halt. "Do not remove that, Mrs. Harrington. Tonight, I want to watch as you follow my directions."

A renegade tear escaped my lid, only to be swallowed up by the satin material. I spoke into the darkness. "Stewart, I don't want to do this. I don't want any part of this."

He brushed my arms as I felt the zipper of my dress go down. "I'll be with you every step of the way. I'll make this as easy or as hard as I choose" His warm breath bathed my neck. "I suggest that you work toward easy: it is what I truly want." Guiding me up toward the head of the bed, he removed my panties and spread my legs. "Tonight it's just us. Nod if you can hear my voice."

I nodded, for the first time fearful of the man I called my husband. *What did he mean when he said that it can be as easy or hard as he chose? What would he do if I denied him this?*

The mattress shifted: instinctively I knew he was gone, though his voice sounded as though he were still next to me. "You're so fucking hot. The whole loss of sight and selective hearing can be incredibly erotic. Give into it. Give yourself over to the sound of my voice."

I shook my head. "Please, Stewart."

"Stop talking," he scolded. "When we're home, you can do and say whatever you want. But here, in this place, it's my domain—my fantasy. You'll do as you're told, when you're told. If you can't follow the directions when they're given, you'll be punished. I have gags for talking out of turn. Is that what you want?"

I shook my head.

"That's a good girl. And as you may recall, our contract contains a do-not-disclose clause. What happens in this place stays in this place.

No one, not even Ms. Madison can be trusted. Nod your head if you understand."

I nodded.

"Now, I don't want you to embarrass me."

What the hell? Me embarrass him?

Stewart continued, "So, at first, we'll practice alone. Once you learn to obey, we'll invite friends."

My fucking choice was to not obey and get punished or obey and be fucked by others. That didn't seem like much of a choice.

"Tonight will be very simple. You know the routine, Mrs. Harrington, work that pretty little pussy of yours and show me how wet you can get."

My fingers obediently found my sex. There was nothing even remotely erotic about what I was doing. At home, in our bedroom, as I watched his blue eyes devour my movements, I could do what he wanted. Though my fingers obeyed, my mind was thinking about my new reality. *How could I look his friends and business associates in the eye knowing that any one of them could have been inside of me?* Names and faces came to mind. The way Parker Craven had looked at me the first time we met. *Did he know? Would he be one of them? Why else was he so intimately involved in the writing of the contract? Business executives, politicians, who would be part of the* they?

I gasped as the mattress shifted and Stewart's fingers plunged deep into my core.

"What the hell? You're fucking dry as a bone. Come on, darling, you're normally so wet." His thumb took over what I'd been doing. "Listen to the sound of my voice. Don't listen to the thoughts in your pretty little head. Listen to me. We're going to work to make you comfortable here. That's it. Think about my cock. If I'm going to let you get all wet and let you come, you're going to do the same for me. Reach out those pretty little hands. My cock is right in front of you."

I did as he said, touching his torso. I could tell that he was now kneeling over me. His fingers stopped moving inside of me as I felt him reach past my head. *Was he holding the headboard?*

"Open your mouth, baby. I'm going to give you a surprise for being a good girl."

I'd given him head many times, but he'd never come in my mouth, always pulling out and splashing my chest or stomach. I tasted the tartness of his pre-come as he glided his cock deeper into my mouth.

"When we're here, you're my whore. Remember that." He pumped in and out of my mouth. "And good little whores swallow." My scalp screamed as he fisted my hair, limiting my ability to move or pull away. "You don't want to disappoint."

My chest hurt. Not from the weight of his body over mine, but from his words. *How could this be real?*

CHAPTER FOURTEEN

Present

MY HANDS GRASPED the cool wrought-iron spindles while *Fatal Lullaby* played in my ears. The familiar tune gave consistency to my darkened world, providing reassurance as my mind searched for answers. Perhaps I should've been questioning my current situation, but I didn't. I'd been here too many times. My thoughts concentrated on Brody's bombshell. I hadn't been able to meet with him yesterday after he'd sprung the news of Stewart's will. I'd visited the Harrington Society distribution facility as I planned, but then Stewart awakened, and I was summoned home.

I wasn't sure if it was the high doses of medication or possibly the pain, but like Val had said, as Stewart's illness progressed, he seemed to be striving for any semblance of control. To that end, I even tried to sleep in his bed last night, but after the second round of nurses came in before midnight, I gave up. Something was up about his vitals and the monitors kept chiming. Everyone was on alert. Honestly, after they increased his pain medication, I'm not sure he even knew I wasn't in his bed.

This morning when I went to his room, he seemed weaker than the day before. As a matter of fact, when I left the apartment, he hadn't yet been moved from his bed to his wheelchair. Nevertheless, he was still his demanding self. When I told him I had errands, he informed me that he'd already made plans. I was to be at the warehouse and prepared for an 11:00 AM visit. Though my stomach twisted, the smile never left my lips as I consented. His friend had requested an early lunch meeting, and we didn't want to disappoint him. *Right!*

As I waited for my husband's voice and his friend's arrival, I held out hope that I could still make it to the Viceroy and meet Brody. It all depended on the friend and what would be involved with today's meeting. Instead of allowing my thoughts to linger in that direction, I concentrated on Brody. *What would he tell me about the will?*

It was undoubtedly after eleven and still no word from Stewart, only the ghostly music coming through my headphones. I fought with the desire to remove my blindfold. Stewart had always been the one to secure it. Now that I was on my own, I momentarily entertained the idea of keeping it loose. If I did, perhaps I could see the friend. But then I remembered the realization of Parker. *Did I want that?* I couldn't get wet for these men. Did I want to truly know their identities?

The bed shifted, bringing me to the present.

Still, all I heard was music.

A cool hand traced an insubstantial trail from my hand to my collarbone. Then, another touch explored my other arm. Again the bed shifted. I knew this person was now straddling my waist. My hyper-alert senses felt each of his knees on either side of me as well as the heat of his presence above.

My mind told me to open my mouth, but ever since this cruel game began, every one of my movements had been choreographed. Never had I been expected to depend on my own intuition—never here, never at the warehouse. Where was Stewart?

Warm peppermint breath skirted my neck and a sense of unexpected relief loosened my overwrought nerves. I knew this man. I didn't know his identity, but I knew his peppermint scent. He was kind, as kind as someone could be having sex with another man's wife.

Some men had preferences and fetishes they enjoyed. Apparently, Stewart enjoyed most of them too. Not Peppermint Man: he was reliably vanilla.

Reverent hands fondled my breasts, pulling and teasing my nipples. I wondered who he was. *Did I know him outside of this room?*

Did I know his wife? As much as I was in the dark, figuratively and literally, with these men, I imagined their wives were too. *Did they have any idea that their husbands enjoyed sex with a restrained partner?*

It wasn't that my hands or feet were ever tied or that Stewart ever used the gag he mentioned on my first visit. No, my restraints were invisible and more binding. My restraints were my sister's future and perhaps even that of the Harrington Society clinics. Yet, as Peppermint Man began to rub his cock between my breasts, I knew those restraints were deteriorating by the moment. If they weren't, I'd be hearing Stewart's voice.

Fatal Lullaby and *Death Dance* had ended long ago as the soundtrack continued its eerie play. Peppermint Man moved his cock to my mouth, teasing my lips and chin as he coated my face with his pre-come saltiness. When I didn't respond, fingers came to my mouth prying and encouraging me to open.

"I'm here, baby." Stewart's voice came through the headphones. I barely recognized his voice, our connection filled with static as if utilizing an old-fashioned phone line and not a technologically advanced sound system. "Nod if you hear me."

I nodded, surprised by my own relief at hearing the familiar command. As much as I hated this, I needed him present. Yet, with each distant sounding sentence, I was reminded of his weakened state.

"Open for him. Let him fuck your mouth."

The music resumed, from the beginning of the track, and I did as he said. Slowly, the cock inside my mouth came to life: growing as it thrust in and out. Course hair scratched my chin and cheeks as Peppermint Man buried himself to the hilt. When his rhythm increased, I prepared myself for his come; however, instead of filling my mouth, he pulled away.

"Roll over," came the direction though the crackling connection. "Let's see that sexy ass."

I did as Stewart demanded and released the spindles and rolled to my knees.

"Up on all fours." The static made his words difficult to decipher. "We want to see those titties swing as he drills into you. Nod if you understand."

Nodding, I worked to right myself. I hated this position. It was difficult to not fall forward. As I fought the blindness to secure my steady balance, Peppermint Man gently pushed my knees apart, fingered my folds, and spread my fake arousal around my entrance. Then without warning, the cock that had been in my mouth—now wrapped—pushed inside my sex. Peppermint Man's fingers dug into my hips, directing me: pulling and pushing, plunging deeper and deeper until his balls slapped my ass. With each thrust my heavy breasts swung forward and back. It was just as Stewart had orchestrated. Even from the distance of our penthouse apartment, or hopefully from the gates of hell, he was able to plan it all.

It didn't take long before the *friend's* rhythm again increased and heat radiated from his hands and body. I was concentrating on staying balanced when Stewart's static-filled plea interrupted the music. "Come on, darling, come for us."

I couldn't come if I'd wanted, and I didn't want. Nevertheless, I'd learned to put on a show. If the *friend* thought I came, it often accelerated his orgasm. Moans came from my lips as I pushed back against the thrusts. Pretending to give way to my impending release, I fell face first into the pillows and let out a muffled scream. Seconds later, Peppermint Man's cock throbbed and his weight came crushing down upon me.

With his face near mine, I felt the slight brush of his cheek against mine. Then the bed shifted. I lay unmoving, waiting for my directions. Over the last nine years I'd learned to do more than fake an orgasm. I'd learned to be Stewart's obedient whore. As I lay waiting for his voice, I envisioned his decaying body. Soon... soon he would be dead. Soon I would be free of this. And then I remembered the will.

Crackling interrupted the music. *Why didn't the music have static? Why was it only there when he spoke?* "Roll over, my Tori. Find those spindles, hold on, and spread those legs. Show me your satisfied pussy." *Yeah, right, I thought, as I listened to his familiar command.*

My body mindlessly obeyed as I opened my legs and exposed myself to his camera. With this friend satisfied, my thoughts returned to Brody's call. Stewart had a new draft of his will. *What does that mean, a draft?* More questions swirled as only music filled my headphones. The soundtrack was all the way to the fourth song when

I allowed my concerns to be drowned away by the music. For the first time in years, I listened, really listened to the notes. The songs later in the track weren't as familiar as the first two songs.

Finally, I heard my husband's voice. "Our friend is gone, Tori. Come home. Don't wash, just dress. Nod if you understand."

It was the same thing he'd said the other day. I'd disobeyed him then; I wanted to do that again. Before he was ill, watching me with his friends made him hard. After his friends were done, he'd usually either fuck me or have me give him a blow job. He'd said that it was his way of reassuring me that even though he enjoyed sharing, I was *his* wife, *his* whore. The friends might get to fuck me now and then, but he could have me whenever he wanted. Bile and disgust created a toxic cocktail that threatened to rise from my throat. I pushed it away, squeezed my eyes shut behind the blindfold, and tried to stop those memories.

"Did you hear me?"

Fighting to stay in the present, I nodded.

As I SETTLED into my warm car, the scent of peppermint and lustful perspiration emanating from my long hair continued to instigate the revolt in my gut. I hated the offending scents; nevertheless, I couldn't wash my hair. If I had, Stewart would've known that I'd showered. It was one thing for Stewart to take me directly after a *friend* when Stewart was right there in the warehouse, but driving all the way home with Peppermint Man's scent on my skin was more than I could stomach. After the quick shower, I reapplied the lubricant, confident that my husband wouldn't know the difference.

Through the depths of my purse, I reached for my phone. My fingers brushed paper-towel-wrapped vials. Val's doomsday scenarios had me intrigued. The drugs held real potential. I was getting tired of Stewart's leukemia taking forever to kill him. I guessed that's what happened when a man as healthy and young as Stewart developed a disease. His body fought. The extra benefit had been his continued suffering. *Did I want that to end?* I did: not to save him from the pain, but to rid me of his presence—forever.

I also knew that my purse was not the ultimate hiding place for the drugs I'd picked up yesterday at the distribution center. There was too great of a risk of the glass vials breaking. If I used them, I didn't want it to be done accidentally. I also wasn't concerned about anyone discovering that they were missing. They'd been accounted for upon arrival to the distribution center, and they'd been accounted for on their way out. Unless there was a case-by-case audit performed at customs, one small tube of each drug would never be missed. Well, not until the cases were opened, and by then, the cases would have gone through too many hands to identify the culprit.

I swiped the screen of my phone. Not surprisingly there was a text from Brody:

"WHERE ARE YOU? I'M WAITING."

Instead of texting, I hit the CALL button.

He answered on the first ring. "Where are you? Are you all right?"

Blinking my eyes at the harsh early afternoon sun as I pulled out of the private garage into the Miami warmth, I attempted to keep my voice calm. "I'm fine. I can't make it. I thought I could, but Stewart's being very demanding. I need to go home."

"Home? You're not home?" Brody asked. "Where are you?"

"Out."

Silence.

"I had to run some errands," I added.

"Vik, I need to see you. If you're already out, run the errands over here. I need to explain this."

"Brody? What did you mean a *new draft*?"

"It's not finalized, not yet. Maggie said that Parker had some more research he needed to complete and then he'd go to your place for Stewart's signature." His explanation came quick. "There's more. I just don't want to do this on the phone."

I fought the battle of my heart and will. Turning the steering wheel toward the apartment, I sighed. "Tomorrow, I'll try for tomorrow."

"Fuck, Vik. Today! If you can't do it now, how about later tonight? Doesn't that cocksucker sleep?"

A faint grin came to my lips. "I'll see what I can do about upping his pain meds."

"I've got this room until tomorrow. I'll go back to work and see what I can learn. I don't care what fucking time it is when you get free. Call and I'll meet you here."

"I'll do my best." Before I was about to hang up, I asked, "Who?"

Brody's end of the line remained silent.

I repeated my question, "Who is Stewart planning on leaving the proprietorship of my contract to?"

"Vik…"

"Brody, fucking tell me. I don't even understand how he thinks he can do this. I mean, if I get everything, all his money and property and Val's education is complete, I don't know why he thinks I'd agree to do what it says in there for anyone else."

"In person, Vik, I'll tell you in person. Make it work."

CHAPTER FIFTEEN

Present

As soon as I stepped off of the elevator into our apartment, I knew something was amiss. Lisa was wringing her hands, as her larger than normal red-bordered eyes turned in my direction. Stopped in my tracks, I steeled my shoulders and asked, "What? What's happened?"

"Ma'am, I wanted to call you, but Travis said you were on your way."

"I was," I confirmed. "Tell me, is it Stewart?" My heart began to race in anticipation. I reached for Lisa's shoulders. "Tell me!"

"The doctors are here. Mrs. Harrington, I suggest you go to your suite and talk with them." Of course, she meant the suite I shared with Stewart, not the one I'd been enjoying alone. Nodding, I tightly clutched my purse and stepped quickly toward the master bedroom suite. When I opened the door, a sea of eyes turned toward me. Immediately, I locked in on Dr. Duggar, Stewart's oncologist. Turning, I also recognized Stewart's cardiologist. Under normal circumstances, I'd assume that most specialists don't make house calls. Stewart Harrington was not *normal circumstances*.

As I continued to scan the room and follow the new sounds, I saw my husband, with a large tube coming from his mouth and a machine that echoed with the sounds of breathing.

My hand went to my mouth. "Oh my God. What happened? He was fine this morning. I was just speaking with him."

One of the nurses came forward and reached for my arm. "Mrs. Harrington—"

"No!" I yanked my arm away. "Someone tell me what happened."

Dr. Duggar turned toward me. "Mrs. Harrington, in cases like this, we don't always have answers. With the cancer alone, your husband could have continued to fight for weeks, maybe longer. Something happened this morning. When did you speak to him last?"

I tried to think. I was supposed to be at the warehouse at eleven. "I'm not sure, maybe about eleven-thirty, eleven-forty?"

Though I hadn't noticed him before, Travis was standing on the far side of the room with his arms crossed over his massive chest and his dark eyes narrowed in my direction.

"Ma'am, that's impossible," the doctor said.

My neck straightened. "Excuse me? What do you mean?"

"What time did you leave here this morning?"

"After breakfast. Stewart was awake." I pointed toward the blonde nurse. "Missy was here with him." I shrugged. "Maybe about nine, give or take." My glare deepened. "Tell me why I couldn't have spoken to my husband when you said."

"Ma'am, Mr. Harrington flat-lined this morning at approximately 9:47 AM. Missy performed CPR while Angela administered the defibrillator."

My knees felt week as I moved toward Stewart's bed. Dr. Duggar reached for my arm. "Your husband does not have a do-not-resuscitate order in place. Missy and Angela brought him back. However, right now he's unable to breathe on his own. That's why he's intubated."

"But? What happened?"

"Without surgery, we won't know for sure. The chemotherapeutic medications that Mr. Harrington has been taking have been known to be detrimental to the heart muscle. I can only venture to guess that it was his heart."

"And…" I looked toward the bed. Stewart's eyes were now open and looking toward me. "…he's conscious?" I took a step toward him.

"Yes," Dr. Duggar replied. "We're sure he can understand. I'm confident he can't speak. That's why I know you didn't speak to him an hour ago."

A gloss of perspiration created sheen to my suddenly clammy skin. I had—I'd heard Stewart's voice. It sounded odd, but who else would have spoken? My gray eyes darted toward Travis. His lips snaked into an evil grin as I now recognized the warning in his still-narrowed gaze.

I turned my attention back to Dr. Duggar. "What's the prognosis? Will you be able to remove this tube?"

Dr. Duggar shook his head. "He's going in and out of consciousness. I don't know of anything else we can do. Earlier, Mr. Harrington shook his head, indicating he didn't want more pain medication, but I think it would make him comfortable until…"

"I have medical power of attorney," I interrupted. "Surely, doctor, we can argue that the combination of medications and recent events has made it difficult, if not impossible, for Stewart to be able to be confident in his ability to make rational decisions—" As I spoke, Travis's arms came down and he leaned forward.

"Doctor," Travis interrupted, "Mr. Harrington left strict instructions—"

I stood taller, strengthened my voice, and addressed the room. "Doctors, the necessary documentation is in my husband's chart. You may call Parker Craven of Craven and Knowles if you have questions. For now, I'm not wasting my husband's final hours arguing a point that very soon will be irrelevant. Right now, I'd like to have some time alone with my husband."

"Of course, Mrs. Harrington. We can monitor Mr. Harrington's vitals from the next room. Just know that if he needs us, medically, we'll come in."

"Yes, doctor…" I said as I looked toward his IV. Multiple bags hung on contraptions with tubes going into one tube that was taped to the inside of his arm. "…the pain medication?"

"We'll check that documentation while you speak to your husband."

I nodded as the room emptied. When only Travis and I remained with Stewart, I turned back to Stewart's open blue eyes and spoke to Travis. "Once Mr. Harrington and I are finished, I expect you to meet me in my office. We have something to discuss."

"I will stay here…"

I spun toward him. "No, you will not. I'll speak with Stewart alone. When I'm done, you will meet me in *my* office." I paused. When Travis didn't respond, I continued, "The appropriate response is yes, Mrs. Harrington."

Clenching his jaws, Travis replied, "Yes, Mrs. Harrington."

Once the door closed, I turned back to Stewart, walked toward him, and sat at the edge of his bed. Leaning closer I spoke in a low whisper. "You do realize this is it, don't you? You are fucking going to die." His blue eyes widened. "Now, Stewart, that isn't enough of an answer. I know you can hear me. Nod if you understand."

Again his eyes widened.

"Tsk, tsk." I touched his cheek. "Before you go, there's something I've been waiting to tell you. You know how you enjoy watching? Nod, motherfucker."

Stewart's head bobbed as much as it could with the restrictions of the intubation tube.

"Well, I have a secret. I've enjoyed watching too."

Question clouded his blue stare.

"You see, the doctors were obviously perplexed by your rapid onset of leukemia. I mean, look at you. Oh, don't look now. Now you look like shit. You smell like shit too, but there was a time, a time you were quite fit and handsome, rather cocky too. Ha!" I laughed. "Cocky sure couldn't describe what you have left. Now," I patted his arm. "Don't let me digress. I don't want you entering hell without truly understanding who put you on the fucking express." I leaned even closer. "I did! Now, as you enter the gates with the fire and brimstone, know that the hell you put me through for the last fucking nine years was nothing compared to the eternity you'll suffer for what you did. Watching you rot away here on earth was satisfying for me." I sat up. "Yes, you're right: watching has been incredibly rewarding. I'm fucking getting wet thinking about it. Over the last year and a half, I've been able to sit back and watch you deny, get mad, spend a fucking fortune to make it go away, sulk, and now… with only hours left… maybe accept your fate."

I stopped and smoothed the material of my dress over my legs. Looking back to his glare, I went on, "I realize this is a lot for your chemo-brain to comprehend, so nod if you understand me."

Stewart's head moved from side to side.

I cocked my head. "What? Am I too young? Am I too dumb? I mean, you didn't want me going to college. However, I'm not fucking stupid. I made a way, provided the perfect source. Did you know that radiation causes cancer?"

Stewart blinked.

"Yes, there are all sorts of documented cases of cancer from radiation. Well, it doesn't take a fucking nuclear-plant meltdown to cause radiation exposure. No." I couldn't stop the grin as my cheeks rose. "Cesium pellets can emit enough radiation to kill cancerous tumors. But..." I lowered my voice as the excitement at my long-awaited confession rambled forth. "...but that's when the cesium pellets are placed within the cancerous tumors. Do you know what happens when healthy cells are exposed to excessive amounts of localized radiation? Do you?"

Stewart blinked again.

"Those healthy cells mutate. That means they change. It was a gamble. I had no way of knowing how they would change. But from your first symptoms, the headaches and hair loss, I knew I was on to something."

Stewart's eyes closed.

"Oh, no, motherfucker. Do not die on me yet. I want you to know that even though I planted the fucking pellets, it was your kinky-assed shit that did you in. Guess where you were exposed to these high doses of radiation."

His head shook from side to side, with his eyes still closed.

"Open your fucking eyes. I want to see what you're thinking. You will fucking understand what I'm about to say and then you will confirm your understanding with a nod. That's the way we do things, isn't it, Mr. Harrington?"

Slowly, his eyes opened and he nodded.

"That's a good boy. The answer to my question was in your fucking chair at the warehouse. Every time you sat your ass in that chair and watched as you ruined my life for your entertainment, you exposed yourself to radiation." I shrugged. "It didn't take long for the symptoms to start, but I couldn't take a chance on your body's ability to fight it. So I continued the exposure."

My smirk returned. "Every time you told me to spread my legs, do you know what I envisioned behind that blindfold? Oh, you can't answer with that tube down your throat. Let me tell you. I envisioned this! I envisioned the look on your face when you finally learned what I'd done. And you want to know my reward? I'm a great wife. I stood by you through all of this. I'm a fucking saint! Driving into the damn ocean would have been too easy for you, besides... I wouldn't have been able to watch. Now, Mr. Harrington, nod if you understand that the day you fucking bought me to be your whore was the first day of the end of your life."

Stewart nodded.

"I do have that documentation, and by the way, your pain medicine is going up. You will never speak again, not of this, not of anything. Consider it our do-not-disclose clause; however, instead of paying you off, I'm the one reaping the benefits. One more thing, Mr. Harrington, that new draft of your will—effective immediately, I'm having you declared incompetent. You will not be signing anything new. My fucking contract is complete, but yours with the devil has just begun."

The beeps from his monitor sped up as I sat back and watched the confusion in his eyes morph into realization. When I heard the door behind me open, I leaned in and brushed my lips against his cheek. "The only thing better would have been hearing you beg," I whispered into his ear. "Because I'm confident that the great Mr. Harrington would beg for his fucking life."

My shoulders shuddered as I lay my head on his shoulder and willed the tears to flow. The warmth of a hand touched my shoulder.

"Mrs. Harrington, we have the medical power of attorney. Do you want us to increase his medication?"

"Y-Yes, anything to help him," I managed through my sobs.

"With the possible strain on his heart, this could cause..."

I looked toward Stewart's cardiologist who was standing near Dr. Duggar. "If we don't do this, can we save him?"

The cardiologist shook his head. "No, ma'am."

"Then do it. Let's make him as comfortable as possible."

Missy, one of the regular nurses, spoke, "Mrs. Harrington, would you like me to contact a counselor?"

"No, I'm not leaving my husband's side."

Such a freaking great wife. But both Stewart and I knew the truth: I wasn't great. I was death. And, I wasn't taking the chance of allowing Travis, Parker, or anyone else to get near Stewart without my presence.

After the medication drip was added to his IV, I sat patiently, drying my tears. Stewart's icy stare stayed fixed on mine, trying to communicate a million things he'd never said or ever realized. I watched but I didn't try to listen; instead, I internally rejoiced in his glare of silence. I'd listened to too many of his words. With each minute, the blackness inside of me grew and illuminated my cold, dead heart. Though I'd been called death all of my life, it wasn't until Stewart's eyes closed for the final time that I'd truly done it, and I'd never felt more fucking alive. The organ within my chest beat with new vigor.

The tears that coated my cheeks were real. They were tears of joy and tears of cleansing. As time passed, each drop that slowly descended my cheeks washed away a memory. It would take a fucking ocean to erase them all, but this was a start.

My days as someone's whore were over.

As news spread, so did the people in Stewart's room. Stewart would never have wanted all of these people to see him in this state so I welcomed each one with open arms. Travis was the first to intrude, and then Parker. There were nurses and doctors, as well as Lisa and other members of the house staff. Val came to comfort me. Even Brody came. As a member of Stewart's legal team, his presence wasn't questioned.

In reality, they all entered to see my good work. Of course, none of them knew that. None of them knew that as the clock struck midnight, I was a black widow.

CHAPTER SIXTEEN

Present

I HADN'T SLEPT, not really. By the time all was said and done and the coroner came and took Stewart's body, it was after two in the morning. There was no need for an autopsy: his disease was well documented. It was just the formalities that needed to be finalized before he was shipped to the funeral home where he would be cremated. The great Stewart Harrington didn't want to be seen in the condition he was in prior to death. He sure as hell didn't want to be seen as he was after death.

Val and Lisa stayed near, helping me as questions came and went. I appeared distraught and overwhelmed. My makeup was gone, and my fine clothes were wrinkled. The bags under my eyes helped project the overwrought widow persona.

Though Parker wanted to discuss Stewart's legal concerns, Lisa told him it would need to wait until the morning. With single-minded efficiency, she cleared the apartment of everyone who didn't live there, directly after Stewart's body was removed. She informed the medical staff that they could return the following day to retrieve their equipment; however, *Mrs. Harrington* needed calm. With an aching in my temples from my self-induced crying, I was eternally thankful for her command of the situation.

The only one who remained was Val. Her compassion and support overwhelmed me. Her good and caring heart had no way of knowing the darkness in mine. I wondered sometimes how I could keep it hidden, especially from her. I knew I had no choice. She could never know the lengths I'd suffered for her future. I didn't want her to know. She only knew what the world knew: I married Stewart Harrington, world-renowned hotel mogul. She saw what they saw: the polished, refined younger woman paraded on his arm—arm candy, as my mother so eloquently described me—who became the steadfast anchor to a man stricken down by an unforgiving disease at too young of an age, and who spent hours working with the Harrington Society to take medical care where none could be found.

When we were alone, Val saw her sister: the woman who longed for the days back at the academy and the simplicity of life. However, never would she know the woman who had signed away her life, the one who was sold to pay a debt she didn't owe. Just before Val left the penthouse apartment, we hugged, and I vowed to myself that no one —ever—would see that woman again. When Stewart's body was placed into the incinerator and his flesh peeled from his bones, freedom would be found in the putrid smoke and I would be free.

It wasn't until I was alone in the upstairs suite that I began to relax.

It was done.

He was gone.

Nine years of hell were over!

In my final act of cleansing, I stepped under the warm spray of the shower and washed away the stench of his decaying body. As I did, the memories of Peppermint Man came back, reminding me that I'd been with him less than fifteen hours ago.

Instead of crying, I laughed. For the first time in years, I laughed. Not just a giggle, my stomach ached at the rolling my emotional swing ensued. I would never endure the warehouse again. As the hot water rained down, I savored the purging fluid. I was Mrs. Victoria Fucking Harrington. I had a few more days to play the grieving wife. It is a new role, but I could do it: shaking hands, smiling sadly, even shedding a tear or two when necessary. After all, the acting wasn't new. I've been doing it my whole life. Only now, the truth I kept buried, the one that ate at me day and night since I was old enough to remember, was a reality. Nevertheless, it was too painful to reveal, too upsetting for those around me. I needed to show them what they wanted, what they needed. They didn't want to see who I truly was... *what* I truly was. They didn't want to know that I'm a killer. But now that I'd done it, I knew without a doubt I could do it again.

The next morning, I awoke with a sense of calm. When I entered the kitchen, Lisa and Kristina, my personal assistant, were waiting. "Mrs. Harrington," Lisa began. "As you know, Mr. Harrington had prearranged his funeral and cremation plans. If you'll allow us, we'll oversee everything and assure that it is all taken care of the way he requested."

I reached out and squeezed Lisa's hand. With eyes that brimmed with tears, I replied, "Thank you."

Kristina said, "Mr. Craven's assistant called. Mr. Craven would like to meet with you this morning. He suggested his office. I told him it wasn't a good time. However, he was rather insistent. What would you like me to tell him?"

I knew what I wanted. I fucking wanted him on my turf, but I knew as a new widow, I should be less decisive. Therefore, I looked earnestly toward Lisa, the woman who'd been so kind to me, and said, "I-I don't think I should be out."

"Of course you shouldn't. I was hoping you would say that." Her neck stiffened. "I don't understand why he thinks this needs to be handled now. Doesn't he understand how distraught you are?"

I nodded toward Kristina. "I think that if he wants to speak to me, he can come here. But I'd prefer he wait until later." Turning toward Lisa, I asked, "Where is Travis? I need to speak to him first."

"He's here. I'll have him go to your office after you eat."

I cocked my head to the side, my lips working to not smile. "Mr. Harrington's office. I believe the important business of this household has always been conducted in the main office. Tell Travis to meet me in there in thirty minutes."

"Yes, ma'am," Lisa said, as she and Kristina exchanged looks.

"And let me know this afternoon the status on all of the arrangements." My command was met with a round of *yes, ma'am* and Lisa's reminder of my waiting breakfast.

~

I'D ALWAYS ADMIRED the view from Stewart's office. The ocean and sky filling the full-length windows brought sunlight to his domain. I recalled the first time I'd seen it, the first time I'd seen him. I was so young and naïve, though I thought I was strong and worldly. Thankfully, the injustices I'd experienced from an early age prepared me for what life had in store and gave me the strength I needed to survive. Oh, how wrong Stewart had been when he saw me as nothing more than his whore. With a smirk, I recalled the look of horror in his eyes as he realized that not only was I a worthy opponent, but I was the victor!

Everything he dangled before me was mine—it was all mine, especially and most importantly, my freedom!

The knock at the door caused me to spin away from the vista toward the opening door. Not waiting for my invitation, Travis entered. Our eyes met in a silent contest of wills. We remained mute as he closed the door and walked toward the desk. I took the seat that used to be my husband's and pointed to the other chair. "Have a seat."

Slowly, he did, his long legs and powerful body folding into the chair. Still his expression was one of superiority. I leaned forward, my long, unrestrained hair cascading over my shoulders. "Tell me how you did it."

He casually relaxed his arms on the edge of the chair. "What, Mrs. Harrington, what specifically are you asking me?"

"You fucking know what I'm asking. How did you make me believe it was Stewart? I know it was his goddamned voice. What the fuck did you do?"

"I'll tell you what I did, if you hear me out."

"You don't get to fucking give me ultimatums. As far as I'm concerned, you're no longer employed by me or by Stewart. I wanted you to come in here this morning so I could tell you to get the fuck out of my home."

Travis pressed his lips together and shook his head from side to side. "That's what Mr. Harrington was afraid you'd do. That's why he tried to mandate that it wasn't possible. He was so close." Travis stood. "I'm not leaving. You're not firing me, and if you'd use your fucking brains half as well as you've used your pussy, you'd want to know more." His glare bore through me. "Oh, fuck it!" He stood and turned toward the door. "It's no goddamn skin off my back. Personally, I'll enjoy watching you fall off your fucking high horse."

"Don't you fucking leave this office," I proclaimed with rising volume. "I asked you a question. How did you make me believe it was Stewart?" I refused to dwell on the fact that he'd watched me have sex with Peppermint Man. I doubted it was the first time. There probably had been cameras there longer than I even knew. My stomach lurched. "You used his recorded voice. Didn't you?"

"You just fired me, Mrs. Harrington. I don't need to tell you a damned thing."

"Where are they? How many recordings are there? Are they only audio or are there video?"

His lips quirked into a slimy, lopsided grin. "Just imagine, you could see all the faces of the *friends*."

I hated that fucking term. There was no such thing as a *friend*! "What do you want? Is this blackmail? Do you want money?"

Looming taller, he sneered. "No, I don't want *money*. I have money. Mr. Harrington made sure of that."

Fucking *déjà vu* hit like a sledgehammer. Stewart's words from ten years ago came crashing back to me: *I have money that I can lend. The thing is I don't need it. Therefore, I decided that in exchange for the money, I wanted something else, something less conventional in return.*

I jumped to my feet. "There is no fucking way I'm going through that again."

"Like with Stewart. I'm not doing that again."

Travis' brows furrowed. "I don't want to marry you. Hell no! Don't flatter yourself. However, you'd be wise to learn that there's a lot about your deceased husband that you don't know or understand. He's made deals, many involving you. If you believe you'll be able to walk away from those deals without repercussions, you really are more pussy than brain."

"I made a deal with my husband, not with anyone else. I've fulfilled my obligation."

Travis shrugged. "I guess you'll find out more when you talk with Mr. Craven. I thought you might want to go into that conversation informed." He cocked his head. "My bad."

I closed my eyes and gathered my strength. Sitting back down I calmly repeated, "I asked you a question. I'm sure it was you yesterday. As your fucking employer, I'm asking you how you did it."

"You just—"

"Tell me and we'll discuss the future."

Travis came back to his chair and sat. Taking out his cell phone, he did what I feared most: he opened an app and held up his phone.

"I'm here, darling." Stewart's voice came back from the grave, taunting me. Travis pushed the button again. "Nod if you understand."

Swallowing my contempt, I asked, "Only audio or video too?"

"This one is only audio. I recorded key phrases. It took me a while to find the one for you to take him in your mouth. That's why it seemed like dear old hubby wasn't paying attention."

Again, my stomach twisted and neck muscles tightened in a familiar way. "This one?" I asked.

Travis cocked his head to the side and raised a brow.

"You said that *this one* was only audio. I'm assuming you have more."

He nodded.

"You don't want money? Everyone wants money. How much will it cost me to make this all go away?" I looked at my watch; Parker Craven was due to arrive in less than fifteen minutes. "How much will it cost to have you tell me what you know?"

"I told you, I don't want money."

I leaned back. "How do I even know you have more information or videos or anything? You may have just shown me all you have."

"I might have. Is that a chance you're willing to take? Did you know about the change Mr. Harrington tried to make in his will? I bet not. But if you did, you'd know that the reason it didn't happen wasn't because he died. It was because Parker Craven was stonewalling. He personally wanted what Mr. Harrington wanted me to have."

"Me?" My voice sounded too meek for my own ears. I sat straighter, my tone more confident. "I did know about it. I also know that you can't fucking will another person. I'm not a damn car or a pet. I'm a person."

Travis' eyes widened. "Oh, the bitch is better informed than any of us knew." He shifted in his chair. "He wasn't willing *you*, only your contract. If you'd open your fucking eyes, you would've realized he was doing that for your own damn good."

I blinked, trying to follow his words. "My own good? Bullshit! There was nothing about my contract that was for my good. It was all about him."

"You're a fucking hot piece of meat. I've watched everyone from investment bankers to politicians fuck your brains out." He lowered his voice. "It's true that I wanted my fucking turn. I've waited a damn long time, but first, listen, and listen well. Mr. Harrington believed your contract was in better hands with me than with Parker Craven. So when he walks in here and tries to convince you otherwise, keep this in mind: I know all of Stewart Harrington's dealings, not just the ones that have been legalized by Craven and Knowles. There's more to Harrington Spas and Suites than meets the eye—much more. There's a whole world that your dear old stepdaddy knew too well. Those men that Mr. Harrington told you about are more than some obscure force: they're the living breathing underground of Harrington Spas and Suites."

I tried to comprehend Travis' meaning. "The loan sharks? The ones who had Randall killed."

He nodded. "Yes and no."

The phone on my desk rang, shattering the intensity of our conversation. After staring, I took a breath and picked it up. It was Kristina. "Mrs. Harrington, Mr. Parker Craven is here."

"Tell him I'm in a meeting. I'll be with him as soon as possible." I hung up the phone.

"What do you mean…?" I asked Travis. "Yes *and* no."

"Loan sharks and high-end pimps, among other things. Randall was ready to work out a trade with them. You. You were the commodity, until Mr. Harrington stepped in. He bought out Randall's deal. He saved you from them. They weren't happy. To pacify them for overriding the deal, he agreed to share you."

"That's bullshit. He enjoyed sharing. It was for him."

"He enjoyed it," Travis agreed, "but it wasn't just for him. It was for you."

"For me? Why? And why would Randall do that?"

"They requested you. Your stepfather didn't volunteer."

I shook my head. "How would these people even have known who I was, ten years ago?"

Travis straightened his neck and squared his shoulders. "That's something I can't tell you."

My gray gaze narrowed. "You can't or you won't."

"I guess, I won't."

"Who are they?"

"They're powerful people and lowlifes. They're the people who run this city, this state, some who even fucking run the country. They are people you see at the country clubs and on the street corners. They're people who know you and those you've never seen. They're people who want to repay you a cruelty and people who don't give a damn if you live or die. They're people who have fucked you and people who have never touched you but royally fucked with your life." He leaned in. "They're your worst nightmare. And believe it or not, now that Mr. Harrington is gone, you're looking at the only one who can save you from them."

"Parker?" I asked with trepidation.

"Is one of them. Just like the *friend* yesterday. Mr. Harrington didn't want to disappoint them. That's why I did what I did. If you hadn't heard your husband's voice, you probably would've freaked out. You're not ready to know whom you're dealing with. Parker Craven is one of the people who's indebted and entranced. You're his way out. That's why he wouldn't complete the will. Mr. Harrington wanted your contract to go to me. Mr. Craven wanted it for himself."

"What am I to you?"

Travis scanned me from breasts to eyes. "You're a bitch. You've been a pain in my ass for ten years. You're also fucking stronger than I ever thought. I want to do what Mr. Harrington never could or would. I want to see those fuckers pay and I think together, we could have the right amount of endurance to see it through. You see, I have my own history and set of issues with those people. Mr. Harrington helped me too. The difference between him and me is that I don't have anything to lose. I think it's time those assholes paid for what they've done to me and to you. Don't you agree?"

My phone rang again. "What?" I asked, my mind reeling from Travis' declaration.

"Ma'am, Mr. Craven…"

"Kristina, tell him I'm too distraught to meet with him today. Tell him that we'll need to reschedule after Stewart's funeral."

I looked up to Travis' smug expression. Hanging up the telephone, I said, "I don't believe you. You've never given me any reason to trust you." Although I did know that Stewart trusted him implicitly. "But I want to think about what you said before I make any—"

The sound of Kristina's raised voice and the opening door stilled my words. My eyes widened as I watched Parker Craven push his way past my assistant, only to be stopped dead in his tracks when he was met chest to chest by Travis.

Chest to chest was not quite accurate. Travis stood a good five, or six inches taller.

"Victoria, this can't wait…" Parker began, doing his best to ignore the mountain in his way.

"Mrs. Harrington, would you like me to show Mr. Craven out?" Travis' smug demeanor immediately morphed to the bodyguard persona, the one that had always somewhat intimidated as well as creeped me out.

Gathering my wits, I stood. "Parker, I appreciate your taking the time to come over last night and this morning. As you can imagine, things are a little out of control right now."

"Yes," his tone dripped with compassion. "That's why I'm here. Stewart had legal matters that cannot be left unattended. All I need is a few signatures. We don't even need to discuss them until later. Just sign and I'll take care of everything."

Did he think I was a fucking idiot? Travis' warning glare had new meaning. Could I trust the feeling that now he was protecting me? I'd always assumed I was the prey.

"May I see the papers?" I asked, ignoring Travis' suddenly clenched jaw.

Parker stepped around Travis, opened his briefcase, and pulled out a folder. "Victoria, you're not making a mistake. This is the best thing for your future and Stewart's memory." He opened the folder to a marked page. "You just need to sign..." He pointed. "...here."

"No, Parker."

He looked quizzically in my direction. "No?"

"I asked to *see* them. Leave them with me. Let me look at them." I cocked my head to the side and forced a grin. "I mean, even Stewart let me review my contract before I signed it. Surely, you'll grant me the same privilege?"

"I would," he began, "however, we're dealing with a tight deadline."

"Oh, I believe I had a tight deadline ten years ago, too. When do you need my answer?"

His brow furrowed as his hand ran through his fine, dark hair. From the light of the windows, I noticed the renegade gray strands. "Now, Victoria, I need it now. This can't wait."

I scooped up the folder and handed it to Travis. "I'm sorry, Parker. I believe that as a grieving widow I should be granted some leniency with deadlines. I'll get back to you after the funeral."

He gasped at my forwardness and assessed Travis, no doubt deciding if he could retrieve the folder. "Listen, you don't understand —"

"Thank you, Mr. Craven." Travis' voice filled the office. "Mrs. Harrington has just given you her answer. She'll get back to you after Mr. Harrington's funeral."

I pressed my lips together, the tips of which were only slightly turned upward. It took every ounce of my strength not to say, *nod if you understand, motherfucker!*

Parker took a step backward. "Victoria, I was Stewart's lead counsel for a reason." He tilted his head silently toward Travis. "My counsel to you is to be careful whom you believe. You owe it to Stewart and the world that he created for you to know all the facts. Don't let emotion override good sense."

Was that the same as saying I was more pussy than brains? I didn't trust either one of these men. "Goodbye, Parker. At this moment, I don't intend to let my emotion or good sense make any decisions. Right now, I'm going to concentrate on burying my dead husband." I sat back down in Stewart's chair. "Would you like Travis to show you out?"

The two men eyed one another. I was thankful for the marble flooring and ornate rugs. They could more easily be dry-cleaned after their little pissing contest was concluded.

With a slight nod, Parker finally turned and said, "No, thank you, I believe I know the way."

CHAPTER SEVENTEEN

Present

"I CAN'T RISK BEING SEEN at some hotel," I said into my phone, behind the protection of my closed bedroom door.

"Vik, I need you." Compassion and desire oozed from Brody's declaration. "You need me, too. Not just to sort out all this legal shit, but I want to hold you. Shit, Vik, you've been through so much. Don't you just want to lean on someone?"

Did I? Had I ever truly had that?

"Brody, I don't know what I want. I know I want to hear that the cremation is complete, and I want to get this damn funeral over. I know I need to know what's in those papers that Parker wanted me to sign."

"He really expected you to sign them and talk about it later?"

I nodded in the privacy of my suite. "He must think I'm pretty stupid." *They probably all did.*

"Vik, I'll come over there. We can go through the papers together."

His reassuring confidence was exactly what I needed; however, with my emotions on a roller coaster, I wasn't sure it was wise. "I don't think it's a good idea."

"Why? I was there last night. Why would anyone question my presence?"

"Oh, I don't know," I smirked, letting my mind take a well-needed break from the stress of my reality. "Maybe when the moans and screams start coming from Stewart's office we'll raise suspicion?"

"Moans and screams? Fuck! I like the sound of it. Where are we doing it? In the motherfucker's chair or on his desk?"

My insides tightened as I considered the possibilities. "I think the desk with the fucking blinds open to all of goddamned Miami. We could even spread Parker's file and papers over the top. I like the idea of soaking the pages until the print is no longer legible. I mean, that would null and void anything in there, wouldn't it?"

"Jesus fucking Christ! You're killing me here! I want to help you and hold you, and you're making me blow a fucking wad. I'm going to need to change slacks if you don't stop."

My cheeks rose into a welcome grin. "You know what you're doing to me?" I ask.

"What? Tell me."

"You're making me smile. Despite all this shit and one fucking bombshell after another, you're making me smile."

"Is that all I'm doing?"

"No," I reluctantly admitted. "No, that's not all. I want to do what we just said. I want to have you take me all over this damn apartment, but right now I need to understand what Travis and Parker are trying to do, what Stewart was trying to do."

"What Stewart was trying to do?" Brody repeated cynically.

I closed my eyes and listened.

"Well, let me help you. Let's start with the fact that he was a controlling warped son-of-a-bitch, who had a damn fifteen-page contract that spelled out specific sex acts you would agree to perform. He let you sign that contract without informing you of what it truly entailed. Then, while he was at death's door, he tried to pass that contract to Travis Daniels, a lowlife, two-bit racketeer who's worked with him for the past fifteen years."

"But why? And why did Parker want it?"

"Why did he want it to go to Travis?" Brody repeated. "I have no fucking idea. Why did Parker want it? Well, I hate to say this about one of my senior partners, but damn, Vik, that should be obvious. He knows there's no way you'll do with him what he spelled out in that contract, without proprietorship of said contract."

"Like I said before, I agreed to Stewart's sick shit because he was able to hold Val over me. I know Marcus and Lyle aren't through college, but the money is mine. I can pay for their education and continue to fund Harrington Society. What does Parker think he has that will make me agree to the contract?"

"I'm assuming the only way to find out is to hear him out."

My already knotted stomach tried for another flip. "I don't want to hear him out today. I don't want to do any of this today."

"Vik?" Brody asked, with a hint of anxiety.

"Yes."

"What did Travis say? Why does he want you to agree to his taking it?"

I laid my head on my pillow and covered my eyes with my arm. I should really close the blinds and allow myself to hide in the dark, away from Parker, Travis, Stewart's funeral, grieving friends, everything...

"Vik? Are you all right?"

"I'm great," I replied sarcastically. "Travis said something about business dealings that would come due. He implied that if I thought I could walk away from the agreements Stewart had made with no repercussions, I was..." *more pussy than brains.* "...dumber than I looked."

"Well, baby, I think you're beautiful. I think you look like you're intelligent and cunning. Shit, I know you are. I know you're more than Stewart ever gave you credit for."

I fucking was. I was *much* more than Stewart gave me credit for. That was painfully obvious as he stared me down, just before I slammed the lid on his urn.

Brody had continued talking. "...he's done to you. Never think of yourself that way. You're amazing in bed, but like I keep trying to tell you, it's not just the idea of fucking you that turns me on. It's the thought of holding you. The other night... falling asleep. Shit! I know there's more to that beautiful body than a tight pussy. You're the whole package. Stewart was the idiot for never realizing that."

I shook my head. What had Travis said? That what Stewart did was to save me. Save me from whom? What wasn't Travis telling me?

"Vik? You keep leaving me. Are you there?"

"Yes, I'm here. I think it's all catching up to me. If I scan these papers that Parker left, will you look at them?"

"Of course, I'll come over and pick them up."

My arm still over my eyes, I sighed as my head shook from side to side. "No, I need to meet with some people from the funeral home. Kristina and Lisa are making all the arrangements, but I need to finalize and agree to everything. Let me email them to you."

"Vik, that's too risky. I'll stop by."

"Meet me at the funeral home."

"I can do that. What time?"

I looked at the clock. "Half past three." I knew I'd have Travis there, watching my every move. I had to figure out a way to get the papers to Brody without Travis seeing me. First, I'd scan them. Then it hit me.

Thank God for technology!

~

TWO DAYS later and wound tighter than a freaking rubber band on one of those cheap, little propeller planes, I stood at the front of the funeral home and continued my perfect-wife role. I wasn't sure when the Academy Awards would be calling, but I expected at least a nomination. Somehow it was easier to meet the lustful eyes of the male mourners without Stewart's whisper in my ear, the one that would ask, *"Do you ever wonder if his cock has been in your pussy? Would you want it to be? Maybe he's never been there, or maybe he's a friend with an affinity for other uses of his cock?"* Then with a brush of his lips against my cheek, he'd add, *"Smile, Mrs. Harrington. I just wanted to give you a little something to think about.*

I pushed those thoughts away and concentrated on the present. I couldn't think about his cruel words and pretend to be mournful at the same time. Besides, even those memories were clouded with Travis' revelations. Stewart had saved me? That seemed preposterous. I mean, I'd been there all along. When had he ever saved me? Well, other than from Travis. And now Travis wanted me to believe that the men from the warehouse and others I'd never met, or perhaps met, but never intimately, were calling for the final bid on Stewart's deals.

Each person who shook my hand or offered a sympathetic hug was suspect. With each contact I did what I'd learned to do. I closed my eyes and inhaled.

It wasn't that I wanted to know. I didn't. But as much as I wanted this to be over, until I came face to face with the truth, I knew it wouldn't be. It never could be. I steeled my shoulders, fixed my façade, and faced the next person. When I gazed upward, it seemed as though the line went on forever.

As each and every person sighed and gave me their heartfelt condolences, I stared into their eyes, judging their sincerity. I knew that life would be better without the great Stewart Harrington, but did they? Were they outside his realm and saw him as the world did, as I may have for a brief time? Or were their words as much of an act as mine? Did they truly know him for the cruel, manipulating bastard whom I had the unfortunate displeasure of knowing and being married to for over ten years?

If that were the case, were their grim expressions no more than masks hiding their true feelings of elation. Mine was. Yet below the elation, I also had confusion. What kind of a mess did he leave me?

"Victoria," Sheila Keene said, pulling me into the present, forcing me to acknowledge her presence. Her kind eyes teared as she shook her head slowly. "We're so sorry for your loss. Your poor, dear Stewart suffered for so long. Cancer is such an ugly thing. And you... you never left his side."

Sheila was one of the first to truly accept me into Stewart's world. She understood the pressure that our sudden marriage would inflict. While her situation was different, being married to a senator, she dealt with similar scrutiny. Perhaps that was why we found common ground with the Harrington Society. She was the president of my board, and thankfully, we saw eye to eye on many of the pivotal issues.

That said, her husband made me uncomfortable. Usually he was too busy to attend couples functions, other than ones that could second as campaign fundraisers. That was what I appreciated about Sheila. She didn't have the single mindset of supporting her husband. She actually had a brain and believed that her time and energy could go to genuine causes that warranted her attention.

Squaring my shoulders I repeat the words I've said over and over, "Thank you, Sheila." Looking up into her husband's cold, calculating eyes, I continued, "And Senator Keene. I just couldn't leave him, not as ill as he was. I didn't want to be anywhere but by his side."

"I'm so sorry they had to call you to the distribution center," Sheila offered. "I'd told that imbecile of a secretary that I'd be home in just a few days. Of course, we cut our vacation short and came home as soon as we received word about Stewart."

"That was very kind of you. Truly, you didn't need to do that."

Sheila patted her husband's arm. "Robert insisted. He said he knew Stewart would have done the same for him."

I looked back up to Senator Keene's ruddy cheeks and less-than-mournful expression. Travis had said politicians—he'd watched me be fucked by politicians. I stiffened my neck and leaned toward Sheila, hugging and thanking her for her support. Her heavy perfume permeated my senses.

"My dear," she continued, "you really do need to get out, now that…" Her words trailed away. There are so many ways to end that sentence: now that *the bastard is dead*… now that *you will have some freedom*… now that *you're filthy rich and can tell the entire world to stick it up their*… Her mouth continued moving even though I was lost in my own world. I'd missed a few sentences, but it wasn't difficult to figure out the meaning. "…very busy with all the arrangements and legalities, but soon, soon…" She squeezed my hands. "…we must do lunch. You need some girl time."

"Thank you Sheila. I appreciate the offer. We will need to do that."

I moved my eyes to the next couple, hoping that Senator Robert Keene wouldn't attempt conversation. That hope was immediately dashed as his hands embraced my shoulders, and his rank, warm breath whispered the appearance of condolences into my ear. "Mrs. Harrington, the loss of your husband will create many voids in our world. I certainly hope you'll make the right decision and carry on."

I didn't need his words or his implications: his acetone breath brought back a rush of memories. *Had I never stood this close? Had I not tried to know, or did I just not want to know?* The answer didn't matter. *Fatal Lullaby* played in the distance as I remembered scenes.

Closing my eyes for only a second, I backed slightly away from his touch and made the most of my five-foot-six-inch frame. With my red-glossed lips pressed into a smile, I allowed my steel-gray eyes to give him the recognition he apparently thought I was too simple to obtain. "Thank you, Senator. I appreciate your concern for my husband's arrangements and for my future. I can guarantee you that my future will be considerably different from my past."

Senator Robert Keene stepped back from the determination of my statement. I'm sure it wasn't what he'd expected. After all, I'd never been allowed to speak. Sheila's eyes flickered back to her husband's and then to mine. As she was about to speak, I saw Travis and his familiar narrow-eyed glare.

"Robert," Sheila began, "this is no place to be discussing business. Victoria has her plate full. I'm sure that whatever you're discussing can wait."

Before Robert could respond, I reached for Sheila's hands. "Thank you again, Sheila. I'm sure Robert meant well. I promise, I'll be fine." Blinking, I focused my newfound disgust into the right amount of emotion and fostered a tear. "I'll see you next week at the Harrington Society meeting. Maybe after that we can get coffee?"

"Oh, I didn't think you would… so soon."

"Stewart would want me to do that. He was so proud of my work with the foundation."

Smiling sadly, Sheila agreed, "You're right. We'll let you get to your next visitors. Once again, we're so sorry for your loss."

If only she knew. I wasn't sorry, but I couldn't help but think that if her husband pursued his current train of thought, he would be.

"Mrs. Harrington…" The condolences continued.

I nodded and responded mechanically, until the familiar aquamarine appeared before me. I had difficulty not reaching up and stroking Brody's cheek as he respectfully extended his hand and began a speech about how much my husband would be missed. There was a comical relief to his words. Though not each one of them registered, I listened, taking in their cadence as a melody to my dark soul. It was the infusion of energy I needed to continue my role.

"Thank you, Mr. Phillips." My hand lingered for a little longer than normal in his warm embrace. Finally, I removed it, afraid of watchful eyes. A similar greeting two days before had been our perfect secret rendezvous for slipping him Parker's information. I had scanned the papers, but not to paper form; instead, I placed them on a flash drive. A quick reach into my pocket and a lingering handshake, and magic: the papers were in Brody's possession. "Thank you for all of your support. We've had a wonderful turnout from Craven and Knowles this evening."

His eyes widened in question. "Well, yes, Mrs. Harrington, your husband meant a lot to each and every one of us at the firm."

I nodded slightly, answering his unasked question. Parker and Maura Craven had both made their way to me. However, with Maura present, Parker had refrained from mentioning the impending legal documents.

Brody tipped his head. "If we can be of any assistance, please feel free to call."

"Thank you, I will."

My insides twisted at the promise of his grin and the shimmer of his smirk.

When the final guest left, I settled into an overstuffed loveseat and retrieved my phone. Before I could look, both Travis and Val were at my side: Val sitting down next to me, leaning in close and offering me her support, while Travis loomed above.

"Mrs. Harrington, would you like me to bring the car around?"

I peered down at the screen.

"I CAN'T STAND SEEING YOU AND NOT TOUCHING YOU. CALL ME."

Turning off the message, I looked up at Travis' narrowing glare. *Did he see that? Fuck it!* I looked over at Val. Her eyes were closed with her head on my shoulder.

"No, Travis. I'm going to stay at Val's tonight. I've had enough of all of this for one day. Why don't you run along, and you can pick me up in the morning."

I saw Val's lips quirk.

"Mrs. Harrington, the funeral—"

I lowered my voice. "I'm well aware that my husband's funeral is tomorrow, thank you. Tonight I want to spend some time with my sister. Need I remind you..?" I didn't finish the sentence.

"Thank you, Mrs. Harrington. I'll be awaiting your call tomorrow morning."

Val and I giggled at Travis' clenched jaws.

"You know," Val began. "If he keeps that up, he could have real TMJ problems. The man needs to learn to loosen up."

"You have no idea."

"I'm kind of surprised that he's still here. I always got the feeling you didn't like him much."

I shrugged. "I guess I want to get through all this stuff..." I gestured toward the chairs and the empty funeral home. "...first."

"So, you're coming home with me? I like that."

"Then let's go."

I waited until we were in her car before I sprung my news. "Thanks for letting me spend the night. Can I borrow your car?"

Val did a double take. "My car? Where do you want to go? I can take you."

I tilted my head to the side, opened my eyes wide, and elongated my plea. "Ple-eea-se."

"Oh, shit! This is horizontal-sleeping-friend, isn't it? Sis, give Stewart a day or two to get cold."

"He didn't need a day or two. He was cold as ice long before he died."

CHAPTER EIGHTEEN

Present

WHILE VAL DROVE us to her apartment, I couldn't help my eyes drifting toward the side and rearview mirrors. In the pit of my stomach, I knew that Travis would be watching. It didn't take long for my suspicions to be confirmed. Nearing the medical center, I spotted his black SUV. *Fuck! Isn't it my SUV? I should have fired him two days ago. Why didn't I? What did he know?* I remembered a long time ago wanting Stewart to fire him, asking Stewart to fire him, and he told me no. He said Travis knew too much. *What the fuck was too much?*

I pushed my thoughts away and concentrated on Val's words. As usual, she was in the middle of some soliloquy. "...come in, unless you're too preoccupied with your friend to spend some more time with your sister."

I sighed. "I'd love to come in, but only if you have a glass of wine. Spending all night listening to everyone tell me what a wonderful man Stewart was has me ready to jump out of my skin."

Val's tone lowered. "You really can't blame him."

My head spun toward her. "Excuse me?"

"I'm not sticking up for Stewart, or against you. Please don't take it that way. I have no idea about the particulars of your life. That's been your decision not to share."

And the do-not-disclose clause.

She continued, "But I have been trying to tell you: those drugs he was on—they make people different. I know it was driving you crazy that he wanted you around all the time and wanted to know where you were, but, Vik, the man was dying. He knew he was dying. That's not something that's easy to swallow, especially for a man as young as Stewart."

I stifled a laugh. "I seem to remember your calling him old when I told you we were getting married."

"Well, hell, I was seventeen years old. You were eighteen. He was old! But for a victim of the rapidly progressing leukemia that he had, he was young. That doesn't usually happen to people until they're in their seventies or eighties."

I took a deep breath, eyeing Travis again in the side mirror. "I know that. I know you think I need counseling. Maybe I do; maybe I will. Right now I just need to get through the next few weeks of shit. My plate is full."

I watched as Val inserted a card into a reader and the gate to her apartment's parking garage opened. I sighed, watching Travis' SUV fade away as we drove deeper into the bowels of the parking garage toward her assigned space.

"I get that," she replied. "I just don't want you to forget the eight-plus good years you had because he was hard to live with near the end."

I shook my head. "Thanks, I promise. The memories of him at the end won't tarnish the other years." *Quite the opposite.*

∾

AN HOUR, A glass of Merlot, and a string of text messages later, and I was out of Val's apartment and on my way toward Brody. Wearing my hair up in one of Val's baseball caps, I drove a loop around the medical center. It was my diversionary tactic. If Travis saw the car leave the garage, I hoped he'd think it was Val. After repeatedly checking my mirrors and looking down side streets, I breathed a sigh of relief that he was nowhere to be found.

As I made my way toward the small, secluded motel, taking the less than direct route, I had the realization: this was fucking ridiculous. Stewart was dead. *Why the hell did I feel the need to hide my activities from my own damn employee?*

Earlier, when I'd brought up the motel's address on my phone, I knew it wasn't our normal type of place. From its pictures it looked like the kind of motel seen on crime shows, the places where prostitutes frequented and often ended up dead.

As I got closer I laughed. Maybe it was the perfect place. Because tonight I wanted to be a whore: not Stewart's whore, but my own. For the first time since I could remember, I wanted sex—pure, unadulterated fucking—and I wanted it bad. So much so that as I drove into the darkness the night before my husband's funeral, all I could think about was Brody Phillips. I thought about his tall, trim, and healthy physique. I remembered him standing in the funeral home all proper and businesslike. I imagined the clean scent of his aftershave.

As miles passed, I embellished the memory:

No longer were we conversing in front of the other mourners. No. I imagined the same scene with significantly different details. In my fantasy, as he stood in front of me and gave me his condolences, instead of nodding, I unbuttoned his starched white shirt. As each button came undone, more of his wide chest became visible. Unable to control myself, I ran my hands up and down his firm abs. His aquamarine eyes zeroed in as each ripple of muscle tightened under the tips of my fingers. When his stare turned sultry, my nails gently raked the surface of his tanned skin. With a quick lick of my fingers, I rolled his nipple and licked my lips. His gaze narrowed as I allowed my hand to fall lower, teasing the buckle of his black leather belt.

He leaned closer as the room of people hushed at our blatant display of disrespect. Seizing my shoulders, Brody growled in my ear, "What the fuck are you doing?"

Instead of answering, I nuzzled his neck, hearing the stir in his throat and feeling growth of his erection. I pushed my hips forward.

"Oh, you want to put on a show?" he asked, his deep voice now raspy.

"Yeah," I cooed, just before playfully nipping his ear.

Grabbing my chin, he harshly captured my lips, holding them hostage until my body melted and I moaned in both pleasure and pain. Pulling away, he reached for my shoulder and in one fluid move, spun me around, bending me over the table—the one with Stewart's urn. My hips bruised against the polished wood as his stone-hard cock met my ass. His stubbly cheek against my neck felt like sandpaper as he snarled near my ear, "If you want a show, I'll give you a fucking show. I'll show all these assholes that you're mine. No one else's, ever. Just mine."

Before I could respond, he reached for the hem of my black dress and pulled it to my waist, exposing my black lace panties, now wet in anticipation. "Is that what you want?" He continued to taunt me with his cock.

Speech was becoming more difficult as the murmurs throughout the funeral home disappeared into the sounds of his frantic heart and warm breath at my ear. All I could do was nod.

Brody snatched my hair, twisted it around his fist, and held my head still. "No, Vik. No more nodding. Fucking talk. Tell me what you want."

My body trembled as I answered honestly. "I want you. I want you to take me right here."

I gasped as he touched my inner thigh and his knee pushed my legs apart. Reaching for my panties, he moved only the crotch and slid his fingers deep inside.

Even though I knew that eyes were watching, I didn't care. Some of them had seen me like this before; others were appalled, while even more were turned on as hell. Moans echoed throughout the room as Brody returned my concentration to him. With one hand he reached forward, rubbing my clit.

"Tell them," he growled.

My mind was a blur. Tell them what?

"Tell them you're mine."

"I'm his," I panted, not loud enough for anyone else to hear.

Fisting my hair again, he repeated, "Tell them louder."

"I'm his. No one else can take me, ever." The words were liberating as my hips once again banged against the shiny table and his thick, hard cock plunged in and out of me. I bit my lip to stop my screams as each thrust hit harder than the one before: dominating and claiming. Brody's upper body pushed forward, splaying me across the surface of the table and sending everything to the floor: the vases, the flowers, and Stewart's ashes.

The road before me came back into focus as I squirmed in my seat, blinked repeatedly, and shook my head. *Damn!* I wonder what Val's counselor would think of that little fantasy. He or she would probably have a field day with it. I didn't want to think about any part of it, other than the obvious. I wanted sex, and I wanted it now.

When I pulled up to the motel, my suspicions were confirmed. This wasn't our normal type of establishment. This was small, secluded, and the rooms had doors directly to the outside. I looked both directions and saw nothing, not even Brody's car. Only a few other cars were in the poorly lit parking lot. Honestly, I didn't give a damn that it wasn't palatial.

Opening the door to the car, I inhaled the cooler evening air, listened to the hum of traffic from the interstate above, and concentrated on my fantasy. A smile graced my lips as I realized that I wanted to scream out like the prostitutes who frequented this establishment. No longer was I Stewart's whore. Now I could choose, and tonight I chose to be fucked.

I turned off my phone. No one was interrupting my plans.

Before the light from Val's headlights dimmed, the door to room number 8 cracked open, and I slipped from the car and walked briskly into the motel. Flickers of light caught my attention as hundreds of candles burned throughout the darkened room. Before I could truly look around, the door closed and the chest I'd fantasized about pinned me against the wall, momentarily pushing the air from my lungs. Brody's shirt was gone and though I still wore my black dress, my flattened breasts tingled from the warmth of his exposed skin.

I couldn't resist touching him as I ran my small hands up his firm arms. The tips of my fingers burned from his radiating heat. When I reached his broad shoulders and my eyes met his, the shimmer of candlelight in the aquamarine sent my already primed core into spasms. I gasped at the seizing of my wrists as my hands were suddenly pinned to the wall above me. Brody silently scanned my body.

Aching for his touch, I tried to move toward him.

"Not yet, Vik. I want to look at you, really look at you. You're so fucking beautiful, and I want to see you as the woman you are now."

What did he mean? Did he know that I was now a killer?

Releasing my hands, he said, "Give me your left hand."

Reluctantly, I did, and I watched as he removed my wedding and engagement rings and dropped them to the filthy, worn motel carpet. "There. Ever since that motherfucker died, I've wanted to do that. Hell, before. Now, I'm going to fuck you, fuck you like the free woman you are."

The tips of my lips rose as he unbuckled his belt, unbuttoned his slacks, and allowed them to fall to the carpet, somewhere near my rings. Protruding from the waistband of his boxers, the head of his erection made itself known. When I started to remove my sleek black pumps, Brody once again seized my wrists and stopped my movement. "No, you're fucking perfect the way you are, the way you looked earlier tonight." He leaned closer and inhaled deeply. "I could smell you at the funeral home. You fucking want this: here, now, against this fucking wall. Am I wrong?"

Oh God! "No," I managed. "I want it. I want it so goddamn bad."

"Well, Vik, you're not getting it *bad*. You're getting it *good*. Leave those hot fuck-me heels on." His sultry gleam fueled the fire that still kindled from my fantasy. "And you have about two seconds to get those damn panties off or they're mine."

Instead of obeying, I reached for the wall, splaying my fingers near my hips.

His brow moved up. "I may have to reconsider. I think you do want it *bad.*"

I sucked my lower lip between my teeth and I inhaled.

"Turn around, baby, and hold on."

When I did as he said, he reached the hem of my dress and pulled it up to my hips. With two hands, he ripped my panties. The shreds fell down one of my legs to my ankle. Suddenly, I yelped as a firm hand struck my exposed ass. Immediately, he began rubbing the cheek, only to repeat the assault on the other side.

"There we go," Brody cooed. "That's all the *bad* for today."

His touch on my inner thigh encouraged me to spread my legs and lift my ass, opening myself up for him. I closed my eyes as one and then two large fingers slid inside me, pumping in and out.

"So fucking wet."

His nose nuzzled my neck as his other hand, pinched one nipple and then the other, creating a rhythm that kept beat to his fingers. With warm breath bathing my neck and his erection taunting my swollen lips, he asked, "Are you ready for the good?"

Fucking beyond ready! "Yes, please."

His fingers disappeared as I heard him reach for a condom.

"I'm on birth control," I offered, wanting to feel his skin inside of me. "I promise, I'm clean. I go to the doctor every six months."

"Oh, I thought… fuck!" he growled as his unwrapped cock sunk deep inside me.

The skin-to-skin contact created a delicious friction as the heat of his cock filled me, consuming every nerve within my body. Unknowingly, I cried out as I held to the wall, my elbows stiffening with each thrust. Brody fucked me like he's never fucked me before, wild and unforgiving, pounding into me, filling not only my core but also my ears with the sound of his balls slapping my ass, and his heavy breathing.

The mountain's ledge was right there. I saw it approaching at lightning speed as he pounded faster and faster. When he once again reached for my clit and rolled it between two fingers, I no longer heard him: the small motel room filled with the sound of my own screams. "Fucking God! Brody, I'm coming!"

"Do it, Vik. Come for me; let me hear you."

I closed my eyes and let myself fall, calling out as wave after wave crashed through me. I waited for the hard reality of the ground; however, the ground didn't come. Instead, the waves continued until my knees and elbows gave out and we both fell to the floor, a tangled mess. The only movement was his pulsating cock, still buried deep inside me.

Brushing his stubbly cheek against mine, he whispered, "Jesus, Vik. That was fucking awesome."

I moaned at the loss as he slowly pulled out of me, unleashing a flood onto my thighs.

Despite the beauty of his candles, I finally saw the dump we were in and contemplated the floor. "Brody, I think the next place for us to go is the shower."

He laughed. "Yeah, this carpet has probably not been cleaned..."

Covering his lips with my kiss, I said, "That's gross. I don't want to even think about that."

Shrugging, he stood and helped me to my feet. "Assuming the shower is better, may I help you remove that dress?"

"Well, since I don't have any underwear to wear home tonight, I guess I shouldn't get my dress wet in the shower."

"You're not going home tonight."

"I'm not?" I questioned as we walked toward the bathroom.

"No, you're not. That smile on your face is the most beautiful one I've ever seen. We're going to work on keeping it there."

"Val needs..." I began.

"You said that Val is off call because of the funeral. We'll get you back to Val's early in the morning."

My lips pursed together in thought.

After turning on the water, Brody turned toward me and asked, "What? Where did that smile go?"

"I was just thinking that I told Travis to pick me up tomorrow at Val's. I have to go home before the funeral. I can't be seen in the same dress..."

"Or without panties," Brody added with a grin.

Blood blushed my cheeks. "That would be a tad uncomfortable."

"Why haven't you fired him? Travis? I know you hate him."

As Brody took my hand and led me behind the cheap shower curtain into the warm water, I shrugged in response and asked, "Before I told you, did you know that Stewart wanted Travis to have my contract?"

Brody nodded.

I went on, "Travis said that was what Stewart wanted. He said that Parker was the one fighting it."

Brody reached for the hotel shampoo. "Look at this. Even at sixty bucks a night, you get shampoo. Oh…" He read the bottle. "…and the conditioner is mixed in."

I turned as he poured the mixture onto my head and began massaging it into my hair. "Brody?"

"Yes, baby?"

"I don't want either one of them to have it."

"They can't. It's over. By dying when he did, Stewart saved you from that."

Saved me? Why did people keep saying that?

"But the way Travis sounded, if it doesn't belong to someone, there could be others, others who claim it."

Brody spun me around to face him. "Vik, no one can claim anything. You're a wealthy woman. No one can make you do anything you don't want to do. Hire the best: the best bodyguards, the best accountants, the best attorneys—that's me by the way…" He smiled a mischievous smile. "…and I work for benefits."

My cheeks rose in a smiling expression as I leaned closer, our slippery bodies sliding against one another.

"What if…" I began.

Brody's finger came gently to my lips.

"Shush. Tonight we'll celebrate your freedom. Tomorrow we'll worry about *what if.*" Leaving his finger in place, he added, "Nod if you agree."

Nod if you understand. The words reverberated through my mind.

Turning away, I nodded. Under the guise of the shower, I allowed the tears I'd kept bottled up for too long to flow. It wasn't until my shoulders shuddered that Brody realized I was crying. Without a word, his strong arms surrounded me and he gently kissed my freshly washed hair.

.

CHAPTER NINETEEN

Present

I WOKE to the sound of Brody's alarm, feeling anxious and nervous about the funeral, yet also rested for the first time in ages. "What time is it?" I asked sleepily.

Fumbling for his phone, Brody answered, "Four-thirty. I wanted to have you back to Val's before anyone was out and about."

My body ached in the most wonderful way as I stretched and started to sit. Before I could, my gaze settled on the handsome, warm man nuzzling closer.

"Where are you going, Vik?"

"To take a quick shower," I giggled, as he leaned over me, his strawberry blonde hair sticking up in the sexiest of bedheads.

"How about if first I help you get ready for your big day?"

My eyebrow peaked. "Help me get ready? Whatever do you have in mind?"

With kisses to my neck, chest, and stomach, Brody moved slowly down my body, his fingers taking the lead as he spread my legs. "Just a little something to start your day off right."

Before I could comment about the *little something*, I fell back to the pillows and whimpered as his tongue lapped my slit.

"You taste so fucking good," he moaned between taunts, pushing my legs farther apart, torturing my already swollen lips and tender thighs.

Fuck! I won't be able to walk at the damn funeral. Just as my mind started to leave the room, Brody's thumb circled my clit, bringing me back to present. My legs involuntarily closed as my insides tightened to a painful pitch.

"That's it, Vik," his words encouraged and pushed me upward as my fingers wove through his hair, craving his touch.

His tongue assaulted my clit, flicking and taunting, until whimpers of words spewed involuntarily from my lips. The heat of my core intensified, and my body took on a mind of its own. My hips bucked and my legs grew rigid. The entire world disappeared as Brody sucked my clit, electrifying me from head to toe. Screaming out his name, my hands flew to the sheets grabbing for something, anything, to keep this incredible ascent from coming to an end.

Just as I was about to fall, Brody stopped and covered my body with his. "I can't take it, Vik, I love being inside of you without protection. I want to feel that tight pussy squeeze my cock as you come."

The next thing I knew, he was gliding into me, pumping and pumping, hitting me in that perfect sweet-spot each time. With each thrust my body seemed to take him deeper. It was as if he knew exactly what to do to make my body react. The freedom of letting myself go and running my hands over his warm skin pulled me higher. There was nothing—no blindfold nor protection—between us. It was raw skin on skin and I couldn't get enough.

When the mountain reappeared, I craved the peak. However, each time he drove into me, I couldn't deny the pleasure of the climb. With our goal in sight, Brody reached between us and pinched my clit as he simultaneously leaned down and sucked my hard nipples. The combination sent me flying. No longer breathing, only sounds escaped my lips. My core detonated and waves of heat radiated from our bodies, dispersing the anxiety from earlier and leaving me satiated.

"Fucking fantastic!" Brody growled as he too fell from our mountain. His shoulders relaxed and his cheek, soft with a day's beard growth, rubbed mine, before he rolled to my side. When I turned toward him, I found myself momentarily lost in the aquamarine.

"Vik," he said, his voice soft and tender, "today at the funeral, I wish I could be with you, holding your hand, supporting you."

We both knew that wasn't possible. "Brody, you don't owe me..."

"It has nothing to do with obligation. I want to be there." His gaze shimmered. "And I will."

My eyes opened in question.

"I'll be there in the crowd. You can count on that. But most importantly, know I'm in you. As you're listening to the amazing attributes of the great Stewart Harrington, remember it's my come inside of you. And if I have anything to say about it, that's not just today." He reached for my hand and kissed my fingers. "I'm not pressuring you. It's just that I want you to know that I've wanted to be the only man in your life for a long time. I want it even more now."

I didn't know what to say. I kissed his soft, fuzzy cheek. "I'll remember."

~

A QUICK SHOWER, and twenty minutes later, I went out into the dark, still morning and slipped into Val's car. I wondered once again about Brody's car. Maybe I should have offered him a ride. Before I could process the thought, Travis' SUV pulled up behind me, blocking me in my space. Sucking in my breath, my neck straightened in rage. *What the fuck!*

I wasn't the only one upset. Watching him get out of the vehicle and stalk over in my direction, I could see the anger emanating from him. I flirted with the idea of hitting the gas and ramming into his SUV, but all that would do was turn Val's car into an accordion, and besides, I owned that SUV. Instead, I tried for my most obvious bitch face, allowed my indignation to flow, and rolled down the window. "What the fuck are you doing?" I asked.

With his teeth together and the vein pulsating in his forehead, Travis nodded. "Mrs. Harrington, I could ask you the same question, but since you reek of sex, I don't need to."

I didn't fucking reek. I showered!

Undaunted by my expression, he went on, "I assume you're on your way to return your sister's car? You might want to wipe down her seat before you do."

Maintaining my glare, I replied, "Need I remind you that you work for me?"

"No," he leaned down and inhaled. Shaking his head, he lowered his voice. "You don't need to remind me. I should've fucking accepted your dismissal, but I didn't. My goddamn job is to keep you safe, just as it was to keep Mr. Harrington safe. Why don't you get your slutty little ass back to Dr. Conway's and then we can be on our way home? I'll explain how you just about fucked up my job for good. Oh..." he added, with a tilt of his head toward the motel. "...you're lucky I found you."

"I'm tired of you talking in riddles. If you have something to say to me, fucking say it."

Travis stood tall. In the light of early dawn, his muscular body in the tight black t-shirt and black slacks looked ominous. His characteristic glare that came at me through the narrowed eyes of disapproval only made him look more daunting. "Don't worry, Mrs. Harrington, I have every intention of *saying it*. By the way, if you weren't so busy getting fucked, you might have looked at your phone. Call your sister before you drop off her car." He reached in his pocket, pulled out a tissue, and threw it toward the open window. "Take this. The good doctor doesn't want to sit in your come." With that, he turned and walked back to his SUV.

I stared as he backed up and waited for me to lead. He was right about one thing: I hadn't looked at my phone. As a matter of fact, I'd turned it off as I entered the motel. I was tired of everyone and everything. And I'd had one goal—but I didn't reek!

At the stop sign, I checked the newly lit screen: four text messages and two voicemails. I hit the voicemail as I accelerated.

First voicemail, from Lisa:

"Mrs. Harrington, I'm concerned. You should be home. Is everything all right? When may we expect you?"

Well, shit. I should have called her.

Second voicemail, from Val:

"Vik, call me. I know where you are, but call me. I just had some weird visitor asking about you. Here! At my apartment! What's happening?"

I hit the CALL button and looked at the clock. It wasn't even half past five, but she was a doctor. They didn't need sleep. Did they?

"Vik," her sleepy voice mixed with alarm. "Are you all right?"

"Shit, Val. Me? I'm fine. Are you all right? I turned off my phone last night. I just turned it on and heard your message."

Through the phone, I heard her moving around before she said, "It was really weird. It happened about an hour or two after you left. This man came to the door." She paused. "I'll be honest: I'm kind of freaked out that he knew where I lived."

"God, Val, I'm sorry." My gaze fluttered to my rearview mirror, seeing mostly the grill of Travis' large black SUV.

Val went on, "He was persistent. He wasn't obnoxious. He said that he needed to speak with you. I told him you were sleeping."

"He didn't believe you?"

"I think he did at first, but he didn't care. He was determined for me to go get you. He said his business couldn't wait."

"I told him I was your sister and your doctor, and you needed rest. Finally, I said I'd given you something to help you sleep. I was getting pissed—he just wouldn't leave."

"What did he look like," I asked.

"Tall, dark hair, a little gray, clean-shaven."

Well, shit, that described about fifty percent of the men I knew.

"He kept referring to you as Mrs. Harrington, never Vik, Vikki, or Victoria."

"He didn't give you his name?"

"No," she replied. "He said you'd know him. I was about ready to call security when Travis showed up."

"What?" I asked, alarm evident in my voice.

"Weird, I know. I mean, usually he freaks me out, but I see why you keep him around. I was glad to see him."

I glanced back again to the SUV. It was a little farther back, and I could see Travis through the windshield. "What did Travis do?"

"What he always does. He talked, all business-like. You know, like 'Dr. Conway, may I be of any assistance? I'm sure Mrs. Harrington has had a difficult day… 'You know, yada yada."

"And this guy left?"

"He did. I invited Travis in. I mean, I didn't feel right saying, hey, thanks for saving me from that scary dude. Now go away."

The temples of my head began to pound. "What did you tell Travis?"

"I started to tell him the same thing, about my giving you a sleep aid… but there was something about the way he looked at me and around the apartment. I'm sorry, Vik. I told him the truth. I told him that I let you borrow my car, and you wanted some alone time."

"Alone time?" I repeated.

"Well, since you're technically a widow, whatever happened with horizontal-friend is legal. I'm assuming. In most states?"

"Go on," I encouraged.

"But I didn't think he needed to know this wasn't a new thing. I just didn't say one way or the other."

I looked around at my surroundings. "Val, I think I'll need something to help me sleep once today is done. I'm almost to your apartment. Is it all right if I leave your car on the street?"

"Sure, sis. What about getting home? Do you need a ride?"

As I slowed down I saw Travis do the same. "No, I'm good. Travis is here."

"Okay, drop the keys in my mailbox. Hey, maybe he's not so creepy?"

I shook my head. "He's still creepy." I thought about his help with Parker. "It just comes in handy sometimes. Will you be over before the funeral? I really liked having you with me yesterday. I know it's not a lot of fun, but if you don't mind…"

"Of course, don't even think about it. I'm there for you."

I hung up as I eased into a parking space right in front of Val's building. Before I locked the doors, I unconsciously checked the seat. *Travis can suck it! I didn't need his damn tissue.* The sound of doors unlocking brought my attention to the big black SUV. Straightening my shoulders, I shoved the tissue in my purse with my phone and walked toward Val's building.

After dropping her keys in her mailbox, I turned back toward the waiting SUV. Taking a deep breath, I walked around to the passenger side door; with each step I was keenly aware that my panties were MIA. Climbing up into the passenger's seat, I made a concerted effort to keep the skirt of my dress tucked around my legs.

"You know, your husband's only been dead for a few days. You might at least consider taking a change of clothes if you're going to go out whoring, especially if you plan to continue to do it in the slums."

I hated his condescending tone, not to mention his words. Straightening my neck, I declared, "I decided at the last minute to spend the night with my sister."

Travis feigned a laugh. "If I'm going to spend my time dealing with your shit, I guess I should get the lingo down. *Spend the night with my sister means whoring?* Do I have that right, Mrs. Harrington?"

My body flew back against the seat as he hit the accelerator. Almost as fast, the SUV swung into a parking lot and I flew forward as he pounded the brake. Instinctively, I reached forward and braced myself on the dashboard. "Jesus Christ, what is your fucking—"

Before I could complete my question, Travis threw the SUV into park, unsnapped his seatbelt and lunged toward me. Faster than I could pull away, he reached my seatbelt, pulled it over my body and latched it in place. Shaking his head, he leaned back, secured his own and put the SUV back into drive. Under his breath, he muttered, "I fucking need a goddamned raise for this shit." Raising his voice, he turned toward me. "Safety. That's my job. Do you think you could help me out a little?"

I felt like a two-year-old being reprimanded. "If you'd given me a fucking chance before you pulled out into traffic like a bat out of hell, I would have done that myself."

"Next time, I'll say *ready, set, go.* Will that work for you?"

I stared at this man's profile. I'd known him for over a decade, but I'd never really looked at him. If I were to be honest that was because he scared me, even more than Stewart. Perhaps it was because with Stewart, from the beginning, I'd felt a small semblance of power. It wasn't much, but even with what he made me do, I felt that part of him cared. I never had that feeling from Travis. From the first time I saw him, when he picked me up at the academy and brought me to the apartment, I had the feeling I was an annoyance, someone he'd rather do without. And then there was the creepy predator feeling: the one that gave me goose bumps and made my stomach lurch. Hell, just the other day he'd admitted to watching me have my *brains fucked out* by all the different men. He'd also admitted to wanting his turn. We both knew how that had turned out the first time.

Lost in my own train of thought, I asked, "Travis? Were you there, at the warehouse, or were there always cameras?"

He didn't look my way; his eyes fixed on the road. "I was there."

"Every time?"

"Almost. I wasn't there the last time. Mr. Harrington had just... I couldn't leave him."

"The time before? The first time Stewart wasn't... were you?"

"Yes."

I inhaled deeply, thinking about that. "Why?" I asked with genuine curiosity.

"It's my job. Mr. Harrington had the contract with those men: I didn't. I was there to make sure things didn't get out of hand. I was upstairs and watched through a closed-circuit network. The other men didn't even know I was there."

"Closed-circuit—like cameras? Did it record?"

"No. Mr. Harrington wouldn't allow that. It was part of the *do-not-disclose*. The friends wouldn't have allowed that either. As you can imagine, many of them have wives and careers. They didn't want to have their pastime come back on the six o'clock news."

"But," I questioned, "you said you had video? I heard the audio."

"I recorded it on my own, with my phone. I saved it all to flash drives."

Resting my elbow against the window, I stared out toward the road, my eyes wide open, yet seeing nothing. "Why did you record it? Did Stewart know?"

"He didn't. I didn't start doing it until Mr. Harrington began to get sick, and I did it for insurance."

"Blackmail."

"Insurance." His volume rose. "Yours and mine."

"If there was no evidence, why would I need insurance?"

His dark eyes looked my direction for the first time since the beginning of this conversation. "Tell me that you're fucking listening. Tell me you understand what's happening."

"I'm listening. I don't understand one goddamned thing! I don't know why all of a sudden you feel this obligation to protect me. I don't know who those other men were or are. As you know, Stewart made sure of that. And I don't know why you think I'm suddenly in danger."

Again with the jerky driving. This time, we pulled onto the shoulder of 95 as gravel and rocks pummeled the underbody of the SUV, as we came to an abrupt stop. My body flung forward only to be pulled back by the restraint of the seatbelt.

"Nothing is *sudden*," his voice was uncharacteristically animated. "Maybe you are just a dumb cunt. Maybe I overestimated—"

Interrupting, my gray eyes glared as I spoke over him. "I'm the dumb cunt?! You don't fucking speak in complete sentences. How about you start? How about you actually tell me more about this mysterious underground of Harrington Spas and Suites? And you tell me who would know or have known of me before I married Stewart?" I took a deep breath, crossed my arms over my chest, looked toward the windshield, and huffed. "I have more questions, but I'd like to start with those."

Travis reached for my chin. His warm touch burned my skin. My neck immediately stiffened and I pulled away. "Do not fucking touch me!" I growled as my cadence slowed and tone deepened. "Ever. No matter what you've witnessed, or what you know, I'm still your employer. You'd be good to remember that."

His hand came back and opened wide. I braced myself for a repeat of the slap I'd received years earlier; instead, what I saw was the universal sign of surrender. "Now that's the bitch I know." His sincerity came through as his tone morphed into one I couldn't remember ever hearing. "What you said before... about *sudden*—nothing is sudden. My job has been to protect you since before the day I picked you up at that highfalutin' academy. I told you that I was at the warehouse to protect you. It isn't sudden. It didn't just happen. Again, you've been in danger even before you were married." He pounded the steering wheel. "*Again*, you've been a fucking bitch about it. Keeping track of you without the help of your goddamned phone has been a royal pain in my ass. Thankfully, Dr. Conway's car has a GPS tracker; otherwise, who knows what could have happened this morning." His dark eyes bore through me. "Get it through that pretty little head of yours. None of this is fucking sudden!"

I shook my head. "Then why didn't I know?"

"Mr. Harrington took care of everything. He made sure with his deals that you would remain safe, as long as he—"

"Shared me?" I interrupted.

Travis nodded. "That was part of it. There's more, but it's a lot to swallow at one time." His eyebrow twitched, and his lips snaked into a grin. "But you can probably handle it."

I fucking hated this man!

"Tell me who: who knew of me before I married Stewart. Who first mentioned me to Randall?"

Travis looked toward me, eyeing my seatbelt, and put the SUV back into drive. As we eased onto the interstate, he said, "Tell me who just fucked you."

"I asked you a question first."

"You did, but I need to know if you trust me."

I shifted slightly in the seat and remembered Brody's words: *I'm with you. It's my come inside of you.* "Do you know who I was with?"

His dark eyes once again focused on the road, as he confirmed, "Yes, Mrs. Harrington, I'll know if you're lying to me."

I considered my answer while Travis made his way through the growing morning traffic. As we approached the apartment and I watched the scenery, I realized that I'd never sat in the passenger seat of this SUV. I'd always ridden in the backseat.

When I didn't respond, Travis nodded. "Very well. Did you talk to Dr. Conway?"

"I did." My head snapped to the left. "Who was it? Who came to her apartment?" I considered the description. "Was it Parker?"

"No."

Dark hair with gray, tall… who? "Are you going to tell me?" I asked.

Travis shrugged his massive shoulders. "I'm waiting for my answer, Mrs. Harrington."

CHAPTER TWENTY

Present

THE FUNERAL PASSED by in a blur. Though I appeared the mourning widow, in actuality I was listening, dissecting, and inhaling everyone around me. As I scanned the large crowd that overfilled the church, I wondered if the people Travis knew, the ones he believed were threatening me, were among the mourners. *Were Stewart's friends in attendance? Could they be wearing a mask of compassion, when in actuality they had other plans: plans that involved an extension on my personal hell?*

My mother, Marcus, and Lyle were seated directly behind Val and me during the service. I hadn't spoken to her since before Stewart's death, though her sufficiently red eyes and blotchy face made for the perfect distraught mother-in-law. Why was I even surprised? I was sure she welcomed the chance to be seen at such a high-profile occasion, even if it did mean being seen in less than perfect condition. Marilyn nodded sympathetically as Val and I took our seats. My unsmiling-bitch-face worked as well as my smiling one.

During the service I wondered about Brody. Was he there as he'd promised? As I'd left the motel this morning, he was getting into the shower. Had he seen Travis with me outside the motel room? I hadn't heard from him since I left. Perhaps he didn't know that my bodyguard had practically accosted me. But then again, was it accosting when Travis claimed to be concerned about my best interests? Was it even possible that he had been protecting me all of these years? Or Stewart?

I refused to entertain the idea. Given my situation and the same opportunity, I'd do what I did. I'd place those pellets in his chair again. As I worried about the idea that my contract could go to anyone else, I wished I still had the pellets; however, from what I knew, their half-life had been exceeded. That meant they were no longer potent enough for therapeutic treatment. Of course, my use wasn't therapeutic. All I could hope was that the chair was still radioactive. Perhaps if anyone else spent enough time there, they too would suffer Stewart's fate.

After the service, Val led me by the elbow as we made our way out of the church and into the finally cooler autumn air. Thankfully, I'd been too lost in my own thoughts to listen to the eulogy. Instead of concentrating on Stewart Harrington's stellar qualities, my mind was filled with questions.

Brody and I had only scratched the surface of the papers Parker wanted me to sign. They weren't a request to bequeath my contract to Parker. It was a rephrasing of the original contract, one that gave Parker Craven dictatorial power over my activities described as payment in exchange for Stewart's withholdings. Those debts were poorly defined, making repayment seem unattainable.

In essence, his new contract pulled me back into the role I'd played for too long with no hope of getting out. What neither Brody nor I could surmise from the new documents, was what I was supposed to reap? As I glanced into Val's steel-gray eyes, I knew what I'd gained from the original contract. I'd lost my body and soul, but I'd secured my sister's future, and together we'd helped thousands of people with more to come. Could any of that—Val, her work, the clinics—be at stake?

"Victoria, dear," Marilyn Sound sighed, as she quickened her pace to walk beside me. I glanced first toward Val, who remained stoic. It was then that my gaze fell on Travis. I saw his first hint of humor as his brows arched and forehead furrowed. He'd just asked me an unspoken question, yet I heard it as plain as if he'd said it out loud: *Mrs. Harrington, would you like me to escort Mrs. Sound away?*

The slight grin that came to my lips was instantly misinterpreted by my mother as she reached her arm around my shoulder. "My dear,

I know what it's like to lose a husband. I'm here for you. I want you to know that."

As we approached the limousine to ride to the cemetery, I fought the urge to tell her exactly what I thought about her timing. Though Stewart wasn't being buried, the cemetery had vaults made of thick marble specially designed for urns. When my gaze met that of Travis, I ever so slightly nodded. Instead of speaking my mind, I whispered near her ear, careful to avoid the multitude of listeners who mingled nearby. "I believe there's another car for you. Allow Travis to help you find it."

"But, dear, I need to speak—"

I didn't hear any more as Val and I moved into the car and Travis directed my mother away. Once the door was closed and we were alone, the cool, dark interior allowed me to remove my sunglasses.

"She probably wanted—" Val began.

"She hasn't been able to talk with me in two weeks," I interrupted. "She wants money, money for Marcus' second semester tuition. The thing that she doesn't realize is that I've already paid it. I'm sure she's worried they'll contact her and put her on the spot."

Val shrugged. "She might want to offer you her support."

"She might," I conceded halfheartedly. "They say there's a first time for everything."

Just then, through the glass panel, I saw the passenger side door open and Travis get into the limousine. Exhaling, I leaned back against the soft leather seat, closed my eyes, and sighed.

"I'd be glad to prescribe something for you. Probably not too strong, but you could use a good night's sleep."

Remembering Brody, I said, "I had a good night's sleep last night. I just want this to be over."

She patted my hand. "It's almost over."

I didn't respond, because I wasn't sure. *Was it almost over?* The car began to move. It didn't take long as we meandered toward the cemetery for me to miss Travis' heavier accelerator foot. I figured, if he and the driver would switch places, we could have Stewart safely behind marble in half the time.

Should I feel guilty about Stewart's death or the way he suffered?

I imagined him as I'd seen him hundreds of times over the past nine years. I imagined him sitting in that chair: his smug expression of pleasure and control when he'd finally allow me to remove the blindfold and headphones. From the very beginning, I knew that when he told me to take them off, my focus was supposed to be on him.

Rising from the chair, he walked toward me, his blue eyes glowing as he sat on the edge of the bed. "Tori, my Tori..." he cooed as the pad of his thumb wiped away my smeared mascara. "No tears. You're fantastic. Our friend was extremely satisfied."

I never knew what to say to that kind of praise. Good? Yippee? Or be honest. I don't fucking care. I hated every second of it. There just wasn't an appropriate response.

His hand dipped down to my sex: his fingers stroking my swollen lips and circling my clit. "You're so fucking beautiful when you come. You should've seen how aroused our friend was as you put on your little pre-show. He got hard before he ever touched you."

I closed my eyes. The blindfold was a blessing. I didn't want to see that. I didn't want to be any part of it.

"Look at me."

With shame and hatred simmering in my chest, I opened my eyes.

"I've told you before to never be ashamed of your body's reaction."

Stewart's hands roamed my naked body, stopping to caress my tender nipples. When he did, I involuntarily flinched. His mouth immediately covered one and then the other. Gently his lips and tongue stroked and sucked. Against my will, my nubs grew hard.

His breathing quickened. "Oh, fuck! You're so responsive." His blue eyes questioned. "Are your tits sore?"

"Yes." My voice cracked. It was the first word I'd uttered in over two hours.

"I'm sorry, darling. Our friend left the clamps on longer than either of us realized. He was just so preoccupied with other parts of you, like that fuckable pussy." His large hands palmed each breast. "Let me make them feel better. Lie back on the bed. I'll make you feel better."

I didn't want to lie back. I wanted to shower and leave. But that wasn't Stewart's plan. He enjoyed round two as much as round one. Despite his tender voice and concerned manner, I knew my place. As long as we were still at the warehouse, I had a role to play. I was his whore.

The word I'd said—yes—was only allowed because he asked me a direct question. If he hadn't, no matter how painful my nipples were or how upset I was, I wasn't allowed to speak. At home I could make advances or reach out to touch my husband. I could run my fingers across his broad chest or over his shoulders. I could wrap my legs around him as he pounded his cock deep into my core. At home, or when traveling, I could get out of bed and go to the bathroom to pee or clean myself. Not here.

Here, I waited for instruction.

Lying back as I'd been told, I left my arms at my side and prayed he'd let them stay there.

"That's my girl. Now hold on to the bars."

Obediently, I reached up, the ache in my shoulders replacing the soreness of my nipples.

"Hold on tight, my darling. Don't close your eyes. I want you to see me, your husband. That's what makes us so much more special than you and our friends. My Tori, we have our connection. Your gray eyes say so much more than your words. I want to see every emotion in those eyes."

He reached for the nipple clamps and held them above my head. My eyes widened. What the fuck? That wasn't going to make them feel better.

"Don't do that," Stewart reprimanded. "You don't ever need to look at me with fear. I'm not going to put these back on, not today." He sucked each nipple. "I'll admit, once I realized the clamps hadn't been removed, I wanted to see your eyes as he took them off. I wanted to know exactly what you were feeling. I miss that with your eyes covered. I miss seeing your thoughts."

If he only fucking knew my thoughts.

Though he tenderly caressed my breasts, the soreness of my nipples rippled through me. I clenched my teeth to keep from crying out.

"That must feel invigorating, as the blood rushes back and your nipples fill."

Invigorating? It hurt like hell. That was why my mascara was smeared. I could stop the tears from the humiliation—I'd learned to do that. However, sometimes stopping the tears from physical pain wasn't possible.

The bed shifted as Stewart stood. "I'm so proud of you, baby. This was an important friend and he wants to visit again. You don't know how happy that makes me. We want to keep our friends happy, don't we?"

Was this a time he wanted an answer? Because if he did, my answer was fuck no! His friends can find their fucking happy place somewhere else.

As Stewart removed his clothes, he said, "I'm over dressed for my gorgeous wife. I mean look at you. Your pussy is still hungry. I love watching you come. You're going to do it again, and this time when you do, you're going to scream my fucking name. Will you do that for me, Tori? Will you scream your husband's name?"

I fucking hate you! "Yes, Stewart, I'll scream your name."

He held his hard cock in both hands. Getting back on the bed, he kneeled near my face and ran one hand up and down the length. "Oh, darling, I'm going to fuck that wet pussy until you do just that, until you scream my name, but I'm not coming inside of you, not this time. I'm going to fucking come on those sexy tits of yours. Then I'm going to watch as you rub my come around those nipples." He leaned closer, nuzzling his nose against my neck. "See, baby, I promised I'd make them feel better. There's nothing like some of your husband's come to cure all your pain. Isn't that right?" He smeared the glistening fluid from the head of his cock over my lips. "Lick your lips, Tori, let me see that tongue."

I did as he said. His unique, salty flavor helped me forget the taste of his special friend. I hated this, yet I wanted more—more to take away the friend. Stewart had done this to me, made me this way. I hated him, but somehow needed him.

"Oh, fuck," he continued, "now I can't decide if I want to fuck your mouth or your pussy. So many choices." Again, he teased my lips. "Open wide, I'm going to start with your pretty little lips. You did a good job with our friend. Every time you swallow, I get hard."

He knelt over my face and reached above me on the headboard. I opened my mouth and moved my chin upward, to accommodate his length.

"So fucking good." He moved in and out; his familiar scent loosened my muscles and involuntarily caused my body to react. Wanting this over, I sucked harder.

"Baby, not so greedy. You don't want to make me come yet. That pussy of yours wants a turn."

"Vik?"

I opened my eyes and turned toward my sister. "What?"

"I was talking and you were totally zoned out."

"I'm sorry. I have a lot on my mind."

No, I didn't fucking feel bad that Stewart was dead or that he suffered. I didn't give a damn what Travis said. Stewart deserved every minute of pain and agony. When the fucking door closes on this vault, I will secretly rejoice. And if there were people who thought they could get me back in that position, well, they didn't know the real Victoria Harrington.

The real Victoria Harrington was not a whore. As I looked down at my black dress, black nylons, black shoes, and black purse, I straightened my shoulders and felt the weight of the large brimmed black hat. No, I was a fucking widow—a black widow—I wouldn't go back without a fight.

Unconsciously, the corner of my lip rose. As it did, I caught Travis' eyes in the rearview mirror. *Did he know?* He seemed to know so much. *Did he know I was a killer?*

"Vik? Hello?"

I looked toward my sister and sighed. "Val, I'm fine, really."

"You're not fine. You're overwrought. I'm coming home with you. I don't have to be back to the hospital until tomorrow evening. I'm staying. I'm also getting you a script for Ambien, the kind that not only helps you fall asleep but stay asleep."

I shook my head. I didn't want that. I wanted to talk to Parker. I needed to know why he possibly thought I'd sign those papers. "I don't need a babysitter," I huffed and tilted my head toward the front of the car. "I already have one and don't forget Lisa and Kristina. I think the position is well covered." I reached for her hand and squeezed. "I'd love to spend time with you, but I just want to go home and get away from all of these people." The car turned into the cemetery and toward the columbarium.

"Are you going to stay at the penthouse, or go out to the estate?" she asked.

"Honestly, I haven't given it that much thought. For now, I'll be at the apartment."

She put her hand on my knee. "I know it's hard to think about the room where he died. Usually they recommend that you don't do anything to it for a while."

I shook my head. "I've already had it cleaned out. It smelled. The furniture is gone. His clothes are gone." Val's eyes widened as I spoke. "I've had a few things boxed, but honestly, I think there are charities that can benefit." The car stopped.

"That's nice, but you shouldn't—"

This time I patted her knee. "Sis, I love you. I know you know what *should* be done. I'm doing what I need to do. If I regret it later, you can tell me I told you so."

The door opened and the sunshine streamed in. Reaching for my dark sunglasses and securing my purse, I scooted toward the door. "Stay with me, Val. Please run interference with Mom. I can't deal with her right now."

Val nodded as we both stood. Under my black hat and dark glasses, my gray eyes shimmered with delight. I wanted to watch the vault close once and for all.

Stoically, we stood, Val, myself, and Travis, Mother, Marcus, and Lyle behind us as well as a few special mourners who'd been invited to this private ceremony. The minister offered more words of praise for the life lost too young. I even caught his mention of the reward in heaven for Stewart's devoted wife. He was wrong. I would never see heaven, and my reward was the sound of the small door closing.

I'd done it. The evidence was gone and so was Stewart.

Walking back to the car, Marilyn reached for my arm and whispered. "Please, Victoria. I need to speak with you. Tell that goon to take Valerie to the other car with the boys. I need to speak to you alone."

"Mother…" Val said.

I looked at Marilyn's hand on my arm and slowly brought my eyes to hers. Through clenched teeth, I whispered, "This is hardly the time or the place for—"

With more spirit than she'd had since Randall's death, since she'd truly become dependent on Stewart and me, she retaliated. "This isn't about money. I know Marcus' tuition is paid."

My eyes widened. Money was our only topic of conversation. *What the hell did she think I'd want to say to her?* She misinterpreted my change of expression.

"Thank you for that, for the money."

Those words of appreciation were spoken for Stewart, not for me. After the first few times of his demanding gratitude from her, she too learned her place, at least with him. The fact she'd just offered it to me was rather comical.

Her complexion paled as she leaned closer. I saw Travis approaching as her next words registered.

"You need to know something. There are things I never told you."

Travis began to speak, but she hurriedly continued, "Your father— your biological father—was at the funeral. I saw him."

The world went black.

CHAPTER TWENTY-ONE

Present

ALONE WITH TRAVIS, within the cool interior of the limousine, he spoke, "I assume that catching your ass before it hits the pavement is an acceptable exception to your earlier mandate?" His dark eyes glistened as he watched my every move.

Instead of answering, I pursed my lips together, smoothed my black dress over my trembling legs, and glared at him.

With Val and Marilyn still outside of the car, Travis leaned closer as his lips quirked into a lopsided smirk. "I believe the appropriate response would be 'well, yes, Travis, thank you for saving my ass. You're so right. This was an acceptable exception.'"

I narrowed my glare. "You seem to have an issue with who's in charge here. It's still me."

"I'm very well aware of that. If it were me, I'd throw your mother's bony ass on the ground and back this fucking car over her. She's a bigger pain in the ass than you."

I couldn't contain my laugh. "Why, Travis, I believe that's the kindest thing you've ever said to me. Who knew that under that asshole exterior you had a personality?"

Pulling a bottle of water from the car's small refrigerator, he handed it to me and asked, "What happened out there?" *Was I actually hearing a genuine hint of concern in his tone?*

Taking the cool water, I shrugged and made myself drink.

"Tell me, Mrs. Harrington, will Dr. Conway or Mrs. Sound be riding with you? Or both? Or neither?"

I sat taller, feeling less shaky after having a couple of sips of water. "I want to hear what my mother has to say. She wants to speak to me privately. Ask Val to ride with the boys." I smoothed my dress again, though it didn't need it. I looked back to his dark, questioning eyes. "Tell the drivers to go directly to my mother's house. I don't want her or the boys coming back to the penthouse with me. After we drop them off, Val can ride with me. She said something about spending the night." I sighed. "Honestly, I think I might want the medication she promised."

Travis' brow rose in question. "Please don't tell me that we're going to add prescription drug use to my list of activities to oversee."

I still had a difficult time believing that my activities were that important to him. I shook my head. "Don't worry about it. Do you think the good Dr. Conway would do anything illegal?"

He shrugged. "I'm less likely to suspect her than others." *What the hell?* "Shall I get Mrs. Sound?" he asked again, giving me another chance to change my mind.

Exhaling, I nodded. "Yes, thank you."

"My pleasure, Mrs. Harrington, although I doubt it will be yours." The last part he added with a smirk.

Next, he opened the car door and stepped out, momentarily leaving me alone in the large space. As the warming October breeze blew through the open door, I listened to the voices. The first ones that came into range were Marcus and Lyle. Their camaraderie brought a smile to my lips. The boys were as close as Val and I. Although they'd been raised considerably differently than we, their closeness shone light on my dark heart. Apparently, having a bitch like Marilyn as a mother caused you to seek a confidant and a friend. Perhaps she had done one thing right in her parenting. She gave each of us that special sibling. I leaned my head out of the car. "Goodbye, Marcus and Lyle. Thank you for being here."

They both smiled, reminding me of their father. They both had his brown hair and green eyes. The older they became, the more Randall I saw in them and the less Marilyn.

"You're welcome, Vikki," Marcus offered as he came near and

reached down to offer me a hug. "Hope you feel better."

I hugged him back. "I will. I need some rest."

While continuing our hug, he whispered near my ear, "I know it's you. Thanks."

I pulled back, opened my eyes wide, and glanced toward our mother.

He shrugged. "She wants everyone to think that she's the one paying for everything, but I'm not as young and stupid as I used to be."

Grinning, I ruffled his hair. "Hey, no one ever said you were stupid. Stupid people don't get accepted to the University of Miami."

As he stood taller and smiled, I saw a man where there used to be a boy. "Val told me that you were accepted there too. I'm sorry you didn't get to go. It's really a great school. I haven't been there that long, but I think I'm going to like it."

At one time attending the University of Miami had been my greatest desire. *Was that me or was it someone else?* As Marcus spoke, Marilyn came near and put her arm around him. "Your father would be so proud of you."

"Marcus," I said, with a sad smile. "Keep me posted. Your old sister is proud too."

"You're not that old," he quipped with a nod as he walked back to the second car.

"What did you tell him?" Marilyn asked as she joined me in the first limousine.

Before I could answer, Travis peered in, shook his head, and shut the door.

"Nothing, Mother. I didn't tell him that I was paying his tuition, if that's your concern. However, I suggest you try honesty with at least one or two of your children. It might work out better for you."

She looked down. "Better than this?" Her voice sounded uncharacteristically weak.

"Yes, better than this. Don't try to play me. I'm not in the mood. You just dropped a fucking bomb on me at my husband's funeral. We're taking you home. Start talking."

"Home? No, Victoria, I'm going to stay with you, to take care of you, to help you."

The car began to move as a laugh rang from somewhere deep inside of me. "No fucking way. I need some peace and quiet. You'd better start talking. Your time is ticking."

She swallowed and stared toward the window. "I understand how you may feel like we're not close—"

"Fucking stop! We're not. You never raised me or cared for me. When I was young, you shipped me off to other family while you lived in a fucking bottle. Then when you got clean and married Randall, you shipped Val and me off to boarding schools."

"It was only because—" she began.

"Because looking at me upset you. I remind you too much of my father and my twin. Hell, I probably still do. I've heard it my whole damn life. I'm not rehashing it all, but you and Randall fucking sold me."

"That's not entirely true."

My head snapped toward her. "Tell me, what part of that statement isn't *entirely* true?"

She became suddenly obsessed with a piece of lint that desperately needed extrication from her dress. "It was a desperate situation. You don't know what it's like. You haven't had to deal with things like—"

My patience was wearing thin. "Marilyn, you have about fifteen minutes until we reach your door. I'll never forgive you for what you did to me. Don't expect it. Move on."

"Victoria, look at you. You're a twenty-nine-year-old beautiful woman with more money than I can even imagine. So you married when you were young; things could be a lot worse. If Stewart hadn't offered to marry you, things would have been much worse."

Offered? Is that what he did or did he buy me? "Really, mother? Worse for whom? For me or for you? And by the way, I'm twenty-eight. Keep waiting for that mother-of-the-year award. I'm sure it's coming any day."

"Victoria, hear me out. You said to try honesty. That's what I want to do. Will you listen?"

There was something in her voice, something I didn't recognize. I nodded.

She straightened her neck and began. "I loved your father—your biological father—like no one else I've ever loved." She moved her gaze toward the window as her tone became whimsical. "Our romance was something like you read about in books. It was, for lack of a better word, intense. He was unlike anyone I'd ever known. We weren't from the same kind of family. Neither of our parents approved of us being together."

"Mother, you've mentioned Johnathon a handful of times in my entire life. Why was he at Stewart's funeral?"

She looked at me, her gray eyes clouded with a veil of confusion. "No, Victoria. Not Johnathon. Carlisle."

What the fuck? Carlisle? Who the fuck was Carlisle? My eyes opened wide in shock. *Would her fucking bombshells never stop?* I was speechless.

Marilyn's gaze again went toward the window, momentarily mesmerized with the streets of Miami as building after building passed by. Finally, she continued, "It's true that I never told you any of this. Part of the reason was that I blamed you for ruining our marriage, but..." Her stone-cold hand reached for mine, its touch sending shivers down my spine. "...I also didn't tell you, because I wanted to protect you."

"From what? I don't understand."

"Carlisle and I were young and madly in love. It was passionate and volatile. I don't know if I'd wish that type of love on anyone. In hindsight, I can say it wasn't healthy. At the time, it was all-consuming. Carlisle came from a different world. He overwhelmed me. Against both of our families' wishes, we eloped. With mine, it meant we didn't talk. His was different. He didn't want to avoid them. He wanted to prove to them that he could be part of the family, the business, and follow his heart."

She took a breath. "God, Victoria, this is so hard."

Did she fucking want me to feel sorry for her? "You're telling me that this man, Carlisle, whom I've never heard of before was at my husband's funeral?"

"Please, let me say what I need to say."

I gestured with my hand, indicating for her to go on.

"Carlisle's family was very male dominated. The only way for a woman to move up the hierarchy was to bear sons. For that reason, older women, like Carlisle's grandmother, were respected. She didn't like me. When we went to her, to tell her that we had married, she claimed that since we weren't married in the church, we weren't really married. She cursed our union and our children. Carlisle was the eldest son. It was his responsibility to have a son, someone to take over the family business. Though his grandmother wasn't involved in the business, she was still revered by the family. Her curse was that we would never have children. You can imagine how excited we were when I became pregnant. It was a miracle. When the doctors told us that we were having twins, we were elated. Carlisle told his parents. At the time his younger brother was engaged. If Niccolo had the first son, the business would go to him." She looked out the window. "It was a crazy and scary life. As you can imagine, the family business wasn't legal."

I nodded, wanting her to keep talking.

My mother's expression darkened. "You know what happened with the pregnancy." She gave me the familiar stare. "Carlisle blamed me." Her gray eyes narrowed. "He also blamed you, and yes, I blamed you.

"When we learned that our son had died, Carlisle found himself in the position, or maybe I should say, with the opportunity, where he could back out of his commitment to me, to us. It was his chance at a fresh start. Like I said, in his world sons were of utmost importance." She added, with noticeable sadness, "Women who couldn't give those to their husbands were disposable. He was still young. If he abandoned us, he had a chance of fulfilling his destiny."

"That's ridiculous," I interrupted. "The woman doesn't determine the sex. Just because my twin died... you could still bear sons. You have, two."

"Please, let me go on."

I nodded.

"Though I begged him and I couldn't imagine my life without him, he left us. After all, with his grandmother's curse, there was no guarantee that I could give him the son he wanted. Months before you were born, he left us and had our marriage annulled. I fell apart. I'm not proud to say that I was ready to blame you for two deaths, your brother's and mine. I was that close. I didn't realize until later that my death before your birth was what his family wanted.

"Before you were born, I met Johnathon Conway. Johnathon knew enough about Carlisle's family to know that I needed to get away. Johnathon and I moved up north and married. We stayed up there until after Val was born. Johnathon was a good man, but if I were honest with him or with myself... I never really loved him. My life was void without your father. There was a hole that no one could fill. Johnathon tried; however, instead of allowing him to do that I turned to alcohol. A little over a year after Val was born he left. He was a good man, but after a while he couldn't handle having a drunk wife and two little girls. I came back to Florida, and tried to re-acclimate with my family. They tried to convince me to stop drinking." She looked my way and back to the window. "I didn't want help. Every time I looked at you, I saw Carlisle and thought about what could have been.

"After Johnathon divorced me, I spiraled even farther downward. It's true: my mother and sisters cared for you when I couldn't."

Too much information. My heart sank as I tried to make sense of her confession. "Johnathon Conway was Val's father, but not mine?"

She looked down. "Valerie doesn't know. She thinks you're both Johnathon's."

Because that is what we'd been told.

"Please don't tell her," she pleaded. "Johnathon encouraged me to tell my family that he fathered both of you." She looked down. "He really tried. I blamed you for the end of that marriage too. I mean, I drank because as you grew, you looked more and more like your father. I kept thinking that if only you had been the one to not survive. If only your brother had lived."

That's fucking great. Sorry to disappoint.

Seemingly unaware of how hurtful she was, Marilyn continued, "We'd already established a ruse about you. There was no sense denying it. According to everything we told people, you died. You were born two months prematurely and didn't survive. Our story was that Johnathon and I conceived you on our wedding night."

"I don't understand what you're saying."

"Victoria, you are twenty-nine. Your birthday isn't in May, it's October ninth of the year before. You recently turned twenty-nine."

"Why? Why would you do that?"

"It was Johnathon's idea. In Carlisle's mind he'd almost lost his place in the family business due to you. Making it seem like you were Johnathon's and not Carlisle's was to protect you. We had the date on your birth certificate changed. According to our story, the baby I was due to deliver in October never lived. She died just like her twin."

I didn't know what to say.

"There was more about your father, but with you and me out of the way, he made his way with another woman, one the family liked. The whole ordeal was a lot for me to handle," Marilyn went on. "I didn't do it well. As you know Randall saved me. You know that we met in group therapy. My addiction was alcohol and his was gambling. I've never drunk again, but Randall continued to fight his demons; however, even those weren't what you thought.

"Your true identity would cause a major wrinkle in their finely constructed nobility. There were some people who would say that because you lived, Carlisle's place within the family wasn't secure. In their business, trust is essential. If it were determined that he'd lied about the identity of his firstborn, it could be the first string to unravel more than they wanted to reveal."

My head ached as I tried to construct this family tree, one that as of an hour ago didn't exist.

"Victoria, Carlisle's family warned me to kill you before you were born. After Carlisle left me, Niccolo, his brother, came to see me. He told me to have an abortion. He even made me an appointment. Johnathon and I left town the day of that appointment.

"It was true that Randall owed the organization money. It wasn't Carlisle's family. It was another family, one who wanted to prove to the world that Carlisle's family lied: to prove that he had a daughter before he had a son. Before you married Stewart, this other family ensured that Randall's debt was insurmountable. They capitalized on his addiction and continued to offer him opportunities that never paid off. It wasn't until they asked for you that we knew."

"What? They asked specifically for me?"

She nodded her head. "I know I've never been a good mother, but I couldn't do that. I couldn't allow them to take you. When I was very young, I saw what happened to women, women who weren't part of the family. If they had you, Carlisle's daughter, they could prove that his family lied about you and they could use you." Her eyes filled with tears. "I don't even want to think about what they could have done to you."

My mind was a blur. *Could any of this be true?*

"How did Stewart become involved?"

Marilyn wiped her eyes and sniffed, before she continued, "Randall had met Stewart through his medical practice. There were rumors that the families that I've mentioned conducted some of their business through Harrington Spas and Suites." She reached for my hand again. This time the cold didn't even register. "I'm not insinuating that your husband was involved in illegal activities. What I'm saying is that he had power, power over some of the business that went on behind the scenes. Stewart Harrington was the only person we knew who could possibly have the kind of money that we needed to save you from those people."

"How much Mother? How much did Stewart pay for me?"

"Victoria, you weren't sold. You were saved."

I sat straighter. "How much?"

"Over six million."

My jaws ached, temples throbbed, and mouth dried. I reached for the water bottle and tried to drink, but, suddenly, the water tasted sour and my stomach threatened to revolt. "I can't... I don't even know what to say."

"My dear, this is too much. The thing is, this isn't all. There's more. Please let me come to your apartment. We're almost to my house. I need you to know everything."

I shook my head. "Not today. I don't think I can handle any more."

She looked around at the street. Ignoring my plea for silence, she spoke fast. "When your husband paid Randall's debt, the organization was upset. They thought they had this perfect plan Stewart foiled it. Randall said there were some rumblings of discontent, but then after you'd been married for a year or so, things seemed to settle down. During all of this, I did my best to distance myself from you. I hoped that they'd still believe you were truly a Conway.

"I can't prove it, but I suspect that Randall's accident wasn't due to unpaid gambling debts. It was a warning to me: a reminder that I know too much. He did owe money, but comparatively it wasn't that much."

"I know Randall asked Stewart to cover it."

Marilyn looked down. "I don't blame you for saying no. I did at one time, but now I don't. I'm not sure how long it would have been before they came back for more." She looked down. "Randall wasn't a bad man. He wasn't."

I couldn't think about Randall being a good man. If he'd never gotten involved with the gambling, this never would have come about. Then again, would those people have found another way to me? *Me who?* I didn't exist. I'd died. My mind spun. "So you're telling me that my father, Carlisle, not Johnathon Conway, was at my husband's funeral, and he's part of some crime family? This sounds like a TV movie, not real life."

"Yes, Victoria, that's what I'm saying. Those TV movies come from somewhere. It's real. As long as Stewart was alive he had power. Now I'm scared."

Goose bumps rose on my arms. "Why?"

The car came to a stop. We were in my mother's driveway. "It wasn't until your actual eighteenth birthday, the one you didn't know you had, that I heard from Carlisle's family. It was the first time in over eighteen years. I didn't hear from your father. I heard from his brother, Niccolo, the same one who wanted me to have an abortion. He wanted proof that you were truly Victoria Conway, the daughter of Johnathon Conway. I gave it to him. I gave him a copy of your second birth certificate. I never heard from them again, but then when Randall was asked specifically for you, we knew that at the very least, the others suspected." She spoke fast. "Stewart was a good man. He knew what he was getting into when he married you. If he hadn't..." Travis opened the door.

"Victoria, please don't share this." She tilted her head toward Travis. "Does he protect you?"

I looked toward the mountain of a man outside the car, the one who only days ago intimidated me. Though I could only see his body as he stood holding the door, I imagined his dark eyes and narrowing suspicious gaze. Looking back to my mother, I nodded.

She covered my hand and spoke soft and fast. "Good. You don't understand what you're up against. Darling, there's more. I know you hate me, but there is so much more. I'm not denying that I've unjustly blamed you for things that truly were out of your control. However, I've also done what I've done to protect you. Keeping you distanced from me was for your own good. You weren't supposed to be born."

"Mrs. Sound," Travis' voice came from the open door.

I didn't speak, unsure what to say as Marilyn moved from the car. A few minutes later, Val was beside me and we were once again on the road.

"Vik?" Her voice overflowed with love and support. "Are you all right? You look pale. What did Mom say?"

What had she said? I couldn't process. *Carlisle and Johnathon… She'd married both of them. I wasn't supposed to be born? I hadn't been—but I had. What was Carlisle's last name? It wasn't Conway, not the same as Val's.* Tears spilled over my painted lids. Before I could speak, Val's arms came around me and I collapsed on her shoulder.

Of all the things Marilyn said, the one that came to the forefront was that my father wasn't the same as Val's. Had I just lost my sister? She wasn't truly my sister as I'd always thought. We were, but we weren't. My shoulders shuddered.

"It's going to be all right," Val soothed. "You'll be all right. I know it's hard. Maybe you'll consider that counseling. You're too young to be a widow. You don't have to do this on your own." Her hand ran circles over my back as she continued, "I'll postpone my trip to Uganda. I won't leave you."

My head moved back and forth. "No, Val, don't." I spoke between sobs. "I don't want you to do that." When her caring gray eyes met mine, I asked, "Can you please give me some of that medicine? I want to sleep. I don't want to think anymore."

CHAPTER TWENTY-TWO

Present

The notes of Fatal Lullaby *faded as* Death Dance *began. I tried to open my eyes, but all I saw was black. Were my eyes not opening or was it the blindfold?*

No! *I wanted to scream. This couldn't be happening. I was never going back again.* Never! *Why was I here?*

The last thing I remembered was taking Val's medicine and going to sleep. I was in my bed, in my suite. How did this happen?

The cold, smooth bars of the headboard felt familiar under my grasp. As my fingers flexed, the indignation within me grew. I wasn't doing this. I wouldn't. Just as I was about to release the bars, Stewart's voice spoke to me, "I'm here, darling. Show us that pretty, wet pussy."

No! *My legs snapped together.*

"Come on, Tori, don't make our friend mad."

This wasn't real. Stewart was dead! I saw him die! My mind searched desperately for answers as the bed shifted. I tried to let go of the headboard, but I couldn't. My hands weren't obeying my mind.

Cold, rough hands reached for my ankles. Uncharacteristically, I kicked, feeling my foot strike something hard. The bed shifted again, the harsh hands brutally seized my ankles and pulled my body farther down the bed. Though I tried to fight, one by one my ankles were secured and tightly bound as my legs were pulled apart to a painful width.

"No!" *I found my voice.* "No! Stop!" *I screamed louder, hoping that my pleas rang throughout the warehouse and beyond. I knew the location was remote and isolated for a reason. Nevertheless, even though I couldn't hear myself with the headphones, I continued to scream. I must have spoken, because as my demands grew louder, a large hand came down and covered my mouth. I tried with all my might to bite, but the person moved his hand, just out of the way.*

"Stop, baby," *Stewart's calm voice came through the headphones.* "You know the rules. No talking."

I'm not doing this! You're dead! You can't make me!

I screamed a muffled scream into the hand, as pain emanated from my hair and the blindfold and headphones were ripped from my head. The onslaught of light momentarily blinded me, making it difficult to focus on the man before me. He was right on top of me, his hand over my mouth and his rancid breath filling my senses.

Senator Robert Keene's voice was low and menacing. "Do you want to fight? Good. I like that." He grabbed a fistful of my hair and snapped my head back. "Keep it up. I always thought you were too compliant."

I glared. Motherfucker, this isn't happening.

"Stewart made promises. If you think I'll continue to support his endeavors without this little incentive, you're as stupid as you are hot."

My heartbeat quickened as panic overtook me. No. I couldn't do this. I wouldn't. I'd never been this frightened before. Stewart couldn't help me. My mind searched for possibilities.

Robert's face came closer. With his hand still over my mouth he leaned in and licked my cheek. My stomach threatened revolt as his wet tongue lapped the other cheek and he spoke, "There we go. Will you be a good girl or do we need to punish you?" Gripping my hair tighter he bathed my face in his awful breath and asked, "What's it going to be, are you going to be a good girl?"

Fucker! I nodded—as much as I could with his hand entwined in my hair. Yeah, I'll fucking be a good girl.

He petted my head, loosened his grip, and slowly removed his hand from my mouth. As he started to move, I fought against the restraints and screamed with everything in me. It was my only hope, my only chance. "Travis! Travis! Help me!"

HANDS CAME to my shoulders and I braced myself for Robert's punishment.

"Vik, Vik. Wake up."

"No way, motherfucker! Travis! Help me. Travis!" My voice was louder than it had been before. My skin dripped with perspiration as my trembling body fought the restraints. Instantly, my hands and feet flung free. The restraints were gone. I pushed past the hands, and rushed from the bed. As I did, the room came into focus. The warehouse was gone. I was in my suite and I wasn't alone. Val was in the middle of my bed, the covers disheveled and her eyes as big as saucers. Her gray questioning gaze stared through me as if I were possessed.

My mind couldn't register what had just happened. My shaking body was no longer naked; instead I was covered in a sweat-dampened nightgown. Robert Keene wasn't with me. I was in my apartment, my suite. Val moved cautiously toward me, as if she were afraid of what I might do. All energy and strength left my limbs as I closed my eyes and fell to my knees.

I was fucking losing it.

Just as Val reached me, my suite door opened. I looked up to see Travis' large frame fill the doorway. In the dim light, I felt his dark eyes assessing the scene.

Val turned toward him. "She's all right. I'm sorry I bothered you. I think she was having a nightmare. The only name I recognized was yours. She was calling to you."

I shook my head. "No, I wasn't. I'm fine."

"Vik, you're not fine," Val said. "You were in the middle of some nightmare or night terror. I couldn't get you to wake up. You almost decked me. What the hell were you dreaming about?"

I stared toward Travis. He'd yet to speak. Trying for a small bit of decorum, I stood and reached for my robe. Securing it around me, I said, "Thank you for coming, Travis. I'm fine. I'd appreciate it if you'd leave my room."

His back stiffened. *Why was I concerned about him seeing me in my nightgown?* He'd obviously seen me with a lot less. Instead of listening, he took a step closer. His customary dark slacks were replaced by gym shorts that exposed his thick, muscular legs, and his feet were bare. "Mrs. Harrington, if you figure out what your nightmare was about, or if I can be of any assistance, I don't mind your call." He turned toward Val. "Or yours, doctor. I'm here."

I exhaled. "I don't think that will be necessary. I probably shouldn't have taken that medicine." I feigned a smile toward my sister. "It was like some horror story, a monster or something." My eyes went toward Travis. "I'm not sure. I couldn't see much."

His eyes closed knowingly. "Mrs. Harrington, are you sure you're *fine*?"

I nodded, standing as tall as possible in my bare feet. "I am."

"Just know, ma'am, I'm downstairs. No monsters will restrict your vision as long as I'm here." With that he turned, and said, "Good night."

Val and I watched as he walked out into the hallway and closed the door. Once he was gone, Val wrinkled her nose and said, "Well, that was kind of weird." Turning toward me, she continued, "I'm sorry that I called him, Vik. I used your phone. You were screaming and you kept calling for him. I wasn't sure what to do."

"Kept?"

She reached for my hand and led me toward the bed. "Yeah, it went on for over ten minutes. Psychiatry isn't my thing, but something is going on. Please let me get you connected to someone who can help you."

Could anyone help me? I thought this would all be over when Stewart died. I looked at the clock. "Val, I'm sorry for waking you so early." I eyed my bed. "Did you fall asleep in here? We do have other rooms."

She grinned. "I know you do. I didn't want to leave you. You wouldn't have left me. That's what sisters do."

I pressed my lips together. Sisters. The term made my chest hurt. We were sisters. We were. Just like Marcus and Lyle were my brothers. *Did it matter that our fathers weren't the same?*

"Okay, then. Climb back in." I patted the mattress of my large king-sized bed. "It's not even three. Why don't we try to get some more sleep?"

"If you promise not to try to kick me again," she said with a gleam in her gray eyes.

"Oh, no. Did I kick you?"

"Don't worry about it. That must have been some monster. You know some people have problems with night terrors after taking sleep medicine. I'm sorry, sis. I was trying to help."

I reached out and touched her arm. My trembling was nearly gone. "It was only a dream." *Was I reassuring her or myself?*

She turned off the light near the bed and the room fell silent. After a few minutes, Val asked, "Vik?"

"Yes?"

"Who's horizontal-friend?"

I turned toward her voice. The darkened scene reminded me of a simpler time, the years we'd spent sharing a room. "Why?"

"I get it if you don't want to tell me. I was just wondering why you'd call out for Travis in your dream and not him, or even Stewart."

I shrugged. "I remember in my dream telling myself that Stewart was dead. Even in my dream, I knew he couldn't help me."

"But you called out for Travis, the guy you used to say gave you the creeps?" Her voice grew higher. "Is he horizontal-friend?"

"No! God no."

Val's laugh filled the room. "Okay, I was just wondering. Is he married?"

I tried to keep up. "Travis, no, he isn't married."

"No," Val corrected, "Horizontal-friend?"

I shook my head in the dark, thinking about Brody. "No, he's not."

"Good."

"Why good?" I asked.

"Because I don't want you having another one of these nightmares and being all alone."

"Maybe this is something I need to explore with your counselor. Good night, Val."

"Night, sis."

Would Brody understand? How could I explain to him what I was imagining? He'd read the contract, but I'd never given him the particulars. He knew there were other men. He knew it was Stewart's idea of fun, but he didn't know any more. What would he think of me if he knew? But then I wondered if I really cared. He was the one spouting things about being the only man in my life. Right now, I didn't care about having a man in my life. I mean, the sex was hot—it was. However, after all the bombshells I'd had dropped in the past few days I didn't want a man. I wanted a life: a normal life. A wishful smile came to my face.

Could I ever have a normal life? Just Brody and I, away from Miami, away from the warehouse and Stewart's deals. Away from Marilyn and Carlisle? I'd never allowed myself to entertain such an idea, but now I did. Could that be my new goal?

The question that arose was what would I be willing to do to achieve it?

As sleep threatened, I knew my answer: anything.

∼

MY NIGHTMARE from the night before gave me new resolve. I wasn't going back to the warehouse. There was no way in hell I could do it. Somehow knowing that if I returned it would be without Stewart made the whole situation seem somehow viler.

Early that next morning, I texted Brody:

"DO YOU KNOW OF ANYONE NAMED CARLISLE?"

The next thing I did was call Craven and Knowles. With each ring, I contemplated my options. Until I knew exactly what I was up against, I couldn't truly form my plan. The answering of my call refocused my attention.

"Craven and Knowles, this is Trish. May I help you?"

"Trish, this is Mrs. Harrington. I need to speak with Parker as soon as possible. Tell him to call me."

"Yes, ma'am, I'll inform Maggie—"

"No, Trish, I'm not interested in his assistant. If I were I'd ask for her. On second thought, tell Parker that if Craven and Knowles plan to be part of the Harrington future, he'll be at my apartment at ten this morning. I'll be waiting."

"Mrs. Harrington, I'm sure he has appointments."

"Then he can cancel them. Good day." I hung up.

Settling into Stewart's chair I opened Parker's folder, the pages burning my fingers. I hated every word as I scanned Parker's contract. No longer was I a naïve eighteen-year-old. Now, I understood the meaning of the words. The innuendos were no longer mysterious but daunting. A knock on the door pulled me away from the torturous words on the page and back to the glass office overlooking the rough seas. I glanced at the clock: only a little before nine.

I didn't think it would be Parker without an announcement from Lisa or Kristina. "Come in," I responded cautiously.

The door opened and the familiar, dark gaze looked my way. "Mrs. Harrington, are you feeling better?"

I sat taller. "Yes, Travis. It was wrong of Val to bother you in the middle of the night."

He came forward and eyed one of the chairs. I nodded as he sat. "No, it wasn't wrong. It's my job to make sure you're all right."

"Fine, it's your job. You can protect me from real things, not nightmares."

His brow rose as his dark brown eyes widened. "But you called out for me?"

"According to Valerie," I clarified.

"So now we're accusing the good doctor of lying?"

I stood and walked to the window. The skies were an uncustomary gray, with thick clouds that billowed toward the horizon as white caps graced the tips of the waves in the raging ocean. It was late autumn, near the end of hurricane season. Only large commercial ocean liners could be seen on the rough waters. The smaller crafts no doubt had heeded the warning about the impending weather.

Was that what I needed to do? Heed the warnings... but which ones? Who could I believe? Without turning, I began, "It was so real. I was there, at the warehouse. I was even reasoning with myself. I knew it couldn't be real. I knew Stewart was dead. I remembered you saying that you'd always been there." I closed my eyes and fought the revolt in the pit of my stomach from Robert's rancid breath. "I tried to fight."

A muffled laugh came from behind me. "As I recall, you're a pretty damn good fighter."

Hugging my midsection I spun and took in Travis' expression. I didn't see pity or condemnation as I'd expected; instead, I saw respect. I continued, "But this time was different. I couldn't fight. My hands and feet were bound."

"It wasn't real," Travis said matter-of-factly.

"It sure as hell felt real. It smelled real. I even saw him. He took off my blindfold. It was as if he wanted me to know it was him."

Travis' neck straightened. "Who? Who did you see?"

Biting my lip, I admitted, "I don't know if I should say."

"Why? You know I know who's been there."

"But what will it mean if I know? I'm not supposed to know."

Travis stood and moved closer. "Who said you're not supposed to know?"

"S-Stewart."

His dark eyes questioned mine. "Mr. Harrington is dead. Right now, no one owns that contract. Right now, the choice is yours to know or not know."

I moved back to the chair, suddenly alarmed at my desire to find solace in his proximity and common understanding. "Why would I possibly want to give anyone, you or Parker, the right to make those kinds of decisions for me again?"

"Because if you don't, there are those who want to suck you into a world that will make your nightmare seem like a walk on the beach."

"Those?"

"Who did you see in your nightmare?"

I closed my eyes and inhaled. Sighing, I admitted, "Senator Keene."

Travis' dark eyes opened wide as a shrill whistle came from his lips. "Damn, how long have you known?"

I shrugged. "Not long. You said politicians. He was at the viewing and I smelled him."

"You smelled him?"

"You know—senses. I was never able to see the men or hear them. Most of the time I wasn't allowed to touch them—not with my hands. That left the sense of smell and taste. Over the years I've identified a few *friends* by their unique odor: particular colognes, aftershaves, their breath. Senator Keene's breath reeks."

Travis nodded. "He's one of the friends who's not happy about the end of his visits. He's supported or rather effectively turned a blind eye to some of the activities that happened within the underworld of Harrington Spas and Suites. He's even been instrumental in expanding the business outside of the US. He believes that he's entitled."

"So how will that change if you or Parker is in control?"

"It won't. However, it will keep you safer. Mr. Harrington had rules. You're right that he enjoyed watching, but he also watched to be sure his rules were maintained. Multiple times throughout the years Mr. Harrington stopped things that you never knew about."

I didn't want to think about that. "Let me get this straight." I looked Travis in the eye. "It doesn't matter if it's you or Parker, you both plan on making me continue this… this… life?"

"I don't know what Mr. Craven plans. I would assume he does. From what I know of him, I would also assume the rules would be significantly different under his watchful eye."

"From what you know? He's one of them, isn't he?"

Travis nodded again. "I don't think that's a revelation, is it?"

"No," I admitted. "I've known that for a while, too." I looked at Travis earnestly, "What about you? What are your plans?"

"To bring the fuckers down. Not all of them. There are a few sick bastards who've joined this party because they could. They have no hidden agenda. They'll go away as quietly as they came. They don't want their good names associated with a possible scandal. A few seconds of carefully selected audio and I can make them go away; however, there are a handful who know exactly what they're doing. They think that by fucking with you, they're helping themselves with other causes. I want to see them all burn in hell. Fuck, I'll probably be there with them, but at least that's a show I'll enjoy."

"Why, Travis? Why do you care?"

"It's a long story." He sighed. "One that began when I was too young to understand. Let's just say that I knew a woman, one who was caught up in something similar to what you've gone through, but worse."

I shook my head. "I find that hard to believe."

"Really? Fucking look at yourself. Look at your goddamned life. You're Victoria Fucking Harrington. You aren't a poor girl with a twelve-year-old kid who's trying to stay alive by playing the kinky games these ass-wipes want to play. You have choices. Mr. Harrington made choices for you, ones that would pacify the powers that be. They won't stay pacified for long.

"You want to know what I'd do with that contract. I'd explain a few more of your choices to you. One thing I'd say is that you have a fucking fortune. Use it. Take it. Leave the goddamn world of Harrington Spas and Suites to rot.

"Do you really want to own a company that is nothing more than a cover for the exploitation of women who don't live the fucking high life you live? I'm not saying that you've had it easy. You haven't. But at the end of each day, you were unhurt and sleeping in a fancy-ass apartment or mansion with a fucking rock on your finger that could feed one of those other women's families for five years."

My stomach knotted. I'd never thought about it like that.

"You were destined for that life. Mr. Harrington made it the best he could. Now is your chance to make it better."

Travis' voice lowered. "I can guarantee that if you choose to not sign a contract with either one of us, my fucking job will get a lot more difficult. They want you."

"Who? Who fucking wants me?"

His dark eyes narrowed. "Who fucked you the other day?"

I no longer felt that I had any secrets from Travis. In a way it was liberating. Without blinking, I replied honestly, "Brody Phillips."

He shook his head. "Jesus, are you fucking crazy? He's part of Craven and Knowles. They're so deep in this shit. Your sense of smell should have told you to stay away."

"No, you're wrong. He does work there, but he's not one of them. He didn't know about the contract, the warehouse, or anything until I asked him to dig into it. All he knows is what I've told him."

Travis leaned back in his chair and crossed his arms over his chest. "So he's the reason you knew about the will?"

"Yes. You see? He's helped me. It's Parker I don't trust."

"Follow your gut... with Mr. Craven."

"He's on his way over."

Travis inhaled deeply, his chest expanding in his tight shirt. "I implore you, Mrs. Harrington, do not sign his contract. Tell him that you've thought it over and want to fulfill your husband's wishes. If you trust Mr. Phillips so much, have him write up a new contract with my name. But above all, under no circumstances should you sneak off without me. You truly don't realize what you're up against."

"Travis, before you go, I want you to tell me something."

His brow rose.

"Who is Carlisle?"

The blood drained from Travis' usually confident expression. "Mrs. Harrington, neither Senator Keene nor Parker Craven is your worst nightmare. I'm not sure how or why you're aware of Carlisle Albini; however, I suggest you forget what you know. He's none of your concern; neither is Niccolo, Wesley, nor any of their family."

None of my concern. Stewart had said that before we married. *Albini?* Wesley Albini, from Kinsley Preparatory.

"Niccolo is Carlisle's brother. Who's Wesley?" I asked.

"Mrs. Harrington, you have no idea what you're asking."

I raised my voice. "Tell me. Who is he?"

"Wesley is his son."

"Niccolo's son?"

"No, Carlisle's."

My head felt suddenly too heavy to hold. Wesley Albini was my brother.

CHAPTER TWENTY-THREE

Present

"MRS. HARRINGTON," Kristina's voice came through the speaker of my phone. "Mr. Craven is here for his ten o'clock appointment."

"Thank you, Kristina. Show him in."

I stood.

"Vic-tor-ia." He elongated my name as he entered Stewart's office, my office.

"Parker, so nice of you to accommodate my wishes. I'm not quite ready to face the world."

"It's my pleasure. I understand that this is still a difficult time for you." He sat across from my desk and leaned forward. "I suppose it will be for a while. I truly wish we didn't need to discuss the matters at hand; however, I believe the sooner we address this, the sooner we can have it resolved."

"Resolved?" I questioned. "I'm not sure what we need to resolve."

"Victoria, you are in a precarious situation. If it weren't so dire, I would gladly wait. However, there are deals that Stewart made, ones he has yet to fully repay."

"Surely you've been in contact with our accountants and bankers. I'm confident that they can take care of whatever it is you need."

I loved watching him shift in his seat. There was no way I was broaching the subject of the contract. I wanted to hear him say it.

His brows rose. "This isn't about money. Don't play dumb."

"Oh, was I playing? You walked in here the other day and expected me to blindly sign documents without reading them." When his lips pursed, I asked, "Now, that was you, wasn't it?"

"I had every intention of explaining them to you at a later date. You don't seem to understand the trust relationship there is between an attorney and client. There were many occasions where Stewart gave me full reign over his affairs."

I sat back and opened my eyes wide. "Really, Parker? Please elaborate. In what areas of Stewart's affairs did he give you *carte blanche* control?"

"Many more than you realize, Mrs. Harrington."

My gaze never wavered as my lips twitched to a grin. "That isn't what I was told. As a matter of fact, I was told your desired activities were constantly monitored." I shrugged. "Then again, one doesn't know whom a woman can trust these days."

"Me. You can trust me. Stewart trusted me." He reached into his briefcase and produced another folder. "I haven't had the chance to show this to you, and Stewart didn't sign it, but he was about to." He opened the document titled: *Last Will and Testament* to a page near the back, and pointed. "Here, Mrs. Harrington, please read this clause, the one under Specific Bequests and Devises."

I looked to where his bony finger pointed:

I, Stewart Allen Harrington, give controlling power over previously verified contract between myself and Victoria Ann Conway, now Victoria Conway Harrington, to the executor of my estate, Parker Craven, until such time as the withholdings upon said contract are complete or agreement is fulfilled.

I nodded. "Yes, that *is* interesting. However, as you stated, Stewart never signed this new will and testament; therefore, it's not valid."

"That is why I gave you the contract. We can fulfill your husband's wishes by completing a new contract, one that is as legally binding as your first."

"You may remember when Stewart and I signed that contract? It was the first time you and I met. You may also have realized that I was woefully uninformed of the true nature and extent of that contract. Nonetheless, I believe you are fully aware that I have followed that contract to the letter. I have fulfilled my obligation. Due to Stewart's untimely death, I am now the sole inheritor of his estate. Tell me, Parker, what incentive do you have to entice me to sign your contract?"

I leaned forward, elbows on the desk, and looked him square in the eye. "In other words, tell me why in the fuck you think I'm that dumb. I can buy and sell you. I can fire your ass and find a new law firm to represent my holdings. Tell me why you think I'd agree to living that hell another day."

Though he seemed slightly put off by my forwardness, Parker didn't miss a beat. "Yes, Victoria, I remember the first time I saw you. I remember many other things."

I maintained my façade though my stomach lurched.

He went on. "I also know about deals that Stewart made. After all, I'm his attorney. Let's specifically talk about this one." He reached down and retrieved another folder. When he opened it, and I saw the document, I knew I didn't need to read it. I knew exactly what it was. Parker watched my expression before he continued, "I'll assume, for the sake of argument, that you recognize this contract, your original contract?"

"Yes."

"Yes, indeed. If I recall, it was the one that Stewart asked you to review only days before his death?"

"It is the one I reviewed only days before my husband's death," I confirmed, changing only a small part of his meaning. Again, he didn't miss what I said.

His eyes flashed knowingly. "I heard a few semantic changes to that agreement." He leaned forward. "If we're to make this work, honesty would be best. Mrs. Harrington, your husband didn't tell you to review the contract, did he?"

"No."

"You weren't with your husband the afternoon in question, as you previously stated. Were you?"

"No, I was not."

His smug confidence grew. "And you know how I know that, don't you?"

"Yes, Parker. If we're going for honesty, I know that you're the pencil dick I spent my afternoon with. I'm honestly surprised that Maura has stayed with you this long."

Crimson blossomed from his neck to his cheeks. "Maybe she hasn't complained because she isn't as experienced as you."

I raised my eyebrows. "It wouldn't take her long to comparison shop. I must say, you can rest assured that your wife is faithful. I mean, all it would take is one other man to show her that she's spent her life with a bargain-basement second, when truly she would be happier with a designer knockoff."

Parker's jaws clenched as the vein in his forehead bulged.

"Again, I'll ask you, Parker, why would I possibly want to sign your contract?"

"Don't act so confident. You have no idea the mess that Stewart left. His dying is your worst nightmare."

"I doubt that. I've already had some pretty bad nightmares."

"Stewart wanted to be perfectly certain of whom he was marrying. He had you thoroughly investigated."

I shook my head. "I was eighteen fucking years old. I'm sure that investigator enjoyed the cakewalk."

Parker sat taller. "No, Victoria, you were nineteen."

Bile bubbled from the depths of my stomach. "I have no idea what you're talking about. I think I know how old I was."

He tapped the desk. "You will sign my contract because if you don't, I'll share that bit of your personal history with interested parties. One interested party will be the US government."

"Excuse me?"

"When you married Stewart Harrington, you claimed to be Victoria Conway, born in May. Whether you know this or not, the birth certificate you produced for your marriage license was false. It was changed, forged. Therefore, if that information were to be made public, you could neither buy nor sell me. Your marriage would be rendered null and void. Stewart's holdings would go into probate. In the meantime, I would be the one, as executor, who would be in control of everything. That would include the foundations, such as the Harrington Society."

A cold sheen of perspiration chilled my skin. *He was bullshitting me and I knew it. I also needed more information.* "That is ridiculous," I proclaimed. "I don't believe you. My birthday is my birthday: it always has been."

Parker leaned back in the chair. "You may think it sounds ridiculous, but I can see it in your eyes. You have at least an inkling that I'm right."

"I'm not fucking signing my life away again on an inkling. I need proof."

Parker scanned me from breast to head. "Very well, I'll get you proof."

"Who else knows about this?"

"Stewart knew."

"Anyone else?"

"Besides your parents, no, not yet," he declared confidently. "The attorney who created the counterfeit birth certificate is no longer alive. The original and a copy of the forged one were found in the bowels of a storage unit. However, don't misjudge me. I will share what I know, and when I do, the US government will be the least of your worries."

I swallowed my disgust. "Parker, I don't believe you. However, I'll give you the chance to show me your proof. If what you say is true, it could undoubtedly have far-reaching implications. What can I do to help you see my side of this?"

His eyes glowed as he stared at my breasts. "I can think of a lot of things. Once you sign that contract, you'll see that I'm much more imaginative than your deceased husband."

"When can you get me the proof?"

"I'll bring it to you tomorrow."

I nodded. "All right, here tomorrow—"

"No, Victoria. What you're experiencing right now is called a power switch. You're no longer the one calling the shots. I personally prefer you blindfolded and mute, but for what I have in mind, it will be more fun if you can see. I think it will help build the anticipation."

I didn't reply.

"See how well behaved you can be." He stood, walked toward me, and caressed my cheek. It took all my self-control to not flinch. "I never expected to receive this opportunity. Ever since I saw you in my office on that fateful morning years ago, I've wanted to be the one to give you the instructions, to be in control of your fucking, your coming, and your going. I know from experience that you've grown in your expertise over the past nine years. I'm confident that in no time at all, this bargain-basement cock can teach you to be more respectful of your friends." He fisted my hair and pulled my head back. "Didn't you enjoy that term: *friends*? Look at me."

I did.

"Stewart liked the term *friends*. I believe you'll learn that respect I mentioned sooner rather than later. If you don't, not all of our visitors will be as friendly."

I waited for the taste of blood as I bit my tongue and listened to his power switch. However, before he could continue, the phone on my desk rang. He didn't release my hair as we stared, hearing the second and then the third ring. Finally, I asked, "May I answer my phone?"

His slimy grin grew, showing his too-white teeth. "You see," he said as he released my hair. "You're a quick learner. Tomorrow, two o'clock, at the warehouse."

I nodded as I picked up the phone, suddenly thankful for whoever was on the other end. "Yes, Kristina?"

"Mrs. Harrington, there's an Officer Shepard on the line. He said it was urgent."

Oh my God. Did they find something out about Stewart's cause of death?

"Put him through," I said cautiously as I turned toward Parker, covered the receiver and said, "It's the police. They said it was urgent."

"Put them on speakerphone."

I gave him a puzzled look.

"Hello, Mrs. Harrington..." The voice came through the handset.

Parker whispered near my ear. "Speakerphone, cunt, I'm your attorney. I need to hear."

I hit the button and said aloud, "Yes, this is Mrs. Harrington."

"Ma'am, I'm so sorry to bother you at this time."

"Yes, it is a difficult—"

"Mrs. Harrington, your mother is on her way to Memorial Hospital. I'm sorry to inform you that she was in a serious automobile accident."

I couldn't process. I'd been thinking about her ever since our conversation yesterday. I'd been meaning to call her, wanting for the first time to call her. This couldn't be happening, I asked, "Excuse me, what did you say?"

Parker spoke, "Officer, this is Parker Craven, Mrs. Harrington's attorney. Can you tell us any more about Mrs. Sound?"

"Sir, Mrs. Sound is on her way to the trauma center at Memorial Hospital. I recommend that Mrs. Harrington go there immediately."

"Thank you, officer. We'll leave immediately," Parker replied.

"Mrs. Harrington, you should know that we did a field sobriety test. Your mother's blood alcohol content was .38 percent. Thankfully, no one else was involved in the accident."

Covering my mouth, I gasped. "No, officer, that isn't possible. My mother is a recovering alcoholic. She hasn't had a drop of alcohol in almost twenty years."

"Ma'am, I'm sorry. She did today. Please get to Memorial."

It wasn't even eleven in the morning. This wasn't right. Why would Marilyn decide to go on a binge early in the morning? She wouldn't. I knew that.

When I didn't respond, Parker did. "She will, sir. Thank you." He leaned over me and disconnected the line. "I'll drive you. Let's go."

"No," I shook my head. "I'll be at the warehouse tomorrow, if I can."

"You will. Unless you're the one in the hospital, you'll be there."

I closed my eyes. "Yes, Parker, I'll be there. Bring your proof." When he narrowed his eyes, I rephrased, "Please bring your proof. Right now I need to get to my mother."

"You're in no condition to drive."

Now he's worried about my condition? *Asshole!* "I won't drive. Travis will drive me."

Parker's jaw clenched. "We'll discuss Mr. Daniel's employment future after tomorrow."

I nodded. He was fucking crazy if he thought this was the way it was going to be. Nonetheless, I could play the role. I'd been taught well.

Though everything within me wanted to run for the door, I sat unmoving, respectful, and complacent, while Parker slowly gathered his things, including the copy of his new contract and placed them in his briefcase. The motherfucker probably never thought I'd made a copy. When he turned to leave, he quipped, "Until tomorrow, Victoria. Best regards to your mother."

Fucker!

My cell phone rang and the screen flashed: VAL.

CHAPTER TWENTY-FOUR

Present

VAL MET me as I rushed from Travis' SUV and ran into the emergency room. The crowd of people didn't register as I looked at my sister's face. She was a doctor; she was supposed to be better at hiding her emotion.

"Oh my God," I said, as sobs erupted from my chest. "Is she dead?"

Val wrapped her arms around me. "No, she's alive, barely." She led me through doors, down hallways, and to an elevator. Next, we walked through more doors and hallways. Finally, we arrived at a small private room with chairs, a fish tank, and too many fake plants. "They know we're here. The nurses will keep us updated as she's in surgery."

On the way to our waiting area, Val explained that our mother had an array of injuries. They'd know more about her internal injuries once all the scans were complete; however, early tests indicated damage to her spinal cord and possible traumatic brain injury. Apparently, she wasn't wearing a seatbelt and flew forward upon impact. The only thing that saved her from going through the windshield was the airbag; however, that caused other problems. Once we sat, I asked the question that had been on my mind since I received the call. "Do you really think she was drinking?"

Val closed her eyes. "I don't want to. I mean, she didn't go back to drinking even when Randall died. Why would she drink now?"

I stood and paced. "She wanted to come to my apartment yesterday. If I would have said yes…"

"Stop that. If Marilyn Sound decided to pick up a bottle of vodka, she and she alone is the person responsible: not you. You've been blamed for too many things in your life. This is not one of them. Don't think that way.

"All I can say," she continued, "is thank God she didn't harm anyone else. As a doctor I see too many innocent people hurt and killed by drunk drivers."

"That's just it," I proclaimed. "I don't think she would do this."

Val looked at me dubiously.

"I know. I'm not the one who usually sticks up for Marilyn. I just don't feel right about this."

"Vik, the sobriety test didn't lie. I didn't want to believe it either, but I could smell it on her. Also, they'll be doing more blood draws here to verify it. We'll know more when they report to us."

My purse vibrated. I looked at my phone. Travis. His text was simple and to the point:

"WHERE THE FUCK ARE YOU?"

I hit the CALL button. "Val, will you explain to Travis where we are? I don't even know. I wasn't paying attention."

She nodded, and as I was about to hand her the phone, his deep voice came through the receiver and echoed through the small room. "Don't fucking tell me you left the hospital?"

Val's eyes widened.

I grinned. "He has a way with words." I spoke into the phone. "We're in some waiting room. Perhaps you could keep your opinions to yourself and speak with Val. She'll explain where we are."

His tone morphed back to the one I'd heard for a decade. "Thank you, Mrs. Harrington, I'd be happy to speak to the good doctor."

Shaking my head with a grin, I handed Val the phone. While she explained our location to Travis, I wondered about the boys. Marcus was at the University of Miami, but what about Lyle? In order for Marilyn's blood alcohol level to be as high as it was, she would have needed to consume a substantial amount. Was she drinking before he left for school?

Val handed me back my phone. On the screen I saw BRODY PHILLIPS. I turned it off and placed it back in my purse. When I turned toward Val, I could tell by the look on her face that she'd read the name. I shrugged. "He's one of the attorneys at Craven and Knowles. It probably has to do with Stewart's will. I'll call him back later." Changing the subject, I spun my large yellow diamond and asked, "Val? How much alcohol would it take to get to a .38 percent? How many drinks?"

She momentarily closed her eyes. "It depends on how quickly she drank and if she'd been eating. But on average a drink is considered one and a half ounces, of hard liquor at least. They said there was a vodka bottle in the car. To reach .38 would probably take at least ten drinks and that would be if she drank them quickly. If she'd been drinking for a longer period of time, it would take more. The body processes about half an ounce an hour."

"Ten! So like fifteen or more ounces of alcohol? A coke can has twelve ounces. You're talking more than that." I shook my head. "For someone who hasn't drunk a drop in over twenty years... don't you find this weird? Has anyone spoken to Lyle? Was she drinking when he left for school?"

"No."

We both turned at the sound of our brother's voice as he, Marcus, and Travis entered the small room. Val and I rushed toward the boys, as Travis explained, "I found these two wandering around downstairs. I thought they should be with you."

"Thank you, Travis."

When Val finally released Lyle from her embrace, we could see his red blotchy face and hear the pain in his voice. "Val, you're a doctor. Why aren't you in there with her? She has to be all right."

My heart broke for our youngest sibling. He'd lost his father. Even I didn't want him to lose his mother. Again, Val embraced Lyle as Marcus reached out and squeezed my hand.

"I can't be in there," Val explained. "They don't allow that. It's too difficult. Doctors need to think with their head and not their heart." She looked Lyle in the eye. "But don't worry. The doctors here are the best. She's in great hands."

"Lyle?" I asked. "What did you mean when you said no?"

"I meant," he said after wiping his eyes with the back of his hand, "she wasn't drinking. She was fine, like normal, when I left."

"What time did you leave?" Travis asked.

"School starts at nine. They just changed it this year. It used to be earlier."

My eyes darted to Travis.

"Mrs. Harrington, may I speak with you?"

"Yes." I turned to the sea of gray and green eyes and said, "I'll be just outside."

Once we were in the hall, Travis and I walked around the corner and found a secluded corner. "What are you thinking?" Travis asked.

"Someone did this to her. Why?"

He started to reach for my hand and stopped. "This is a warning. This was what I was talking about. Those people want your attention."

"They've fucking got it. But who and why?"

"We need to reestablish the communication that Mr. Harrington had."

I looked down and whispered, "At the warehouse?"

Travis' large hand captured mine. "You're shaking."

I didn't fight his touch. It was warm and reassuring.

"I'm cold."

"No, you're not. You're scared and I don't blame you. These are dangerous people. But I've been thinking about this. I think there are two different things happening. I could be wrong, but I don't think that the people at the warehouse, the friends... I don't think they would stoop to these tactics."

I nodded. "All right. Who are the others?"

"Why did you ask me about the Albinis?"

"I heard the name and was curious?"

At first, Travis didn't speak, but his dark eyes narrowed. "Then I suppose it is just a coincidence."

"What?"

"That it was Niccolo Albini who was at Dr. Conway's apartment the other day."

My gray eyes snapped to his. "Tell me why you think the Albinis would want to talk to me, or get my attention."

Travis turned toward a sound in the hall, then reached for my shoulders and shifted so that he was between me and the noise. I watched around his shoulder as two women in scrubs passed by. Once they were gone, he replied, "I've been trying to figure that out since the night at Dr. Conway's. I think it has something to do with the business. Mr. Albini's family had an agreement with Mr. Harrington. Now that you have the ability to make decisions, they want your support."

"They try to kill my mother to get my support?"

Travis shook his head. "I know... it doesn't make sense. We're missing a piece of this puzzle."

"What about Parker?" I asked.

"After what you told me he said, if he produced documents to nullify your marriage, he would be in a position to make those business decisions."

I thought about that for a moment. "How does this all work? I mean, did Stewart pay them?"

"No, they paid him for the cover. They paid him a lot."

"So if Parker proves that my marriage is invalid, he stands to profit?"

"Yes," Travis agreed. "But if he gets you to sign the contract, he can keep people like Keene happy and also convince the Albinis that he's in control of your decisions. My assumption would be that the payoff would never see your bank account. It's really the best-case scenario for him. That way if the shit ever does hit the fan, his hands are clean. You're the one with the business dealings that need to be explained."

I peered again around Travis to see a tall man with dark but graying hair, and dark eyes staring silently in our direction. With his nice black suit and shiny shoes, I knew he was the man who'd been to Val's apartment. "Travis?"

There must have been something in my voice, because immediately Travis followed my line of sight, and spun around. Instantly, he became a wall, standing between me and the rather handsome yet imposing stranger. "Mr. Albini," Travis said with a nod.

Who was this? My uncle? The one who told my mother to have an abortion?

"Mr. Daniels," the tall gentleman replied. "I heard about Mrs. Sound's unfortunate accident. I came to offer my support to Mrs. Harrington."

Support?

"As you can imagine, with the death of her husband and now her mother's accident, Mrs. Harrington is not in the condition—"

I stepped out from behind Travis, extended my hand, and offered Mr. Albini my firmest handshake. "Hello, I'm Mrs. Harrington. I apologize, however, I don't believe we've been introduced."

"Mrs. Harrington," Mr. Albini's voice took on a silky strain. "You are lovely, like your mother."

My neck stiffened. I didn't look like my mother, Val did.

He went on. "My family... we were sorry to hear about your mother's relapse and accident. I hope she will have a full recovery."

"So do I Mr. Albini, as do the rest of her children."

"Mrs. Harrington, I would like to speak to you, in the future. There are things... things I'm not sure your husband explained."

I stood as tall as I could, all the while accepting the strength Travis' presence behind me offered. "My husband was very informative, and I am aware of a few things. Perhaps you can enlighten me to a few more?"

His dark eyes shone. "It would be my pleasure."

"Thank you, Mr. Albini. Please feel free to contact me, or Mr. Daniels, and we'll continue to honor Stewart's obligations."

His lips twitched to a grin. "That is music to my ears. Please, please call me Niccolo. You are a lovely woman. I'm sure your parents are very proud of the woman you've become."

"I can only speak for my mother."

"Your father?" he asked.

"Johnathon Conway has been a missing member of my family for as long as I can remember. Randall Sound was the only real father I knew."

Niccolo nodded. "My condolences, Mrs. Harrington, it seems as though your family has had a string of unfortunate events."

"I really must get back to my siblings."

He extended his hand. "Yes, you do that. We will talk. Let me say, I'm pleased with your promise to continue our arrangement."

After again shaking his hand, I replied, "My husband was known for his good business sense. I see no reason to make any abrupt changes. I do hope that I won't be sidelined by any future unfortunate events."

"Mrs. Harrington, the Albinis help those who help the Albinis. We will talk."

"Yes, Niccolo, we will. Now if you'll excuse me." I nodded and stepped around my uncle.

~

NEITHER TRAVIS nor I discussed the hallway meeting until after my mother was through surgery, recovery, and into a room. It was dark by the time we finally left the hospital. Once we were in his SUV, I checked my messages. There were multiple text messages from Brody. I'd told him about Marilyn and he'd offered to come to the hospital. It was more than I could deal with; instead, I asked him to come over to the penthouse once I got home.

"I need to text Brody to have him come to the apartment."

"Really, Mrs. Harrington, it's late. You've agreed to go to the warehouse tomorrow. Can't you wait until then to get fucked?"

My head spun toward Travis. His jaw was clenched and his knuckles blanched. *What the hell was his deal?*

"It's not what you think," I replied, keeping my voice calm. "I'm going to ask him to write up another contract, one with your name."

"Why? You surprised the shit out of me in the hallway. You keep that hard-assed businesswoman shit up and you don't need Craven or me."

"Not for the Albinis, but I do for Keene and Craven and whoever else wants a piece of me."

"You're willing to put my name on it?"

"I am, but as your employer, it's never happening."

"As the proprietor of the contract..." he began.

"I don't give a fuck. We're going to work this shit out somehow and bring this to an end. The way I see it is that if he forces me to sign his contract, it won't be valid if I'm already under obligation from another contract. I'm just not letting him know that until I get his proof."

"That's fucking genius." Travis lifted his chin and peered momentarily in my direction. "You know, what you did this afternoon... you may have played this perfectly."

"How so?"

"I'm sure that Craven never suspected that you'd have the balls to work directly with Niccolo."

Shaking my head, I tried to sort everything out. "I'm standing by my accusation that someone besides Marilyn is responsible for her accident. I don't think she willingly drank fifteen ounces of alcohol in, what? Less than two hours? According to Lyle there wasn't even any alcohol in their house. That would mean she'd have had to go buy it and basically guzzle it. I don't get it. Why would the Albinis try to kill my mom? If Niccolo is going to walk up to me and talk to me in person, why hurt her?"

Travis shrugged. "It doesn't make sense, other than that he couldn't get a hold of you the other night. You remember, when you were fucking Phillips or he was fucking you."

"Stay on the goddamned subject. Do you think it was them? If not the Albinis then who? Why?"

Travis replied, "I suppose it could be Craven. I didn't think it was his *modus operandi*, but then again, I don't know. Maybe he didn't expect you to cave so fast. Maybe this was his backup plan."

"Did Stewart always work with the Albinis?"

"As long as I've been around." Travis cocked his head to the side. "People talk. The Albinis have been in charge of this area for a long time, but they're not the only family. It wasn't even them who your dear ol' stepfather owed the money to. And each generation there are new names trying for power. Your mother's accident could have been a setup, to make you think it was the Albinis and break off the agreement."

"This fucking sounds like fiction. This shit doesn't really happen, does it?"

"It's your mother in the hospital and your stepfather who drove into the ocean. You tell me if this shit really happens?"

"Whom did you pay the money to? To whom was Randall indebted?"

Travis' expression filled me with a sense of pride. "Your listening skills have improved. You're following along."

"And you're doing a better job of talking in complete fucking sentences. How about you keep it up? If you know who it is, tell me."

"The family's name is Durante."

I blinked as I tried to remember people and faces. "Why does that name sound familiar?"

"Your friend Sheila—it's her maiden name."

I fell back against the seat, a wave of nausea hitting me like a sledgehammer. "Is she involved?"

"No. I can say that with confidence. She knows about her family and its businesses, but she's not involved. I'd suspect that's why she's so engaged with charities like the Harrington Society. It's her way of balancing out what others do. However, her husband is a different story..." Travis' dark eyes left the road and stared toward mine, probing and encouraging me to use my brain and connect the dots.

"Fucking Senator Keene, he's the brother-in-law to a crime family that wants to overtake the Albinis?"

"Yes, Mrs. Harrington, congratulations."

I looked at him with utter bewilderment. "Are you fucking joking?"

"No, I'm dead serious. With your little show of unity with the Albinis, you for the first time officially are the one to fuck Senator Keene. My guess is that he won't be happy when he realizes that he's the one with a dick in his ass."

I tried to remember my mother's confession. "Is Niccolo the top one? I don't even know how to phrase it. The head of the family?" It reminded me of a fucking episode of *The Sopranos*.

"No, he's not. Carlisle is. He's Niccolo's older brother."

"Didn't I read somewhere about firstborn sons and shit, or is that all TV crap?"

Travis shook his head from side to side. "I don't know all the ins and outs. Honestly I think the daughters are revered too. But either way, Carlisle has the oldest son." He gave me a sideways glance. "His only child, named Wesley."

"Really?" I knew Wesley and I were in the same grade, but then again, I was older, wasn't I? If I'd had my real birthday, I'd have been two grades ahead of Val. "Does Niccolo have any sons?"

"Two, but they're younger. I heard a rumor that Carlisle's wife was at one time engaged to Niccolo. I don't know if that's true, but it doesn't matter. If Niccolo offered you the Albini family support, you have it. Fuck! You impressed the shit out of me. Maybe you can use your brains as well as your pussy."

Asshole! Against my better judgment, I grinned. "Thanks, I have other plans, too. First, I need to take care of Parker."

"With your pussy?"

"I don't plan on it."

Travis' forehead furrowed. "Interesting, Mrs. Harrington. By the way, it's *we*, not *I*."

"We what?"

"You're not going to the warehouse alone."

I sighed, honestly thankful for his presence. "Parker insinuated that he would demand that I fire you after I signed his contract. I don't think he likes you very much."

Travis shrugged. "Well, you did fire me a few days ago. So I don't give a fuck what he likes and what he doesn't like. You don't like me either. I'm still here."

I looked out the passenger window. The morning storms had cleared and the familiar blue of day had turned to the black of night. As cars and buildings passed, I thought about the view. "How come I never rode up front before?"

"I think the better question is why are you doing it now?"

"I don't know. I like it." I tilted my head toward the backseat. "It's lonely back there."

"You like it?"

"Yes, I do. I can see better up here, better than I can in the back."

Travis nodded.

"And maybe," I confessed, "you're not as big of an asshole as I previously thought."

"The sentiment is mutual, Mrs. Harrington."

I rested my head against the seat and watched as glimpses of ocean shone between the buildings. The moon was full over the water, creating reflections like millions of small mirrors bouncing the silver rays back toward the sky. As we neared the apartment, I tried to make sense of everything, but nothing made sense.

According to my mother, if the Durantes could prove that I—her and Carlisle's daughter—was alive, they could use that as proof that the Albinis lied, that Wesley wasn't Carlisle's first born. Stewart knew all of this. Had he helped to propagate the idea that I was a Conway to both families? After all, one would assume that even in a male-dominated world, a daughter of the Albinis, the strongest family around, wouldn't be shared, and certainly not openly, by the man who provided one of their biggest covers.

I couldn't think straight. Fucking forget asking me my name. I truly didn't know.

CHAPTER TWENTY-FIVE

Present

"ARE YOU FUCKING CRAZY?" Brody asked, running his hand through his strawberry blonde hair and walking the length of Stewart's office.

When he stopped near the window, I saw his reflection against the night sky. On his face I watched the bewilderment I heard in his words. Instead of answering his question, I leaned back against the chair and let him digest all that I'd said. It wasn't even the tip of my iceberg, but since I'd spent most of the day at the hospital, I didn't have the strength or the time to explain all that had happened since we'd last been together.

"Let me get this straight: you want me to construct a contract, like the one Parker wrote, but instead of Parker's name, you want Travis Daniels? Vik, that doesn't make any sense." He spun toward me, his aquamarine eyes boring a hole into my soul. "If you're going to trust someone, if you truly feel this is necessary, trust me."

"I can't, Brody. You don't know what this is like."

"Fuck! And Travis does?"

I stood and walked toward him, stopping just outside of his reach. "I don't want you to see it."

"I've read the damn contract. I know it involves other men. You've told me the basics. I don't care." When I looked down, Brody came closer and lifted my chin. "Vik, what I mean is that none of that matters to me. Don't you get it? You're more than the person who signed that contract. I know it. You do *not* need to go back to that. I don't care what Parker has that you consider a threat. I don't care how many other men want to get you back there." He pulled me close and wrapped his strong arms around my shoulders. With the steady beat of his heart and fresh clean-scented aftershave, I allowed myself a momentary reprieve and melted against his chest. "Don't you trust me?"

I nodded. I did trust him, but I couldn't expose him to that side of me. It was one thing for him to think he knew. It was another for him to see it.

Brody pushed me back by my shoulders and looked deep into my eyes. "Vik, does this mean..." Once again, he turned away. "Fuck. Tell me this doesn't mean that Parker is one of those men." His volume rose. "Fucking tell me that Parker Craven wants this contract to help you, not because he's been one of the men Stewart watched fuck you."

My chest ached. Brody thought he could handle the contract. He can't even handle a small part of the truth. I shook my head and sat on the sofa.

With his hands once again going through his hair, Brody stomped from one side of the room to the other. When he was almost back to the windows he turned and said, "I want to kill him. Just let me kill him. Fuck, I'll kill them all. Do you know the others?"

"Brody, you're not killing anyone. I have a plan. Part of my plan is to have the contract with Travis. If I do, the one I sign with Parker will not be valid."

"But Vik..." He came to the sofa and sat facing me. "...don't you get it? If you sign one with Travis, he has the same control over you that Stewart did."

"No, he won't. Travis works for me. He can't make me do anything."

"Then why? Why have the contract?"

"Please, Brody. It's getting later by the minute. I'm tired. It's been a long fucking day. I'd do it myself and use the contract that Parker wrote and just change the names, but Parker will be able to tell if it's not exactly the way it needs to be. I need it to be perfect and legal."

"None of this is fucking legal. And no."

"No?"

"Vik, you're not answering me. I won't do this. I can't do this—not to you, not after everything Stewart did to you. You deserve better. What are you afraid of? Who are you afraid of? Tell me." He stood again and paced. "I'm a fucking attorney. If you believe in Travis so damned much, keep him around. I don't care. The man is as big as a fucking mountain. No one is coming near you with him by your side. For fuck's sake, do not go alone to the warehouse with Parker." He spun, unable to find the room to expel the energy coursing through his system. "I fucking swear, if he lays another goddamned finger on you."

"Brody, stop. I promise my days of being anyone's victim are done. I've already made my presence known in a world I didn't even know existed. I'm tougher than any of them thought. I've been underestimated for the last time."

He collapsed to his knees in front of me. "Then let me write the contract with my name on it?"

I shook my head. "No. If you do that, Parker will know that you're helping me. He might even suspect that we've been working together for a while. I can't do that to you. You could lose your partnership." I reached out and brushed my fingers against his cheek, relishing the sensation of the soft, stubbly growth. "I'm not worth it."

Brody seized my face between his large palms. "Don't you ever say that! You are fucking worth it! You're smart, fucking beautiful, and…" His smile grew. "…never to be underestimated. You are so worth it. Damn, Vik, I'd walk away from Craven and Knowles in two seconds to go away with you and get you out of here, away from all these fuckers."

I sighed, enjoying the warmth of his hands. "Where?"

The aquamarine clouded. "Where what?"

"Where would you take me?" With all the shit I'd had thrown at me, a momentary daydream seemed like the perfect medicine to calm my overwrought nerves.

He released my face and nuzzled his cheek against mine. Again the clean scent filled my senses and brought a welcome smile to my lips. Taking my hand, Brody stood and repositioned me. Next, he settled on the sofa behind me. Sighing, I laid my head back against his chest and listened as his words vibrated through me. "Sweetheart, I'd take you anywhere you wanted to go. How about our own tropical island?"

I'd read a story once where the couple went away to a tropical island. It was hot—both kinds of hot. I was tired of heat, though. After living my entire life in Florida I dreamt of cool. I shook my head from side to side.

Brody continued, "All right, no island. How about the mountains?"

That sounded cool. I nodded.

"Wherever I take you, I want it to be remote, so it's just us."

"I like that idea." I listened to my own voice. It sounded foreign. In it, I heard hope, hope that I'd never before heard or never allowed myself to project.

"Then that's where I'll take you. We'll go somewhere in the mountains, somewhere secluded. We'll have a house on a lake. I've always liked lakes. Have you been around lakes?"

"No, just the ocean."

"Lakes, especially lakes like our lake, are clear and clean. We can skinny-dip in there whenever we want."

I giggled at the thought. "Will it be cold?"

His lips found my neck. I craned my head to the side, allowing him full access. "Don't worry, beautiful, I'll keep that sexy body of yours warm." His warm breath bathed my collarbone. "I can see you now: dripping wet as we come out of that lake, a cool breeze against your fucking soft skin. It makes your dark pink nipples pebble. God, I like that." From the growth of his erection against my back, I knew he did. "We have a blanket, a big fucking blanket. It's laid out on the grass and the mountains... they surround the lake on all sides. Even though it's summer..." He nuzzled my neck again and whispered, "...there's snow on the peaks."

"Snow?" I'd only seen snow when Stewart and I traveled. I'd never really experienced it.

"Yes, baby, snow. Even in the summer there's snow on the peaks of the mountains. In the winter there's so much snow we can't go anywhere. All we can do is spend our days and nights making love by the fireplace, with a big roaring fire. In the summer, we can go up to those peaks and ski, but I like having you on that blanket."

"Do we have neighbors? Is anyone watching?"

"No, no one's watching. No more watching. It's just you and me. You're on your back. Those hard nipples are staring up at me from those fucking luscious tits. As I look down at you, I see your silky hair fanned out behind your gorgeous face and notice that your pussy is wet, but not from the lake. No, you're wet and ready for me."

I closed my eyes and imagined the scene he painted. "Brody, what do we do on that blanket?"

His erection twitched, and I wiggled against it.

"Oh, fuck, Vik. We're going to fuck like rabbits in heat."

I laughed. "Do rabbits go in heat?"

"They do, and when they do, they fuck all day and all night. I mean, it's quite an incredible display. You see..." His hand brushed over my stomach and down to my thighs. "...they only stop to eat. They need their energy..." His rapid heartbeat pounded against my back. "...because each time they fuck and the male rabbit's cock fits perfectly inside the female rabbit's tight pussy, they both find the best fucking release they've ever had."

My breathing quickened as my insides clenched. "Do they come even harder than on a wall at some cheap hotel? Because, let me tell you, if they do, they're fucking lucky. It was the best orgasm I've ever had."

"Ever?" he asked.

"Ever," I repeat. "That doesn't mean I doubt those little rabbits. They might know something I don't."

"Did you know the female rabbit screams when she comes?"

"She does? How does the male rabbit feel about that?"

"He fucking loves it. He loves to hear her scream. He loves hearing all the sounds she makes."

"Does the male rabbit make sounds?"

Gently pulling my lips to his, Brody answered my question with a moan and a kiss: a hot, long kiss. A kiss that twisted my insides as my face tilted back toward his and my ass ground against his cock. When his tongue probed, I willingly opened, giving him entrance, feeling his warmth, and tasting his sweetness.

I'd forgotten how much I enjoyed kissing. It wasn't the same as fucking. Kissing was passionate and deep. For it to truly be a kiss, the kind that reached from your lips to your core, there had to be a give and a take. It was something that never happened at the warehouse, well, with anyone except Stewart. And even then it felt more like a take than a give. Brody's kiss didn't only take: it gave me strength and power. I told myself that I'd remember it tomorrow at the warehouse. I'd hold onto it and hide it. That was my thought as I pulled away from his warm embrace.

"God, Brody, I can't do any more than this tonight. And if we keep this up, we will."

The gleam in his uniquely hued eyes disappeared. "You still want me to write that contract?"

"I do."

"And you still want Travis Daniel's name on it?"

I nodded.

Brody reached for my hand. "I'll find that lake, Vik. When I do, it will only be you and me. No fucking Travis, no Parker, no one but you and me and that big-assed blanket."

Smiling, I tilted my head to the side. "Thank you. Thank you for writing the contract. The lake sounds truly magical, but there's something else I want to have there."

"What?"

"The rabbits, because I think they sound fucking hot."

"Oh, they are, beautiful, they are."

～

LEAVING THE HOSPITAL I SIGHED. Even though it was halfway through October, the summer heat was back. I dreamed of the damn lake and the fucking snow. As I placed the dark glasses over my eyes, I imagined the snow-covered mountains and a smile floated across my face.

I thought about my mother. Thankfully, she was improving. She still hadn't awakened, but Val explained that it was the way they wanted it. She needed rest and the swelling in her brain needed time to decrease.

As I got into my car, I looked in the backseat at the present I'd gotten for Parker. From what Travis said, Parker and Stewart had argued about Parker's desires at the warehouse. I fucking hated to hear Travis talk about it, like he was describing a damn TV show, but the information was helpful. I was confident Parker would like my gift.

As I drove toward the warehouse, my mind spun in so many different directions. My mother had a housekeeper who promised to be there for Lyle. I thought about bringing him to my place, but his school was closer to his house. Besides, I had a few other things to deal with. Though Marcus was at the university, he said that he'd pick Lyle up each day and bring him to the hospital. Lyle had his permit, but he couldn't drive alone. I looked at the clock and hoped that my time at the warehouse would go fast. I wanted to make it back to the hospital when the boys arrived.

With so many swirling thoughts, it wasn't until I arrived at the warehouse, parked my car in my usual spot, and turned off the engine that the reality struck. When it did, it hit me like a fucking anvil, like one of the ones in those old cartoons, immobilizing me. While my mind spun, my body sat motionless. With each passing minute my skin grew moister from the growing heat. My brain told me to open the door and get out, but my body was paralyzed. It wasn't until my phone rang that I was even aware of the passing of time. I looked at the screen: TRAVIS.

Taking a deep breath, I swiped the screen and said, "Hello." I knew my voice sounded weak and when I glanced in the rearview mirror I saw my pale complexion.

"Mrs. Harrington, where are you?"

It was much kinder than his normal *where the fuck are you?* greeting that I was used to receiving. "I'm in my car."

"The GPS said your car has been here for nearly ten minutes. It's after one-thirty. Don't you want to be inside before he arrives?"

Tears threatened my eyes. "Are you here? I don't see your car."

Travis chuckled. "Have you ever seen my car here?"

I shook my head from side to side. "No, I guess I haven't."

"But I've been here, and I'm here now. Do you want to change your mind?"

"No, I can't change my mind. I have to do this."

"You know his threat is bullshit. You didn't know about your birthdate. He can't take away your marriage. Mr. Harrington made sure it was all legal."

"I know," I exhaled. "But Parker thinks I believe his shit. I have to make him keep believing."

"Mrs. Harrington, you're not alone. I don't give a damn about his plans or even yours. I promise if I think things get out of hand, I'll make my presence known."

"Victoria," I whispered.

"Excuse me?"

"You're about to watch me get fucked—maybe—if I can't convince Parker otherwise, so fucking call me Victoria. You've been watching for years, and the Mrs. Harrington thing is getting on my nerves."

Travis laughed, really laughed, and said, "Certainly, Victoria, if the way I address you is the one thing that's on your nerves with this whole situation, by all means, I'll call you Victoria. By the way, you may call me Travis."

My lips quirked to a halfhearted smile. "Thank you, Travis, I think I will. Mr. Daniels seems formal, considering the circumstances."

"Don't forget, I'm here. I can be downstairs in seventeen seconds flat, faster if I just jump the banister."

"I'll remember." I took a deep breath. "I'm coming in."

"Do you want to hang up or do you want to talk to me as you come in?"

Getting out of the car, I grabbed the package from the backseat as I held the phone between my shoulder and ear. "You know, I didn't think I'd ever be back here. I really thought once he was dead…"

"What did you plan to do with this place?"

Entering, I looked around at the tall brick walls and began to descend the stairs. "Do you think it would burn?"

"Not well," Travis replied. "Too little wood."

"Speaking of *little wood*… can your cameras see outside? Will you know when Parker is here?"

Travis chuckled again. "It's nice to hear your humor. No, I can't see outside, but I'll know when he pushes the code on the door."

I made my way to the bottom of the stairs and flipped on the lights over the bed. "How does he know the code?"

"They all have their own code. It was Mr. Harrington's idea. He also didn't want to leave you alone downstairs to open the door."

I didn't want to think about Stewart remaining in his chair to protect me—I couldn't. "What can you see with your cameras?"

"Everything. Not just the bed area—I can see the entire interior. Part of my job was to be sure that the friends or Mr. Harrington weren't interrupted."

"But no one other than Stewart, not even Parker, knew that you were here?"

"I never had to make my presence known."

I looked around and sighed. "I guess that was a good thing."

"Yes, Mrs.... I mean, Victoria, it was a good thing. Someone is entering the code. Remember, you're not alone."

I ended the call and nodded toward the ceiling, not knowing exactly where the cameras were located. I placed my gift for Parker in Stewart's chair. It was a long silver box with a big white bow. It might have been overkill, but if he fell for it, I would be showing the *new owner* of my contract how compliant I could be.

"Victoria," Parker's voice billowed throughout the cavernous room as he reached the bottom step.

I turned toward him, my eyes open wide.

"My, my, I'm not used to seeing you here fully dressed."

"I'm not used to seeing you here at all," I replied.

He came closer and brushed his fingers against my cheek. I fought the revulsion growing within as I remained statuesque. His voice was thick with anticipation. "I believe before we leave here today, we'll need to revisit some of those fond memories. You do know where the blindfold is, don't you?"

"My proof, Parker. I need to see this birth certificate you talked about."

He slowly walked around me, scanning me from my Christian Louboutin heels to the scooped neckline on my Versace peasant-styled blouse. His voice continued to echo against the brick wall. "It will be a rude awakening for you, Victoria, to lose all that money and all the possessions that my dear friend was so willing to give to you." Parker's cold finger traced a path along my collar, tugging my blouse sleeve off my shoulder onto my arm. "No bra strap." His eyes widened. "That's a good girl. Perhaps that will earn you some leniency during our hours of education."

"Parker, please, show me the proof."

Pulling the other shoulder of my blouse he stood back and assessed. "I have friends, lots of friends. If you decide to fight me on this contract and force me to make your real birthdate public knowledge, I just want you to know that they're interested in your expertise." He looked down at my shoes again. "It's not like you'll be able to afford shoes like those, but you'll be able to survive. I've steered many cunts like you their direction. I already know that they're particularly interested in you." His forehead furrowed. "You have a famous pussy. The friends are calling me already."

Silently, I remained still as he pulled my blouse down, exposing my breasts. "You're being very compliant. I was hoping for a little more fight." He pinched one of my nipples. "I must admit to enjoying a little fight."

Oh, asshole, I can fucking fight. "Please, Parker, let me see what you have. I know what's at stake."

Parker placed his briefcase on the bed and opened it wide. I gasped at the contents. There were papers, but there were also sex toys, the most noticeable was a whip, coiled into a circle.

"Do you like what you see?" he asked with a slimy, toothy grin.

I momentarily closed my eyes and gathered my strength. When I opened them, I stood taller, reassured myself that I wasn't alone, and reached for my blouse. Before Parker could say a word, I pulled it over my head, reached for the zipper of my skirt, and allowed it to fall to the floor. Standing in only a black thong and heels, I smiled my best smile, and said, "I do. I like all that I see." I took a step toward him and ran the tips of my fingers over his shoulders. "I wasn't sure what your plans would be for today, but I have to tell you that so far your bad-boy routine is making me all hot and bothered." I reached for my breasts and twisted my nipples. "But I guess that's obvious."

Parker reached for my hair but before he could grab a hold, I took a step backward and shook my head. "Parker, Parker, show me your proof and I'm all yours. You don't need to be rough… unless that's what you like."

He mumbled something under his breath about bitches and

playing him as he rummaged through his briefcase. Finally, he pulled out a familiar-looking folder.

As he began to hand it to me, I shook my head again and allowed my long, dark hair to sway over my back. "The one thing this warehouse lacks is…" *Wood.* "…a solid desk to review contracts. You know, your good friend Stewart liked doing it on his desk. Do you like that?"

"You're not fucking playing me. I've got your goddamn proof," he said, as he followed me toward the kitchen, in the far corner of the warehouse. I didn't know how much the friends saw of the building. I only knew that this area wasn't visible from the bed.

I reached for a robe that was draped over one of the bar stools and wrapped it around me. "Here." I patted the stool beside me as I sat. "First, let me see your papers."

Never taking his eyes off of me, Parker sat and opened the folder. Turning his smug expression on me, he pointed to a Connecticut State birth certificate. "Victoria, you were born on October ninth. This little illegal change has far-reaching implications, as you yourself said." Next, he held up a copy of the forged birth certificate. "You lied."

Reaching for the birth certificate, my chin fell to my chest and my fingers went numb. Even though I knew it was true, seeing it in print ripped something out of me. I ran my fingers over the seal. It was me, and it wasn't me. The implications meant that everything I'd always known about myself was a lie. I wasn't really a Conway. My identity was gone.

I bit my bottom lip to stop the trembling as Parker roughly seized my chin and pulled my eyes to his. "What do you have to say?"

I willed a tear to fall as I tried to shake my head while in his grasp. "It's true. How can this be? Why didn't Stewart tell me? Why didn't my mother tell me?"

"It doesn't fucking matter how it's true. It is. And I have no fucking idea why they didn't tell you." Leafing through the papers, he located the contract and placed it on top of the birth certificates, and reaching into the breast pocket of his coat, he handed me a pen. "Sign."

With sobs resonating from my chest, I did. I signed in each of the places I'd done last night. The only difference with Travis' contract was the clause that now made it impossible for me to sign anything without him as a co-signer. Each time that Parker pointed and I penned Victoria Harrington, it was a lie. It was my plan B. I prayed I would never need it.

When the final page was signed, Parker picked up the pages and put them back into the folder. Leaning back in the chair, Parker sighed. "Victoria, I'll enjoy having you as my pet."

My skin crawled at the thought.

I stood and dramatically swallowed. "I didn't know what would happen. I'd hoped…" I took a deep breath. "…but that doesn't matter anymore. I brought you something, something to show you that I can behave. I can be respectful." I looked down. "It's something… well, from what I saw in your briefcase, I think you'll enjoy."

Parker's brow rose. "You have me intrigued. What did you bring me?"

I reached for his clammy hand and led him back to the chair by the bed. Lifting the box, I said, "Please have a seat. I guess this is your chair now."

As Parker sat, I removed my robe and knelt at his feet. Demurely, I handed him the silver gift. Without a word, Parker removed the bow and opened the box. Moving the tissue paper, he eyed the black leather fingerless gloves, like those worn by weightlifters, and the long sleek riding crop. His eyes opened wide.

"Stewart enjoyed this. I thought you might too." I turned toward his briefcase and the whip. "I know what you brought, and the choice is yours, but I'd like to work my way up to that. I've never…" I let my words trail away as my face fell forward and I willed more tears.

"Fuck!" Parker said as he eyed my gift. "Stewart was into this shit?"

I nodded. "Yes, are you surprised?"

"Fuck, no—yeah. I didn't realize he was such a selfish bastard."

I wiggled my ass against my heels. "He called it our special time."

Parker looked back into the box at the gloves. "Why—"

Before he could finish I offered, "Sometimes Stewart would really get into it. He said the gloves helped his hands with the leather handle. You don't have to wear them. It's up to you."

The slimy, toothy smile returned. "No, I like them." He motioned toward the bed. "I fucking want to give this a try."

I nodded. "May I go to the bathroom and prepare myself for you?"

"Yeah. Don't take too long."

I could see his pencil dick protruding under his slacks. "Do you want me to help you with your clothes?"

"No, go and hurry."

Slowly, I stood and walked toward the bathroom. Just before closing the door, I turned to see Parker unbuttoning his shirt and removing his slacks. Once inside, I sat on the edge of the shower and tried to regulate my breathing. I had no idea how long it would take for the Cytoxan inside of the gloves to penetrate his skin. By leaving the package in the car, the heat coming through the windows caused the powder to be absorbed into the porous leather. I knew to make it most effective I needed his hands to sweat. Though I hated what I was about to do, I knew it was my best option. After a few minutes, I braced myself, took a deep breath, and I made my way back out to the bed.

Seeing him standing in his boxers, socks, and shoes, I wished for the blindfold: this was an image I'd never be able to erase. Even with the leather gloves and riding crop he looked less like a Dominant and more like a pencil dick. I looked at the bed and noticed the satin restraints at the same time that Parker turned toward me.

I weighed each word, reminding myself that I needed his hands to sweat. I also knew the most important part of my plan: he couldn't touch me. Even though the drug was on the inside of the gloves, there was no guarantee it wouldn't leach through the leather. Making my presence known, I said, "Parker, I know this is your show. Believe me, I know how that works. But if you want me to, I'll tell you what Stewart used to do."

When he didn't respond, I picked up the thick satin ribbon and ran it through my fingers. "Stewart always said that the strongest restraints were in my mind. He said he could tie me, but that didn't teach me to obey. By not tying my hands or feet, I had to maintain his positions even when it was difficult. He said that physical restraints were too easy on me." I raised my brow. "Didn't you ever notice that I was never tied?"

Parker nodded. "Maybe Stewart was better at this than I thought."

I went on. "He would tell me what to do." I leaned over the bed, pressed my breasts into the soft cover, stretched my arms above my head, and keeping my ass in the air, spread my legs. "This was one of his favorite positions."

Parker walked closer and ran the tip of the crop between my shoulder blades and down my back.

I moaned. "Oh, God, Parker. I don't want to tell you other things that Stewart liked to do. Please don't make me say it."

The crop came down hard on my ass. I yelled, "Fuck!"

"Tell me. Tell me what you don't want to say."

I shook my head from side to side.

The crop came down again with a crack. "You'll do as I say the first time." Another crack. "Don't fucking make me repeat myself." The crop landed again. "Nod if you understand."

Motherfucker! I nodded, and hurriedly said, "Stewart liked to tease me. He'd get me all hot and make me wait. He wouldn't touch me, even when I begged." I turned toward Parker, with real tears in my eyes, praying that he was really this dumb, and begged, "Please don't tease me. I never thought I'd be back here but now that I am, I'm so fucking horny. I want you inside of me."

Another strike. I felt the welts mushrooming on my skin as I fought to maintain my position. "My pencil dick?" Parker taunted. "You want my pencil dick inside of you?"

Crack. My ass was on fire.

"Yes, please, Parker. Please, I'm sorry I said that."

Another crack and then another. As the crop teased my inner thigh, my cell phone rang out, penetrating our bubble.

I stood, my ass screaming, and raised my hands. "Parker, I'm sorry. I know the rules, but it could be about my mom. Please let me see if this is the hospital."

I glanced at the screen: TRAVIS.

Sweeping my finger, I watched Parker's eyes as I spoke into the phone, "Hello, this is Mrs. Harrington."

The voice in my ear spoke low. "If that motherfucker hits you again, I'm going to jump the fucking banister and kill him with my bare hands."

I let my head drop to my chest and turned away from Parker. "Oh, no! When did it happen?"

"I took care of the paperwork. Good job on the distraction, Victoria."

Our plan had been to have Parker leave the birth certificates and contract in the kitchen and while I had Parker's attention, Travis would steal the birth certificates and replace the contract with a new generic Dom/sub contract. If our plan worked, we didn't want anyone going through his papers and finding something with my name.

I nodded. "Of course, I'll be there as soon as possible."

"Make sure he doesn't touch you," Travis cautioned as I ended the call.

I turned back to Pencil-Dick. "Oh, Parker, I'm sorry, but that was the hospital and it's my mother. Something happened and they want all of us there. I can't let Val and the boys do this alone."

I watched the indecision in his eyes. Finally, he grunted, "Fine. We have forever to play my games."

I sure as hell hope not!

While one gloved hand rubbed his little wood through his boxers, he added, "And some of Stewart's games, too. Next time, you will tell me more."

"I will," I reassured as I grabbed my things and ran toward the bathroom. Once inside, I washed my hands for what seemed like forever. If I'd gotten any of the Cytoxan on them, it wouldn't help. Nevertheless, it made me feel better.

Fully dressed, I reentered the large room and watched as Parker rubbed his hands together.

Securing my phone and my purse, I asked, "Is everything all right?"

"Yeah, I liked the gloves. I think I'll use those again."

Not if the Cytoxan works like it's supposed to. "Leave them here if you want. We'll use them next time." I lifted my brows up and down. "Unless you think Maura would like them."

Parker scowled in my direction and growled, "*We'll* use them again. Don't ever mention—"

Walking briskly away from him and toward the stairs, I called back over my shoulder, "I'm sorry, Parker, but I really need to run along. Until next time." I opened my eyes wide. "Lock up, won't you?" Without waiting for his answer, I squared my shoulders and walked up the stairs and out the door.

I was fucking done with this place. Let it burn or crumble. I didn't give a rat's ass!

CHAPTER TWENTY-SIX

Present

"Travis?" I spoke through the Bluetooth of my car.

"Excellent job, Victoria. Are you all right?"

A tight-lipped smile graced my lips. *Was it the sound of his concern or hearing him use my first name?* "Thank you. Well, my ass hurts like hell, but if it's one of the last things that motherfucker ever does, it's worth it."

"Tell me that he didn't touch you with those gloves."

"He didn't. Please tell me he hadn't touched the bed with the gloves."

"He hadn't," Travis confirmed. "I watched him like a hawk. He put the gloves on after he was undressed. After you left, he jacked off. The gloves were off, but one can only hope…"

"Jeez," I said, scrunching my nose and fighting the mental image. "I thought seeing him in his boxers, shoes, and socks was bad. You're going to need to scrub your eyeballs after watching the pencil dick get off."

Travis laughed. "I've seen worse. I just kept thinking, that's it, buddy, rub that shit in."

"Now all we can do is wait. If it works like Val said, it should happen fast."

"Where are you going?" Travis asked. "I don't like you being out alone. This isn't done."

I blinked my eyes, working to stay focused on the traffic in front of me. "I'm headed back to the hospital. The boys should be there soon. I want to check on my mother."

"I should clean this place up, but now that Craven left, I think I'll leave it and meet you at the hospital."

I agreed, "Fucking leave it and light a match on your way out. I'm done with that hellhole."

"Oh, not so fast, I seem to remember a contract..."

If I hadn't heard the hint of sarcasm in his voice, I would've crashed the damn car. "No fucking way!" I interrupted. "That will only see the light of day if Pencil-Dick lives to argue the contract he can't find."

"Victoria," Travis' tone was back to business. "I'll see you at Memorial."

"Yes," I said, as I nodded and hit the END CALL button on my steering wheel. Seconds later, my cell phone rang. The screen on the dashboard flashed: BRODY PHILLIPS. I hit the CALL button.

"Hello, Brody."

"Jesus, Vik, I can't think about anything else. Are you all right? What happened?"

I bit my bottom lip. I couldn't let him know... know what I was, what I'd done again...

I worked to lighten my tone. "He didn't show."

"What?" Brody asked, obviously confused.

"Parker didn't show. He told me to be there at two. I was. I waited until a few minutes ago. I don't know what this all means with the whole contract thing. I don't know what happened."

"So he didn't touch you?"

"Brody," I said, slowing my words. "Parker didn't show up to the warehouse. I didn't see him. He didn't touch me."

"Oh, thank God!" he exclaimed. "But now, now you've got that fucking contract with Travis."

"Don't worry about it. Nothing will happen with that."

"Don't worry about it? I'm fucking beside myself. I haven't slept. I need you. I need to see that you're all right."

I thought about my ass. There was no way I could see Brody, not the way he wanted to see me, not for a day or two. "I'm fine. I'm on my way to the hospital to see my mom. Hey?" I had an idea. "You could come to the hospital. I mean, she's been accused of driving while intoxicated. She needs an attorney. Come by to start representing her."

"Vik, her blood alcohol level was almost four times—"

"I didn't say you'd win, but maybe you can help her. Brody, I know it doesn't make sense, but I don't think she did this."

"You think someone poured the booze down her throat and put her in a car?" He didn't try to hide his sarcasm.

I sat taller. "I do."

"Vik, I'm not a miracle worker."

"Fine," my words were clipped. "If you don't want to represent her, I'll call Parker."

"No fucking way. I'll do it. I'll see you there."

I grinned. He was so easy to sway. "And when you do, you'll see that I'm fine."

"Oh, you're *fine* all right. But a few glimpses of you at the hospital won't do it for me. I spent half the night worried sick and the other half thinking about fucking rabbits. I need you alone."

A laugh escaped my throat. How could I be laughing after what I'd just done? Maybe it was because as I eliminated these assholes one by one, my dream of a normal life in the mountains seemed suddenly obtainable.

"See you at the hospital," I said as I ended the call.

~

ARRIVING BEFORE MY BROTHERS, Val met me in the hallway outside of our mother's room. "She's waking up," my sister said.

I nodded, knowing that by the look on my sister's face, there was more.

"She isn't speaking coherently, which isn't unusual. However, it's what she is saying that has me concerned."

"Why? If it isn't coherent?"

Val leaned closer. "She keeps saying no and begging someone to stop. Then she starts to cry. Vik, I asked them to give her a tranquilizer. They did. In a minute or two she won't be talking at all. I

261

didn't want Marcus and Lyle to see her like that."

"Isn't it good that she's talking?"

"It is," Val agreed. "I just kept thinking about what you said. Maybe she didn't do this herself. Who would? Who would do this to our mother?"

I straightened my neck and inhaled. Looking each way down the hall, I saw no one except the nurses at the large circular station, too far down to hear. "I don't know, Val. I really don't. And I know I've never been a Marilyn cheerleader. Hell, I've been the exact opposite—Stewart could have attested to that—but I don't think she'd suddenly throw away almost twenty years of sobriety. She was too proud of what she'd accomplished."

Val nodded as we both turned down the hall toward the sound of our brothers' voices. She squeezed my hand and whispered. "Let me go back in and make sure she's calm. I'll come out and get you."

I nodded as she disappeared behind the door and Marcus and Lyle flanked my sides. Plastering on my signature smile, I turned and wrapped my arms around each of their shoulders. They were both so tall that I had to reach up. My little brothers were men. "Hi, I'm glad I made it here for your visit. Val said…"

It wasn't long after the boys and I were allowed in Mom's room that Travis knocked and entered. "Mrs. Harrington, I wanted to let you know that I'm right outside."

"Thank you, Travis." It surprised me how the tension eased from my shoulders at the sound of his voice. Nothing had happened since I'd left the warehouse to raise my suspicions; nevertheless, with Parker's promise of friends and the whole Albini-Durante world all happening outside of my bubble, having Travis near eased some of my anxiety. It wasn't until later, after the boys had left, that my phone rang.

"Hello?"

"Mrs. Harrington, this is Trish from Craven and Knowles."

I looked at my watch: nearly six. Questions came faster than answers. Where had the day gone? Why hadn't I heard from Brody? And what had they done to get this stupid woman to work past five? The only answer that came to me was the one to my last question: perhaps she was too busy under someone's desk to realize the time.

Suppressing the smile from my voice, I answered, "Yes, Trish."

"Ma'am, I'm sorry to bother you. Mr. Craven would like you to come to the office right away."

I glanced at my sleeping mother. "Trish, I'm currently in the hospital with my mother. This is not a good time. Mr. Craven will need to wait."

"Ma'am, he said it's urgent. He said it's about your husband's will."

Fucking asshole! My shoulders once again went rigid as my spine grew taller. *What the fuck was his deal?* After exhaling, I conceded, "Fine, tell Mr. Craven I'm on my way."

"Yes, Mrs. Harrington. And..."

I waited; finally, making no attempt to hide the irritation in my voice, I asked, "And what, Trish?"

"I don't think Mr. Craven is feeling well. If you could hurry—please."

I couldn't have suppressed the smile if I'd wanted. "Perhaps he'd like to reschedule."

"No, I asked him and he said this was urgent."

"I'm on my way."

Gathering my things, Travis and I started down the long corridor toward the elevator. We were almost there when I noticed two men standing to the side of the hallway talking. As soon as the younger one turned, I felt the rush of *déjà vu*. He was someone who I knew, or had known. My mind searched as I unsuccessfully tried to look away. When he turned, our eyes met. Immediately, I knew that I was seeing my brother. The ramification made my stomach twist. I no longer saw the handsome young man I'd dated. There was so much more.

"Victoria?" Wesley's voice echoed through the hallway, deeper than I remembered. As I scanned him up and down, I assessed that he too had indeed matured from a boy to a man. His dark hair was now tamed and trimmed, and his shoulders were broader. He'd grown up well, and even more handsome than I remembered. I had the sensation of looking at Marcus and Lyle as I've seen them over the years. There was nothing remotely sexual about my feelings toward this man. The fact that I'd ever had those types of feelings made me slightly nauseous.

Travis and I both stopped walking at the sound of my name. As I kept my expression in check, I innocently replied, "Yes?"

"You're Victoria Harrington?"

"I am." I allowed my eyes to widen. "Wesley? Wesley Albini?" Through my peripheral vision, Travis grew inches taller and suddenly broader. Without a word he'd made his presence known.

"When my uncle asked me to..." Wesley shook his head. "...I've been out of the country, and I didn't realize."

My head tilted to the side. "Niccolo is your uncle?"

"Yes, he asked me to watch you." Wesley nodded toward Travis and extended his hand. The two men silently shook, until Wesley turned back to me. "I can see you're in good hands. We didn't mean to insinuate otherwise. It's just that when my uncle asks, there's usually a good reason."

"I've learned it never hurts to have an extra layer of protection. Please tell your uncle I said thank you, and I hope this won't be necessary for long."

The taller man beside Wesley turned. He was older and very looked very distinguished. His fine black hair had a hint of gray. The family resemblance to Niccolo was undeniable. My heartbeat quickened as I looked into my father's eyes for the first time. *You were never supposed to be born.* My mother's words rang through my head. Extending his hand, my father said, "Mrs. Harrington, it is a pleasure."

I gave him my hand and replied, "I'm sorry? Have we met?"

He bowed slightly, with my hand still in his, and kissed the top. "Mrs. Harrington, it is I who should apologize. Your husband was very important to our family. I was wrong not to have introduced myself to his lovely wife before his sad passing." Releasing my hand, he continued to speak, sincerity emanating from each well-planned word. "I'm sorry for your loss. I was at your husband's funeral when I saw you for the first time. You were with your family." His dark eyes softened. "It wasn't until I saw your mother..." He shook his head. "...I didn't want to intrude." Squaring his shoulders he said, "Mrs. Harrington, I am Carlisle Albini." He glanced toward Wesley and lightened his tone. "It sounds as though you know my son."

I looked back to Wesley. "We did, sir. Years ago."

Playfully, Carlisle pushed against Wesley's shoulder. "Before she was married? And you let her go? What's wrong with you?"

Crimson graced Wesley's cheeks.

Carlisle looked back to me. "Perhaps one day you'll forgive my son. We all make choices when we're young that we regret with time."

"I'm afraid, sir, it wasn't that serious. Wesley and I were friends."

"Pity," Carlisle said. "A beautiful woman like you would be an asset to our family."

My chin rose indignantly. *He knew. I knew he knew.* However, his words didn't feel like a threat, more like a show of support.

Before I could respond, Wesley said, "Victoria, please forgive my father. He seems to think the family name is dead. I've told him that twenty-eight isn't that old, but he married my mother young."

Finding my voice, I smiled. "Please, Mr. Albini, since I'm only twenty-eight, I hope you don't consider that age too old. As you know, I'm now a widow."

He nodded and looked down. When our eyes met, the spark I'd seen only moments ago had extinguished. "Niccolo tells me that your husband's passing will not affect our business? I wanted to discuss it with you myself."

"Your brother is correct. I have no plans to make any rash changes. I'd be glad to discuss it further; however, I'm on my way to a meeting."

Both Wesley and Carlisle nodded. "Another time. Good day, Mrs. Harrington." Carlisle reached out and gently seized my arm. Quietly, he whispered, "Your husband's passing opened a few doors that were better left closed. Please know that your allegiance to our family is appreciated. I'm sorry about your mother. I believe that was meant for me. The two of us..." he nodded toward Wesley. "...were also friends a long time ago. Rest assured, those doors I mentioned will soon be closed and you have nothing to fear."

"Thank you, Mr. Albini."

"Carlisle," he corrected.

I nodded as I swallowed the lump forming in my throat. "Carlisle."

Reaching into the breast pocket of his silk suit coat, he handed me a card. "Mrs. Harrington, this is my personal number, one I rarely share. If you need anything, call."

I wrapped my fingers around the business card and did my best to remain stoic as I asked. "That lack of fear you mentioned? I'm new to all of this, but does it include my family?"

Carlisle and Wesley nodded in unison.

"Thank you, Carlisle… Wesley." I nodded to each of them. "I hope that call isn't necessary."

"From now on, Mrs. Harrington, the Albinis will be there for you, as if you were part of this family. Mistakes have been made, but rest assured, we do not abandon family."

I smiled. I'd already said thank you a thousand times. As I watched Carlisle and Wesley walk away I thought I heard *Speak Softly Love* playing in the background. Shaking my head I decided it was a definite improvement over *Fatal Lullaby*. When I didn't move, Travis touched the small of my back directing me toward the elevators. A moment later, I felt his hand tense. When I looked up, my eyes met the aquamarine I'd been waiting to see.

I turned toward Travis. "Give me a minute. I know Parker's waiting, but I asked Brody to be here for my mother."

Though I was speaking, Travis' narrowed gaze never left Brody.

"Yes, Mrs. Harrington," came from his clenched jaws.

Asshole! What the fuck was his problem? That damn contract wasn't real. Travis had no right to judge whom I saw or didn't see. I could be with whomever I wanted. I didn't say that, standing in the hospital corridor, but I made a mental note to mention it once we were in the car. In the meantime, I bit my tongue, shook my head at Travis' evident disapproval, and walked toward Brody. When I neared, I smiled up at his beautiful eyes; however, the closer I came, the more obvious it was that my pleasure at seeing him wasn't reciprocated.

"Brody? What's the matter? Where have you been?"

Seizing my hand, he pulled me down the hall. The first small room we came to was occupied by an older couple. Silently, we moved down the hallway until we came to a family bathroom.

"What the fuck?" I murmured as he pushed me inside with him and secured the lock. Scanning the tile bathroom I wrinkled my nose and said, "This is gross. What are you doing?"

"Vik, a better damn question is what are you doing?"

I opened my palm and read Carlisle Albini in scrolled lettering. Shrugging, I tucked the card inside of my purse. "I'm on my way to your office."

Brody paced the incredibly small space. "My office? Craven and Knowles, why?"

"Parker called... well, Trish called. She said he wants to see me. It's urgent."

Brody moved toward me. His hands palmed the wall on either side of my face, creating a cage with his strong arms. Pushing his body closer, he pressed me backward. When my sore ass hit the wall, a moan escaped my lips."

"What's the matter, baby?"

I reached up and caressed his cheek. His soft stubble felt familiar under my fingertips. His warm skin and fresh scent filled my senses, easing my aches and pains. He was my normal, my promise for a real life. "Nothing, Brody," I sighed. "I just don't know what has you all uptight?"

"Vik, you were talking to the Albinis. Do you even know who they are?"

I shook my head, allowing my fingers to graze his warm neck. "I didn't. I didn't know anything about them until the other day. They've been very nice."

Brody pounded the concrete wall near my head. "Nice! Vik, those people are not fucking *nice*. They're dangerous. You shouldn't be talking to them. You don't understand. Why wasn't Travis dealing with them?"

Indignantly I stood taller. "I don't need Travis or you or Parker or anyone else to do my business. Stewart left it all to me. I can do it."

"Stewart? The ass-wipe who treated you like a fucking commodity? Well, God knows we don't want to disappoint him."

"Brody." Again I reached for his cheek. "Brody, you're upset. I've never seen you like this."

"You fucking told me you didn't see Parker."

"I didn't," I lied. "I'm guessing that's why he wants me to come to his office."

Brody's eyes closed as he exhaled. Releasing the wall, he ran his hands through his strawberry blonde hair and paced in a small circle. His actions reminded me of watching a caged animal. When he looked back in my direction, his anger was gone. I saw the love and adoration I didn't deserve but longed to have. It was the look I envisioned on that big-assed blanket near our lake surrounded by mountains.

"Baby." He captured my cheeks and covered my mouth with his. The temperature of the small bathroom rose as his tongue danced with mine. When our kiss ended, he looked deeply into my gray eyes and said, "You don't know how fucking worried I've been. I didn't sleep last night. I'm like a crazy man. All I kept thinking about was you with Parker or Travis or anyone else."

"I've never been with Travis. I know that for certain."

"How do you know?"

"I just do."

"But now… now you're talking to the Albinis. Fucking Vik! You're jumping out of the proverbial frying pan into the goddamned fire."

I shook my head. "No, I'm not. I can't tell you all of it, but I trust them. I do."

"Jesus, you don't know them. You trust them and you don't know them. And you wanted Travis Daniels' name on a goddamned contract instead of mine. You don't trust me."

"I do. I trust you. The contract with Travis isn't enforceable. I told you that. He works for me. Nothing is going to come of it. I'm going to go see Parker." I wrapped my arms around Brody's tight abs and pressed myself against his chest. Freshly cleaned sheets came to mind as I inhaled. "Brody, this is almost done. When it is, can we find that lake?" I tucked my head under his chin and listened to his erratic heart. Even through his shirt I felt his warmth, such a stark contrast to how Stewart had been, especially toward the end. Stewart had been cold, always so cold.

Brody kissed the top of my head. "Yeah, Vik, just you and me and some fucking rabbits."

I grinned. "I think that means there'll be a lot of rabbits."

He squeezed me tight.

I looked around. "Brody, although this may be cleaner, I have to say, it's more disgusting than that damn motel. How about we get together tomorrow?" I hoped my ass would be better by then. As long as I didn't bruise, the welts would be gone.

"Sure, Vikki, tomorrow." Again, he cupped my cheeks. "No more deals with the devil. You did that once. Let Parker handle the business. You just sit back and enjoy your freedom."

Closing my eyes, I nodded. My only concern was that my time in the warehouse was done. "I don't care about the business," I said, "but I promised the Albinis—"

His finger came to my lips. "Baby, I'm a fucking attorney. Don't tell me anything you promised those lowlifes. Just promise me that you'll concentrate on that big-assed blanket."

My insides twisted in the most pleasant of ways at the promise. "I will. Now, I need to find out what Parker wants."

Brody leaned in, giving me one more parting kiss that left my lips burning with thoughts of a future. I righted my skirt and blouse and unlocked the door. Just as I was about to open it, Brody offered with a grin, "By the way, Mrs. Harrington, I'll represent your mother."

"This was an interesting consultation appointment, counselor."

"Wait until you get my bill."

When we stepped into the hallway, Brody walked in the other direction, toward my mother's room, and Travis' dark gaze scanned me from head to toe. Walking back to the elevator, he leaned nearer and inhaled. As he stood straight, he whispered, "Well, at least you don't fucking reek."

Asshole! "You work for me."

"I'm painfully aware." He shook his head. "Painfully aware."

CHAPTER TWENTY-SEVEN

Present

Travis told me that he'd arranged for my car to be taken back to the penthouse. I didn't mind. With everything that had transpired, I would have a difficult time concentrating on driving. In his SUV, I settled against the passenger seat and tried to make sense of my afternoon. I couldn't process the entirety: Parker at the warehouse, the Albinis... and then Brody. Parker was a dick—a pencil dick—but that wasn't a revelation. The Albinis—a few days ago, I'd never heard the name. I'd never heard of Carlisle Albini. Now, we'd spoken. Though my knowledge level was only slightly elevated, I felt a surprising sense of calm. Then again, Brody didn't. He was upset that I spoke with them. Why?

"Victoria," Travis' deep voice pulled me from the depths of my thoughts and questions. "The way you've handled the Albinis, I think Mr. Harrington would be proud. Honestly, I think he'd be shocked. I'm sorry to say, he probably underestimated you."

You have no fucking idea. "I don't think he's the only one."

Travis' lips went together in a straight line, before he said, "He did care about you. I see how you would doubt that, but he did."

I didn't want to think about Stewart caring for me; nevertheless, I asked, "How do you know?"

"I know. He worked to keep your identity hidden from both sides. He believed that if Carlisle knew who you were that you'd be in danger."

I turned toward Travis. "My mother had said the same thing, but I didn't sense that. Did you? Just now?"

He shook his head. "No, I didn't. I think Mr. Albini respects you."

"Oh, God!" My stomach lurched as nausea struck with a vengeance.

"What?" Travis' dark eyes flew my direction. "What's the matter? Are you getting sick?"

"No, it's not that. It's just... I had a thought. Oh, God, please, please Travis... please tell me that the Albinis aren't *friends*."

He reached over and placed his hand on my suddenly trembling knee. Feeling the warmth, I stared at the size as I waited for his answer. After a moment, he pulled it away. "Sorry, I remember: no touching, ever." His lips morphed into a lopsided grin. "No, the Albinis weren't among Stewart's friends. I'm pretty sure they have plenty of women in their business. However, the more I see of them, the more I'm inclined to believe that they may be a few of the more honorable men in a world of filth. It's no doubt why they're the most successful." He looked back toward me. "Nothing against you, but I'm not sure they would've wanted to be one of Stewart's friends."

"You did." I wasn't sure what made me say it, but once it was out I couldn't bring it back.

Travis shrugged. "I'm not honorable."

"I'm beginning to question that. A while ago, I would've agreed with you, but now I'm not too sure." I turned toward him and studied his profile. His hard chin flexed as his jaw clenched. "You did it on purpose didn't you?"

"What?" he asked.

"You were an ass to me. That day at the warehouse; you wanted me to know it was you."

He forced a laugh. "Yes, because I'm into being bitten until I bleed, and kneed in the balls. It's one of my favorite pastimes."

"No." I shook my head, closed my eyes, and turned away. I remembered that day. I remembered his scent and his warm breath. I was so fucking scared. After that incident, it took a while for Stewart to invite his first friends; instead, Stewart spent more time and worked with me, encouraged me. That day also gave me a sense that even with what he was making me do, Stewart had my back. Maybe he did, but now I knew that Travis did too. Travis was always there, even today. "You knew I wasn't ready. You did what you did: you purposely made sure I knew it was you. You did that so I'd have more time. You also wanted me to know that through all that shit, I was protected."

Travis' knuckles blanched as his grip assaulted the steering wheel. "You're wrong. I wanted to fuck you. I'm the only fucking man who's been at the warehouse who hasn't had his cock inside of you. I was too energetic. I screwed up."

"I don't believe you."

Travis turned his narrow dark gaze back toward me. "Are you calling me a fucking liar?"

Smugly, I nodded. "Yes, I am."

"You're wrong. I wanted to fuck you before and I still do. Maybe when we get to Craven and Knowles we should check out the legality of my contract."

"You're a liar and that's not happening. If you really wanted it, Stewart would have caved. He would have let you."

"Mrs. Harrington, you're dead wrong."

I grinned toward the window. "Victoria, asshole, my name is Victoria, and I'm not wrong. You've been a nice guy all along. Ha! Who knew?"

I glanced at the clock in the SUV as Travis parked outside of Craven and Knowles. It was nearly seven-thirty: almost five hours since I'd left Parker in the warehouse. As we approached the leaded glass doors to the ostentatiously large entry of the esteemed law firm, Trish sprang from behind her desk, her eyes wide as she rushed toward us. Opening the doors, she said, "Mrs. Harrington, I'm so glad you're here."

No doubt, the surprise at Trish's gregarious greeting was evident on my face. Never once had she been as welcoming. "Trish." I nodded.

"Mrs. Harrington, let me show you back to Mr. Craven's office. You'll see when you get there..." She added in a whisper, "He needs to go home. I'm afraid we'll all be ill if he doesn't."

I stopped in my tracks. "Trish, if Mr. Craven is that sick, perhaps

—"

Her long neck, visible with her dark hair twisted behind her head, moved from side to side. "No, he said he's not leaving until he speaks with you…" She eyed Travis up and down. "…alone."

I looked to Travis and back to Trish. "That's fine. Mr. Daniels will wait outside. Shall we go to the conference room?"

"No, ma'am. Mr. Craven wanted me to bring you to his office." I followed a step behind as she led us past the normal fish bowl and down a long hallway. As she did, I realized that I'd never been back to the partners' offices. Only once had I been in Brody's office; it was always better for us to meet away from the firm. After only one rap on the shiny wooden door, Trish opened it wide, revealing the grandeur of the senior partner's private workspace.

The customary bookshelf lined with volumes of legal jargon filled one wall. Fleetingly, I wondered with today's technology if that were truly necessary. Wouldn't it be easier to do a computer search to locate a specific precedent than search through a wall of dusty journals? Two of the walls were floor-to-ceiling glass, looking out onto an impressive ocean view. It was in front of one of those spectacular windows where my eyes were suddenly drawn. I couldn't look away from the man behind the desk. His normally olive complexion was pale and his face was covered with a sheen of sweat. More perspiration dripped from his temples, running down the length of his face and plunging from his quivering chin to the depths of his dampened shirt. Even his eyes were clouded with a veil of infirmity.

"My God, Parker, what's happened to you?"

The clouds before his eyes parted, as a dark, menacing stare looked my direction. "Sit down, Mrs. Harrington. Trish, leave us."

I turned toward Trish who looked at me with raised brows. I nodded, confirming her earlier concerns. Parker Craven was obviously ill.

When I looked back, Parker said, "I believe I told you earlier today to not make me repeat myself. Sit."

I considered arguing. I'd spent the better part of the day standing, thanks to him, but seeing his pallor, I nodded and perched myself on the edge of a chair. When I did, he smiled sadistically, and asked,

"Are you comfortable, Mrs. Harrington?"

"No, I'm not. Did you call me here to gloat?"

"Hardly. I called you here…" His words were interrupted by a hacking cough. "…I've received some troubling news. There are rumors that you have made the unfortunate decision to entertain…" More coughing. "…a business venture, which I feel would be better…" Coughs. "…discontinued."

"If you're talking about Travis—"

His fist pounded the desk as his other hand then went to the collar of his shirt, loosening the top button and his tie. Parker continued, "Don't interrupt and don't play dumb. You've been talking to Niccolo Albini."

He again began to cough.

I waited. With my eyes open wide, I implored, "Parker, this can wait. You're obviously ill. I hope it isn't contagious. We'll discuss it when you're feeling better: maybe when we discuss the will. Right now, I'm Stewart's wife and I'll talk to anyone I want."

He took a drink of water and wiped his brow with a handkerchief. "You will not make any more promises or deals with the Albinis. With our new contract, I'm in charge of all of those decisions. To that end, unless you want your birthdate and all it implies made public, and believe me, you don't, you'll sign this power of attorney."

More coughing. His chest convulsed as he hacked into the handkerchief. I grimaced at the red seeping through.

Shaking my head, I pursed my lips. "My goodness, you're getting worse by the minute. Has anyone called Maura? She should take you home."

"Victoria, the Albinis don't know who you are. If they did—"

I stood. "You see, Parker, that's where you and Stewart were mistaken. Carlisle, my father, and I had a nice little chat this afternoon at the hospital. Apparently, you were all misinformed. I don't know what you or the Durantes think you know, but I'll assure you, Carlisle Albini is an honorable man. His brother Niccolo has pledged his protection on me and my family. Carlisle has confirmed that. For the time being, I believe this discussion is over."

Wearily, he shook his head. "No, you can't do that. You can't do any of that. You don't have the power." He again wiped the perspiration as it dripped near his eyes. "I have your contract."

"Parker, you're delusional. I'm afraid your fever is making you forget. I never signed a contract with you." As I spoke he reached down near his feet to where I assumed he had his briefcase. "I haven't seen you today until now. Harrington Spas and Suites will not be run by you. And very soon, I will be seeking legal representation elsewhere. Oh..." I added while he searched through the folder now open on his desk. "...and the warehouse is closed."

"You can't..." he choked.

"I can and I did." I pulled my phone from my purse and found Maura Craven in my contacts.

Speaking into the phone, I said, "Maura, dear, hello. I'm sorry to bother you. But I came to your husband's office to talk about Stewart's will, and dear, your husband is sick. He's being too much of a man to admit it, but I'm worried."

I smiled toward Parker as Maura replied.

When she was done, I said, "Yes, we will need to have that lunch. I think you should come and get him. We don't want him working himself to death, now do we?"

"Goodbye, dear."

I disconnected the call and leaned closer, lowering my voice. "One more thing: I heard the most interesting thing on television the other day. They were saying that it's not smart to try to turn wild animals into pets. They said it can be dangerous." I tilted my head to the side and scanned his pathetic, shivering body. "Oh, that was just some random trivia I wanted to share. Unfortunately, I think it might be too late for you.

"I do want to thank you for calling me in here tonight. I would've hated to have missed this." I pulled the generic Dom/sub contract from the folder and placed it on top. "You may want to shred this before Maura arrives. We don't want her to know what a pencil dick she married." I waved my fingers as I turned to leave. "This time, I'll be the one running along. Goodbye, Parker."

CHAPTER TWENTY-EIGHT

Present

I woke the next morning to the ringing of my cell phone. MAURA CRAVEN flashed on the screen.

"Maura," I said sleepily. "What's happening?"

"Victoria, I'm sorry to call so early, but you need to get to Memorial Hospital right away."

My tired mind was suddenly wide awake. "God, Maura, is it my mother?" *How would Maura Craven know about my mom?*

"What? No, Victoria, it's Parker. He's very sick. The doctors don't know what's wrong, but they want to monitor everyone who's been in contact with him."

"Jeez, Maura, I'm sorry." I sat up, assessing my body. After only a moment, I decided that I wasn't ill; as a matter of fact, even my ass felt better. "I feel fine."

"Parker felt fine yesterday morning too. Now… oh… Victoria, now he can't even breathe. His hair is falling out, and they have this tube thing in his throat. It's awful." I heard her holding back the tears.

Oh, just like Stewart. "Maura, how are you?"

"I'm beside myself, but physically, I'm well. Well, for now at least, but the doctors are monitoring me. Please come. Trish said you weren't with Parker long, but if you start to have symptoms, maybe they can catch it early."

"I was five feet away."

"Was he coughing?" Maura asked.

"Yes," I admitted.

"Victoria, please come, I don't want anything to happen to you."

I closed my eyes. "Thank you, Maura. I'll be there as soon as I can."

Travis drove us to the hospital in silence, both keenly aware of our roles in this tragic chain of events. As the SUV approached the hospital, Travis reached out and touched my leg. "The fucker deserved this."

I nodded. "I know. I don't feel bad for him; maybe I should, but I don't. I'm not relishing the idea of facing Maura, but one day she'll realize she's better off without him."

"And his pencil dick," Travis added with a lopsided grin.

"Yeah, and his pencil dick."

"I had no idea it would work this fast," Travis said as he searched for a parking spot.

"Me either. I think the other one takes longer. I don't exactly remember."

"The other one?"

"It's a red liquid. I think if it's ingested, it works slower. The symptoms are noticeable, like the hair loss, but once it's in the system it can't be stopped. I used the powder. Val said it was toxic, that even a little was disastrous to the immune system. I may have overdone the amount I put in the gloves."

Travis looked at me, his gaze narrowing. "I'm glad the doctors are going to watch you. Are you sure you're feeling all right?"

I covered his hand that was still on my leg and sighed. "I am; even my ass feels better. If Parker got that sick, that fast, I think I'm in the clear." Then I thought about Travis. "You didn't touch anything... you're not feeling ill, are you?"

He shook his head. "No, like I said yesterday, I was going to clean up, but I decided to just leave it and get to you at the hospital."

"And you're feeling..."

"Mrs.... Victoria, I'm feeling well." He parked the SUV. "May I escort you to the infectious-disease unit?"

"Oh, Mr. Daniels, does that line get you laid, because it's uniquely intriguing?"

"No, believe it or not, it's the first time I've used it. However," he said with a gleam in his dark eyes, "I may hold on to it. You never know when it might come in handy."

"Indeed." I pressed my lips together and searched for my mask of concern: the one I'd worn for months while nursing my dying husband. With the recent revelations, I felt less self-assured about what I'd done. As we walked through the doors of the hospital, I wondered if it was time for karma to bite me in the ass.

With my façade securely in place, we arrived at the nurses' station. "Excuse me. I'm Victoria Harrington, Mrs. Craven called—"

The nurse's eyes widened. "Yes, the doctors would like you to come back. We have an area with others. It's a makeshift isolation." She looked to Travis. "I'm sorry, sir. It's only for those people—"

"I was with Mrs. Harrington at Mr. Craven's office last night," he declared.

"Oh, and your name?" she asked as she checked her list.

"My name is Travis Daniels."

"Sir, I don't see—"

I turned my gray eyes toward the woman before me. "Ma'am, why would he lie? Will this *makeshift isolation* be that enjoyable that you have to stop the crowds from entering?" I obviously wasn't making a friend, but I also wasn't ready to be alone with Parker or anyone else without Travis.

"No, ma'am. It's just that by allowing Mr. Daniels entry we may be unnecessarily exposing—"

"You needn't worry. If Mrs. Harrington was exposed, then so was I," Travis interrupted.

Perhaps it was his size or his tone, regardless of the reason, after a brief look from Travis to me, and back to Travis, the nurse sighed and reluctantly led both of us through some doors and down a long hallway. After a few turns and a few more doors we came to a door with a lovely picture of three incomplete circles and a sign warning us to not enter without proper safety equipment.

"You both may enter here."

I looked to Travis and raised my brows. Silently he nodded and we entered. Once inside, we were met by Trish and other members of the Craven and Knowles staff. "Trish," I asked, "where is Mrs.

Craven?"

"She's with Mr. Craven." Trish's eyes were red.

"How are you feeling?" I asked, feigning concern.

She nodded as she swallowed. "I'm fine. We all seem to be fine." She assessed me. "And you?"

I nodded.

"I knew... yesterday... I just knew..." Trish's words trailed away as another woman hugged her and led her away. Travis and I found two chairs. We sat as time crawled. Through a series of text messages with my sister, I learned that Parker had the hospital in an uproar. Whatever he had was progressing extremely fast. The good news was that no one else had gotten ill.

As I was nearly asleep from boredom, the door opened and Senator Robert Keene entered. Immediately, his beady eyes found mine. Unconsciously, I reached for Travis who too had been lulled into a false sense of serenity. He sat taller as I offered sarcastically, "Senator, welcome to our party."

"Mrs. Harrington," he acknowledged with a nod.

"Senator, will your lovely wife be joining us?"

"No, fortunately for her, it was only I who had a brief meeting with Parker yesterday afternoon. She wasn't present."

I tilted my head to the side. "I would assume a man of your importance has a lot of meetings without your wife, or even perhaps without her knowledge."

He moved to the chair beside me and lowered his voice. "Mrs. Harrington, you would be wise to keep your knowledge to yourself. Parker told me about a new agreement—a new contract. It's my understanding that once he's well, certain business situations will be nullified." He stared for a moment, moving only his eyes from my face to my breasts and back. "I must say, I'm also pleased to hear that your husband's other obligations will continue to be met. Word is, the rules have changed." He furrowed his forehead knowingly. "Are you comfortable sitting? Or would you rather stand?"

It wasn't only his words that made my skin crawl: it was his breath. I fought the urge to retch, not because I didn't like the image of him covered in my vomit, but because I didn't want the doctors to misconstrue my symptoms. Instead, I smiled appealingly, and leaned closer. With a whisper, I said, "It seems that Parker misinformed you. I have no idea what you're talking about. And as for business, my husband's business dealings will continue as he planned."

"Mrs. Harrington..." with each word his ruddy cheeks grew more and more red. "...I'm certain you don't understand the connections —"

I placed my hand on his. "Apparently, you don't understand mine." I tilted my head to the side and used my sweetest voice. "However, if you push me again, I will use them. Senator, as I'm sure you're aware, blood is thicker than water."

"And I am—"

"Water, Senator. Sheila is blood. I know more than you think. Don't push me."

As he was about to respond, a woman entered our room wearing something that looked more like a space suit. "I need to take all of your vitals. Is anyone feeling ill?"

"No," a woman I didn't know said. "This is silly. We're all fine. When can we go?"

"I would have said soon, but there's been another case. I'm afraid everyone from Craven and Knowles is considered infected."

"Excuse me," I said. "I'm not from Craven and Knowles."

"Neither am I," Senator Keene interjected. "Who else is infected?"

"I'm sorry. I'm not at liberty—"

Trish began to cry. "It's Mr. Phillips. Isn't it?"

My heart stopped.

Before I could speak, Trish went on. "I couldn't reach him this morning. Everyone else answered their phones. Not him. He was with Mr. Craven yesterday afternoon. I bet it was him."

"What do you mean he was with him?" I asked.

"I don't know. Mr. Craven had a meeting, and Mr. Phillips had a follow-up meeting. They used to do it all the time."

I bit the inside of my cheek to stop from changing my expression. My imagination was running wild. I told myself that it couldn't be... it had nothing to do with the warehouse. I knew it didn't. Brody didn't know about that.

A FEW HOURS LATER, still symptom-free, Travis and I were released. When we made it to the main information desk I asked, "Excuse me, I'm here to see Brody Phillips."

The woman searched her computer screen. "Ma'am, I'm sorry, Mr. Phillips can't have visitors."

He was there. *Oh my God!*

"Ma'am, are you friends or family?"

"I'm a *friend*." The word stuck in my throat.

"We have no record of his family. If you have any information it would be helpful."

I shook my head. "I don't. I'm sorry."

As I turned to leave, my eyes were met by my own gray. It was Val. "I wanted to catch you before you left," she said, her tone soft.

It was all too much. I closed my eyes. "Is it Mom?"

"Yes." She reached for my arm. "It's not bad. It's good. She's awake and talking. She's even talked to the police. She remembers everything. Her story is pretty far-fetched, but they're listening to her."

I looked up to Travis' dark eyes. We were both exhausted. I was worried about Brody, but I needed to see my mother. For the first time since I could remember, I wanted to see her. "I'll go see her for a few minutes."

Val nodded. As we walked toward the elevators, with Travis a step behind, Val whispered, "She's even had some interesting visitors."

I lifted my brow, silently imploring her to continue.

"That man, the one who was at my apartment looking for you? Well, I guess he knows Mom. The nurses said that at first she seemed apprehensive, but I walked by and saw them talking. It was him and another man who looked a lot like him. I guess they were all right. Mom was smiling."

As we approached Mom's room, Val's pager went off. "I'm sorry. I'm needed somewhere else."

I tried to ignore the compassion-filled glance she shot my way as she walked quickly down the corridor. I approached the room, wondering if I'd see my mother and father together. It was a thought that only two days ago would've seemed preposterous. I opened the door and found Marilyn alone, sitting up, and looking out the window. When she turned toward me, I saw her tear-coated cheeks.

"Mom, are you all right? What's the matter?"

Shaking her head, she looked away.

I walked to her bed and sat on the edge. "I've contacted an attorney. His name is Phillips, Brody Phillips. He can help you." I reached for her hand, praying that he could help her, that he wasn't as ill as Parker: he couldn't be. I reassured myself that there was no way for him to be exposed. When my mother didn't respond, I reached for her hand. "Val told me that you spoke to the police. I know this whole thing seems absurd, but I believe your story."

Her moist gray eyes turned back toward me as her head slowly shook. "I've made so many mistakes. I was young and believed the stories I heard. I thought..." Her words trailed away as her petite body shuddered.

Straightening my neck, I asked, "What? What Mother? What did you think?"

She looked down to where my hand covered hers. Turning hers palm up, she laced her fingers with mine. "I thought he would reject you or that his family would hurt you. I've wasted so much time. I'm so sorry. I know you hate me and you should."

I inhaled, waiting to exhale. "Hate's a strong word. There were times when it was probably appropriate, but not now."

She squeezed my hand. "He knows. Your father knows."

I nodded. "We spoke. He didn't say that, not in so many words... but I got the feeling that he knew."

Her chin fell to her chest. "He said that he had no idea. He never even assumed that I'd lied about you until Stewart's funeral. I thought he was there because of you." She shook her head as her gaze met mine. "He wasn't. It was a coincidence. He was there because of Stewart, but then he saw me with you. You look so much like him, he knew."

"But didn't you say that Niccolo—"

She nodded. "He apologized to both Carlisle and me. He said that he suspected, but when I produced the birth certificate, he didn't pursue it. He never mentioned it to Carlisle."

I turned away, gazing around her hospital room. The sun still shone outside the window. As I scanned the small space, I noticed a suit coat draped over the corner chair. It was gray and I recognized it immediately.

"Mom, did Brody Phillips come and see you last night?"

As if pulling her from a fog of memories, she looked at me and her eyes cleared. "What? Phillips? Yes, the attorney you mentioned. He stopped by here last night. I was still pretty out of it. I'd just awakened. He said he'd come back. Why?"

I tilted my head toward the chair. "I think that's his." I got up and walked toward the jacket. Reaching for it, I inhaled the fresh scent of clean sheets and my chest ached.

"I don't know," she said. "I didn't even see that. I'm sorry, Victoria. I'm sorry for so many things."

I hugged the jacket as my thoughts went back to Brody. "Mom, we'll talk more. You need your rest." I looked toward the door and saw Travis' broad shoulder through the small windowpane. "I think I need to go home."

"Victoria?"

The sadness in her tone pulled me silently to her.

She reached for my hand. "You *were* supposed to be born."

I straightened my neck as I swallowed the emotions bubbling up from the pit of my stomach. It was a direct contradiction to what I'd heard all of my life. In one sentence she was telling me that I was wanted, that I wasn't a killer, but she was wrong. I was a killer. I'd killed my twin, Stewart, and soon Parker. I couldn't respond. A renegade tear fell from my gray eyes as I turned toward the door.

When I stepped into the hall, I found Val standing by Travis. Both of their expressions were grim. I braced myself, unsure of what was happening. All I knew was that I didn't think my emotions could take anything else. "What?" I asked, Brody's jacket hanging over my arm.

Val shook her head. "I wanted you to know that I'm sorry."

Did she know about our fathers? Did she know that they were different? "You're sorry about what?"

Travis took a step back as Val put her arm around me and lowered her voice. "The other day, I read the name on your phone. The night you were flipping out... I may have searched your text messages. I know that Brody Phillips was Horizontal-Friend."

"What do you mean, you're sorry?" I gasped. "What do you mean *was?*"

"We don't know what happened. The CDC suspects some kind of homegrown terrorism, maybe a disgruntled client. They're checking into all the business dealings of Craven and Knowles. Vik, the reason I was called away as you came up here was because they were notifying all of the doctors that both Parker Craven and Brody Phillips are dead."

"No," I whimpered. Tears fell and my chin sagged to my chest as I surrendered the valiant fight I'd been battling with my emotions. It was all too much. I tried to form thoughts into sentences. "No. There's been some mistake."

My sister hugged me tighter. "I'm so sorry, sis. They will try to figure out what happened. The hospital is keeping it quiet, but I wanted you to know."

Holding tight to the jacket in my arms, I nodded, unable to speak.

As Travis quietly led me back to the SUV, I lost sense of time and space. Instead of opening the back door as he used to do, he opened the passenger door. The drive from the hospital to the penthouse was a blur.

When we entered my apartment, I blindly walked to my suite. "I want to be alone," was all I could say. I couldn't form other words. There were none that made sense. Nothing made sense. *How could Brody get ill?* I didn't get ill. I saw him yesterday at the hospital. He was fine... or was he? I remembered his intense warmth.

The jacket in my arms was all that I had left of my dream of a normal life: all that was left of the only man to love me for me. I unfolded the jacket, laying it upon my bed, and inhaled. Brody's aftershave emanated from the fabric. My chest heaved at the sense of loss. I should've felt this way for my husband, but I hadn't.

The reality struck: I was death, slow and insidious. I killed everything around me. That was what I'd been told since before I could remember. My mother had been right. I shouldn't have been born. Now, karma was paying me back. Just when I had the promise of love and a normal life, it was snatched away. All Brody had ever done was love me, love me like no one else.

I hugged the suit jacket. I didn't have the chance to say goodbye.

At least with Stewart I had said goodbye. Was that what I said? Oh, why the fuck had this happened to Brody? I was the one who deserved to die, not Brody. My knees gave way as I fell to the floor. Lowering my head, I hugged his jacket using it for my pillow as my tears permeated the fabric.

Instead of being soft, the garment was bumpy. Wiping my eyes, I opened the coat. As I did, the scent of clean, fresh aftershave mixed with a new scent. Candy canes and little round mints filled my thoughts. I reached into his breast pocket and pulled out a half-dozen individually wrapped peppermints.

No! Fuck no! He couldn't be! It couldn't be him.

My body trembled as I jumped to my feet and ran for my door. "Travis! Travis!" I screamed, as I raced down the stairs to the main level. "Travis!" My legs barely held my weight as my eyes overflowed with tears. The salty remains flowed freely down my cheeks. "Fucking Travis, where the fuck are you?"

He and Lisa met me as I rounded the corner to the kitchen. Seizing my shoulders he held me still. Both of their eyes opened wide.

"Mrs. Harrington, what is it?" Lisa asked.

Staring only at Travis, I held out my hand and opened my fingers to reveal the peppermint candies. My voice cracked with disbelief. "Tell me. Please tell me that he wasn't one of the…" I couldn't say the rest: that Brody was one of the *friends.*

Travis didn't speak; instead, he closed his eyes and nodded.

"Noooo!" I couldn't—didn't want—to—process; my knees gave out.

When I awoke, I was in my bed. Though the room was dark, I knew I wasn't alone. "Travis?" I questioned.

"Victoria?" the deep voice came from the darkness.

"What happened?"

The bed shifted, and I knew he was near. As my eyes adjusted I saw his profile: his tall, muscular body against the moonlit sky.

"I had to catch your ass again."

I rubbed my cheek against my pillow as the memories came back. My chest ached with loss.

"Lisa and I brought you up here," he continued. "Dr. Conway came over and gave you something: a shot. You've been asleep for about six hours."

The emptiness was unbearable. "Travis, how?" Sobs came from deep within me. "How did Brody...?" I couldn't even finish my sentence. I couldn't say the word *die*.

"I'm sorry," he offered.

"No, you're not!" I screamed. "You didn't like him. I saw the way you looked at him."

"I didn't like him because he lied to you."

My tears resumed, stinging my swollen eyes. "I don't want to hear this. Why are you even in my room? Get out of my room!"

Large warm hands seized my shoulders.

"Don't touch me. I fucking told you not to touch me ever!"

He didn't let go; instead, Travis moved nearer as his warm breath skirted across my face. "He lied to you. I never lied to you."

I knew that what he was saying was true. I didn't want to believe it, but deep down I knew it. My body shuddered with the truth that was on the tip of my tongue. With Travis still holding my shoulders, I whispered, "He was Peppermint Man."

"Peppermint Man? What do you mean?" Travis asked, puzzled, as he released me.

I sat up. Realizing that I was still wearing my blouse and panties, I pulled the sheet around my waist and tried to explain, "There were some of the *friends*—I fucking hate that goddamned term—some who I identified by scents. One of them was kind..." My shoulders shuddered as I wiped my eyes with the sheet. "...or seemed comparatively kind. I named him Peppermint Man. He was the one I was with the day Stewart died."

"Yes."

"That was him... Brody."

Travis nodded.

I shook my head in disbelief. "But he never told me he was there. He led me to believe..." I couldn't stop the pain in my chest or the tears. I hated tears. Tears were weak. I wasn't weak. I didn't want to be weak, but the pain was unbearable.

"Victoria?" Travis said, gently wiping my tears with his thumb. "He was one of them. He worked with the Durantes, just like others at Craven and Knowles. He's so fucking entrenched in their shit. I'm not saying he didn't help you. Hell, he may have even had feelings, but you're a fucking wealthy woman. There are assholes out there who'll say and do anything. You weren't the one to tell him about what happened at the warehouse: he knew what you were doing. He was fucking doing it to you."

"How Travis, how? How did he get ill?"

The bed moved as he shifted. "I don't know. The only thing I can figure is that he went to the warehouse after we left. I can go check it in the morning and see if anyone has been there. I'll be able to tell if anyone's used their code. If he did... if he went to the warehouse, maybe he found the gloves and shit."

"And *shit*? Like the crop and Parker's fucking come when he jacked off?" *If he did, he knew I lied.*

"Victoria," Travis said. "I didn't clean up *anything*. If he went down there and started handling things, hell, even the crop, I don't know. He could have exposed himself to it."

"You said I can't trust assholes, they'll do or say anything. You're an asshole. Can I trust you?"

A large hand found my face and smoothed back my hair. "Have I ever claimed not to be an asshole?"

"No," I replied, relishing the warmth of his hand as well as his honesty.

"I don't know if you can trust me, but I can tell you, I've always been straight with you."

"No, you haven't."

"What?" Travis asked, "When wasn't I?"

"In the car, when I accused you of being nice."

He leaned closer. "Oh." His tone dropped an octave. "I wasn't lying. I'm not nice, and I do want to fuck you."

Oh fuck!

CHAPTER TWENTY-NINE

Present

"But you're not allowed to touch me," I whispered. "Ever," I added, unsure of my own voice.

"I told you..." Travis' large hands caressed my arms sending trails of fire and desire straight to my core. "...I'm not honorable." He lowered his voice: it was the tone I used to find intimidating. "I want to touch you, and I fucking want you to touch me. However, if I'm going to be straight with you, I did lie about one thing."

"What?" I asked breathily.

"I'm not into biting and getting kicked in the balls."

A small grin came to my lips.

"So..." His hands continued roaming the length of my arms. Finding my hands, his fingers intertwined with mine. "...I want you to see me..." He brought my hand to his lips and sucked the tip of each finger. "...and I want you to want me, as much as I fucking want you."

I bit my lower lip. "Travis, I-I don't know."

"I understand." He moved toward me slowly, pushing me against my pillows. Inhaling deeply, he nuzzled my neck. "You talk about scent," he whispered, his warm breath on my collarbone. "You said it was the way you could identify people."

I nodded.

"Do you know how you fucking smell?"

I shook my head.

"You fucking smell like freedom, like sunshine and wind on the goddamned beach."

I looked up at his dark eyes. "I don't understand."

"For years you've smelled like a prisoner in a fucking dungeon." He inhaled again. "Not that you haven't had all your fancy-assed perfumes and lotions, but that place hung around you like a cloud. It's gone, all of it. You're fucking free and I can smell it."

I felt my cheeks rise.

"When you're ready, *if* you're ready—because, Victoria, it's your choice—I want to taste it."

"It?"

"Your freedom. I know everything. I know things you thought you'd kept hidden from Phillips. This is freedom. When someone knows everything and wants you for you, for your fucking strength, for the way you faced Albini, for the way you screwed Craven, for everything you are and despite everything you've been through. I want to taste that freedom, to drink it from your sexy as hell lips, from your perfectly round tits, and your fucking inviting pussy."

My insides twisted as I listened to his deep voice.

"That's what I want. What do you want?" he asked.

I couldn't talk. I didn't know what to say; instead, I lifted my lips toward his.

"No, Victoria, I want words. I want hands. I want you to be with me one hundred percent. No fucking nodding, or doing as you're told. Show me the bitch with a brain who's gotten under my fucking skin like no one else."

I held my head still, looked into his dark eyes, and said, "I want you to kiss me. After that, I don't know."

With the light from the rising sun, I saw his lopsided grin. "I'll take that. I'll fucking take that. I want more, but I'll take that."

With one large hand on my cheek, our lips met and the fire I questioned roared to life. The twisting I'd felt earlier turned painful as moans came from somewhere deep inside of me. Inch by inch he pushed closer, his massive chest covering mine, smashing my suddenly sensitive breasts. Slowly my hands moved up his shoulders, touching what I'd never imagined feeling. He was so big, so much bigger than anyone I'd ever known: tall, muscular, and strong. My body dwarfed beneath his. With each passing second I longed to touch the skin below his shirt.

"Travis?"

"Yes?"

"Will you take off your shirt?"

"Fuck yeah," he said, and his shirt flew over his head.

The chest I'd admired from afar was directly in front of me, solid and perfect. I traced the defined muscles with the tips of my fingers as a masculine-scented cologne, one that was neither heavy nor ghostly familiar, filled the suite. When I realized I was ogling, I bit my lip and bashfully raised my gray eyes to his. "I've never seen you. You've seen me, but I've never seen you."

His lopsided grin morphed into a full smile. "Do you like what you see as much as I do?"

"I do."

"So do I." He leaned back and scanned my body from my waist to my eyes. "I've never seen you like this."

I raised a brow.

His tone was velvet. "Oh, you've always been fucking hot, but this is different. This is you, all you." He teased the neckline of my blouse. "I want to see more, more of you. Will you let me see more? Just me, no one else?"

I nodded, knowing that once I removed my blouse, he'd see my hard nipples. He'd know what his words were doing to me.

"No, Victoria. Remember, no more nodding."

"I remember," I said, as I lifted my blouse from over my head.

"I tasted those luscious lips. Now I want to taste your perfect tits."

I reached up and cupped his cheeks. "You're fucking killing me. I'm using my words. I want you to taste me, and I want to taste you. Now shut the fuck up and do it."

His smile grew before my eyes, radiating from his whole expression: from his firm lips to his dark, gleaming eyes. "There's my bossy bitch," he quipped before his lips seized one nipple and then the other.

I threw my head backward as my spine arched and goose bumps appeared. Whimpers came from my lips as my insides clenched. After nibbling each pebbled nipple, Travis's large hands caressed each breast while his thumb massaged, the combination created an excruciating need deep inside. Each time he sucked or tweaked my hardened nubs, electricity surged through me, straight to my core. Without getting near my sex, his words and actions made my panties wet as I unconsciously rolled my hips, silently begging for more.

When I thought I couldn't take it anymore, he found the waistband of the only remaining obstacle. Reverently, he pulled my panties down over my hips and down my legs, moving down my body as he did. "You smell so fucking good." He looked up, his gaze settling on mine. "This is your last chance, Mrs. Harrington. If you don't tell me to stop now, I'm not stopping until I'm satisfied." His warm breath teased my inner thigh. "And I've fucking wanted this for ten years. I'm not rushing."

He wasn't rushing, nor was he the man from long ago in the warehouse. This monster of a man between my thighs was worshipping every inch and taking an agonizing amount of time to lavish me with reverent attention. I wove my fingers through his fine, dark hair. "My fucking name is Victoria! And I don't want you to fucking rush. What I want is for you to take me slow and hard. Make me come and do it again."

His lips quirked. "Bossy!"

"Oh God!" I moaned as one and then two fingers plunged deep inside of me.

"You're so wet, so ready." In and out his fingers plunged. He lifted my hips, creating a rhythm that sent my body into spasms. "Oh fuck!" My mountain was right there, both literally and figuratively. I had never realized that Travis was my mountain, my high.

Kissing the inside of my thighs, his fingers disappeared. I watched as he sat up, his eyes never leaving mine as he removed his gym shorts and revealed his giant cock. "Fucking hard?" he asked, as he stroked himself. "You want it hard? I've got it hard."

Holy shit! He did! I reached out to touch it.

"Not yet, Victoria, not yet. I still have pussy to eat. Remember, I'm taking this slow."

Oh my God!

I laid my head back and spread my legs wider. "I remember," I uttered through labored breaths as his tongue found my now swollen lips and lapped my wetness. When I reached for the soft sheets, he sucked my clit. The room around us dimmed as nothing mattered but his actions. Each tug on my hypersensitive bundle of nerves pulled me higher and higher. I was in a dark tunnel, a vacuum, and only Travis could pull me out, toward the light and toward my figurative mountain's peak.

When he added his fingers to my delectable torture, he brought me suddenly to the top. The edge was right there. "Fuck, Travis... Oh my God!" I was incapable of complete sentences as my hips bucked against his strong grip. He continued to suck as my legs became rigid, a vise around his head. I no longer controlled my body or my words. They were coming from my lips, but I couldn't process them as I heard myself beg. I begged for him to stop, and begged for him to never stop. It wasn't until all my strength dissolved and I floated back to earth that the room finally reappeared.

When it did, Travis was above me, looking down into my eyes. "You're fucking gorgeous when that's real. Fucking gorgeous. I want to see that again."

Again? I don't fucking think I can do that again.

Before I could articulate words, he was on top of me, spreading my legs and coaxing my entrance with his cock. A whimper left my lips as he teased my clit and moved only the head of his massive penis inside of me. "Please..." I begged again.

"Please what? I love hearing your voice, your words."

"Please fuck me. I want your cock inside of me."

I gasped as he did exactly what I asked. My hands reached for his shoulders as he thrust deep inside. With all my strength I clung to him, the man who'd been with me through it all. Harder and harder he plunged, hitting that spot, the one that pushed me back up my mountain. *Fuck!* He hit every spot. I couldn't remember feeling so full. As the wonderful scent of masculine musk filled my suite, he pounded me against the mattress, deeper and deeper until I didn't think I could take anymore.

"So fucking good!" he growled as our bodies fell into a rhythm: in and out, in and out, each thrust brushing my clit and filling my core. The mountain grew and grew. I wrapped my legs around him. He grabbed my ass and pulled me closer. The ledge appeared out of nowhere. When his fingers dug into my skin, I let go, and screamed. Lights flashed and my body convulsed. I was there but not there. I was lost as wave after wave of heated contractions rippled through me.

"Oh my fucking God!" Travis yelled with one final thrust that tore me to the core. We landed in a bundle of sheets, his cock throbbing inside me.

When our breathing quieted, I asked with a grin, "Travis?"

"Yes?" His nose nuzzled mine.

"I've changed my mind."

"You have? About what."

I reached up and ran my hand over his cheek. "You can touch me."

"Fucking A." He ran his hand down my side, finding my hand, and intertwined our fingers. Bringing them to his lips, he showered each one with kisses. "I'm glad I have your permission, because after this, I don't think I could stop."

"Don't. Don't fucking stop."

CHAPTER THIRTY

Eight months later

EVERY NOW AND THEN, when I reached into my jewelry box, my fingers would brush the old paper napkin that still surrounded the small vials. I knew there was no reason to keep them; most of the Cytoxan was gone. Nonetheless, the tightly wrapped vials that I'd taken from the Harrington Clinic Distribution Center a lifetime ago remained. Travis and I both knew they were there, and we knew that there was no immediate threat or reason to keep them. Yet, for some reason they remained.

We'd talked about ways to dispose of them. It wasn't like we could just throw them away. A smile fluttered across my face as I thought about how Travis rid me of the warehouse. If we would've been thinking at the time, we could've put the vials in the building before the explosion. Stewart's chair was still there.

It didn't take long for the police to rule that the blast was caused by a gas main break. Thankfully, the area was uninhabited and no one was injured. When the warehouse was declared a total loss, I had no trouble telling them to bulldoze the whole fucking place to the ground.

As I sat at my desk midmorning, I pushed those memories away and concentrated on our now. We were still in Miami: Travis wanted to run the Spas and Suites. Truthfully, he'd stepped into the role well.

"Mrs. Daniels, your mail is here," Kristina said as she handed me the stack of letters.

"Thank you, Kristina. Have you seen Lisa?"

"Yes, ma'am, I can get her for you."

I fumbled through the letters as Kristina left and Travis entered the room. Looking up, I became momentarily preoccupied with the way my husband's tight shirt accentuated his chest and arms, as well as the way it tucked into his customary dark slacks. For only a second I thought about what was under those slacks, what was deep inside of me just this morning. By the time my eyes moved to his, his lopsided grin told me that I'd been caught. "Mrs. Daniels, may I help you?"

I reached out to hold his waist and looked up at his dark eyes. "I think you did this morning, twice as I recall."

He shook his head. "Have you talked to your mother?"

Rolling my eyes, I said, "Yes, she called again. I'm glad she's doing well, but I could do without the daily updates. I do think it was smart of them to make her go through rehab again as part of her parole. I mean, we know she was forced to drink the alcohol, but in some ways it's like she's starting all over."

"She's still a pain in the ass."

I smiled and tilted my head, my gray eyes opened wide. "A bigger one than me?"

"Most days," Travis replied, kissing the top of my head and pulling playfully away.

I looked back down at the mail and remembered something I'd read. "What's happening with the Harrington Spas and Suites in London?"

"Nothing, don't worry about it."

I pursed my lips together. "I'm great with your taking over all of that. I mean, you worked beside Stewart and know a hell of a lot more about it than I do, but don't shut me out."

Travis sat down opposite the desk, his long legs folding as his large frame filled the chair. "I'm not shutting you out. Nothing's happening. There was a big-assed summit, and they needed extra security. It's over. Nothing happened."

We both turned as Lisa entered. "Mr. and Mrs. Daniels, Kristina said you were looking for me?"

"Stop that," Travis said, looking directly at Lisa.

Her suppressed grin made her blue eyes sparkle. "You know, I do it because I know it drives you crazy."

"It does. It fucking pisses me off. My goddamned name is Travis. It was for fifteen years, and it didn't suddenly change just because I'm fucking—"

Lisa put up her hands. "Stop. Way too much information."

"Then call me Travis and I won't give you the details of what happened this morning..." He winked at me. "...or last night or..."

"Travis, Travis, for Christ's sake," Lisa pleaded in surrender.

I shook my head, happy that we'd all made the transition as well as we had. "If you two are finished?"

Lisa turned toward me. "Yes, ma'am, your husband can be a real pain..."

"...in the ass, Lisa. Yes, I'm well aware." Before Travis could speak, I turned my gray eyes toward him. His and Lisa's friendship went way back. I didn't trust him to not bring up a few of the ways I enjoyed him being a pain in the ass. Glaring, I warned, "Shut up."

He dramatically pressed his lips together and lifted his brow.

I turned back to Lisa. "I wanted to be sure that you remembered Sheila Keene and Maura Craven were coming over today for lunch."

"Yes, ma'am. Everything will be ready."

"Thank you, Lisa."

After she left the room, Travis leaned back and said, "Oh, I forgot. Today is the monthly widows' club luncheon."

I nodded. "It's kind of weird now that I'm remarried and Maura's seeing someone."

"She is?" He lifted a brow. "I wonder if he has a pencil dick?"

I shrugged. "I'm glad I don't know."

"Sorry, Vik, I didn't mean it..."

I waved him off. "No, it's just, I'm glad that I don't know. And Sheila's doing better. I think she's had the most difficult time. I mean, suicide is a tough pill for the wife to swallow."

Travis nodded knowingly. "With all the shit going down at Craven and Knowles, after the CDC started investigating and the feds got involved. Shit, Senator Keene's clean, shiny reputation suddenly got pretty fucked up. The Durantes didn't fare much better."

"I suppose I should feel as guilty about Robert as I do Parker. I mean, the more Robert kept threatening me, well…" I sighed. "…at least I know that Carlisle meant it when he said he'd be there for me."

"The insulin overdose was genius," Travis said.

I nodded. "Yeah, they officially called it an accident, so at least Sheila got the insurance money. But she's confided that he did it on purpose. Apparently, he'd been diabetic for a long time, and she finds it hard to believe that he'd suddenly mess up his medication dosage." I shook my head. "Sheila thinks that the scandal was all too much for him to handle. That's why she's been so immersed in the Harrington Society. She and Val have secured grants for Harrington Cancer Clinics in five different U.S. locations. They've been working on permits. Hopefully construction will begin soon."

"You told me about that. I know you'll be happy to not have Dr. Conway traveling overseas as much."

"I will," I agreed. "Hey, she's your sister-in-law now, maybe you could call her Val or Valerie or something other than Doctor Conway?"

Travis grimaced. "I like your sister, I really do. I like her a lot more than I do your mom."

I giggled.

"And," he continued, "I respect her. I feel like Val isn't enough for all she's accomplished."

I shrugged. "Whatever. There's always Doc?"

"I like that. I can do Doc." He stood. "I came in here to let you know I'm heading out. I have a few meetings with some investors. I've promised Carlisle and Niccolo that we'd continue to work together, but I'm working to make some more connections for them." He leaned down and kissed me. "Legit connections. They've got a lot more legal shit happening than I ever realized. The prostitution shit was mostly the Durantes.

"I'll tell you what. The Albinis are smart as hell. I think I'm learning as much from them as I did from Mr. Harrington."

I wanted to tell him to call him Stewart, but damn, this name thing was a never-ending battle.

"I'll see you tonight."

He kissed me goodbye. "Have fun at your luncheon."

With my mind still lingering on our morning workout, I looked at the letters from our new legal firm. Getting everything changed over from Craven and Knowles was taking for-fucking-ever. With the on-going investigation every document was read under a fucking microscope. I opened the letter addressed to me:

Dear Mrs. Victoria Daniels,

Enclosed please find the approved and verified copy of your late husband, Stewart Harrington's, Last Will and Testament. I'm pleased to report that everything was as you assumed. The bulk of Mr. Harrington's assets were bequeathed to you.

The only other individual specifically named by Mr. Harrington was Travis Daniels, Mr. Harrington's only remaining blood relative. You will see that he was individually bequeathed ten percent of all cash assets. That did not include business holdings or investments.

As I'm sure you're aware, since you and Mr. Daniels' chose not to have a prenuptial agreement, the division of assets is no longer significant.

If our firm can be of any further assistance to you or Mr. Daniels, please do not hesitate to contact us.

Sincerely,

cc: Travis Daniels

I reached for the envelope addressed to him. It felt the same. I was sure it was his copy. I wasn't shocked that Stewart had left money to Travis: the two were obviously close. What shocked me, surprised me, and fucking blew me away was that they were related. *How? A fucking cousin?*

Travis was thirty-nine. Stewart was fifty when he died. Travis couldn't be Stewart's son. Besides, their coloring was all wrong. Stewart was blonde with blue eyes. Travis had dark brown eyes and brown hair.

Then I thought about Val: her light brown hair and my long dark hair. Now that I knew the truth, I knew my hair and skin tone came from my father's side of the family. We looked different because we had different fathers. Travis' last name was Daniels, and Stewart's was Harrington.

The only thing Travis had told me about his mother was that she was the woman with the twelve-year-old son: the one who was sucked into the Durante hell and the one whom Travis felt he righted by helping to expose their dealings. The only other thing I knew about her was that she was deceased. I was confident that Stewart didn't share the same mother. He was raised in the lap of luxury with both of his parents.

As my mind searched for answers, more questions arose. Why didn't one of them tell me? How had Travis been a part of my life ever since I met Stewart and I never knew that they were related? Why wouldn't Travis tell me?

I got a sickening feeling in the pit of my stomach. Travis had never mentioned his father. When I asked, he told me that he didn't know him. Since I could relate, I never pushed it. But now I wondered if Travis and Stewart could have shared a father. Could Stewart's father have been one of the Durantes' *friends*? The whole thing made my stomach lurch. I didn't want to imagine Travis' mother with friends. A cool sheen of perspiration formed on my brow.

Travis had told me that he wasn't honorable, but he'd also said he'd always been straight with me. I asked him if I could believe him and he'd told me that he didn't know. What the fuck did that mean? If his father was the same as Stewart's, could I possibly be nothing more than a way for him to get to Stewart's money and power? Was that what he had planned all along?

I didn't want to think like that. I couldn't. I'd finally gotten my normal, as fucking normal as I could. I mean, I was a killer and as painful as that truth was, both Travis and I knew it. He didn't know what I'd done to Stewart, but he knew about the others. I tried not to think about it... I refused to think about it...

Opening Travis' envelope, I removed the letter, placed Stewart's will back inside, and laid the envelope on the corner of my desk. As I watched both letters shred, I told myself, I would have my happily ever after. I fucking deserved it. I'd earned it, and I had no intentions of losing it. Karma could kiss my ass.

EPILOGUE

Future

WITH MY BACK against the tile wall and the warm spray assaulting our skin, I peered out behind veiled lids and watched as Travis lathered his chest. As his large hand covered in soap went lower, sudsing the fine trail of dark hair that led to his gorgeously engorged cock, I couldn't think about anything but having him inside of me. When our eyes met, I saw the familiar dark, narrowing gaze, the one that sent my insides into spasms.

"Mrs. Daniels, is there something you want?"

"Fuck, yes," I moaned as I reached out and grasped his cock. Despite my thumb and finger not touching, I moved my hand up and down creating a rhythm as my other hand reached for his heavy balls and rolled them between my fingers.

"Fuck! Vikki, you're killing me."

"After what you did for me this morning, I think it's my turn," I replied with a grin, falling to my knees. With the spray of the shower, I tilted my head to the side and rinsed the soapy foam from his rock-hard penis. With both hands on his shaft, I opened wide and took him inside my mouth. My tongue ran circles around the head as I tasted his salty dew. Moving my head up and down, I listened to the sound of his breathing.

As it quickened, I slid him out of my mouth and licked his length. My tongue lapped the pulsating vein, as his balls tightened and he fisted my hair. With a growl, he plunged deep inside my throat.

Just as his cock began to throb, Travis reached for my chin. "Fuck this, Vik, I want to come inside that pussy. Stand up."

When I did, he turned me around. "I'm fucking you from behind, babe. Hold on tight."

I was already wet from our earlier round and sucking him had my sex primed. Holding on to the wall I spread my legs and lifted my ass. In one hard thrust, he filled me, stretching my core to the brink. "Oh fucking God, that feels so good!" I moaned, as my fingers splayed and I tried desperately to hold on to the smooth surface. Over and over he pounded, deeper and deeper until all I could do is call out his name, "Travis, oh my God!"

"That's it. We're coming together."

I nodded as he reached for my swollen clit. "Oh, fuck!" The tension inside of me continued to build. Each thrust was harder than the last and I knew he was almost there. "Turn me around," I begged, needing to touch him.

Travis did, pulling out of me, and lifting me up. My legs wrapped around him as his cock impaled my sex. I held on to his shoulders as he held my ass. Only a few more thrusts and I called out, "Jesus, Travis, I'm going to come."

"Not yet, babe." Again, he reached between us and teased my clit, his hips moving with mine. Our wet skin slapped one another and our breathing labored.

"Now! Fucking now!" he growled in my ear as my body ripped into a million pieces.

I melted against him, my body limp. Holding me under the spray, Travis kissed my neck, his cock still inside of me.

When my words returned, I looked up, the spray still covering us. "I was supposed to be thanking you for earlier."

He flashed his lopsided grin. "You did, sweetheart, you did."

As he lowered me to the shower floor I looked down at my feet and the pooling water. My legs were Jell-o and my body felt enjoyably sore.

"What are your plans for today?" I asked.

"I'm at your service, Mrs. Daniels."

Kissing his cheek, I looked back toward the drain. No wonder the water wasn't emptying: it couldn't, not clogged with all of that hair.

-The End-

THANK YOU

Dear Readers,

Thank you for reading Insidious. I hope you enjoyed this stand-alone sexy thriller and will remember the twists and turns as your head hits the pillow tonight. If you do, I will have accomplished my goal. Although we have seen the last of Victoria, Travis, and all of the amazing characters in Insidious, there are more stories to tell and new characters to meet in future novels in Tales From the Dark Side.

This is a unique series of stand-alone, smart, sexy thrillers.

If you have enjoyed Victoria's story, you will want to follow Aleatha Romig for news of the next Tales from the Dark Side. Each book in this series will have its own characters, its own thrilling roller coaster of a story, and none will overlap with any of the other books.

If this is your first time to read my work, please check out my Consequences series, a five-book series with two reading companions. The Consequences series is also a dark thriller. While it is not as explicit, there is a relationship that connects the series and has been embraced by dark romance readers. Also, for more thrillers, please check out my Light series, coming in June of 2016 and my Infidelity series, five books, the first published in October of 2015. The Infidelity series is not about cheating.

Thank you again for reading and being part of Victoria's story. Please tell your friends and leave a review. It is the nicest thing you can do for an author you enjoy.

Sincerely,
Aleatha

ACKNOWLEDGMENTS

First and foremost I want to thank my family. Without your support and patience I would never have been able to make my passion for writing and telling stories into a career. My love for each one of you grows daily. A special thank you to my mother who, from a very young age, encouraged me to use my imagination. We've all heard the stories of my imaginary friends throughout my childhood. I believe that without those, I wouldn't have been able to embrace my imaginary friends in adulthood.

Thank you to my friend Debra, RN, for her medical knowledge especially with off-label uses of medications. I can only imagine the faces of others who could overhear our fun conversations! Thank you for helping me make INSIDIOUS real.

Thank you to my trusted betas who've stayed and grown in knowledge with me as we continue to tackle new stories and new genres! Sherry, Val, Kirsten, Stephanie, and Angie, your help and encouragement brought INSIDIOUS to life. Thank you, also, to my dear friends who read and willingly gave me advice that has helped to make the final INSIDIOUS even better than my first draft. I can't tell you how much I appreciate your words of praise as well as those of advice! Pepper Winters, Kathryn Perez, Tia Louise, Kiki Chatfield, my fantastic editor Lisa Aurello, and my amazing agent Danielle Egan-Miller, I listened to each and every one of you—and did what I wanted! lol… Thank you. The expertise of each one is reflected in the final product!

I also want to do a shout out to all of the wonderful readers, bloggers, and authors out there. I know without a doubt that if it were not for each one of you, no one would know the name Aleatha Romig. I can't thank you all enough for your love and support. I shudder to name names. There's no way I can call out each and every one of you. Please know that if you're reading this, I'm talking about you!

Now, I hope you enjoy my jump into the world of smart, sexy thrillers! Here is INSIDIOUS!

What to do now...

LEND IT: Did you enjoy INSIDIOUS? Do you have a friend who'd enjoy INSIDIOUS? INSIDIOUS may be lent one time. Sharing is caring!

RECOMMEND IT: Do you have more than one friend who'd enjoy INSIDIOUS? Tell them about it! Call, text, post, tweet...your recommendation is the nicest gift you can give to an author!

REVIEW IT: Tell the world. Please go to the retailer where you purchased this, as well as Goodreads, and write a review. Please share your thoughts about INSIDIOUS on:
   *Amazon, *INSIDIOUS*, Customer Reviews
   *Barnes & Noble, *INSIDIOUS*, Customer Reviews
   *iBooks, *INSIDIOUS*, Customer Reviews
   *Goodreads.com / Aleatha Romig

ABOUT THE AUTHOR

Aleatha Romig is a New York Times and USA Today bestselling author who lives in Indiana. She grew up in Mishawaka, graduated from Indiana University, and is currently living south of Indianapolis. Aleatha has raised three children with her high school sweetheart and husband of nearly thirty years. Before she became a full-time author, she worked days as a dental hygienist and spent her nights writing. Now, when she's not imagining mind-blowing twists and turns, she likes to spend her time with her family and friends. Her other pastimes include reading and creating heroes/anti-heroes who haunt your dreams!

Aleatha released her first novel, CONSEQUENCES, in August of 2011. CONSEQUENCES became a bestselling series with five novels and two companions released from 2011 through 2015. The compelling and epic story of Anthony and Claire Rawlings has graced more than half a million e-readers. Aleatha released the first of her series TALES FROM THE DARK SIDE, INSIDIOUS, in the fall of 2014. These stand-alone thrillers continue Aleatha's twisted style with an increase in heat. In the fall of 2015, Aleatha moved headfirst into the world of dark romance with the release of BETRAYAL, the first of her five-novel INFIDELITY series. (This series is not about cheating) Aleatha has entered the traditional world of publishing with Thomas and Mercer with her LIGHT series. The first of that series, INTO THE LIGHT, will be published in June of 2016.

Aleatha is a "Published Author's Network" member of the Romance Writers of America and represented by Danielle Egan-Miller of Browne & Miller Literary Associates.

Do you love Aleatha's writing? Do you want to know the latest about Infidelity? The Light? Consequences? Tales From the Dark Side? and any new projects from Aleatha?

Do you like EXCLUSIVE content (never released scenes, never released excerpts, and more)? Would you like the monthly chance to win prizes (signed books and gift cards)? Then sign up today for Aleatha's monthly newsletter and stay informed on all thing Aleatha Romig.

NEWSLETTER SIGN UP
recipients receive exclusive material and offers.
You can also find Aleatha at:
Facebook | Twitter | Goodreads | Instagram
Website: www.aleatharomig.com
Email: aleatharomig@gmail.com

ALSO BY ALEATHA ROMIG

INFIDELITY SERIES:

Betrayal, Book #1

Cunning, Book #2

Deception, Book #3

Entrapment, Book #4 (September 2016)

Fidelity: Book #5 (January 2017)

CONSEQUENCES SERIES:

Consequences, Book 1

Truth, Book 2

Convicted, Book 3

Revealed, Book 4

Beyond the Consequences, Book 5

Behind His Eyes - Consequences, Book 1.5

Behind His Eyes - Truth, Book 2.5

THE LIGHT SERIES:

Into the Light, Book 1 (June 2016)

Away from the Dark, Book 2 (October 2016)

TALES FROM THE DARK SIDE SERIES:

All books in this series are standalone sexy thrillers

Insidious

Duplicity, (Completely unrelated to book 1) Release TBA

You may also listen Aleatha Romig books on Audible:

42397322R00187

Made in the USA
Middletown, DE
13 April 2019